NOT IN THIS WORLD

JANE SCOTT STUART

WITH ELAINE FLOWERS

BeforeYouPublish Book Press
We Publish Books

Before You Publish — Book Press
Addison, TX

Cover Design: In house at BYP
Edits: EBM Professional Services
Published and printed in the United States of America

Scott Stuart, Jane
Flowers, Elaine
Not in This World — First edition
www.beforeyoupublish.com

*To **James Stuart** for his invaluable help on the RAF and war chapters: our gratitude knows no bounds.*

With love, Jane, your devoted wife
With deep appreciation, Elaine, your entrusted friend

CONTENTS

PART THREE

NOT IN THIS WORLD

JANE SCOTT STUART

WITH ELAINE FLOWERS

ADDISON, TX

PART ONE

1

Paul Carew woke early, not looking forward to facing another endless summer Sabbath. Inside the church, he sat feeling angry and sad. It was past noon and hot. He was sure Elijah had preached longer than usual. Seems, after the ham auction, the holy-picture window fund had raised well over the three hundred dollars needed to make the payment. His father spent a great deal of his sermon thanking God, thanking Jesus, for choosing to pour down blessings upon his own worthy head. Paul took notice that the last thing Elijah remembered to do was thank his loyal congregation.

After church, as they always did, the Carews got together at Cousin Lorene's house for lunch. But Paul couldn't find his appetite and scooted little mounds of mashed potatoes and chicken breast under his untouched biscuit. He kept an eye on Elijah, now in his shirtsleeves, sweating authority.

After a while, he couldn't bear the sight of his father's grease-covered chin, moving up and down like a string-pulled dummy, so he matched up his knife and fork, stood, and took his plate into the kitchen.

"Paul, you come back over here, get you a piece of my coconut cake, allow me to put this spoon of vanilla ice cream on top." Lorene dug her scoop down deep, came up with a perfect round ball.

As soon as she handed him the plate, Paul tiptoed well behind his father's scowl and found a place next to Lorene's daughter, Arletta, took his cake, cut it up into small pieces, and divided tiny blobs of ice cream to spoon onto each bit.

"Paul, you just so delicate," Arletta whispered.

While Lorene passed coffee, Paul slipped out the door into the two o'clock sun, walked around the corner, home to his wooden house, held up by gray concrete stilts under the front porch. He was alone. All was still in the house. So, he set to picking up clothes Elijah dropped while in a hurry to get ready for church. He folded, placed, and hung them back into the cupboards.

On his way to the bedroom, carrying Elijah's tobacco-stained overalls, his eye caught the folds of his mama's second-best dress from Lorene. It was a hand-me-down she'd gotten from the big house over the tracks where she worked, a giveaway after spring cleaning. This was his chance to follow his feelings and he took it. He peeled off his Sunday shirt, unwound the pink lace and cotton dress from its hanger, and pulled it over his head, where it fell to below his knees. He followed himself in the dressing-table mirror, then sat down to unroll Mama's Pink Lady lipstick from the five and dime.

He pursed his mouth, flattened his lips in a big O. He traced and filled in the color, not stopping until he'd reached the deepest pink. A small, brown powder puff carried rouge onto his thin cheeks. He unhooked the colored beads Mama'd hung over the pointed tops of her mirror, wound them over and over around his neck, turned on her radio, snapped his fingers to the tune of "Sweet Georgia Brown." He knew it by heart, like he did every other hit song of the day.

No gal made has got a shade on Sweet Georgia Brown,
Two left feet, but oh so neat...

He wasn't a second away from tapping his feet, his mama's pink dress swished with the beat, he swayed from one side to the other, moved backwards and forwards, arms gently swinging, until he was dancing and singing with his perfect partner, the boy in the mirror.

Fact is, Paul could croon the words to most songs by the light of any old silvery moon. Every day he sang one into his mama's mirror. He reached over to turn the music up and heard the bang of the front screen door. Paul was scared to death it might be Elijah. He dived down, scrambled under the double bed, trying to pull Lily's pink skirt with him, as he lay there flat on his stomach, holding his breath. He peeked out. His hot eyeballs could see a pair of black shiny-leather preacher shoes. Time went by, the shoes never moved. Blood pounded in his ears, and he was praying Elijah hadn't seen him.

Then, in a low voice, "I see your mama's pretty pink dress hanging out. Might have called you Paula, that's more like it." He knelt, looked at his son.

Paul caught one of his father's rare wide smiles, and with relief, started to breathe again, until Elijah hooked a hand under his arm, squeezed hard on his chicken wing, and pulled him out from under. One of the strings of Lily's necklace broke, spattering beads all over the floor, and for a minute Paul thought of scooping up all the different colored glass balls. He could smell the stale breath when Elijah put his face up close against his.

"Take off that dress, wipe your face." Elijah stood waiting with his hands on his hips.

Paul fumbled with each pink-covered button, pulled down the side zipper, and lifted the dress carefully over his head. Then, he took a towel hanging over the basin, spat into it, and scrubbed off as much makeup as he could. He stood in his underpants, shivering in fear.

"You know what God would say, don't you, boy? Or is it girl? God would say to me, loud and clear: 'Beat out those demons, Reverend Carew. Beat them until they fly down to Hell!'"

Elijah unhooked his brown-leather belt with the big brass buckle and with the other arm, threw Paul across the bed. At first the strap came down in slow, sharp slaps, then fury gathered steam and on they came harder, faster.

Paul tried to wriggle away, but Elijah pulled him back with one hand, and with his other, turned the belt to the buckle end and kept on beating as the metal clip dug deep into Paul's skin with each blow. Trickles of sweat rolled into his eyes, mixed with his tears, and with his agony he could feel the slipping sweat and blood on his back. Then, just as Paul nearly lost himself in a dead faint, the bedroom door opened.

2

Paul Carew never took on plump—just got longer and longer, thinner and thinner. His fingers reached from fine hands, and a long neck swept up into a dimpled chin under large brown eyes. When he began to walk, his unsteady shuffles gave way to his own rhythm. As a child, whenever he'd helped himself to a biscuit or a square of cornbread, thumbs and forefingers broke the pone into little pieces before he allowed it near his lips.

In time, his nails grew longer and longer. He filed them into points with his mother's emery boards, and if she tried to cut them, he'd run away. It didn't take Paul long to see from the way folks looked at his long nails that they thought there was something funny about him. So, he kept one single little fingernail, long and filed, hoping no one would notice it. He was happiest hanging around the folds of his mama's skirts, and when he heard his father, Elijah, coming back after a day in the fields, he found a dark corner and stayed quiet.

As the 1930s passed in the Kingdom—the section of Horse Cave, Kentucky where the Black people lived—more babies came along after Paul in the Carew family. First came James, then Ernest, then finally the twin sisters: Tallulah, and Tabby five minutes younger than Tallulah.

Every morning, when the twins were babies, Paul waited for his father to hitch up the mules and clatter off to work before he felt free to pick up one of his little sisters, rock her up and down, croon the songs he'd learned from the radio, dancing away any quarrelsomeness by dipping and twirling the bundled child around the room. By the time he was ten years old, Paul's mama said he could make the best cherry cobbler in the world and kept him busy in the house, folding, polishing, and fluffing anything he could find into "pretty." He loved the expression: "Mama, let's get it pretty."

Just before it got dark, Paul hurried up, finished his ironing, keeping an eye on his bubbling pot of chicken and dumplings with his ears tuned for the rattle of Elijah's wagon on the old dirt road in front of the house. His father's mules snorted. When Elijah undid their harnesses, Paul heard the pull of the outside pump, followed by a swoosh as his father ducked his head under the cold water, cleaning off sweat and dirt.

Paul watched Elijah come in and strut around the house without his shirt. His skin was a deep rich brown, and when the light caught it, almost purple. He was two inches taller than Paul's mama, so well over six feet. His face was wide, his neck thick. He had sharp brown eyes and a flat nose. No beauty. But when Tabby and Tallulah tried to reach their hands around his bulging biceps, Paul caught his mama looking at her husband with pride.

Paul's mama, Lily, on the other hand, was light molasses, stalk thin, her long frizzy hair piled in a bun on top of her head. He knew where he came from when he looked at his mama. Sometimes, he wondered just before he fell asleep, if her White blood had turned him into a girl. He knew he wasn't weak, and was sure Elijah was wrong when he said to his mama, "Lily, all that White blood's turned our boy into a sissy."

Paul's mama held a basin of hot water, a towel draped over her arm, and waited while Elijah scrubbed his hands with awful-smelling lye soap. Before his father sat down to supper, he picked up the little ones, gave each one a kiss and then patted the heads of Paul's brothers and sisters. When it came to Paul's turn, same thing every night: "Cut your hair, boy. File them nails." All he wanted was for Elijah—he could never call him Daddy—to pay him some mind, to put his arms around him and say, "Paul, I never noticed what a handsome boy you are."

As time passed, the routine stayed the same. As soon as Elijah left for work on the White side of the town of Horse Cave, where he was an overseer for Mr. Jackson, Paul hurried to finish washing the breakfast dishes and got busy looking after his sisters and brothers in time to go to school.

Tallulah pointed her finger at the dresses the twins wanted to wear in the morning and was sure she knew which to choose for them both. Before Tabby opened her mouth, Tallulah said it for her. Tabby was a thoughtful girl, a gentle dreamer, and from the beginning she understood how much easier it was to agree with Tallulah. They played around the heels of their brother and grew into his shadows.

Paul braided his sisters' hair this way and that, and sometimes laid a pressing comb on the top of the wood-burning stove, waited for it to heat up, so he could straighten the strands. "Hold still, girls," he said, "I promise I won't burn you."

James and Ernest, on the other hand, belonged to Elijah. As soon as their father kissed them goodbye in the morning, the two boys began tearing around, upsetting Paul's careful order. One day, when they got up on a chair and knocked over his two baking tins of rising bread, Paul gave each one of them a smack on the bottom.

The boys ran out to tell Elijah that evening before he'd even climbed down from his wagon.

"Daddy, Paul hit us."

Lily was right behind. She pulled James and Ernest up by the scruff of their necks. "Elijah, the two of them knocked the bread tins off the kitchen table, pulled the dough out of the tins, played with it all over the floor. Got none left for our supper."

In the house, Elijah finished drying his face. "You boys oughta know better than that." He put an arm around each of their shoulders. "Ain't that right?"

Ernest and James nodded. "Yes, Daddy." All the while, glaring at their brother.

Elijah turned toward Paul. "I'll be the only one smack my children, you hear me?"

Paul heard.

———

Moses Daniels, Paul's best friend, was born the day after Paul and lived next door. No one was sure what had happened to his daddy. Samuel Daniels left the house one morning when his son was two days old and was never heard of again. Every morning of the week, Lily leaned out the back door, called over to Moses's mother, Coralee.

"All right over there?" Lily would ask.

"We're fine," Coralee would answer.

And every evening after Elijah unhitched the mules, he marched over to the old broken-down fence between his shack and Coralee's and shouted out, "Y'all fine?"

"We're fine," Coralee shouted back.

Most afternoons, their neighbor rushed home from work to spend time with Lily, who for the first time all day set her work aside and made a cup of tea for the two of them. They sat at Lily's neatly arranged kitchen table and chatted, mostly about their sons. Coralee fretted and worried about Moses, being brought up without a father. More often than not, Lily and Paul kept a couple of plates of that day's cornbread, biscuits, fried chicken, cake, pie, or cobbler all covered with white tea towels, ready for Coralee to take home for supper.

Moses had soft, dark brown skin so smooth that when they

played together as small children, Paul could hardly keep himself from reaching over to touch his friend's face. Coralee loved to tell him, "Son, your skin's like the belly of a newborn puppy."

By the age of eight, Moses was five foot eight with no sharp edges but well-developed muscles. He had a high forehead, perfectly shaped halfmoon eyebrows, and large brown eyes with long silky lashes. His stand-up hair haloed his head. Nobody tried to tame it.

On Sundays, Paul joined Moses and Coralee for breakfast, and grinned when she smiled at her cuddly boy over steaming bowls of cornmeal and molasses.

"Morning, son. You must've slept well 'cause you has the look of an angel."

———

When both boys were nine, Lily gave them fishing poles she'd cut from a willow tree, tied lines with hooks onto the poles, and taught them how to dig in the dirt for worms to go catfishing.

Dave Strickland, a poor White farmer with a few good acres, lived on the edge of the Kingdom. He allowed the two nine-year-olds to fish in his pond.

"Fish all you want, boys, as long as I gets all you catch, 'cept the one you take home for your supper."

Paul kept his eyes shut when Moses was threading hooks with the worms they'd dug up that morning.

"Paul, you're such a scaredy-cat," Moses said. "Open your eyes, it's done."

Paul held his rod in one hand and quickly tossed the line. The bobber flew in the air following the weight, and the wiggling worm on the hook landed on the water, almost without a ripple.

Moses sat next to him, chewing on a piece of couch grass, shaking his head, and admiring the way his best friend threw out his line. They waited.

The bobber began to shiver, dipped a little, was quiet, until a tug pulled the cork under water, and, with a strong jerk, Paul's pole bent double. He stood up and strained to pull in the whopper of a six-pound catfish. They hadn't noticed Dave Strickland standing behind them, ready to claim the catch.

That evening, two small filets sizzled in Lily's frying pan.

"You should have seen how big he was," Paul bragged.

Elijah carefully divided the fish before handing small pieces to the children. "We do the work, have to put up with what they gives us." He sighed. "Way it's always been."

As long as they could dangle their worms over the water and talk all day, the boys didn't mind giving up most of their catch. They never tired of each other's company, but that did not mean they were alike. Paul got out of bed in the dark, before the first cock crowed. He pumped cold water from the outside tap, brought bucketsful into the house, washed his face, put on clean blue pants and a freshly ironed white shirt. He laid the table for breakfast and fired up the old cast iron stove. But Moses had a hard time opening his eyes in the morning. Coralee fussed and chided. She'd laid the table before she went to work, put her sweet, precious boy's breakfast on top of their old iron stove and laid out his fresh clothes at the end of his bed. Once he was up, Moses got busy, washed up his dishes, took out the old scraggly broom, swept the whole house, finished on the front porch where he gave a holler over to next door.

"Ready? Let's go fishing, Paul."

Without a husband at home, Coralee tried to stretch every cent. For thirteen years, six days a week, she did work for the Larkins. They owned the Horse Cave grocery store on Main Street. Everybody in town bought groceries at Larkin's. The family were strict Baptists, tried to live by the rule, "Do unto others as you would have them do unto you."

One early morning in June 1935, after waking up the four Larkin children, making sure they were washed and dressed, and then cooking the family's breakfast, Coralee found the courage to ask the question she'd been rehearsing all week.

Bruce and Ida Larkin were on the front porch, enjoying a cool morning breeze, finishing their third cup of coffee.

"Sir, Ma'am, my boy Moses needs a job. He looks up to his friend, Paul Carew 'cause he's got book learning. Moses needs to feel good about himself, earn a little money."

Coralee stood there for a minute, trying to find the words for the next part of the question. "He'll work for learning how—wouldn't have to pay him hardly nothing."

Ida and Bruce knew fourteen-year-old Moses was a good and thoughtful boy.

Bruce spoke up, "Let me think on that, Coralee. We'll let you know."

Coralee waited for a minute then turned and took their empty cups to the kitchen.

Bruce looked at his watch, and said to Ida, "Rather have Paul Carew, but I could use Moses. I got plenty of work for a strong boy. I'll start him off at a quarter a day."

Ida Larkin swept her naturally curly blonde hair with determination into a large tortoiseshell barrette on the nape of her neck, wearing no powder or lipstick. She was tight with the wages but believed part of her Christian duty was caring for her Colored help. She looked up at her husband sweetly. She prided herself that theirs was a kind, fair, and harmonious family. "No need to give the boy money right off, Bruce. You heard what Coralee said. See if he's any good before you pay him."

The following week, Paul walked Moses to his first half day of work. "I'll pick you up at noon for fishing."

A few hours later, on their way to Strickland's pond, Moses told Paul about his morning. "I had to carry heavy boxes, stock the shelves, and keep them tidy. Weren't too hard. I reckon they liked me."

When Moses was fourteen, he left school to take up his duties full time, putting together orders, unlocking the store in the morning, locking it last thing at night. Once he learned how to drive,

Moses made his deliveries with confidence in the Larkin's 1925 Chevy Superior-K truck. With pride, he kept that Chevy polished to a mirror shine.

"Hi, it's Moses, from Larkin's."

After a while, every household in Horse Cave recognized his gentle knock on their back doors.

———

Coralee wasn't the only one who found a way to earn extra money. Paul would always remember that September afternoon when Cousin Lorene, who did work for Sally Jackson, came to their front door in Mr. Jackson's new Model T Roundabout truck. Lorene was sitting in the back, cradling a second-hand Singer sewing machine, with its table wrapped separately in a blanket in the bed of the truck. Eddie and Lorene lifted it out of the back and carried it into Elijah's shack.

Lorene sat at Lily's kitchen table and took a slice of Paul's coconut cake, closed her eyes, and sighed with the first heavenly bite.

Paul said, "Know why it's so good, Cousin Lorene? 'Cause I picked the coconuts off my tree in the backyard."

"Quit that." Lorene giggled along with Paul. "I ain't born yester-day." She took another bite, sighed as the icing touched her tongue before saying, "You all want to hear how we got this machine?"

Paul and Lily nodded.

"I was rolling out the biscuit dough for lunch when Miss Sally come into my kitchen, opened the refrigerator, pulled out a pitcher of cold lemonade, poured a glass, and sat herself down at my kitchen table.

"She called my name, but I kept right on rolling my dough. She says she'd ordered herself the new-model lightweight Singer. I said, 'Yes, ma'am. I can't raise a hem, but we all know Lily Carew sews the finest stitch in the Kingdom.' I keep on rolling, dusting with flour and cutting, all while smiling to myself, waiting for Miss Sally to hit on her own idea.

"She said, 'Lorene, why don't we give the old machine to your cousin Lily? I'll ask Eddie to run it over in the truck. You ride in the back and hold it down, and when you get there, you show Lily how to run it.'

"Miss Sally was having a hard time holding up her halo. When she got up from the table, I knew what was coming. She said, 'By the way, Lorene, don't you forget to ask Lily if she would run up a few new white aprons and maybe some tea towels? Of course, I'll pay her.'

"'Yes ma'am,' I said. 'Good idea. I reckon she could use it, all those mouths to feed.'

"Miss Sally finished her lemonade, handed me the glass. Lily's got her a Singer."

From that moment on, Paul called the sewing machine "Mama's golden trophy." She earned extra making dresses and mending the unmendable. Lorene made sure she gave Lily Miss Sally's castoff dresses, and there wasn't a maid in the Kingdom who didn't bring in her own unwanted hand-me-downs. Pretty soon, Lily had baskets full of different-colored cut-out materials. Mrs. Jackson kept her busy making dark blue cotton dresses and plain white aprons for Lorene, and white handkerchiefs bordered with lace for Sally herself. And she didn't forget to pay.

Paul showed Tallulah and Tabby how to help cut out the patterns, even managing to coax Ernest and James into carefully putting the different colored threads away in a cardboard box. All day long, the whirring of the sewing machine, the needle going up-and-down jabbing into the cloth, the cock-a-doodle-doo of their brand-new rooster, tunes from Lily's radio, and the smell of Paul's cakes and cobblers... Those were the moments, free of heartache, Paul would try to remember.

3

Ten minutes from the Carew shack, school was held every day in the Children of God Third Baptist Church, where Elijah Carew preached on Sundays.

Each morning before her oldest son left, Lily patted Paul's freshly ironed shirt collar. "Paul, you hear me, pay attention to Miss Bessie. Only way for you to get out of the Kingdom is learning to read and write."

Lily looked at her beautiful boy and sighed. "I been chewing on it. You're too fine to be a porter on the train, lifting bags, waiting for tips. You say you don't want to be a teacher. Only way out is to go work for White folks: clean, iron, make the best cherry cobbler in the world. That's most all us Colored folks can hope for. You'll never be right to work in the fields. You might work in an office. You could be a writer, the way you have with words. Only way out of our lives is book learning."

Paul put his arms around Lily's shoulder. "I love to sing. I love to dance. You never know, I could be a movie star. Meantime," he laughed, "if I have to work for White folks, I'll do my best, make you proud of me. Quit fretting."

That Monday morning, Paul was dreading school. Miss Bessie had asked him to make up a story and tell it in front of the class. He'd been practicing in front of Lily's mirror all week, pausing at certain moments, waving his arms for dramatic effect. The more he practiced, the more nervous he became.

When Paul and Moses arrived at the church, ready for school, Paul sat on the front-row bench, as their teacher had asked any pupil telling a story to do.

Miss Bessie, her eyes cold and fierce, walked out onto the wooden stage in front of Elijah's pulpit, clapped her hands, and called out, "Order, order." Her class settled.

Paul's teacher was short and fat with fans of black hair sticking out all over her head, like a wild woman; when she bent down stiffly, her body seemed to be stuck in the middle from her too-tight corset. Miss Bessie favored her friend Lily's handsome boy Paul, and made sure he learned to read and write.

Paul stood in front of the class, cleared his throat, waited for his heart to stop pounding, and began, "One night, I dreamt I turned into a butterfly. When I woke up, I was sitting on a red rose in a patch of sun. I looked all round me. I saw a flutter of butterflies swooping and gliding. One of them says to me, 'Come on out, Paula. Why are you sitting there? Join us.'

"I say right back, my voice all funny, sounds as if I'm singing in a whisper, 'Who are you?'

"'Name's Leslie.'

"She was a pretty butterfly, with long legs, wings of all different colors. A rainbow.

"Another one flies in, this one's smaller, more delicate. 'I'm Muriel. Lookahere, now, ain't you the painted butterfly?'

"I say, 'What do I look like?'

"She says, 'You have bright-orange, red, and yellow velvet wings.'

"I ask, 'Can I fly with you?' She says, ''Course you can, silly. Just flap your wings.'

"'I ain't sure, Muriel.'

"She ruffles her own wings, says, 'You'd rather stay there sitting on a red rose for the rest of your life? You're a butterfly. If you don't try, you never fly.'

"Soon as I look at myself in the mirror, I start laughing. She's right. I got purple and red wings. I *must* be a butterfly.

"I bat my pretty wings, and sure enough, up I go, join up with the flutter, keeping up between Leslie and Muriel.

"We fly higher, catch a breeze that takes us over Old Man Strickland's pond. We drop down into his melon patch full of flowers, light on the biggest and the prettiest, stick out our tongues, find it's all sweet and warm inside. We light on one flower, dance a little, light on another. Leslie says, 'We got to mind for birds so keep your eyes open 'cause if we don't see them, they'll see us.'

"We're playing, dancing, swirling, I want to stay there forever, when all of a sudden, Muriel flies in beside me.

"'We don't settle for nothing. Come on, Paula, wind's up, let's catch us a ride to Hollywood.'

"I tell her, 'I'm dying to fly to Hollywood.'

"When no sooner had I said that then I hear Elijah yelling, 'Get up, boy, where's my cereal?'

"Soon as I get out of bed, what do I see, sitting on the edge of my pillow? A butterfly, sad, all folded up. She climbs onto my finger. Carefully, I carry her to my open window, her orange, red, and yellow wings opening, shutting slowly. Then they start sweeping faster, I blow under her, harder and harder, until, sure enough, she catches a breeze.

"'Paula,' I say, 'better get out of here.'"

The young ones listened, fingers in their mouths, wide-eyed. The older ones with their chins in their hands. When classes were over, Jake and Sam Farlow, the undertaker's sons, teased Paul and called him "Butterfly Boy."

On their way home, Paul waited for Moses to say something about his story.

They'd almost reached home, when Moses teased, "I expects you have to start off as an old, ugly caterpillar before you ever get to fly 'round like a butterfly."

4

Most of the time, Moses and Paul stayed away from trouble. When they were let out of school for the summer, Moses worked in the grocery store from eight A.M. until noon. He hurried home to join Paul, and the two boys ate lunch together at Moses's house, then rested on the porch, waiting for the afternoon to cool before they ran to the railway tracks on the edge of the Kingdom to wave at the five o'clock Louisville & Nashville train speeding through Horse Cave. They counted down to the second for the train to come, and when it did, the cars rattled by with whooshes of cool air, and the two boys jumped up and down, waving to the passengers behind the windows and waved even harder to their own when the green segregated car went by.

One day, Moses shook his head, and said, "Paul, that train ain't stopping for nobody."

"Stopping for nobody" gave Paul the idea.

They'd celebrated their birthdays in Paul's backyard, with Coralee, Lily, and Paul's brothers and sisters, sipping fresh lemonade and eating a fudge cake made by Paul. Afterwards, when they went over to sit on Moses's front porch, Paul outlined his idea.

The next day was Friday, a hot June day, not a cloud in the sky. They'd been up since dawn, chewing on licorice sticks under the chestnut tree in Moses's backyard. They filled a pair of Moses's outgrown overalls and an old white shirt of Elijah's with fresh leaves. They stuffed, patted, and shaped it to look like a body and tied the bottoms of the arms and legs with string to hold the leaves inside. Paul ran over into his yard and picked a small red watermelon to make the head. By the time the two of them finished, Clarence—that's what they called him—almost got up and walked away by himself.

They were ready.

"Come on, Paul, we don't have much time!"

Moses folded Clarence in half, Paul carried the watermelon head under his arm. They ran as fast as they could to the crossing, then hid in the thick bushes alongside the tracks to put the finishing touches on their dummy. It was 4:50 P.M.

"We got ten minutes," Paul said.

They ran out and arranged Clarence across the hot steel tracks, their hearts racing.

"If he don't look like a person, I ain't never seen one. We did it, Moses!"

Paul put his ear to the rail. "Tracks are humming. She'll soon come a-thundering."

The boys ran back over the crossing to get behind their bushes, doubled over, laughing so hard they hardly heard Blessing Macrae, rechristened by Elijah as "the Whore of Babylon," until she came up alongside.

"What are you boys up to?" She was on her way to business, wearing a tight red cotton skirt, a fringed black off-the-shoulder blouse, and her hair was combed into a stiff black pageboy with shiny barrettes on either side.

"We're putting Clarence on the track—stopping the train."

They pointed to the dummy.

"You boys' crazy, you'll get your asses put in jail for this," she warned.

"Ain't got time for talk," Paul answered, out of breath.

The three of them scooted behind the tall thick bushes and waited. Paul wondered what Moses was hoping for when he saw how close his friend had huddled up to Blessing. He took a careful look as the late afternoon sun picked up the shadows on her pretty plum-black face. He remembered that two years earlier Elijah had turned her out of his church after he'd found out how she was earning her money.

At this very moment, Moses looked like he was ready to take a bite out of Blessing's full red lips. She giggled and slipped her arm around his friend's neck. Sweat trickled down Paul's back. He felt a flicker of excitement; pictured himself wearing Blessing's tight red skirt and tried to imagine what kind of business it was she'd be doing. He wondered then what would happen if he crossed the tracks for business. Would Moses look at him the way his friend was looking at Blessing now? In the midst of his confusion, he heard a rumbling.

"Pay attention, Moses, it's coming."

Faraway whistles turned into two loud shrieks. The great black engine, cowcatcher in front, was bearing furiously down the track, a white column of smoke and steam pumping out of the funnel. She was almost on top of them. They heard the grinding of brakes, followed by an almighty screech as the engine stopped.

Paul, awestruck, whispered, "Moses, we did it."

When they heard angry voices from the tracks, Blessing put her hands over the boys' mouths. Through the thick leaves and branches, they could make out the engine driver walking along with the conductors, picking up the leftover pieces of Clarence, shaking their heads, and flinging his watermelon head away.

"Somebody's going to jail for this." The engine driver, fat, red-faced and sweating, took off his hat to mop his brow with a dirty red-

and-white handkerchief. "When we catch 'em, we'll teach 'em a lesson—maybe even hang 'em."

They watched the huddle of men nodding.

Blessing whispered, "What did I tell y'all?"

Moses started to shiver, and Paul began to shake. What had they done? They were far enough away that no one could hear their voices, but despite that, Blessing whispered, "Stop shaking so hard. Ain't no one seen you boys. Go on home, shut your doors, and keep your mouths shut, too."

That evening she was late for business with Ernie Price. Six months had passed since Elmer Peabody retired and Ernie had taken his place as Horse Cave's one and only policeman. Blessing had been doing business with Ernie since he started his new job. She opened the back door of the station, left unlocked as usual and on purpose.

A few minutes later, he rubbed his baby pink face with its thin, light-brown mustache into Blessing Macrae's straight up, seventeen-year-old breasts. "Blessing," he moaned, "you got tits like a young calf." Afterwards, a little ashamed, he peeled off a dollar bill carefully and handed it to her as she wiggled into her skirt and slipped back into her high heels.

Ernie never stopped talking, "Blessing, lucky you was over an hour late. You missed that old fool Billy Joe Brandstetter, rushing through my front door with his hair standing on end. First time something big ever happened to him. You shoulda seen him, red in the face, stuttering, trying to get his words out. He said, 'Some damn fools stopped my train, put a dummy on the tracks.'"

Blessing reached over and rubbed Ernie's thin, wiry hair. "What if I told you I saw who done it? What if I told you that's why I'm late?"

Ernie stood up, reached for his gun belt, strapped it around his waist. "Seriously? Out with it, girl. Otherwise, you'll be withholding evidence."

Blessing took her time, smoothed under her ruffled hair. "Well, I ain't sure, and I ain't saying, but on my way over the tracks, a little before the train was due, I saw two White boys, looked like the Weavers, running away as fast as they could skedaddle. You couldn't make me swear to it, 'cause I'd say I never saw any such thing. You and I both know their granddaddy rides with the Klan. What's more, you know they'd kill me, ever found out it was me who told you."

He reached over, patted her shoulder. "I wouldn't want nothing to happen to you."

Only months into this job, Ernie knew this investigation was going nowhere. Who in his right mind would mess with Old Man Weaver or his two brats? And Weaver's other boy, Earl, was an up-and-coming lawyer in Munfordville, might even become the district attorney. Wouldn't pay to get on the bad side of him. Ernie rubbed his hands together. "I guess that's it then."

On her way out, Blessing turned back. "Now you know where not to look."

He laughed. "Reckon you're right."

On down to Horace Nickel's Drugstore to let herself in by another unlocked backdoor, Blessing thought about how to teach those boys she'd taken a special liking to a lesson.

Next day, she woke up just before the noon whistle, boiled up a cup of coffee, and sat down to eat a piece of the peach cobbler she baked twice a week. She knew Ernie Price believed her, knew she'd saved a lot of Black folks from having their doors kicked down by the police, and certainly saved the skins of her two favorite young boys.

After breakfast, Blessing set out in a newly ironed full pink cotton skirt, a white buttoned-up blouse, and her hair tied back with a pink ribbon. She found the boys under the chestnut tree in Moses's backyard.

"Howdy! I'll be surprised if you two ain't already shaking and quaking." She sat on the ground beside them and spread her pink skirt. "Moses, run on in the house, get me a root beer."

While they waited, Blessing picked up one of Paul's hands, stroked his fingers. "Be fun to paint those pretty nails." She picked a couple of leaves off the tree. "Y'all stuff your dummy with these?"

Paul nodded.

Moses called out from the back door. "Paul, help me carry these root beers and the plate of your sugar cookies." Paul baked every week and took half of the cookies and cakes next door to Moses and Coralee.

Blessing put down her bottle of root beer as Paul and Moses edged in closer to the circle of her skirt. In a low, steady, serious voice, her head almost touching theirs, she said, "Pay me mind, boys, and just maybe you'll get through this here world alive." She took a small delicate sip of her drink.

Moses's cheeks burned, aware of her red lips around the bottle.

"White folks' law ain't for us."

Paul saw her undone hair ribbon, watched it hanging and tickling her neck. "Let me do it," he said.

She turned her head, waited for Paul to tie her pink bow, and felt Moses's eyes burning. She said, "Pretend you're lying on those railroad tracks, tied up like your dummy, feeling a hot sun, burning steel tracks against your necks. You ain't moving any which way. You hear a whistle, you close your eyes, nothing you can do except wait for the train to cut you to pieces. You know that train ain't stopping for you like it did for Clarence."

Her words sank in.

"Maybe this time you got away with it. But it's the last time. You don't mess with the White men's train 'less you asking for them to throw you under it."

"Blessing, how do you know they won't come after us?"

Moses echoed Paul, "Yes, how can you be sure?"

"When can we stop being scared?" Paul pressed.

Blessing, licking away the cookie crumbs from around her mouth, chose her words carefully, "Never stop being scared."

5

Sunday morning, Elijah got out of bed, taking his time, making sure his black suit was brushed before he put his jacket over a freshly ironed white shirt—Paul's handiwork. He set off early for service at ten o'clock, on foot to church with Coralee, who sang in the choir.

Next door, Moses, his hair untamed, dressed in a white shirt and fresh blue jeans, came down the steps of his shack to join Paul, his brothers and sisters, along with all the other Baptists in town who set off along the hot, dusty-red road that led to the Children of God Third Baptist Church. It was a simple white-clapboard building on stilts, standing in the middle of the Kingdom with one front colored-glass window—sadly, as Elijah fretted, "without divine pictures." Elijah, Lily, the deacons, and the sisters of the church had been planning a picnic to raise money for two more windows.

When they arrived at the doors of the church, the ushers—stone-faced keepers of the peace in white gloves—led Lily and her family to the simple wooden front pews, behind the sisters, a few rows back below the pulpit. The Baptist Carews almost took up half the church.

Moses, an honorary member of the family, sat next to Paul. On the other side was Lily, straight-backed, her small, yellow straw hat perched on top of a severe black bun, curly hair pulled so tightly there wasn't a wrinkle in her face. Sideways, she had a straight nose, round chin, a long neck with her soft brown eyes and full pink lips. She might have been called a beauty if she'd paid any attention to her looks. It was Elijah who said, "Lily, you walk like you carrying the Bible on top of your head," then he added, "With the Lord himself inside."

James, Ernest, Tabby, and Tallulah were marched off to the Sunday school room, minded by a very strict Miss Hetty. Paul wished he could go back to the good old days when he too was led off instead of squirming with the congregation for the next two hours.

Without turning her head, Lily slid her warm hand over Paul's. She gently stroked them, one by one, pulling each of his fingers until she reached the little one with the long nail, the one he tried to keep hidden. She stopped, tapped the nail, and smiled sideways at him with a flash of her gold tooth. One of their many little secrets.

Lorene, Paul's favorite cousin, sat behind them with her little girl Arletta, tickled Paul's neck with her church fan, and every now and then, slipped him a piece of her homemade toffee. Sometimes she and Paul got together on Saturday mornings, fixed Sunday lunch for all the Carews at Lorene's house: caramel cake, fudge cake, yellow cake, fried enough chicken for an army, bowls of potato salad.

"You're almost getting to be as good a cook as I am," Lorene told Paul. "But you ain't there yet, boy."

Paul was too hot under his white shirt, now marked by the lines of sweat trickling down his back. What if someone besides Blessing had seen him and Moses putting Clarence on the tracks? Why had they done such a dumb thing? Paul hardly heard the choir singing.

"On a hill far away stood an old rugged cross."

It was the first Sunday that Lily's grandmother, Abilene, had missed church since she was five years old. On Friday afternoon, she'd cut her eightieth birthday cake, one of her own famous yellow cakes, surrounded by her seven children and her twenty-two grandchildren. When she laid down the knife, she looked straight across the table into Elijah's eyes and pronounced, "Preacher, I'm through sitting on that hard bench for two hours every Sunday." Grandma Abilene's chin went up and her neck stretched as she looked down on Elijah. "Mean little eyes" was how she'd described them when he and Lily were courting.

Paul wished his Great-grandma Abilene could still be here beside him. She'd seemed to him to be the queen of the world. She sat straight in the pew, her grape-colored cotton dress running up to her neck, secured with small pearl buttons, her black wide-brimmed straw hat with the elastic band under her strict bun held in place with the real pearl hatpin, which looked to Paul as if it stabbed right through her head. She wore little black boots laced up above her ankles and, best of all for her great-grandchild, she kept a pocketful of bear gums and saltwater taffy.

Paul fidgeted, listening to the choir warm it up for Elijah. The congregation stood to sing a hymn he loved: *"What a friend we have in Jesus, all our sins and griefs to bear."* And heads turned when Paul's voice, one Lorene was sure "could melt the horns off the devil," poured out, filling the church.

It seemed to take forever before his father strode out upon the small stage and opened his arms wide to bless the congregation before climbing behind his pulpit, where he was soon threatening the same wide-eyed audience with everlasting Hell and fury.

For the next two hours, Elijah whipped it up, came out of his pulpit, got down on his hands and knees, stomped his feet, and shook his fists.

He looked straight at Paul when he said, "Do you not know that the wicked will not inherit the kingdom of God? Do not be fooled. Neither the sexually immoral nor idolaters nor adulterers nor male prostitutes nor homosexual offenders will inherit the earth. I see darkness all around me here."

Moses leaned over, whispered into Paul's ear, "What's he talking about, male prostitute?"

Paul whispered back, "Ain't never heard of one, reckon he got it wrong."

Lorene leaned forward. "Shhh, y'all, hush."

With that, Elijah pulled out a white handkerchief freshly ironed by his son, sighed, and wiped his brow. "The devil's pushed you all down into a deep, black hole." Elijah ran his hands through his crinkly black hair as if he wanted to tear it all out. "Who's coming to get you out?"

Then the reply from the congregation, "Sweet Jesus is coming for me." Arms were up and waving in time to Elijah's words.

"He's looking, you hear me, sinners? God sees your evil and God rains demons down on your head. His arrows will find you."

"Oh, Lord Jesus is looking," the congregation shouted back, as the church fans whipped faster, cooling hot faces.

Paul tried to move closer to his mama. But it was never close enough.

Elijah brought down more fire and brimstone until the spirit entered and moved one Baptist after another to shout, to scream, even to fall on the floor.

With Elijah preaching, all the Whores of Babylon with Christ's blood flowing out of their terrible wounds, would come raining down for the next hour and a half.

"God is good."

And back it came. "God is good."

"All the time."

Soon as Paul thought it was over, Elijah would start up again.

"Let me hear it!"

Paul was beginning to sweat. How much longer, O Lord? He leaned over, whispered into Moses's ear, "Can't stand another minute."

As he gave his final blessing, Elijah's last ounce of pent-up fervor was spent with a long sigh and an "Amen." When the church doors finally opened, it was way past noon and so hot, Paul had to catch his breath. All the ladies in their straw hats and white gloves filed out to shake the Rev's hand.

Finding a little shade underneath the leaves of an ash tree, Lily stood tall, thin, and upright next to her husband, and as many hands came forward to touch hers as to shake the pastor's.

6

Paul and Blessing sometimes found each other, him on his way home from school, Blessing on her way to business. She had taken a shine to the fifteen-year-old boy, looked him up and down, put her hands on her hips, when she answered his, "Howdy, ma'am," as if she didn't expect it. She said God-fearing folks crossed to the other side of the street when they saw her coming.

Sometimes she invited him in for a cup of bourbon. Those 'sometimes' fired up Moses, who begged Paul for every single detail of what she was wearing, whether she was in a good mood, if she mentioned his name, and who she had been seeing across the tracks.

Inside the one-room shack, her bed was covered with an orange and red quilt, different-colored dresses lay over a chair, and high-heeled shoes were lined up against a wall. In one corner, a dressing table was heaped with creams and paint of all kinds.

Most of the time, Paul would sit and listen to the stories she shared with him about her White customers. There was one about Ernie, the policeman. Ernie had gotten together a bunch of his good ol' boys in town. They all chipped in and hired Blessing to give them a show with Tommy Barber, the drooling Horse Cave idiot.

"Paul, I did it right there in front of them. Took poor old Tommy a while to get the hang of it, but when he got it, he ain't stopping for no one! I give them their money's worth."

Truth was, stories like that made Paul uneasy. He didn't pass them on to Moses.

On one particular day, Blessing invited Paul to watch her paint her face. He wondered how she knew he would love that; she seemed to know a lot about him.

"Paul, I ain't sure 'bout you. You so handsome... Why do I get the feeling you're like my girlfriend? Ever wonder what it's like, doing it with a girl? Like me to show you?"

He didn't want her to show him anything.

She poured out two China coffee cups of bourbon, double for her, Paul sipped a little.

"Come on, sit over here beside me. I'll show you how I put on my paint." Blessing became softer with each sip of bourbon, didn't seem to mind what she said. "I like pretty boys better'n rough men. Come over here. Do you think maybe you'd like me better if I put on a pair of pants?" Then she threw back her head and laughed.

Paul pulled up a chair next to Blessing, looked at both their faces in the mirror. Without turning her head, she reached sideways, put her hand on his pants, and began rubbing.

He put his hand softly over hers and moved it away. "Maybe we'll try all this another time, Blessing."

"All right, scaredy-cat."

Slowly she twisted her crimson lipstick all the way out, while fixing him with a smile. With her finger, she traced red onto the outline of her lips. She leaned forward, mouth open. He could see her pink tongue.

In a soft, low voice, she asked, "Want me to show you something else, Paul? I know what you like. I likes it, too."

"Not ready, Blessing." He'd heard Lily and Elijah grunting through the thin walls of their bedroom. Something about it seemed unnatural, but what, he didn't know exactly.

Blessing laughed, then patted him on the head. "I got a big bag of tricks, you can take your pick, Paul. You're gonna be missing the best part of your life, boy, if you don't try out what I got to offer."

Paul shook his head. "I reckon I'll wait awhile. Maybe Moses is your boy."

"When it happens to you, Paul, there won't be any wait *awhiles*. As for Moses, you both are my boys."

On his way home down the old dirt track, he had to wonder: Would he ever be ready—for Blessing or for anybody?

7

"Hold still, Miss Fancy Pants."

Tallulah was the one. She swirled around the room in her full-skirted, pink-cotton Sunday-school dress while Tabby quietly allowed Lily to raise the hem. Paul was at the hot stove smothering pork chops for supper, while James and Ernest tugged at his pants.

"Come on, come on, Paul. Tell us a butterfly story," James said.

Before he had a chance to sit down with the boys, they were interrupted.

"My old stove is a heap of garbage," Coralee said, as she came in with Moses.

Then Elijah came through the back door looking tired, home a little later than usual from the fields. "We got enough work pulling tobacco for ten men, only five of us."

Coralee unwrapped old newspaper around five new-laid eggs, from her small batch of hens. "Appreciate y'all feeding me and Moses. That stove's always breaking down. I can eat cold cornbread with buttermilk for supper, but not for my boy."

Elijah pulled at his braces, knew he had a duty to look after his neighbors. "Don't you fret, Coralee. I'll send Cousin Eddie over tomorrow. All he has to do is look at something broke and it fixes itself."

When Paul turned around to say hello to Moses and Coralee, he saw his father looking at him with a smile instead of his usual scowl.

"What's for supper, Paul? I'm awful hungry. Let's eat." Taking his usual seat, he continued, "I want you and Moses to sit down aside me."

Moses had tenderness for Elijah. He'd looked up to him as a father when he was a boy. Elijah had taken the time to care for him, brought him into the family. But after seeing how Elijah treated his own son, Moses was a little more careful of him these days.

Paul smiled at Tabby, hurrying to scoot her chair right up next to Moses. Everyone sat down.

Elijah put his arms out as if to hug the table, and half sang, half spoke grace in a deep, loud voice, "For this and for all we are about to receive, may the Lord make us truly thankful." After serving himself a good helping of smothered pork chops, fried apples, and greasy green beans with fresh-picked beefsteak tomatoes, he got to the point.

"I know you boys are smarter than most. I need your help with putting on a picnic... And not just any old picnic." He pulled a piece of paper out of his overall pocket. "You all know we got more Baptists than Methodists, but they got richer people in their congregation. You see water dripping down on to Becca May Cherry's hat on Sunday? We got to get our roof fixed, and we need another stained-glass holy window. We need one hundred and fifty dollars for the roof, and one hundred and fifty dollars for our window.

"We need to lift the spirits, raise lots of money. We got to look for a place big enough to hold everyone in the Kingdom, not just Baptists, a picnic with goods for sale so folks'll put their hands in their pockets, only take them out when we earn that three hundred dollars." Elijah's eyes were shining, out of his own fired-up spirit. "What do you say, boys?"

Paul nodded in dumb amazement. "Yes, sir."

Moses was ready. "We'll all get busy."

Coralee and Lily were already planning.

"We'll help too, Daddy," came from the little ones.

"Happy I can count on my family," Elijah said.

Moses, Paul, James, and Ernest got up to clear the table.

"Mighty good dinner, Paul. Coralee, I reckon we got us two fine boys."

Paul felt the first rush of warmth he could ever remember towards his father.

Lily, sitting at the other end of the table, shook her head, sure she was dreaming.

After supper, the boys finished the dishes and went over to sit on Moses's front porch.

"We need to get busy," Paul said.

"First thing tomorrow, we go to Strickland's and talk to Auriol. She's our girl. She's got the say over at Old Man Strickland's."

"Remember, Moses, how you couldn't take your eyes off her in Sunday school? Bet you never thought she would end up living with a White farmer twice her age."

Auriol Simpson was a lively little girl whose pigtails were laced with bright-red ribbons. Her hair was pulled back from a high forehead over big brown eyes and a nose that was too long for her face. She was fifteen years old when she'd gone to work for Dave Strickland. After a few months, she took charge of the house, made his bed, and lay with him.

"Strickland's farm is the only place to have the picnic." Moses brought out a notepad and a pencil. "We can talk to Auriol. Too bad she wasn't there when we were fishing."

"You can't see a thing in the dark, Moses."

Truth was, they could see to write by the light of a round full moon. They sat, ideas tumbling out and sparking up others. They would go around the Kingdom, find as many Baptists as they could to make and donate dishes for the picnic table. They'd ask Lulu Belle

Baines, who fashioned homemade dolls for all the children in the Kingdom, to set up a sales table. Dead Eye Farlow, the Kingdom's undertaker, could find blocks of ice. Paul suggested they could even ask Grandma Abilene to bake a couple of her caramel cakes. And of course, when the time came, Paul and Lorene would cook up a storm.

"We'll go 'round, ask everyone who keeps chickens to donate some eggs. We'll devil some and we'll sell the rest."

When Paul finally got home, he tiptoed into the bedroom where all the children slept together, put on his night shirt, and waited for the last of the giggles, whispers, and rustling bedclothes to die down. It was almost high summer, and he looked forward to taking his sheet and mattress and sleeping on the front porch. Now he had a goal: Three hundred dollars was the magic number and then he'd become his father's special, bright boy. He could still feel the warmth of Elijah's hand on his shoulder.

———

Old Man Strickland's ten-acre farm lay on the edge of the Kingdom. Dave Strickland wasn't more than forty years old, but Colored people called any White man who didn't shave every day, Old Man.

Auriol was the only child of strict, born-again Baptists, John and Mae Simpson. Auriol's life of sin, living with a White man, cast a shadow over John and Mae. Their beloved daughter was living with a man who was not one of their own.

Word had it that Old Man Strickland was shy of washing. He swatted flies, and if they still wiggled after swatting, he cracked them between his fingernails, even during meals. After Strickland's daddy drank himself to death, his mama died of a stroke a week later. He'd kept up the farm but allowed the house to fall down. Auriol did the best she could to keep it clean and to pester Strickland to fix whatever needed fixing.

For the last month, every Sunday, Auriol had been listening to the Reverend Carew.

"Sweet Jesus, find us a place for our picnic, Lord God Almighty, You listening? We need enough room for every Christian in the Kingdom."

Sitting beside her daughter, Mae Simpson whispered, "Auriol, can you help?"

"Paul and Moses already asked me. I told them I'll try."

Dave Strickland's farm lay under the shade of Kentucky tulip trees, white oak, white ash, and yellow buckeye, and there was plenty of room in the yard around his old farmhouse for every good soul in the Kingdom.

But he told Auriol, "I ain't doing something for nothing." He buttoned up his new clean white shirt, washed and ironed by her, lifted his cap, and took out his handkerchief to wipe away the sweat. "Auriol, I ain't doing it."

When she heard that news, Sister Betty Lamont, who headed up the Baptist church picnic committee, asked Auriol to let them know what Dave Strickland wanted.

Auriol replied, "Sweeten it up."

After two hours of iced tea and hot discussion, the committee came up with several proposals.

Auriol read them out loud to Dave. "Enough hands come over to you a week before the picnic, pick your tomatoes, bring the bushel baskets into the house. They'll clean up your yard, cut long grass, fix up a fishing contest with all the caught catfish going back to you."

Dave pushed his chair back, put his feet up on the kitchen table. "Be interested if you put some more sugar in the pot. How 'bout I get some of the hard cash?"

Auriol took it one step further. The previous year, Dave, a good carpenter, had made himself a small rowboat, neatly crafted, with enough room for four in it. You couldn't throw a stone across his pond where the boys use to fish. It was plenty big enough.

"Dave, float the boat out there, a dime a ride. Baptist Church gives you back a nickel out of every ten cents."

He took his feet off the table, sat up straight. "Sounds all right. Anything else you got in mind?"

Auriol finally softened him up with chicken-fried steak, hash-brown potatoes, and as many "rides" with her as he wanted.

Every Baptist who crossed the tracks to work for White folks asked them to donate a prize for the good cause of the Baptist Church roof and the holy window. Most of the stores in town offered something. Larkin's put up a stack of out-of-date movie magazines and Moses, thinking that was a little stingy, asked outright for some Hershey bars. The five and dime gave a bunch of coloring books and crayons taken off their shelves with their dented yellow boxes. The Hidden River Cave office, in the middle of town, offered their beloved Baptist maid, Severine, a crystal onyx paperweight and a shirt with "Hidden River Cave, largest cave entrance in the world," printed on the back. Walter Jackson asked Lorene to unhook a "good-sized ham" from the Jackson smokehouse, known to be the best in the county.

By the end of the week, Lily had sewn ten white handkerchiefs, the Force family gave six baby chickens, Coralee collected bundles of sassafras root. Fresh eggs were snatched every day from under cackling hens. And most everybody in the Kingdom carried fat envelopes full of loose change they'd been collecting to spend on whatever took their fancy from the six well-advertised wooden sales tables.

————

On the day, a hot July Saturday morning, Lily, Paul, Moses, the twins, James, and Ernest had been up since sunrise putting the cooked dishes and cakes wrapped in tea towels on top of Lily's folded blue-and-white tablecloths into the back of Elijah's wagon. When everything was fully loaded, Paul and Moses took the mules by their reins and slowly walked the mile from their shack to Strickland's farm. Lily sat on the wagon with Tabby and Tallulah and held onto the dishes while Ernest and James sat way in the back, to make sure the baby chicks were covered with a white tea towel, to keep them out of the sun.

"Mama, Ernest done stuck his finger in the caramel icing." Tallulah's slap put an end to that.

Elijah, up at dawn, had gone ahead to give directions. Long wooden tables were set up over wet dewed grass and covered with white sheets. Sister Evangelina, head of the picnic committee, borrowed a chair from Dave and Auriol to count the takings. Paul and Moses stood at the end of the road leading to Strickland's farm to collect the twenty-five-cent entry fee for the tickets. Tallulah and Tabby had worked hard making tickets, cutting them out from different pieces of colored paper.

By eleven o'clock, the Baptist church had already made fifty dollars.

One of the last to buy a ticket was Blessing Macrae, dressed in yellow with an orange straw hat. She handed Paul and Moses a dollar.

"Hold on, girl. We got change," Paul said.

Sister Evangelina's nose was raised a little, as she counted out fifteen nickels to put in the palm of Blessing's hand.

Blessing smiled sweetly. "Keep the change, Evangelina."

Moses shyly stammered, "Eat lunch with us, Blessing?"

Blessing patted his cheek. "We'll see." Straight-backed and head up, jingling her purse, she strolled over to join the crowd at the sales tables.

Paul closed his ears to the sound of the crowd and was standing quietly looking out over the fine bright layer of dust on the top of the pond when he heard Elijah's deep, loud voice behind him.

"Seems we made over two hundred dollars already, son, and we ain't finished counting."

Could it be, from the look on Elijah's face, that he was pleased with Paul?

When it was time to eat, the crowds headed across the grass to the picnic tables where red ripe watermelons lay over blocks of ice in zinc tubs and Dead Eye Farlow—so named after the loss of one eye when he was chipping ice to cool down a corpse—was at it again with his ice pick, getting ready to fill everyone's tin cups, before his wife, Biddy, poured in sweet iced tea over crushed mint.

"O Lord God, bless this food we are—"

Before Elijah could finish grace, the crowd began jostling before the tables: Paul, Moses, Lily with the children, Coralee, and Lorene with her mama, Severine, who cared for Lorene's seven-year-old Arletta, and all the rest of the folks who had spread their blankets under the shade of the white mountain ash and locust trees.

The good Christians stood in line, carrying their own plates and knives and forks they'd brought along with them. Those plates were heaped with fried chicken, coleslaw, potato salad, homemade pimento cheese, cornbread, cold biscuits, salt-rising bread, and that was only the beginning. There wasn't a plate not piled high with fine home cooking.

Paul saw Blessing waiting in line, talking to no one. He didn't want to see her eating alone. He looked over, saw his father. Why should he worry so much about what Elijah thought? He and Moses had planned the picnic. Looked like money was rolling in. After all, Blessing was their friend.

"Blessing, when you get your food, come on over and eat with us."

She stood holding her plate, a little shy about sitting down with Lily and the children.

Paul took her arm, led her over to their blanket, and made a place for her between him and Moses. "You're welcome here, Blessing."

Moses jumped up to take her plate and make a place for her, too tongue-tied from excitement to say much about it except, "Let me fetch you some iced tea."

At first Lily hesitated before handing the girl a napkin. Then her own fine manners took over. "Nice to see you, Blessing. Welcome."

Coralee put out her hand. "I don't think we ever met each other. I'm Moses's mama."

Tabby and Tallulah, in matching pink-cotton sundresses, scooted over closer to the fine-looking girl in the yellow dress with the orange straw hat.

"Pretty hat," Tallulah said.

Blessing smiled at her. "Here, try it on." She whipped off her hat, placed it on Tallulah's head, and fished in her bag for a mirror. "Look at you, honey. It's your color, suits you."

Lily tapped her daughter gently on the wrist. "Now you quit that, Tallulah. You all leave Blessing alone. She needs her hat."

Tallulah, with adoring eyes, handed it back.

Elijah, ready to address the crowd, stood waiting for silence. "Let the rain roll off our roof and light shine through our new holy window and let us all remember a day when Christians dug down deep in their pockets, for the sake of Jesus Christ and the Baptist Church. I reckon we met our target. Lots of hard work went into this, but we won the day. God bless you all. Amen!"

Moses nudged Paul and whispered, "Sounds like your pa did all of our work."

Paul shook his head. "Ain't surprised, but I hoped for better."

"Ain't that Sissy Cole standing over there with Elijah?" Blessing said, in a low voice to the boys.

Sharp-eared Lily overheard, shaded her eyes against the sun. "Sure looks like it."

At first, Paul wondered if it really was Sissy with Elijah holding their plates, gazing into each other's faces. She wore a wide-brimmed purple straw hat. But after another good look, he recognized her sinewy legs and tight little bottom.

Sissy was the only daughter of Abe Cole, the richest man in the Kingdom. It was whispered that his granddaddy had kept a slave on his farm in Bear Wallow. No one knew if it was gospel, but it was yet another reason to dislike and distrust Sissy, who made no secret of her interest in Elijah Carew, caring nothing for his wife's feelings.

———

They got home from the picnic in the late afternoon. Paul unloaded the cart, brought in the empty dishes, and washed up. He felt low. For the last month, he and Moses had been excited. Every morning they'd woken up looking forward to reaching their target of three hundred dollars. Now they had it and more. But what difference did it make? His dream was over; he'd seen his father acting like a fool with Sissy Cole.

Their family supper of picnic leftovers was over long before Elijah finally got in after dark. Paul saw by his scowl and red eyes that he was riled up.

"Ain't that Blessing Macrae I seen sitting, eating lunch with my family, on my blanket?"

Bitterly disappointed, Paul looked with disgust at his father, and wondered why he'd worked so hard for this man's love and approval. For once, he answered back sharply, "Every time we hoped you were coming to eat lunch with us, we seen you talking to that Cole woman."

Elijah snarled back, "I wasn't fixing to come over and see my family with that little whore on our blanket!"

Lily, one of her headaches pounding, looked over sadly at her husband and remembered Grandma Abilene's warnings: "Elijah's got too much fire, not enough tender. He'll not be faithful, you'll see."

8

Paul woke early, not looking forward to facing another endless summer Sabbath. Inside the church, he sat in his usual place, feeling angry and sad. It was past noon and hot. His father spent a great deal of his sermon thanking God for choosing to pour down blessings upon his own worthy head. Paul took notice that the last thing Elijah remembered to do was thank his loyal congregation.

After church, as they always did, the Carews got together at Cousin Lorene's house for lunch. But Paul couldn't find his appetite and scooted little mounds of mashed potato and chicken breast under his untouched biscuit. He kept an eye on Elijah.

After a while, he couldn't bear the sight of his father's grease-covered chin, moving up and down like a string-pulled dummy, so he matched up his knife and fork, stood, and took his plate into the kitchen.

"Paul, you come back over here, get you a piece of my coconut cake, allow me to put this spoon of vanilla ice cream on top." Lorene dug her scoop down deep, came up with a perfect round ball.

As soon as she handed him the plate, Paul tiptoed well behind his father's scowl and found a place next to Lorene's daughter, Arletta, took his cake, cut it up into small pieces, and divided tiny blobs of ice cream to spoon onto each bit.

"Paul, you just so delicate," Arletta whispered.

While Lorene passed around coffee cups, Paul slipped out the door and walked home to the Carews' wooden house held up by gray concrete stilts under the front porch. He was alone. All was still. He set to picking up clothes Elijah dropped while in a hurry to get ready for church, folded or hung them back into the cupboards. On his way to the bedroom, carrying Elijah's tobacco-stained overalls, his eye caught the folds of his mama's second-best dress, a hand-me-down from Lorene who'd gotten it from the big house where she worked. This was his chance to follow his feelings and he took it.

Paul peeled off his Sunday shirt, unwound the pink lace and cotton dress from its hanger and pulled it over his head, where it fell to below his knees. He followed himself in the dressing-table mirror, then sat down to unroll his mama's Pink Lady lipstick from the five and dime.

Paul pursed his mouth, flattened his lips in a big O. He traced and filled in the color, not stopping until he'd reached the deepest pink. A small, brown powder puff patted rouge onto his cheeks. He unhooked the colored beads his mama'd hung over the pointed frame of her mirror, wound them over and over around his neck. Finally he turned on her radio, snapping his fingers to the tune of Sweet Georgia Brown. He knew it by heart, like he did every other hit song of the day.

No gal made has got a shade on Sweet Georgia Brown, Two left feet, but oh so neat...

He wasn't a second away from tapping his feet, his mama's pink dress swishing with the beat, he swayed from side to side, arms gently swinging until he was dancing and singing with his perfect partner, the boy in the mirror.

Fact is, Paul could croon the words to most songs by the light of any old silvery moon. Every day he sang into his mama's mirror. He reached over to turn the music up and heard the bang of the front screen door. Scared to death it might be Elijah, he dived under the double bed, trying to pull Lily's pink skirt with him as he lay flat on his stomach, holding his breath. He peeked out, seeing a pair of black shiny preacher shoes.

Time went by; the shoes never moved. Blood pounded in Paul's ears, and he was praying Elijah hadn't seen him.

Then, in a low voice, his father said, "I see your mama's pretty pink dress hanging out. Might have called you Paula, that more like it." He knelt down, looked at his son.

Paul caught one of his father's rare, wide smiles, and with relief, started to breathe again, until Elijah hooked a hand under his arm, squeezed hard on his chicken wing, and pulled him out from under. One of the strings of Lily's necklace broke, spattering beads all over the floor, and for a minute, Paul was tempted to scoop up all the different colored glass balls. He could smell his father's stale breath when Elijah put his face up close against his trembling own.

"Take off that dress, clean your face." He stood waiting with his hands on his hips, voice booming.

Paul fumbled with each pink-covered button, pulled down the side zipper, and lifted the dress carefully over his made-up face. Then he took a towel hanging over the basin, spat into it, and scrubbed off as much makeup as he could. He stood there in his underpants and shivered in fear.

"You know what God would say, don't you, boy? Or is it girl? God would say to me, loud and clear: 'Beat out those demons, Reverend Carew. Beat them until they fly down to Hell!'"

Elijah unhooked his brown-leather belt with the big brass buckle and with the other arm threw Paul across the bed. At first, the strap came down in slow, sharp slaps, then fury gathered steam and on they came, harder, faster.

Paul tried to wriggle away but Elijah pulled him back with one hand, with his other, turned the belt to the buckled end and kept on beating until the metal clip dug deeper into Paul's skin with each blow. Trickles of sweat rolled into his eyes, mixed with his tears, and in his agony, he could feel sweat and blood sliding down his back. Then, just as Paul nearly lost himself in a dead faint, the bedroom door opened.

Lily saw her boy lying soft and quiet like a ragdoll. She took in the belt buckle, the splashes of Paul's bright-red blood. She reached for her gold-and-white figurine of Christ the Savior and brought it down so hard on Elijah's head, he dropped his belt and stared stupidly at the pieces of ceramic scattered all over the floor.

Just then, the screen door slammed shut and in came Lily's brother, Bill, carrying a plate of Lorene's leftover coconut cake. When he saw his nephew half naked in his underpants, bloody welts all over his body held close against a sobbing Lily, he ran as fast as he could, back to Cousin Lorene's for help.

————

Dr. Jimmy Wilkes snapped his black bag shut, watched his young patient's fingers uncurl from fists as the morphine flowed in. Cuts and bruises, washed and dressed in bandages, all anyone could see of Paul were his cheeks.

"He'll live. In the morning, I'll be back. And you, Elijah, better keep your head down, along with that temper of yours." Dr. Jimmy stood as blue flashing lights beamed in through the front room window of the Carew home.

Ernie Price came up the porch steps and through the screen door, hand brushing the top of his gun. Behind him was Walter Jackson, who'd driven over from his tobacco farm.

As he clinked and snapped the handcuffs around Elijah's wrists, Ernie Price said, "You're lucky we're not taking you in for first-degree attempted murder, Carew. If you didn't kill your boy, it wasn't for lack of trying. You'll spend some nights in a cell."

Walter Jackson patted Lily's shoulder. "Don't look so sad. I'm going to ask Lorene to bring Paul up to the house when he gets better. Mrs. Jackson's been after me for extra help, someone to work with Lorene in the kitchen. Why, there's even a little house out back where the boy could live. Of course, the final decision rests with Mrs. Jackson."

Beneath the bruises and bandages, Paul felt a flutter of hope.

The sun had gone down but folk still came out to sit on their porches, and when the wailing sirens were turned back on, there was no one in the Kingdom who did not see Reverend Elijah Carew, of the Children of God Third Baptist Church, mashed into the back seat of the police car in his bloody Sunday shirt.

———

Through his pain, Paul remembered his father that very morning stepping into his pulpit, inviting down the sword of righteousness on all sinners. He saw that sword stabbing right through his mama's pretty pink dress. Now that Elijah knew his secret, all Paul could hope for was that his father would be too embarrassed to tell anyone.

Paul brushed away the hand on his forehead.

"Paul, it's me, Moses," said his friend. "Why did Elijah do this to you?"

Through his pain, Paul understood he'd better be careful how he answered. "He got mad when he caught me singing and dancing on the Sabbath, playing Mama's radio." Paul struggled to open his swollen eyes, hardly seeing Moses staring down at him with shock and anger.

"That ain't no crime. You can't stay in the house with a man like him." Moses smoothed Paul's rumpled sheet, pulling it up under his chin. "Let's make us a plan. Soon as you're better."

Paul whispered, "Moses, reckon I already have one. Mr. Jackson might have a job for me, living up at his house. Soon's I get better, I'll go up and meet Mrs. Jackson."

Meanwhile, a few days later, Walter Jackson telephoned Ernie

Price. There was no mistaking the note of command in his voice. "Ernie, tobacco's ready to cut. I need all my men in the fields. Elijah's best overseer I got. Let him out of jail."

When Elijah came home a day later, he went about his business, acting like nothing had happened. From then on, Lily stood guard over her boy with a fierce look in her eyes.

9

It was two weeks after the picnic, the day of Paul's meeting with Sally Jackson. By then, his wounds had turned into scars. Early morning, he stayed in bed, waiting to hear Elijah's wagon clatter off down the road to work. The air between his father and him felt thin and starved, leaving them barely enough to breathe.

Paul had been lying with his eyes wide open most of the night, planning what he might say to Miss Sally. He heard his mother's voice saying, "He gone. You can get up now."

Paul dressed slowly, white shirt, blue pants, almost-new shoes.

Lily never allowed her handsome boy to look shabby. "Time to go," she told him. "Last thing we want is for you to be late."

Paul crossed the tracks, traveling by foot, over into town. The stores were closed except for Larkin's. Paul waved to Moses who was unlocking the front door of the grocery.

By the time he climbed the hill and reached the Jackson house, his nerves were sweating up wet patches under his arms. He hoped the lily of the valley powder he'd dusted would keep him fresh. This was the first time he'd ever crossed through the White part of town;

no Colored people on those sidewalks, not unless they were on their way to work.

The white clapboard house with its colonnaded porch was set back, away from the street. Maple trees, sycamores, and one enormous flowering chestnut hid the front porch. How grand it all seemed to him.

On his way up the drive, he tried to remember exactly which door Lorene had told him to take. He reckoned he'd keep walking until he reached the back garden, where at last, he saw the screened-in porch and caught a strong breeze of gardenia from the flowering bushes outside the door.

Inside, his eyes blinked at the new world of the Jacksons' big kitchen: two refrigerators, up-to-date ovens, endless counters for working. He could only imagine what he might cook up in there given the chance.

Lorene was in her uniform: white apron over a simple dark-blue dress, shaping patties of hot country sausage, ready for the iron skillet. "What you waiting for? Come on in here, help me fix their breakfast." She handed him a white apron that was too small. "Pass the test, we'll get you some bigger ones."

Paul took over and began turning strips of sputtering bacon and at the same time, minding the heat under the other skillets. While Lorene was cutting their grapefruit, he dropped his fork, and when he bent down to pick it up, he smelled the beginning of her sausages browning. He stood up, quickly pulled off the skillet, and turned over the patties before the harm was done.

"Paul, quit acting so jumpy, the woman ain't about to eat you." Lorene laughed, flashing a gold front tooth. "She'll be done with eating anything or anybody when they finish all this breakfast."

Paul tried to stop his heart thumping. Instead, he concentrated on holding his spatula ready under four perfect fried eggs, crinkly around the edges, sunny-side up, yolks nice and wobbly. One by one, he lifted them out and laid them gently beside Lorene's hot buttered toast. She took a clean tea towel and wiped around the edges of the two plates.

"Look here, ain't that pretty? Can't wait till you get yourself up here for good and help me."

Paul went out onto the screened porch while Lorene served breakfast. He looked out onto the back garden and wondered at all the colored flowers. Dazzled, he imagined the thrill of arranging them in vases.

"Paul Carew, you quit that daydreaming, get on in here! Miss Sally's ready for you."

Inside the dining room, the walls were covered with silver-and-gold wallpaper. At one end of a heavy mahogany table with a shining silver bowl in the middle, sat a plump fifty-year-old lady with a head of thick, white, curly hair and fierce blue eyes. Sally Jackson was drinking her second cup of coffee.

Paul stood at the far end of the table, his heart pounding.

"Come here, Paul Carew. Let me look at you. I see how you favor your mama."

He stepped closer to her chair.

"Tell me, what made your father give you that terrible whipping?"

The question he'd been dreading.

"My daddy's a strict Baptist, ma'am. Was me who did wrong."

"And what was that wrong?"

"It was Sabbath and when I turned on Mama's radio, it's playing 'Sweet Georgia Brown' and I had to sing along with it. I didn't know he was in the house till it was too late."

Miss Sally had known Elijah ever since he came to work for Walter. He was one of the best hands. She'd also heard he had a hot temper.

"Do you have a mind to obey your elders if you come to work for me?"

Paul swallowed his first flicker of anger with Miss Sally. "Yes, I do."

Sally Jackson thought that she was looking at one of the handsomest boys she'd ever seen, about six-feet-two, thick wavy black hair, thin, fine looking. "Have you ever spent any time in the garden or a greenhouse?"

When he heard that, he was sure he was doomed. "Yes, ma'am," he stammered. "Least, always wanted to learn. Ain't sure about a greenhouse, never been any in the Kingdom, and we don't have real gardens—not like yours." He tried desperately to find a way to show her he had some gardening experience. "I planted zinnias in front of our shack. Now we have so many, I cut them all the time and put them in jam jars all over the house."

"Why, Paul, I'm happy to hear that. Seems you like to arrange flowers."

"Yes, ma'am, I do."

He was so tall, it was hurting her neck to peer up at him. Miss Sally pointed to the chair beside hers. "Sit down a minute." She spoke as if she were telling him a secret. "Paul, in our front yard, I planted everything white and green, for peace and calm. I grow my colored zinnias, my flocks of hollyhocks, my gladiolus, every single one of my hundreds of mums and dahlias, in the back yard. Lots of color. It's all a big show in the back."

She said, "in the back" as if Paul would understand her secret meaning.

"You'll be able to go out there and cut flowers for every vase in the house, and I like to keep every room filled with flowers. I keep the pale-colored peonies in a bed right up against the front porch, mind you." Her voice sank, almost to a whisper. "Only the very palest ones."

Paul kept a smile to himself. Everything pale up front, but hot, colored, and beautiful in the back. Not quite everything—he remembered those gardenias. It seemed in this house some rules were made to be broken.

"Paul, I can teach you anything, long as you're interested. And what about cooking? Lorene tells me you can read and write, so of course you can look in my recipe books, and let's not even mention what she has to teach you. Of course, as she will be the first to say, I taught her."

He began to feel flickers of hope. As long as he was talking about food, he was sure of himself. "Yes, ma'am. I try out new recipes all the time, that's what I love to do most. Mama says I've been cooking since I was old enough to walk. I can do country food, but most of all, I like to make up my own recipes."

Miss Sally put two teaspoons of sugar into the third steaming hot cup of coffee Lorene poured out for her. "Lorene, this boy's going to be a big help to me in the garden, and heaven only knows, you could use him in the kitchen. Didn't you tell me Paul was your favorite cousin?"

"He's the one."

Paul understood who'd been cheering for him.

"And, Paul, you think you could serve at the table?"

"I reckon I can learn, Miss Sally."

With that last question answered, Paul watched Miss Sally press her hands down on the chair, until, slowly and stiffly, thanks to her arthritis, she finally heaved herself up. His trial was over.

"Paul, you'll do fine," she said, with a firm voice. "We'll see how it goes when you start working. You can begin in two weeks, enough time for you to get everything together."

He did not throw up his hands and praise hallelujah. That would come later.

"One more little thing, Paul. In two months, sixty-four days to be exact, as Mr. Jackson reminds me every morning, our daughter, Emma, will be coming home. She's been away for a year, on a world cruise."

"Yes, ma'am." Paul wondered if Miss Sally expected an answer, then saw she was waiting. "I saw Miss Emma one day when me and Mama were buying thread at the dime store. You all were talking to Miss Ruth on the sidewalk, in front of the Cave office."

Paul knew Miss Ruth was Miss Sally's sister and that she owned most of the caves in the county. He decided not to tell how Emma had stood out on Horse Cave Street or how interested he had been in her short blonde hair and hip-hugging, ankle-length, blue-linen dress. He wouldn't say anything about her.

"Is that so?" Miss Sally paused for a moment, "Well, the news is, she'll be arriving in India any minute. Of course, I would have loved to have gone on a world cruise myself. Never mind. What I will tell you is how our daughter has a mind of her own, tries to tell everyone what to do. When she comes home, remember—I'm the one who gives the orders here." She ambled over to the dining room window. "Lorene will show you the little house out back where you'll stay. I reckon you won't mind saying goodbye to Elijah and leaving home. Lily can visit you here, bring your brothers and sisters, and of course you'll have a day off every now and then."

"Yes, ma'am."

"Paul, you haven't asked me how much I intend to pay you?"

"No, ma'am."

"To begin with, I'll give you forty dollars a month. Of course, you will have your room and board, so you won't be counting the hours. Your day will begin at six and end when Mr. Jackson and I finish dinner. You and Lorene will share every other Sunday."

He wondered how many days off he would get but decided not to ask.

"Might be the beginning of a new life for you, Paul."

"Yes, ma'am, I hope so."

10

P aul counted each finger. In ten days, he would be leaving home, maybe forever. He tried to concentrate on the hum of Lily's sewing machine, Tabby and Tallulah's giggles, young Ernest and James tugging at his shirt sleeves.

We want Paul to tell us a story... We want Paul to make us caramel cake... We want Paul to play with us.

Who would cut out Lily's patterns? Who would get up and fix everyone's breakfast, including Elijah's? There would be no one to iron their clothes on a Sunday morning, no one to set the table, make the cornbread, fry the chicken.

Lily must have read his mind. "Don't worry, son. We'll get along."

The anger he felt then came from the deepest part of him and lodged in his throat. From the moment he took his first step, he'd been helping his mama. He'd minded after his brothers and sisters, cooked, cleaned, washed, and ironed. Lily was delicate, she needed him; and now, because of his father, he had to leave her. He'd give her half his pay, he decided. Even so, how would she manage? He looked over at Tabby and Tallulah, who'd just turned eleven years old. He'd shown them what to do.

When Elijah came home, Paul kept quiet. He knew where the burden would fall.

On her way to the kitchen, Lily stopped, put her arms around Paul's neck, and the look she gave her husband dared him to make any objection.

"Don't you forget, Paul. Tomorrow's Saturday, your day to visit your great-grandmother. You'll be saying goodbye to her for a while."

Without a word, Elijah banged the screen door behind him as he went out to unhitch the mules.

———

Great-grandma Abilene belonged to a higher order of things, always treated like the Queen of Sheba. She had green eyes, not brown. She carried her chin tilted high and proud, on top of her long neck. Her head was never still, an eighty-year-old bird looking for worms. Abilene kept a bucket of dirt by her chair on the front porch. From time to time, she'd bring a handful up to her nose, sniff it, then let the earth slide through her fingers.

"Feels cool, smells fine, does you good. I like to remind myself, it's who we are."

Every Saturday, on Paul's day to visit, she told him scary tales, gave him advice, sifted handfuls of dirt, and taught him how to bake cakes. Now that he was leaving to live with the Jacksons, Paul wasn't sure when he would get another chance to visit.

A little past dawn, he heard a gentle, "Whoah," followed by a soft whistle. Uncle Bill was outside. Paul climbed up on his wagon and sat next to him as Bill spat brown tobacco all the way out of the Kingdom until they got to Bear Wallow, the small hamlet on the other side of Horse Cave.

It was early morning, before the dust got up. The air smelled fresh. Paul kept his eyes on the road straight between the mule's ears, listened to Bill complain about his sore back, worrying that his days in Walter Jackson's fields would finish him off. Took them a good, long time bumping along, and when they finally got there, Abilene was waiting with hot baked cinnamon rolls and coffee.

She lived in a done-up shack at the end of a narrow dirt road in the middle of Walter Jackson's property. Inside, her own quilts were hung all over the walls and her favorite was spread out on her bed. Braided rugs lay over the floors and Paul could feel the heat from the kitchen where a woodburning stove was all lit up for cake business.

"Yellow cake today, Paul, with caramel icing."

In the kitchen, pine shelves lined the walls and were stacked with Abilene's collection of different colored dishes, painted tin cups, bowls, one sitting inside the other, every kind of shape of baking tins, and cornbread molds. Black iron skillets hung on heavy steel hooks and a great woodburning stove took up half a wall.

"Long as I got one of my children to fire up my oven, I reckon I'll be all right."

Paul knew his way around her kitchen by heart. He cut up into small pieces the fresh churned butter brought in every few days by Abilene's daughter Belle.

Great-aunt Belle lived with her husband, Jake, on a tenant farm down the road and delivered enough milk, butter, and cream from her three cows to keep a succession of Abilene's famous yellow cakes coming out of her oven. Paul took a bag of unrefined cane sugar down from the shelf and added two cups to the bowl. Abilene made him go at it, beating hard, while she slowly added half-a-dozen egg yolks. She wasn't satisfied until the mixture turned pale yellow. Then she reached into a cupboard, pulled out a bottle of her precious vanilla essence, and added a few drops. After that, the mix was poured into a tin, and, as always, Paul was left to lick the bowl before he washed up the dishes.

After sliding the cake pan into the oven, they went out onto the porch. He patted his great-grandmother's pillows, put his arm around her shoulders, and watched over her, while she eased herself down into her rocker. He sat in the white wooden swing the way he always did while the breeze brought the smell of yellow cake baking.

"Paul, most of my life's been spent in a kitchen—lately the one belonging to Miss Sally Jackson's sister, Annie Straker, living out at Hiseville. I can tell you, no one ever said no to lunch there while I was cooking." Abilene set to rocking, then she looked at her great-grandson as if she knew every detail of what had happened with Elijah. It was said his great-grandmother could see the past, and the future too.

They watched Uncle Bill in the field in front of the house, spanking his mules from behind the plow.

She sighed. "You don't know how deep down goes them White pockets? You're 'bout to find out, ain't you? Around here, Jackson family got the deepest. And the softest."

She didn't wait for him to answer.

"I'm old now, Paul. I've passed all my days, all my years, working in White pockets. Who knows who I might have been somewhere else? You're mighty sweet, my most precious boy. I want you to be safe. Ain't easy in this here world."

The old lady leaned back in her chair. "Your great-granddaddy told me a tale I never forgot. He heard it from his sister from Bardwell, Kentucky. She saw it with her own eyes." She pointed. "Grab one of them swing cushions, lie back, close your eyes." She shifted a bit. "See yourself riding on a train?"

"Ain't never been on a train."

"Well, now you are, sitting peaceful, eating a sandwich, minding your own business. Looking out the window, somewhere in Missouri."

"Missouri?"

"All of a sudden, your train stops. Two policemen get on, ask every Colored man to stand up. Then they come to you. 'Stand up, boy.' So, you do. 'Here he is, look at his blue pants,' one of 'em says. You're scared, don't say a word, even when you feel cold steel hand-cuffs. You look down at your blue pants, wonder what it's about. They put you in a police car, drive you to St. Louis. All the while, they're sitting up front talking soft, you're sitting in the back, sweat-ing, shaking."

Grandma Abilene took in a couple of deep breaths. Was almost like she sang the rest of the story. "They put you on more trains, until at last, you stop. 'Last call for Bardwell, Kentucky.' 'Member this place?

"They take you to the jail. Sheriff says you raped and killed two White girls in this town. 'But... I ain't never been to Bardwell,' you stutter.

"No one's listening. They lock you up. You lie on a hard bench, go for business in a bucket. Outside, you hear shouting, hoots. They open the door, hold you up, you're too weak to walk. Then you see them, hundreds of them, a White mob yelling their heads off. 'Burn him! Burn him!'

"Before the Sheriff gives you over to them, he does you a favor. 'Folks, don't burn this man. Maybe he's not guilty. But you can hang him.'

"They drag you outta town, wrap a heavy chain round your neck, ties the other end to a telegraph pole, pull you up, leave you a few seconds to dangle, then you drop."

Paul opened his eyes, sweat pouring down his face.

Abilene rose from her chair and stood at the edge of the porch. "Look here at these chickens, Paul, scratching up deep yellow yolks for caramel cake. But right now, while we're waiting for the icing to cool, I want you to think why I told you this story, all gospel. Goes to show—Colored you're guilty. Poor man ain't never set foot in Kentucky. Shout that over his grave." Stiffly, she leaned forward to stand. "Meantime, let's cut us a big piece of cake."

Paul could only nibble at crumbs and lick the caramel icing as he wondered what was waiting for him outside the Kingdom.

She had more to say as she sliced herself a second piece, "Light skin," she said. "Hmm... I still remember my mama's stories," she continued, "I used to sit with her, same way you sit with me. I still remember her telling me my daddy weren't my daddy. Ever wonder why your skin and your mama's so much lighter than everybody else's?"

Abilene went over to her oak chest, opened the lid, and took out an envelope. "Take this letter. It's the story of Odella. She was a slave, and she was my mama. Carry it with you. I told Lily I was writing to you about it. She says, 'It's 'bout time. Paul looks so like her.'"

"Why didn't you tell me about her before, Grandma?"

"'Cause you'd only be asking me questions I can't answer."

The mules hurried along on their way home, Uncle Bill half asleep, reins loose in his hands. By the time Paul had washed the dishes and helped put the children to bed, it was too late for the letter. With only a half-moon overhead, it was too dark for him to read.

After breakfast the next day, he found some quiet time on Moses's porch. He opened Abilene's envelope and read:

Dear Paul,

My grandmama Adeah, fetched from Jamaica, was sold in Kentucky. Her child, Odella, was my mama. She was a slave on the Zachary Taylor farm near Louisville. General Taylor, before he was the President, often left his family in Louisiana and came up to visit his property here in Kentucky. Odella was a prize—tall, wavy hair, lots of it, looked exactly like you, handsome but pretty at the same time, with fire in her. Just like you, she got out of bed before dawn to help her mama, and ever since she was little, she carried wood into the big house, fired up the stove, and took turns stirring the porridge. General Taylor had a delicate stomach, needed his oatmeal. He was a tough man, didn't say much. Folks have it he didn't care for slavery, but he never let his slaves go.

On the morning of Odella's fifteenth birthday, she carried up the General's breakfast tray, found him sitting in bed reading newspapers.

This time he looked at her peculiar, said, "Wait here till I finish my breakfast."

So she stands, uneasy, watching him eat every bite of his porridge. He says, "Odella, take my tray. Put it on the table. Come over here, sit beside me." Mama did what she was told. She sits with him, no choice, lies with him, no choice. She ain't got no power. Afterwards, down in the kitchen, she was sobbing in her mama's arms, and not for the last time. Not long after, she suffered to bring me into this world.

How she finally got our freedom, I don't know, but she did, helped by Baptists, and we settled here in Horse Cave. Mama goes to work for the Owens family, walked five miles there and back, six days a week, raised them Owens children, did all their cooking. She was free, but that ain't the end of slaving. As for me, you know how at first I cooked for the Owens family, after that for Annie Straker, Miss Sally's sister. I been doing the same thing Mama did, day in day out, all my life. By time we're ready to leave this earth, we're too worn out to care. You want to work like me and Mama all your life? No. Take your chance when it comes. Lord knows how many times I missed, thinking there'd be another day, another chance coming. That's all I has left in me for you, Paul. I hear you're going to work for the Jacksons. Don't you get old, close your eyes, wonder who you might've been. Pay mind to me and Odella.

Great-Grandma Abilene

Paul's next visit with his great-grandmother never came. Lily brought the news she'd died on the following Wednesday. She told Paul the last time she'd seen Abilene, her head was propped up, hair brushed, lying on a white satin pillow. Lily told how she'd dropped her lids with a deep, soft sigh. That was it, out she went.

Meantime, Paul kept her letter under his bed, hidden inside his secret box with his movie magazines. Many times, he tried to figure out why Lily was almost white. Wanting to ask his great-grandmother, but he never got the nerve. All he knew was that he colored himself with a light touch, kept inside the lines because he'd already figured out there wasn't much room for him to move around.

After supper, when he'd finished the dishes, Paul, as usual, slipped out of the back door and joined Moses on his porch. Each sat thinking his own thoughts until Moses broke the quiet.

"We'll keep our eyes on your mama. I'll be seeing you every day when I deliver."

Moses could say what he wanted, Paul thought to himself, but nothing would ever be the same again.

11

The night before Paul left home, Cousin Lorene carried over a suitcase for him. He folded his clothes, ironed three shirts, fished deep into the back of his mama's drawer where he kept his secret things: pale pink lipstick, face powder, Maybelline mascara, Pond's Cold Cream, Vaseline, and three pairs of stockings. Every night he rolled up one of the stockings and put it on his head, training his shiny, crimped waves.

Mr. Jackson picked him up the next morning in a new 1936 Buick. Paul hugged his brothers and sisters, kissed his mama who folded a dollar into his pocket on his way out. Elijah had gone long before dawn, not a word coming out of his sullen face. Eyes glaring, he'd hitched the mules and giddy-upped off. Next door, Moses was sweeping his porch before going off to work. They'd talked until dawn.

Paul rode in the plush passenger seat as Mr. Jackson drove along Horse Cave's main street, past Hidden River Cave. He knew all the caves in Hart County belonged to Miss Sally's sister, Miss Ruth. They carried on past the Bee Lovely Beauty Salon, then Dorsey's Drug

Store until they were almost out of town. This time, Paul knew where he was going.

Before the cemetery, the car turned into a drive leading up to the white clapboard house with its front porch wrapped with white columns. Its owner, Mr. Walter Jackson, spoke quietly. He never raised his voice, but people heard him.

Many families in the Kingdom owed him their living, and he rewarded loyal sweat. Mr. Jackson owned the Jackson Tobacco Company, raised cattle, and still found time to be president of the biggest bank in the county. The country was in a Depression, but Walter never let on he had been touched by it. None of his people were laid off. Folks said he would rather dip into his own pocket than see his hands in the fields or his workers in the tobacco re-drying plant not paid properly every month.

At the end of his driveway, Mr. Walter stopped, put on the brakes, turned to Paul, and said quietly, "I know you'll miss Lily, and your brothers and sisters. You may come to me any time, ask for a day off, go visit them. This is a new life. You'll make of it with what you have in you."

Paul wasn't afraid of work. He knew he had plenty in him to make his job with the Jacksons a success. "I'll try my best, Mr. Jackson."

———

It was the middle of the afternoon. Miss Sally was asleep. Lorene showed Paul his way out the back kitchen door, down a little path planted with blue delphiniums on either side, to the white-painted clapboard cottage.

"You're lucky to be living in this fancy place. Miss Sally did this up for a guest cottage." The two stood at the door, and with a satisfied grin on her face, she added, "Better unpack your suitcase. I'm going down to iron in the basement for a couple of hours. After you settle, come help me fix supper."

Inside, he looked around at pale yellow walls, blue-and-white-striped curtains covering four windows, two each side of the room, facing the back garden to one side, the other not too far from the chicken run closed in by a picket fence covered with honeysuckle. A white chenille bedspread, a present from one of the women in the mountains whose baby Miss Sally had helped deliver, lay over the double bed. Mr. Jackson had seen to electric lights, put in a toilet and a real porcelain bathtub with claw feet. There Paul was in a real guest house, now his little home, a comfortable bed, with a real mattress, upholstered chairs, and his own beautiful bathroom. He was shaken by a wave of guilt when he thought about his family's shack, his narrow bed in a room shared with the rest of the children, fussing or giggling. A sudden breeze blew the brand-new curtains inside the window, carrying a smell of roses, fresh air, and new linen.

He unpacked his suitcase: three pairs of blue pants, three white shirts, four pairs of socks, and right at the bottom of the case, his secret things which, along with Abilene's last letter, he tucked well under the mattress.

He closed his eyes and all he could hear was the gravelly clucking of a hen. He noticed the door had a lock and realized no one could see him if he pulled the curtains.

Trying to get his thoughts together, he sat in one of the good-sized stuffed armchairs, covered with the same blue-and-white linen as the curtains. He and Moses had celebrated their fifteenth birthday the day after Abilene died. He wondered what she would think of this room. He could almost hear her voice carried on the breeze through the half-open window. *"Sit with me a while, Paul. Watch out. You're getting too comfortable."*

He closed his eyes. He hadn't cried at her funeral, but now he felt tears. He promised right then to keep her close and remember her warnings.

———

The next morning, Lorene was waiting in the kitchen, holding a big white apron. She reached up to put it over Paul's head, waited for him to turn around, and tied it behind his back. "Scramble those eggs, keep an eye on the bacon."

He put the pot on a low flame, cut up small squares of cold butter, lightly beat the eggs, and stood over them with the wooden spoon. In the other hand, he held a spatula, with one eye on the spluttering bacon.

"What you doing there, Paul? I like to put the eggs into bacon fat."

He knew he better be careful. Lorene had a hot temper. He answered, "This makes them soft—hoping you let me try it?"

"We'll see how the old folks feel about that."

Paul fetched a pretty white bowl from the cupboard, ladled in his scrambled eggs, and arranged crisp strips of bacon on top. Ten minutes after serving breakfast, they heard the bell. It was Miss Sally ringing from the dining room.

Paul took off his apron and went in.

Miss Sally was sitting with the empty white bowl in front of her. She and Mr. Jackson had finished their breakfast. "Who made these delicious eggs?" Miss Sally asked, forking up the final bite.

Paul looked behind him at the open kitchen door.

"Ma'am, me and Lorene decided to try out a new recipe."

Miss Sally smiled happily at him. "Mr. Jackson and I are looking forward to having some more soon."

Paul put his hands all the way up to his elbows in hot sudsy water while Lorene took one of her beautifully ironed tea towels to dry the dishes he'd carefully washed. Afterwards, they sat at the kitchen table, poured two cups of coffee, and gathered up the left-over toast and bacon. They dipped into the raspberry preserves, took extra pats of softened butter, and smiled at each other as they crunched through pieces of toast.

Lorene said, "I was sixteen when I came to work for the Jacksons. Now I'm thirty-two. Don't you sit there with your bare face hanging out and tell me you don't know all the rest. You've heard it like everyone else has."

Paul poured himself another cup of coffee the way he liked it, hot and black. He wished he could not hear his father's voice in his head, saying: "By the time Lorene was eighteen, that girl'd had two abortions. One of the daddies was married, the other one no one ever knew what happened to him." He also knew Lorene's mama, Severine had raised little Arletta so that Lorene could go to work and support them.

Paul remembered his mama's sharp answer to Elijah's harsh judgment.

"Your great-uncle Franklin took to moonshine and died, leaving Severine on her own to bring up Lorene. 'Cept she wasn't brung up, she fell up, passed from one good neighbor to another, while Severine went out to work. Lorene's a fine woman who made a few mistakes on the way, like we all do. She's lucky to have her mama to look after her daughter. Her mama's happy to do it since she never had the chance to look after Lorene."

Backed up behind Lorene's easy laughter, there was a well of pain, but she laughed harder when Paul turned up his sass. The veins on the back of her legs bulged out over her flat feet mashed into old brown loafers, and with every step was a shuffle, leaning from big toes to inside heels. When not working, a wet cigarette usually dangled from one side of her mouth. She mashed it out hard before coming into the kitchen, because even if Walter Jackson grew tobacco, and had one of the largest re-drying plants in the South, he despised the smell of cigarette smoke.

The years had run away from Lorene so quickly the only place she could detect them now was in her throbbing joints. Mostly, she tried not to let on, except with a wince here or there. Since the age of fifteen she'd been getting up before dawn to get to work at 6 A.M., every morning walking the one-and-a-half miles over rough tracks and then through the town, up the hill to the Jacksons'. And now, at the age of thirty-two, her knees hurt constantly, and her bad, old shoes mashed her arthritic toes. When she finally got to work, she'd spend the rest of her day, face blazing over a hot stove, or else killing and plucking chickens, sweeping, ironing, washing floors. After all that, she'd trudge her way home when the Jacksons were served supper, so tired she could barely tend to her own house or have the spit in her to talk to Arletta. Severine had supper on the table. She'd eat and fall into bed. Early mornings, she left for work before Severine and Arletta woke up.

There were times when Lorene took a tray of freshly made lemonade out to the front porch, found Miss Sally rocking peacefully, smelling of bubble bath, all dressed up, thinking about who was coming to see her that day and would wonder if Black folks were put on this earth for nothing else than to make sure White folks were kept happy. She tried to keep in mind what Elijah preached, that God has his own purpose, that God's got a plan, that He's fixing for every Colored person suffering on earth to go right up to a sweet paradise, that He sees everything, and He's looking after birds of every colored feather—but that didn't seem to soothe her. It wasn't right, and Lorene knew it.

No one else ever knew about her third abortion. She let some old witch shove something, looked like a plug of tobacco, up inside her, and between the pain and the bleeding, it kept her sitting down on a stool in the kitchen for weeks. The men in her life couldn't stand up to be counted because, as she would say with a sigh, "they were all no-count like her daddy."

Lorene took a knife and scraped the crumbs on the table into a little pile. "We need to get busy. You set that hen to boil while I clean up the house. We're having chicken and dumplings for lunch."

Within a few weeks, Paul folded himself into the Jacksons' routine. He felt his way slowly, dared a little, every now and then, but mostly he listened patiently and with respect to Miss Sally teaching him how to prune roses, dig holes, make sure he packed in enough ripe manure. He stood beside Lorene in the kitchen, watching how she seasoned, learning what dishes the Jacksons liked and disliked. Paul saw at once that in the garden and the kitchen, he would soon be able to make a difference.

Almost every day after lunch, Moses delivered the Jacksons' groceries. With Walter and Sally sound asleep on the front porch, the two boys had a chance to visit. They sat on the back porch, drank cold Coca-Colas, and enjoyed the sweet-scented air of flowers wafting through the screened-in porch.

It was Friday, cloudy, felt close like a storm might be brewing. Moses shook his head as the boys peeled off the wrappers from two Hershey bars.

"I deliver to the Baynor house, round five-thirty, 'cause it's last on my route. Mr. Baynor's the new florist—you know the one? Or maybe you don't. He ain't been in Horse Cave for long, lives with his mama. Every time I take my box of groceries into the kitchen, he's waiting for me, looks me up and down, hands me a Hershey bar. Says, 'You're a fine-looking boy, Moses.'"

Paul nibbled the end of his Hershey bar, wanting to make it last. "Kenneth Baynor, or Mr. Pittypatt, as Lorene calls him, comes up here all the time, in that funny wooden-trim car of his. Got Miss Sally wrapped round his finger like a wedding ring."

"What's wrong with that?" Moses asked.

"Maybe nothing, can't put my finger on it. But something don't feel right 'bout him."

Paul finished the chocolate, folded the wrapper into quarters, again and again until it was a tiny square. His last words to Moses were, "Keep an eye on him. Probably means no harm. Remember, though, you're bigger than he is."

12

One morning, Paul came in from the garden carrying a bunch of peonies; Lorene was filling Ball jars with bread-and-butter pickles when they heard an old truck coughing and sputtering up the back drive.

"Must be that young piece of White trash, Terry Weaver, with Sally's sacks of manure for the garden," Lorene said.

A young boy, fair-haired, skinny, wearing thick glasses with a bookish-looking face and a torn white T-shirt, opened the screen door, saw Paul holding flowers.

"Who's this?" the boy asked, staring at Paul.

"My cousin, Paul," Lorene said, glaring at him. "He's working fulltime for Mr. Jackson."

Terry sniffed at Paul as if Paul were the one hauling manure. He sharply turned, stepped out onto the back porch, letting the screen door slam hard behind him.

Lorene waited till she heard the truck gunning up. She pulled up two stools, sat Paul down, her face right up next to his. "Old Man Weaver's chief of the Klan in this county. I see his boy looking at you, I see you looking right back at him. Watch out. Here you safe. Out there, with the likes of Terry Weaver..." She sighed, stabbed a pickle, shook her head, while Paul laughed and pulled it off her knife.

The next day, he slipped out the back door, grateful for the still cool air of the morning, looking forward to planting all the new geraniums, now in pots behind the greenhouse in front of the garden shed. He lined up fifteen earthenware pots, got out his trowel, and went to work. He was packing down the earth around his fifth pot, stopped for a moment, pulled out a handkerchief to wipe his brow, when he heard a voice behind him.

What Lorene had told him came back to him then, sharp as a stab in the back. "Weaver boy's fixing to come over sometime tomorrow morning, bringing in more sacks of manure. Won't be the only shit he'll be carrying. Ain't sure if you got it into that head of yours how his family hate us Colored folks. Mess with him, your life ain't worth a red nickel. I see he's already taken agin' you."

Now here he was, Lorene's "Weaver boy," shouting at him, "Hurry up, get this open," kicking at the shed door, red in the face, eyes popping with the weight of a huge sack of manure.

Paul stayed on his knees, didn't look round. He smiled to himself and dared, "Give me a second. Gotta finish this pot." He enjoyed the extra moment, Terry Weaver straining and sweating with the heavy load.

Then it came.

"Goddamn, boy! There's no fucking 'gotta'! Git off your knees, open this fucking door!"

By the time Paul had opened the shed and he'd dumped his heavy sack, Terry's face was purple and wet with sweat. He followed Paul back to the greenhouse, looked down at the pot of geraniums Paul had just planted and kicked it over, spreading soil and young plants across the hard red dirt.

"Whoops! Sorry 'bout that, boy. I didn't mean to do it." Smirking, he kicked again, and another pot crashed over, so the dirt floor began to look more like a ploughed field.

Paul closed his eyes, tried to swallow his fury, and it was in the swallowing he felt the real pain begin.

"Next time I come here with a sack, boy, better know to jump!"

Paul looked down at the broken bits and pieces. He couldn't tell Miss Sally. He might stir up trouble for himself. He'd have to buy more pots with his own money. He only earned forty dollars a month for a twelve-hour day every day.

When he got down to the hardware store, he fished out his roll of money, and peeled away ten dollars for fifteen pots. He might as well be peeling off his own skin, that's how much it hurt.

Later that afternoon, Paul came back from town, struggling with a stack of pots, wondering when he would have the time to run back and forth to the hardware store to fetch the rest. He tried to sneak around, reach the greenhouse before Lorene caught a glimpse of him. Too late.

"Where you going with them pots?"

When he confessed what had happened, she sat down heavily on a kitchen chair. "You riled him up. I told you not to mess. You go'n and did it, putting one more worry onto my head. My head don't need it. What's the matter with you, boy? You think you're living outside the rules? That ain't gon' be the end of it. You hear me? Meantime, you get to running back down to the store, fetch those other pots."

Next time he'd pay her more mind.

13

Lorene watched Paul pick up finely chopped parsley and drop it onto deviled eggs—and they were his own deviled eggs because he was the one who hit on whipping up the yolks with mayonnaise, heaping in a teaspoon of curry powder and a quarter-teaspoon of maple syrup. It was Paul who made the air swirl in Lorene's kitchen: cutting perfect biscuits, spooning cornbread into black-iron molds, chopping squeaky newly-picked scallions over beefsteak tomatoes, twirling fried chicken over in the cast-iron skillet to bring it up golden out of the hot fat. Lorene taught him all she knew; he took it, used it as a base to hammer out new ideas, inventing flavors, and playing around with spices.

"Walter will like that." Lorene watched him add cardamom to the bread dough.

"*Walter?*" Paul wondered aloud. "Why do we call him by his first name in here?"

"Brings him down a peg or two." Lorene laughed. "But don't let me catch your ass doing that outside of this kitchen. Here's where White folks all get called by their first names."

A month after Paul got to the Jacksons, he was slowly slipping the old folks into his ways, feeling the ground, trying to please. He was busy working beside Lorene, when one day she turned to him.

"Can't stand these flies. Hand me the swatter. By the way, your rival's back, his hair puffed up more than yours."

It was getting worse. Paul was beginning to feel he was in the shadow of Kenneth Baynor. Three o'clock, four times a week, Miss Sally sat on the porch, fresh powder under circles of pink rouge, peering through her ferns, waiting for the man Lorene called "that jackass" and Paul called "Hershey Bar Man." Almost every other day, you could count on seeing him: red hair worn a little long, freckles sprinkled across a snub nose, molasses voice mellowed into precious. Kenneth Baynor had quickly become Hart County's most prominent florist. Every Horse Cave funeral saw his pillows of white lilies, roses braided into silver and green leaves tenderly laid over caskets. When he wasn't selling cut flowers, he had an expensive line in potted plants.

Out of breath after running up the steps of the front porch, he'd take both of Miss Sally's hands in his. "Oh, Miss Sally, look at you, a vision of beauty in your purple voile. I declare, you look like you're ready for a Viennese ball." Then he'd sigh and pull out his handker-chief, shake it right out to show its sheer-silk luxury. "I've just come from the funeral home. Earl Rafferty looks better lying down in satin than he ever did standing up in his seersucker suit." He wiped his forehead. "They just don't stop, do they? Keep on dying every five minutes from cancer. Why, I reckon it's an epidemic."

Miss Sally remembered the first time she saw Kenneth Baynor. It was a year earlier. He'd strutted down the aisle of the Methodist Church with his mother, Priscilla's, feeble arm resting on the sleeve of his fine, cream linen suit. Of course, Miss Sally had heard about the florist, who, when he arrived from Alabama, had paid outright the asking price of Emily Bateman's old house. Emily had died a few months before, a rich widow without any children. The house was furnished with fine antiques, and since moving in, Kenneth was on his way to becoming an established member of the Methodist

Church, accepted by Horse Cave and Hart County's higher social orders.

Kenneth courted Sally Jackson, paying her a visit every other day, as if he was striving to win the hand of a beautiful young heiress. His soft voice, fine white hands, along with a gentle, almost demure Southern demeanor, were beginning to win her heart.

Sally Jackson was eager to see him succeed. She ordered new plots of the large field beyond her back garden dug out to make way for the pots of flowers and flowering bushes Kenneth sold to make a living.

Paul watched Miss Sally scoot her chair forward, closer to Kenneth's. How those two chatted, sipping iced tea, nibbling sugar cookies.

"How's that funny-looking new Colored boy working out?" He frowned, wrinkled his little nose, sniffing the air around Paul's flower arrangement—white roses with green parsley sitting in the middle of a white wrought-iron table on the front porch.

Paul had his ear to the door, as well as eyes through the screen. He wanted to catch a closer glimpse of the man who was handing out Hershey bars to Moses.

Kenneth reached for the frosted glass of tea, crooked his little finger as he took a delicate sip, leaned forward in his chair as far as he could, his face next to Miss Sally's. "Got to keep your eye on these niggers. I have stories from Alabama to curl your toes. Can't trust none of them." He leaned back and took another sugar cookie, all the while looking at Paul's flower arrangement.

Miss Sally frowned, as if she'd smelt something unpleasant, stood up as quickly as her arthritic knees allowed, and looked down at Kenneth, still sitting innocently in his chair finishing the last of the refreshments. When she spoke, her voice was as cold as the ice in their tea, "Mr. Baynor, I do not welcome remarks on the nature or the honesty of the people who work for me. Furthermore, we call our help 'Colored' in this house. That's how I was always brought up. I'll let you know if I need any more flowers."

Kenneth, sitting dumbly in his chair, understood he might have lost his most important client.

Standing behind the door, Paul had heard part of what Miss Sally was saying to Kenneth in her low voice, but he knew for sure that the florist was saying things about him. By the way Kenneth had turned up his nose at his flowers, he knew the florist was jealous.

From the beginning, he'd felt the bitch in Kenneth. Now, there was something else, a danger he couldn't put his finger on. He thought again how and why Moses had been opening two new Hershey bars every day when he came up to deliver groceries. His stomach felt sour, uneasy.

————

Moses Daniels double-locked the door of Larkin's Grocery at five o'clock as he did every weekday. Main Street was almost empty. Folks in Horse Cave liked to have their supper early.

From sunup, Moses had been delivering all over town. He looked forward to the ten-minute hike home across the railroad tracks over into the Kingdom. That evening, it was raining hard. Moses shivered, stood on the front porch of the grocery store where the newspapers were stacked, taking the *Horse Cave Gazette*, he folded it up to make himself a rain bonnet. He buttoned up his jacket, Larkin's Grocery written on the back. By the time he crossed over the railroad tracks, he'd wadded up his soggy newspaper and thrown it away.

There came such a cloudburst, Moses didn't hear the Ford station wagon until it was right beside him. The driver rolled down the window and inside, Moses recognized Horse Cave's florist.

Baynor leaned over, opened the passenger door. "Give you a lift home?"

"No, sir. I'm happy to walk. It ain't far."

"Come on, Moses. Get in."

It sounded like a command. Rain was pouring down. Moses didn't argue. He got in.

Kenneth drove on into the Kingdom but didn't slow down as they got near Moses's house.

"Mr. Baynor, you're going right by my shack," Moses said.

Kenneth drove on into the dark, past the homes at the end of the dirt road. He'd been going too fast. He took his foot off the gas, let the station wagon slide right to the end of the row of shacks, slowly turned off onto a muddy track under some overhanging trees and pulled on the handbrake. He kept the engine on, the wipers thwacking against the rain, now thumping down on the hood. The rolled-up car windows were steaming; heavy rain bounced noisily.

Kenneth turned to Moses. "Whenever you delivered groceries, I told Mama what a fine boy you are, Moses. That's a fact. Just thinking we'd get to know each other." He opened the glove compartment, pulled out a Hershey bar, tore it open, broke it in two equal pieces. "See, share and share alike, I say."

Moses said, "I need to get home." When Kenneth thrust half the chocolate bar at him, he again waved it away. "Thank you, sir. But..."

"Here! Take it, boy."

Kenneth pushed the half-bar forward again. "You know something, Moses? Sometimes a boy like you might say no to something he doesn't know he wants until he tries it. Isn't that right?"

The rain had eased up, the wipers were still swishing steadily, leaves beaten down from trees hanging above the car were now pasted all over the hood. Kenneth's question hung there waiting for an answer.

"I reckon," was all Moses came up with before adding, "Like what, sir?"

Kenneth ran his fingers through his red hair and turned square on to Moses who had turned in his seat, pressing up close against the door behind him.

"Well, the way I see it, Mo, it wasn't the Hershey bar that opened the car door for you."

"No, sir."

"Right, Mo. It was me giving you a ride."

"Yes, but—no, it was... The rain, sir."

Kenneth cut in, "So we understand each other. Right, Mo?"

"Well... Yes, sir."

"Good for you and good for me then."

"I guess so, sir."

14

End of October. Fall, that's the word for leaves raining down. One morning, Lorene arrived at half past five with the awful news.

"I can't stand tellin' you, Paul, what you ain't heard. You ain't heard what I can't bring myself to say out loud. Sit." She pulled out a chair for him. "I'll bring you some coffee, whisper my news."

Paul's first thought was that something had happened to his precious Lily as he stirred in his seat, waiting for Lorene to bring the cup.

She sat across from him, elbows on the table, fixing him with her eyes.

"Are you ready?" She let out a long breath. "Kenneth Baynor's dead. Our Moses has been arrested, charged with murder."

Paul closed his eyes and shook his head.

"Ready for the rest?" This time she didn't whisper. "Kenneth Baynor's been strangled." She pursed her lips. "They found Moses sittin' in the front seat of Kenneth's car, a dumb look on his face, with Kenneth right beside him, eyes open, tongue hanging out, dead."

Paul rubbed his head, put his face in his hands. "Where's Moses now?"

Lorene didn't answer, handed him the pan for poaching eggs.

"Tell me."

"The jailhouse in Munfordville's full. Moses is locked up in the Horse Cave police station for today and tonight. After that, he'll be up for trial."

Lorene wasn't making it up. It was early in the morning, the day lay ahead of them, and Paul could see from the way Lorene was looking at him, she was worried.

She shoved the pan in his direction again. "Don't fall apart on me, Paul Carew."

He would have to swallow the pain and go about his business.

Before Miss Sally had time to sit down and try Paul's wobbly poached egg on toasted salt-rising bread, he heard the dull sound of a ringing phone in the dining room. Paul did his best to concentrate on the breakfast to serve.

Miss Sally sat upright with the phone away from her ear as she heard Evie take a big breath and begin.

"Oh, Sally wait till you hear what happened. Ernie, the police found Kenneth Baynor murdered."

Miss Sally interrupted, "Wait a minute, Evie, let me sit down, my breakfast's getting cold in the kitchen."

"Our brave Ernie," Evie went on, "Found the station wagon up that alley at the end of the Kingdom with poor dead Kenneth inside. Moses sittin' beside him with his face in his hands, talking crazy."

Paul came into the dining room, poured a steaming cup of coffee for Miss Sally, and waited.

Miss Sally looked up and slammed the receiver down on Evie's voice. "I'm ready for breakfast any time you are, Paul." Before he had time to go back into the kitchen, she added, "I knew it was a mistake to put a telephone in the dining room, no more calls before breakfast."

Everything had been going so well, except for her arthritis, and now, here were shocking and distasteful goings on, which made her feel uneasy. Why would young Moses want to strangle Kenneth?

"Paul, please ask Lorene to come in here and tell me what you both know about all this."

The two of them stood, sad-faced, quietly looking at Miss Sally, and told her what they had heard.

Paul began softly, "Miss Sally."

Lorene's eyes were firing into his, willing him to be careful.

"Miss Sally," he began again, this time he wasn't asking, "I've got to see Moses. He's sittin' downtown in the jailhouse for tonight, cause the jail in Munfordville's full."

Miss Sally was mindful that Paul and Moses were best friends. She waited, took a sip of ice water followed by a taste of hot coffee. "I can't for the life of me see why you shouldn't. Run down there after lunch, and make sure you get back in time to help Lorene with supper." She was reaching for some words of sympathy but couldn't find them. Instead, she carefully folded her napkin and put it back in its silver ring.

"Fix Moses a plate of fried chicken and biscuits. Lord only knows who's cooking at the jailhouse." She let out a long sigh. "Kenneth was the best florist we ever had in this town, but there was something fishy about him."

"Yes, ma'am," Paul's voice was flat. "Knew a lot about flowers." Paul smelled toast burning just as Lorene turned and ran back into the kitchen.

Miss Sally said, "As for Moses, why I've known that boy ever since he started delivering groceries." Sally found another sigh, this one deeper than the last. "I'm mighty sorry, he's a good lookin', gentle, sweet boy. Why, I don't know anyone who didn't look forward to saying hello to Moses when he made his rounds. Remember Paul, it was only last week when I got up from my nap, I saw you boys eating Hershey bars together on the back porch. What in the world do you think happened?"

Paul choked, held back his tears. "Moses told me Kenneth Baynor gave him Hershey bars every time he delivered groceries."

Paul saw from Miss Sally's face that she didn't want to hear any more about that.

Later on in the morning, when he went out to water the plants on the front porch, Paul found Miss Sally asleep. He stood for a few minutes watching the slow rise and fall of her purple cotton dress, hoping her heart would keep on beating for him, reckoned the older you got the less you should allow yourself to get too upset.

He remembered what Lorene had told him about Miss Sally in the kitchen. "All the woman has to do when she not satisfied with you is to give you one of her looks, and when she talks to you, in her low voice, it's always with respect."

Old-school Sally Jackson ruled with a fly swatter and a Methodist church fan. All the way down from the Cumberland gap, she counted her ancestors: Stonewall Jackson, Daniel Boone, but most of the time, she acted like she was her own ancestor. She was struggling to lift herself over and above this terrible crime, trying to keep herself from dwelling on any notion of why Moses was found in a car with Kenneth Baynor. It didn't feel healthy, and she knew it.

In the kitchen, Lorene filled a large white plate with fried chicken, a thick cut of country ham and cornbread, and piled on a thick layer of turnip greens cooked with a ham hock. She unfolded a clean white fresh ironed tea towel, tied up four corners into a double knot and handed it to Paul on his way out the door. "Mind you don't drop it."

Paul was already halfway down the path holding up his knotted towel, when he stumbled a couple of times over bumps in the sidewalk where weeds had pushed up the concrete. He was grateful for a fresh cool wind to dry his sweat, all the while telling his thumping heart to quit it.

———

The jailhouse looked like any other red brick downtown building with the windows painted white. By the time Paul reached the front door, and went inside, his head was throbbing.

In front of Ernie Price's desk, Blessing waited, tall in high-heeled black patent leather sandals, wearing a tight black satin skirt, with a geranium-red stretchy strapless top, her hair stuck back with little bobby pins of artificial flowers. She looked worn out. Paul thought she might have been in the police station all night. Coralee, Lily, and Elijah were standing over at the other side of the desk—Elijah making sure he took his distance from Blessing.

Paul put the plate down before Lily hugged him. Coralee, sobbing, took her turn to throw her arms around him.

She begged, "Save Moses."

Elijah, cap in his hand, kept his voice low, head bent, while Ernie scribbled on a piece of paper. Elijah pleaded, "Moses is a fine Baptist. He's like a son to us."

Ernie did not look up. It was only a few months since Elijah himself had been behind bars.

Blessing walked behind the desk, stood beside Ernie's chair, and pleaded, "Paul needs to see Moses. They're the closest."

Ernie said, firmly, "Murderers can't have no visitors."

Blessing tapped her long red fingernails next to Ernie's hand on the desk. "Just this once. You're the boss here." She undid the top of Lorene's tea towel, lifted the pieces of fried chicken. "Miss Sally Jackson sent this food and ain't hidin' nothing in here."

Ernie looked up at Blessing and laughed. "Reckon you ain't quittin'. He can't have two visitors, it's Paul or his mama."

It only took sobbing Coralee a second, "Better be Paul."

Ernie unlocked the cell door. "You all ain't got long."

Moses sat in the corner of his small cell on the edge of a narrow cot; his circle of frizz dampened down from running his tear-soaked fingers through his hair.

Paul sat beside his friend and put his arms around his slumped shoulders. "What happened?"

Moses shook his head, over and over, looked at Paul, tears running down his face, and said, "I told everything to Mr. Price while he wrote it down."

Paul took hold of Moses's hands, looked into his eyes.

"Now get a hold of yourself. You need to tell me what you said to Ernie. Go back to the beginnin'." Paul gave him his handkerchief.

"It was after work... Mr. Baynor offered me a ride. It was dark—rainin' hard. He rolled down his window, I said 'no, thank you, I'll walk', but he kept on at me, and I couldn't see the harm in it. I showed him where I lived, only a few minutes from where he picked me up. I started to get worried when he drove right by our place, parked his car in that empty field. Remember the one where we used to play. I looked at him, asked him what he wanted. He just handed me a chocolate bar, got angry when I said, 'no thank ya'. Then, I knew something was funny. I was fixin' to get out of the car and run back in the rain to my shack, when Mr. Baynor leaned across and put his hands on my pants, right on you know where."

Moses stopped talking, wrung Paul's hands, gave another choked sob, and asked, "Will they hang me, tell me? You think they'll hang me?"

Tears rolled down Paul's cheeks. He steadied himself. "Tell me exactly what you told Ernie. Did you tell him Mr. Baynor put his hand on your cock?"

Moses answered, "I had a bad time telling it, but I said to Mr. Price, when he asked me, 'Yes sir, that's where he put his hand'. Mr. Price got mad at me all of a sudden. He said, like he was angry, 'Well get on and say it, boy.' I shouted at him, 'On my cock, sir'."

Paul said, "Go on Moses, what happened after that?"

"Mr. Baynor said to me, 'Is this what you're asking for, boy?' I shouted back, 'No, what the hell are you doin'?' I pushed him away."

Paul stood, pulled out a lone wooden chair in the cell, and sat across from Moses. "Go on."

"He seemed to be enjoyin' me pushin' him. He said, 'Wanna get rough, boy?' He was laughin'. He start climbin' all over me, with me fightin' him off. He wouldn't stop, punched me in the stomach. I'm stronger than he is, so I grabbed him by the throat, throw him back, and all I remember is the last thing the man said."

"What did he say, Moses?"

"He said, 'You little cocksucker.' Next thing, I opened my eyes, my hands were around his throat, and he ain't breathin' no more."

Paul turned his head. He didn't want Moses to see the fear in his face. "What did Ernie say after you told him all this?"

"He say, 'Sit up in your chair, boy. Drink this glass of water.' I gulp it down, Ernie takes my empty glass, stands up, goes over to the tap, fills it up, but before he hands it to me, he tells me to sign the piece a paper with all I've been tellin' him written down on it."

Paul's stomach gave a lurch. "Did you sign it?"

"I signed it."

"Then what, Moses?"

"After that, he handed me the glass of water, looked at me, said, 'You're done for, Moses.'"

"Y'all got three more minutes," Ernie shouted from his office.

Paul stood, so did Moses. They reached out and hugged each other, clung to one another, sobbing in each other's arms.

"Promise me, Paul?"

"Anything, Moses."

"Let's say goodbye now. I don't want you to be there when they put the rope around my neck, promise me that."

Paul choked, hugging his friend even closer. "I promise you."

Moses put his hand on Paul's cheek. "Tell Lily, Elijah, and Blessing to look after Mama."

"I will."

"I love you, brother,"

"I love you, too, Moses."

Ernie was rattling his keys at the door.

Later on that afternoon, after Ernie Price had finished eating the prisoner's untouched plate of food, the Horse Cave police officer remembered how he'd locked the report into a drawer, gathering dust for over a year, from the Mobile, Alabama police, concerning a suspected pervert called Kenneth Baynor. Ernie had thought long and hard about how to handle it, but in no time at all, Kenneth had become friendly with most of the important people in the town. Besides, the man could be innocent, after all. He'd never been convicted, and only been seen picking up young Coloreds.

15

In the kitchen, Paul watched Lorene scorch the skillet, pour in her mixture, scrape out a brown crusty envelope of cornmeal, crisp outside, soft-centered when you cut it.

"Hot-water cornbread will cheer Miss Sally up, and you too, Paul." Lorene cut off a piece. "You ain't ate a bite all day."

Paul shook his head. "I feel sick too far down to swallow anything on top of it." Taken down at his lowest, Paul could not get used to the idea of living without Moses, and to make matters worse, Lorene kept on all day long.

"Can't keep a rope from his neck—won't happen. He did it. How? We know. Why? Makes no mind. One of us kill a White man, there'll be hell to pay. They won't care why. Be just like a lynchin'. They'll make it look like it's the law."

Next morning, Lorene told Paul that when she got home from work, she'd put a tea towel over a plate of fried chicken and cornbread for Coralee.

"I knocked on the door, Coralee peeked out like she didn't recognize me, hair standin' on end, a cane of skin and bone. She's put on thirty years, hardly see the plate I put in her hand. Half crazy, she said, 'A White devil attacked my boy.'"

Paul tried not to pay too much attention to Lorene's recounting as he kept right on chopping fresh parsley and tarragon for his chicken stock, dreaming he was sitting on Moses's porch, chatting like they used to. He remembered their long days in the summer fishing, sitting next to each other quietly, smiling as they watched a pair of white ducks gliding in with the swoop of swallows, taking insects above the water.

News came two days later. Mr. Jackson kept it quiet until after supper. Lorene overheard him say to Miss Sally, "Mo faced a judge in Glasgow, Barren County. Admitted he killed Kenneth Baynor. I'm sorry this happened. He'll pay the price."

That night, on Paul's way to the little house, cold air froze a gold bracelet around a thin moon. When he went to bed, he sat for a few minutes, rolled his stocking like a tight casing on a sausage around his head, then pulled the covers up under his chin. He closed his eyes, tried not to see Moses's feet kicking at the end of a rope. Lorene said it would happen. He saw his friend's beautiful bushy hair, baggy overalls. Moses was as much a part of him as he was a part of Moses.

He felt hot tears falling down his cheeks, put out his tongue, caught the wet salt. Right then and there, he made up his mind, made it up good and true. In the morning, he'd get up his courage, risk everything. He lay flat on his back, arms by his side, all night long, talking out loud to himself, making up all the different speeches he would give to Mr. Walter at breakfast the next morning.

At four-thirty, before he ran a hot bath, he sneaked out by the first early light, into the hen house, where he picked up four warm, brown newly laid eggs, for the Jacksons' breakfast. In his bath, he scrubbed, all over, and over again with Palmolive soap. After he dried himself, he tied the towel around his waist, sat, and polished his shoes with spit and determination. He chose a pair of new dark blue pants and unhung a crisp white shirt he'd ironed the day before, brushed his waves flat, buttoned up his shirt. He'd look sharp.

He got into the kitchen a little before Lorene and put the coffee pot on the stove to percolate. He poured the milk in the pan for the oatmeal he'd soaked the night before. He tasted the Straker's dairy raw cream to make sure it was fresh. Raw milk, cream, and fresh churned butter was delivered every week by Ian and Annie Straker, Miss Sally's sister. By the time he put the bacon in the iron skillet, Lorene arrived.

"What you doing here so early, with your waves all combed flat?"

"Couldn't sleep, that's all."

On the days Walter Jackson paid a visit to his farms, he woke up at five A.M. and came into breakfast before Miss Sally. Paul was ready. He stood and watched quietly as Mr. Jackson picked up his cup of hot coffee, rested himself in his thoughts of what he just ate, smelling the cool, sweet air coming through the screen from the back porch.

How should he begin? He had to get it right the first time, or else what chance would Moses have? Now that he was in front of him, none of his speeches, with their heartfelt pleas for mercy, seemed right for Mr. Walter. He was a man who kept his tie on and jacket buttoned, a man who disliked displays of feelings in himself, or anyone else.

Paul swallowed hard. "Sir," he said, "Somethin's on my mind."

Walter, still resting in the peace of the moment, was suddenly aware of Paul standing beside him. He raised his eyes from his second perfectly fried egg.

Paul wished he had waited a little bit longer.

"What is it, Paul?"

Paul's words fell out, one on top of the other, "Well, sir, could you, sir, save Moses? Ain't his fault, Mr. Baynor's a pervert. He attacked him. Moses is innocent—just trying to protect hisself." As soon as he started, Paul knew he had made a mistake.

Walter put on his glasses, reached for his newly-ironed white handkerchief, and said with a sigh, "Now, Paul." He folded his paper, picked up his cup of coffee, and took a small sip. He might have been talking to a naughty child. "You've been raised by good people. Elijah and Lily know what's what, but you haven't learned it yet. Let me put you straight. Moses killed a White man, and what's more, he admits it. There will be a quick trial, and he'll hang a few days from now. I can't save him, but I can help you." Walter looked down at his now cold egg, laid his knife and fork on his plate to show he had finished breakfast, and looked up at Paul. "This is a lesson you better learn. Drop any idea of helping Moses. Let it lie. That's how it works, and I'll forget you ever asked me," his voice was quiet, his eyes cold.

———

Back in the kitchen, over her skillet, Lorene shook her head. "Lost your mind? I heard every word. Those old folks have had enough of this." She stomped over to Paul, put her hands on her hips, and spoke softly. "Save yourself a heap of trouble. Don't go askin' for what you know they're not gonna give you. Stay safe."

He didn't bother answering her. There wasn't any point. How could he not say something to Mr. Walter? He closed his eyes, imagining God's fire lighting up the dust on Moses's dead face, his head of angel's hair, flattened. And there was Paul, climbing up to meet the hangman, alongside Moses, nooses looped around both their necks.

Lorene rubbed it in, the way she was rubbing cloves and black pepper into a new ham. "Better face one thing, Paul Carew, Moses Daniels was a jackass, and he got what was comin' to him. All he had to do was punch that White pervert in the face. Didn't have to put his hands round his neck and choke him to death, no siree. That was extra." She hung her head and softly said, "Mind you, I wish I could have done it myself."

Paul did not pay much mind to Lorene's mean talk. She'd tended to Coralee when Moses was born. And it was Lorene who'd kept a plate of her own homemade sugar cookies and a glass of cold lemonade, placing it all out on the back screened-in porch when Moses came up every afternoon to deliver groceries and visit. She loved the boy.

16

Ever since breakfast, Lorene had been in one of her silent moods. She didn't smile, kept on scrubbing the sink over and over again with Ajax powder, muttering to herself. "I can't stand we have feelings, get hurt and bruised all the time. I'm lookin fo'ward to the day when I don't feel nothin'."

Paul picked up a watermelon from the bushel basket he'd carried in from the garden. He took a knife, rolled the melon on the counter, getting ready to cut up and put into the refrigerator.

"What's wrong?" he finally asked her.

Lorene kept right on scrubbing, this time it was the top of the stove, with a sudsy brush, dipped in ammonia. If he waited long enough, he'd find out what was on her mind.

And sure enough, out it came. Each word fell from her mouth like it weighed a ton, "Moses is dead. They hung him yesterday. Lily went over to lend a hand to Mo's mama, said Coralee near tore every hair out of her head after she got the news."

Paul looked at Lorene dumbly as if he hadn't heard her.

"Seems that little whore, Blessing Macrae, stood up at the trial, yelled out how she knew about Kenneth Baynor's drivin' round the Kingdom evenings, lookin' for Colored boys. No one paid any mind, just shout at her till she sat down. The jury took ten minutes, say all the evidence show Moses be guilty of a cold-blooded murder."

Paul sat dazed, waiting.

"Lily says she heard when they slipped a rope around Moses's neck, he looked like he didn't know what was happenin'. He didn't even look scared. He dropped hard, being such a big boy and all. I'm sorry, Paul. Moses had nothin' to lose and everything to gain. That's if you believe what you hear in church. Way they'd have it, minute he dropped, he shot up to Heaven." She mumbled, "We'd be more than fools for believin' that."

All the while Lorene was telling Paul this awful news, she finished wiping down the stove, she then poured cornbread batter, filling her molds. She banged the oven door, shoved them in, making as much racket as she could, crying and mad as a hornet, all at the same time.

Paul grabbed his watermelon before it rolled off the counter. Without a word, he plunged in the knife, and began hacking it open. Instead of neat wedges, seeds and flesh flew into the air and covered the counter. As he kept on ripping it to pieces, a sea of red mush covered the floor.

"Stop it, Paul. We got to clean up this floor before she comes in."

Paul put his head down on the kitchen counter in the cradle of his arms and buried his face, sobbing into the wet red fruit.

Lorene looked over at Miss Sally standing at the open door. Hard to tell how long she'd been there. Miss Sally and Mr. Walter had already heard the news Lorene had been putting off telling Paul most of the morning. Miss Sally put a finger up to her lips, looked at Paul, shook her head sadly, and gently closed the door.

Lorene wiped Paul's eyes with a cloth she'd dipped in a bowl of ice. "Miss Sally says for you to take some time. She understands how you're hurtin'.'"

Paul slammed the screen door on his way out to the garden.

What kind of world was he living in? He looked up into the hot sun, just to feel his eyes burning through the tears. "Moses, maybe you gone to a better place, but you left me behind bleeding."

By the time nine o'clock came and went, he'd cooked supper and washed the dishes, told Lorene, he had to be busy doing something. He sent her off early, carrying a heavy basket of roast chicken, cornbread stuffing, country ham, biscuits, and with his own deviled eggs, wrapped in wax paper for Coralee. Food they knew she most likely wouldn't have an appetite for.

On his way to bed, he stopped on the back porch, sat for a few minutes in the wicker chair Moses had sat in only a week ago. They'd unwrapped Hershey bars, drinking lemonade, and nibbling sugar cookies, when Moses had said, he thought there was "something funny about that man."

How had he missed it? He should have been aware of the desires and feelings of someone like Kenneth Baynor.

He got up, took the back path that led through the kitchen garden, and sat next to the poplar tree outside on the steps of his little house. There were no more tears to cry, just the dry racking pain of the lifetime he knew awaited him missing his closest friend. The two of them had sat together every evening of their lives before Paul moved to the Jackson farm, except for the week when Paul was laid up with measles, and even then, they'd sneaked out after dark to talk to each other.

Paul called into the night air. "Moses..."

With a whiff of breeze, the leaves of the poplar fluttered out the flapping sound of a captive butterfly. A whisper rustled from inside the tree became clearer, and Paul heard a familiar voice.

"It's Moses."

"Where you at, Moses?"

"Right here."

Paul got up and stumbled closer to the tree. "You mean, from now on you're with me, way it always was?"

Moses answered, "Just the two of us."

"Stay, don't leave, talk to me while I get ready for bed."

"I'm here," Moses whispered.

Paul, hanging onto a hanging branch, closed his eyes. "Good night, Moses."

"Good night, Paul."

17

Early next morning, Paul opened his eyes, and called out, "Moses, you there?"

A rooster crowed. He heard Lorene banging the screen door. Moses didn't answer, Moses was gone. Paul was left with the new heartache and legs so wobbly he had to drag himself out of bed.

In the kitchen, Lorene handed him a cup of coffee. She said, "Elijah and Lily askin' for you to come home Saturday mornin' for the viewin' and the funeral."

After he finished serving breakfast, Paul asked Mr. Walter for a day off.

Mr. Walter told him to take it, spend the night at home, and to be sure to come back the next day for breakfast. As an afterthought, he smiled kindly. "You've settled in here. I told your father in the fields yesterday; we think you're a mighty fine boy."

Paul did not thank Mr. Jackson. He felt too raw when he remembered how he had turned him down when he asked for help. He cleared the dishes, leaving the coffee pot and the Jackson's coffee cups, and slowly left the room.

On Saturday, at the crack of dawn, Paul crossed the tracks not far from where he and Moses had so tenderly laid Clarence. He felt someone had taken his head off, the way they had Clarence's. How could he live in this world without Moses?

Coralee, what was left of her, was standing on her porch, uncombed hair sticking out in every direction, wearing the black cotton dress Lily had run up for her on the sewing machine the day before.

"Oh Lord, Paul, make them bring back my baby." Coralee laid her head on his chest, and sobbed into his newly ironed white shirt. After a while, she looked up. "He's over at your house, lying in a casket."

Paul took her bony arm and led her down the porch steps. "Let's go see him."

Next door, in the Carew house, Coralee sank numbly into a chair at the kitchen table, staring at a bowl of warm milk toast as Lily tried to place her old black church hat over her dear neighbor's wild, unruly hair.

"You have to eat, keep up your strength, 'cause in a few minutes, we expectin' everybody in the Kingdom."

Tallulah and Tabby, with tear-stained faces, were dressed in full skirted Sunday school organdy. James and Ernest, in shorts with their hair slicked down, were quiet and solemn.

When it was Lily's turn to give Paul a hug, she whispered. "Elijah's heart's broken."

His father was standing beside the wooden coffin, in the middle of the room, away from the hot woodburning stove. This time, instead of the usual scowl, Elijah allowed tears to soften his face.

When Elijah saw his son, he reached out, touched Paul's shoulder, and took him by his hand. "You boys have been playin' together since you was babies. Moses is like one of my own children." Elijah pulled out of his pocket one of Lily's white handkerchiefs and wiped his face. "You help carry the casket with the other pallbearers."

"Yes, sir."

There was more on Elijah's mind. "We're all chippin' in for Coralee. She ain't doing for the Larkins no more."

Paul didn't take a second, "I'll send her five dollars a week."

Before Elijah turned to greet the first of the mourners streaming in, he added, "We all gotta stick together."

———

Paul looked down.

Moses's body filled the blue pleated satin lining inside the simple casket. Dead Eye Farlow had insisted that the coffin, and all the arrangements, were his gift to Coralee in memory of her son. Moses's arms were folded across his chest, his hands flat, a red silk scarf neatly wound around his neck, covering the rope burns. The undertaker had teased out the thick springy bush of hair around his face. His eyebrows had been filled in, and arched, his lips painted an unnatural pink.

Paul was aware of angry whispers, folks saying Moses had been "lynched." He heard Dead Eye, standing over in the middle of the room asking out loud, "What if Moses had been a White boy?"

Paul couldn't make out who answered, but he heard, "Be sure he wouldn't be swingin' at the end of a rope."

Paul, full of anguish, felt faint. With the woodburning stove, it was hot enough in the room to melt the waxy look on Moses's face.

"It looks like the Lord's holy ironin' smoothed out all the signs of the poor boy's sufferin'."

Paul looked coldly up at Sissy Cole with her big straw hat, showing off her put-on sadness, remembered her flirting with Elijah at the picnic and how Moses had despised her. Then he heard a sweeter voice whisper in his ear and wondered how his father had allowed Blessing through the door.

"I loved him, too." Blessing was wearing a white dress, her hair down around her face, without any makeup. He heard the catch in her voice as she reached down to touch Moses's made-up face, brushing his too-pink lips with the tips of her fingers. She looked up sadly at Paul. "You always was the one for painted lips."

He shook his head. "Should'a been me lying there."

Next in line, Miss Bessie, eyes watering, without her glasses. She hugged Paul, put her hands on his shoulders. "I'll never forget how much Moses, and all of us, loved your stories about Muriel, your butterfly. That's where Moses is now, flying away with Muriel. Don't you go away and forget us, Paul. After all this, we all need you more than ever."

Next in line, Dave Strickland, the only White man in the room, eyes downcast, sweating, looked at Moses, and said, awkwardly, "I seen how you boys been the closest brothers. I remember Moses was obliged to put your worms on the hook, and how you both sat together all day fishing my pond. I'm sorry."

Lines of people seemed to stretch on forever, until at last, Elijah, standing in the middle of the crowded room, called out, "Folks, time for church."

Coralee, after several hours of greeting the mourners, had to be held up by Blessing, who brought her over to take one long last tearful look at her son. She leaned down and kissed his cheeks before Elijah closed the lid of the casket.

Moses's coffin felt heavy on Paul's shoulder, despite help from five deacons of the church. Elijah's wagon waited outside the front door, the mules brushed, their harnesses gleaming, the coffin covered with masses of fresh flowers, picked by every soul in the Kingdom from any roadside bushes or small patches of garden. With Elijah driving, Paul sat beside Coralee with the rest of the Kingdom on foot behind them for the ten minutes it took to reach the church.

They carried the casket to the front, while the choir lead the congregation in the hymn, "Jesus, Keep Me Near the Cross," and with folks sitting on every bench, people standing inside and out, the hundreds of voices sang.

In the cross, in the cross,
Be my glory ever;

Till my raptured soul shall find
Rest Beyond the river

Hats began to quiver, hands moved up and down waving powers, flinging it all out, lifting Moses's soul to Heaven.

Paul, sitting with the family on the front bench, heard his own voice, gathering strength. When it was over, and everyone sat on the wooden pews, Elijah climbed up to his pulpit, looked down at Blessing, who was sitting in the place next to Paul, where Moses had sat before, shook his head, and began in a slow deep voice.

"Moses sacrificed up his young life to cut the horns off the devil."

Cries echoed from the congregation. "Tell it, brother Elijah, tell it."

He carried on in a slow deliberate voice with carefully chosen words, "Moses Daniels gave up his life for all your children."

He stepped down from the pulpit, stood at the coffin, putting his hand on it. "Every brother, every sister in this church knows we got no justice. Men, callin' themselves Christians, sent our seventeen-year-old brother to hang for killin' a pervert." Elijah's voice rose, he shouted, "WHY? WHY?"

Folks shouted back, "WHY?"

"There ain't no laws in this here world to protect us. Only time we folks in the Kingdom gets near to freedom's when we die." He turned and backed up slowly into the pulpit. "Hear me, God." Elijah raised his arms. "One day, and it's coming soon, You will rain down punishment upon these wicked men who murdered our boy." Elijah clapped his hands. "Are you ready for good news?"

"We're ready," they shouted back.

"I see Moses there, standing at the gates, in Heaven. He's tellin' me, 'Elijah, I'm free'." He shouted, "Free. Give it back."

The congregation shouted back, "He's free."

Paul listened to his father. He'd seen that angry look on Elijah's face before when he was worked up. Where did that leave Paul? There was no fooling himself. He felt like a girl, wanted to dress up, put on makeup. All the people in the church shouting back to Elijah might turn on him if they knew who he really was. Hadn't his father tried to "beat the Devil out of him" for having "unnatural feelings."

Lily must have seen his worried thoughts, she picked up his hand and put it between hers.

Back up in his pulpit, Elijah raised his eyes, saying, "Let's sing together."

"Precious Lord, take my hand,
when the darkness appears
and the night draws near,
when the day is passed and gone,
at the river I stand.
Guide my feet, and hold my hand."

The hymn over, Elijah raised his arms to give the blessing. "In the name of our Lord, Jesus Christ, I bless you all."

How many times had Paul heard his father call on our Lord Jesus Christ? Paul whispered quietly to himself. "Come on, Jesus. Let's see you, Jesus, with your long brown hair, eyes full of love. Where were you, Jesus, when your son Moses needed you?"

———

Paul joined the other pallbearers in the front of the church, to carry his brother to his final resting place. The wagon was waiting, but the flowers had fallen onto the dirt road and wilted.

The Baptist cemetery was a ten-minute walk out towards Strickland's farm on the edge of the Kingdom; two acres of green grass, surrounded by a white picket fence. Driving the wagon, Elijah looked straight ahead.

Paul stayed quiet.

At the grave, Coralee, with Lily and Elijah, stood on the edge of the deep hole, while Paul and the deacons lowered the coffin, let go of the rope, slipping it through their hands, slowly, as the casket swayed, and scraped stone, before finally hitting the bottom.

Paul pulled out his handkerchief to wipe his forehead. The sun was already sinking behind the warm November day. All you could hear was moving air, a breeze had found its way through the almost bare branches of a sycamore tree. He picked up a hand full of dirt, and with Elijah's words, "Earth to earth. Ashes to ashes," threw it into the grave.

At great-grandma Abilene's funeral. Moses had leaned over, and whispered in Paul's ear, "That's what's waitin' for all of us, dirt in your mouth, and no more meals."

18

Pancakes were on the menu for breakfast. Paul had been turning them into tender irresistible temptations, whipping up the egg whites and folding them into his batter.

"Extra fluff, Lorene." He jived around the kitchen.

She laughed and teased, "You ain't nothing but a bit of extra fluff yourself. Feeling better? You can't bury yourself with Moses."

Paul whistled softly as he turned each pancake in the frying pan, stacking them on top of each other, butter and syrup on each layer. He decorated the plate with lots of crispy bacon, and carried his creation into the dining room where Miss Sally and Walter were waiting.

"Paul, looks like you outdid yourself," Miss Sally said.

He'd noticed a blue envelope in her hand, and on his way back to the kitchen, he waited behind the open door and listened.

"Here's her letter, Walter. You've been worrying and fretting, lying awake all night long, radio up against your ear with that awful country music. You're dreaming up problems your beloved Emma might be facing halfway across the world."

Her voice was rising by the minute, "Well, you're the one to blame, Walter, sending our daughter away for a whole year like that with a silly bunch of spoiled debutantes and their even sillier chaperone, Louisa Peabody. Now look where it's got Emma! Soon as we finish these pancakes, I'll read you her letter."

Paul, back in the kitchen, whispered to Lorene, "Better stand behind the door with me and wait for this."

"Well, Sally?" Walter sounded impatient, "Just get on and read it."

Lorene tiptoed close behind Paul. They listened hard.

"'Dearest Daddy and Mama, right to the point, I'm engaged to be married.' Oh, Walter."

Lorene nudged Paul in the ribs, whispered, "Ain't that exciting?"

Sally read on, "'I wrote and told you we'd soon be sailing on the SS Karachi Maru in the Bay of Bengal. Well, we got on board—superb cabins, thank you, Daddy! Curtains and cushions made of divine Indian cottons. You would never believe our first night. Try to imagine a full moon, orchestra playing, and we're all sitting around the table having dinner. I lifted my glass of champagne. There HE was, the handsomest, most distinguished man you've ever seen, in a uniform, sitting across from me at another table. Our eyes met and that was that.'"

Paul listened, excited by the Bay of Bengal, a full moon, and glasses of champagne.

"Stop, Sally," Mr. Walter's sharp voice interrupted, "Read that last part again."

"'He asked me to dance, the orchestra was playing 'Night and Day,' and three days later, he asked me to marry him. Of course, I said yes. Oh, I almost forgot. He's called Flight Lieutenant Henry Lindsey Gordon.'"

Mr. Walter reached for his handkerchief, wiped his forehead, and sighed. "At least we know his name."

Miss Sally put the letter down, fanned herself with the envelope, and rang the bell for more hot coffee. When Lorene carried in the pot, Miss Sally burst out, "Emma's getting married."

Lorene carried on pouring her coffee. "That's good news."

Miss Sally frowned. "We'll see about that. Walter, want another cup?"

"No, Sally. Please, get on and read me the rest of that letter." Walter was grim-faced, still as a stone.

Lorene left the dining room to join Paul at their listening post.

Miss Sally read, "'He's English but says we have to call him British. He's half Scottish and very particular. Nothing more to say except he's an officer in the Royal Air Force, and I love him.'"

Walter winced.

"'Don't worry, Daddy, I'll write in a few days when we know our plans. Your Emma.'"

Lorene shook her head.

"She's lost her mind. An Englishman," Walter said.

Miss Sally's voice was low and soft. "She's lost her heart. Give him a chance, Walter. Remember what you always told Emma?"

He rubbed his forehead. "What was that?"

"Your choice is my pleasure."

Walter rolled his napkin carefully and put it back into the silver napkin holder. "Did I say that?" He rose slowly from his chair. "We'll talk about this later. I'm off to the plant."

Lorene took a fresh percolated pot of coffee off the stove. "This'll kill Walter. Sally will start planning a wedding. He'll hate every minute of it."

A week went by with Paul and Miss Sally busy in the garden. She pointed to new plants while he dug out the dirt, put them in, and molded earth around each one. He thought how that had always been the way. White folks point, Colored people shovel. However, recently she was at least asking his opinions and following them.

He took off his gardening gloves and patted the last bit of compost around a newly planted magnolia tree while Miss Sally admired a cloud of swallowtails around her buddleia bush.

"I ain't never seen so many butterflies." She saw his raised eyebrows at her choice of words. "Might interest you to know my grandmama, like all our people in their day, said *ain't*. Ain't nothing wrong with *ain't*."

Paul got up off his knees and took hold of the shovel. "Well, ma'am, must be where we picked it up."

"That's right. Besides," Sally went on, "I've always tried to talk just like my mammy, Aunt Tildee. I miss her to this day, and most of the time when I'm thinking to myself, I think about the way she talked."

He remembered what Miss Bessie had told him in class: "Try and speak the way I do, Paul. I learned in school, and so can you. The right words and the right grammar can always change the way people think of you."

Miss Bessie wanted to talk like a White woman. Miss Sally pretended to sound Colored.

As his shovel thudded against the packed dirt, he thought about the people he loved, the way they talked, how their language had its own music. He said it out loud, "'Not' doesn't sound as good as 'ain't.'"

"Ain't that the truth, Paul?" Miss Sally laughed and pointed to another plant.

Paul got out the hose and Miss Sally watered until she went inside. He stood listening and looking at the bees, thousands of them swarming and buzzing. He was young but could feel his life buzzing by. With his rising mood, he felt like a bee, pulling out nectar, putting it into his hive, storing it, waiting for the day he could turn it into honey.

19

One afternoon a few weeks later, Lorene sat with her face in her hands on the back porch. "Shut up, you damn crickets. Hotter it gets, more the fools rub their legs together. Sun's burning up the day, me with it."

Paul pulled up a chair. "I love those crickets."

"Fancy that. Now you get to shelling. I need these peas for supper."

Paul took the bowl she handed him.

"Here's the latest. Emma's getting married in Louisville. No wedding dress, just plain and simple. I overheard Sally telling Walter her Englishman's got no money. But, hell, that girl's twenty-three, time for her to get married. You'll be walking on a tightrope with her ups and downs when they get here. Old folks ain't going up to Louisville for the ceremony. Sally has to kiss a Horse Cave wedding goodbye. Just as well, put Emma and Sally together, they'll fry and sizzle."

Paul rolled his fingers around in the bowl of shelled peas. "How come?"

"That's a long story I ain't got time for today. I remember the old days. I turned sixteen when I first come to work at the Jacksons'.

Emma was only six. She had a mammy called Aunt Hattie Curry, lived in Bear Wallow, a friend of your Great-grandma Abilene."

Paul stopped shelling and took a sip of his cold root beer. "I remember Abilene talking about her. She was Rowland Curry's grandma, lived with him. I remember his little farm. He scratched out a pretty hard living." Paul wondered and asked, "What's this got to do with Emma?"

Lorene stuck her neck forward, peered at him. "Better learn one thing, we Colored folks got everything to do with the way White folks' children turn out.

"In those days, Sally Jackson was young, in her thirties, busy all the time with good works. Once a week, she'd hop in her buggy, drive herself to the mountains to help poor White trash push out more of the same. After lunch, Hattie counted on Walter having a nap on the front porch, while out here on our back porch she'd pull Emma up on her lap, stroke her hair, tell that li'l thing a heap of ghost stories. They got scarier and scarier. I remember how Aunt Hattie draws back like a rattler, waves her fingers in front of Emma's face. Emma didn't move, she's under her spell, scared to death."

Paul emptied his full bowl of peas into Lorene's. "I still don't understand."

"When I got here in the morning, I find Emma's sitting up in bed, face white as a ghost, rubbing her poor little eyes, 'cause she ain't slept all night. Sally knows about it, but she don't do nothing. They're all scared to death of Aunt Hattie's powers. Sally Jackson tiptoed around her. Walter stayed out of it, and nobody but Hattie looked after that little girl. Funny thing, Emma keep on and on asking for more ghost stories."

Paul tried to imagine little six-year-old Emma sitting on Aunt Hattie Curry's lap. Who hadn't heard about Aunt Hattie? "A skinny spinster woman six-foot tall" was how Abilene told it, with big dark-brown eyes, the nose of a hawk, and an orange turban wound around her head. Aunt Hattie could stop a baby crying just by laying her hand on its head.

"Want to know how she came to work here? Miss Sally heard tell of Hattie's powers. She needed someone for her colicky little baby and, sure enough, Hattie's touch was enough to stop her fussing."

Paul smiled happily at Lorene as he gave her another bowl of shelled peas. "Puts me in a good mood to think of Aunt Hattie scaring all the White folks to death."

Lorene frowned. "Didn't do Emma no good. Times she acted just like Aunt Hattie, all high and mighty, with her bad moods."

On his way to the greenhouse, Paul passed by the chicken run, marveling, as he peered through the wire at the five new fluffy yellow babies running after a black-and-white speckled hen. He thought about Emma and wondered how she got all mixed up, trailing after Aunt Hattie.

———

Miss Sally and Mr. Walter were dressed to go out for supper. Every week, they were invited to Miss Sally's sister Annie and her husband Edward's house. They produced all the milk, cream, and butter for the county from their Jersey herd on their dairy farm in Hiseville.

Walter, ready an hour early, sat waiting for Miss Sally on the front porch. Rocking back in his chair, he was thinking. He took thinking as serious business, and that man used his time to figure out problems. When the sweet smell of Miss Sally's potted lilies floated in with a light breeze, he allowed his thoughts to be interrupted and to dwell once more on the unhappy prospect of a foreign son-in-law.

While serving their lunch earlier, Paul overheard Walter complaining to Miss Sally, "Henry's British, an airman. Over here, we keep our feet on the ground and our heads out of the clouds."

Miss Sally chided him. "Walter, most of our ancestors came from 'over there,' as you call it. They did pretty well."

Walter gave a long sigh, slowly buttered his bread. "That's

because the good ones left." He lined up his knife and fork. He'd eaten enough.

"We'll see, Walter."

Miss Sally had been looking forward all day to going out for dinner. Preparations began at four o'clock with a bath full of sweet-smelling oils. She lay soaking until the hot water cooled down. After that, she looked through every dress in her closet until she found one appropriate for that evening. She put on what she had chosen, looked at herself—front, back, around, and sideways—in her long mirror. After that, she sat at her dressing table, spent at least half an hour powdering, putting on rouge and brushing her thinning white hair into endless fluff-ups, trying to bring back her long, thick, blonde-haired glory. By the time she bent down and tied up her shoelaces, it was six o'clock and time to go.

Paul was arranging a vase of white store-bought lilies. He always waited around to see what Miss Sally was wearing. He thought you could tell a great deal about how a person felt inside by what they put on. He was different. No one could tell by looking at him who he was or how he felt. He could only dream of satin, ruffles, red lips, and long, curly mascaraed lashes.

Finally, Miss Sally arrived downstairs, smelling of lavender, wearing light-blue voile, an amethyst brooch clutching at the waves of her white lace collar. Paul was sure this showed how far Miss Sally would go not to expose even a tiny flash of flesh. She was holding a filmy chiffon handkerchief, sewn by Lily, and wearing the old-lady white lace-up shoes he'd polished that morning. He stood looking at her, not daring to pass a compliment.

She broke the silence, "Seeing you reminds me I have a pile of dresses that needs to be carried over to Lily next time you go." She smoothed the tight corset around her hips, looked at herself in the full-length hall mirror. "I'm so fat, I can't fit into a thing these days. Your fault, Paul, all those pancakes." She tugged at her sleeves. "I've put the dresses in a pile on my bed, with some old belts on top."

Paul waved until the car's taillights disappeared. He was alone.

He went into the Jacksons' bedroom on the ground floor, looking forward to examining the dresses.

Two large four-poster beds stood side-by-side. There were two hanging cupboards, two chests of drawers smelling of camphor. In a corner of the room, facing a long French window, a large gilt mirror hung over a dressing table covered with pots of creams, lotions, silverback combs and hairbrushes. A full, frilly white apron brushed the floor.

The bathroom door was open, so he stepped through and saw jars of bath salts and flacons of different oils sitting on the shelf next to her bath. He opened the bottles one by one, and whispered out loud as he read each label, "Rose of Damascus, French Lavender, Geranium Bourbon." He dabbed a little of each heavenly scent on his wrists and sniffed.

He did not pick up the sound of a car in the drive until he heard Miss Sally's voice calling.

"Paul, Paul, are you there?"

Terrified, he closed the bathroom door, and grabbed the pile of dresses from Miss Sally's four-poster bed. The door to the bedroom opened.

"Oh, there you are. Silly me, I left those two jars of chutney for my sister on the kitchen table. You're quicker than I am, Paul. Please run, pick them up for me."

Still clutching the pile of dresses, he hurried into the kitchen, wishing he could scrub his wrists.

Miss Sally stayed on the steps of the front porch, waiting for the package. "Whew, I can smell my bath oil. I must've gone way overboard."

Sally hurried out to the waiting car, leaving Paul to dab the sweat from his brow. He wondered what would have happened if she'd returned five minutes earlier?

In her bathroom, he screwed the tops on each of the bottles and put them back carefully. With a sigh of relief, he locked the kitchen door and made his way down the grassy path to his house.

It was dark and there was a cool wind blowing through the poplars.

He turned on his bath, looked through the dresses, and found a red-and-white-striped silk dress with a scoop neck. He'd never seen Miss Sally wearing it. Must be an old favorite from her younger days. He held it up to his shoulders. Maybe he'd try it on after a long soak in a hot tub, practice a few songs, and dance a little. He looked around. He was safe, the door was locked, his curtains were pulled, no one could get in, and no one could see him.

20

"They'll get here when they get here, and with that old fool, Luke Moss driving, Lord only knows when they *will* get here," Lorene grumbled.

Luke Moss, a way-back-when cousin, the kind Miss Sally said you never called kin, had been sent to collect the honeymooning newlyweds from the Brown Hotel in Louisville.

The very idea that Emma and her husband would soon arrive in Horse Cave threw the house into an uproar, and Miss Sally into a tizzy. She told Lorene, "I'm all worn out just thinking about getting ready for my new son-in-law."

They were coming. The house smelled of fresh flowers and beeswax, and for two days Paul and Lorene had been baking, curing a ham, dressing fresh-killed chickens, and rubbing T-bone steaks with garlic and black pepper. Miss Sally dithered about what to wear, finally settling on a green-and-white dress, and when she had looked for the last time at herself in the mirror, she went out to wait on the front porch with Walter.

In the hall, Paul snipped the stems off the first of spring's white lilacs before putting each one into a big crystal vase. After that, he moved on to parsley and white roses, arranged carefully in Miss Sally's Paul Revere silver bowl.

When Emma arrived in the hall, followed by Luke Moss chewing on an unlit cigar, carrying their suitcases, Paul turned. A red-felt cloche hat covered most of her thick blonde hair. A dark-blue silk dress hugged her body and stopped just above her ankles. When he saw the flash of her red fingernails and lipstick, he remembered Lorene's words: "You'll see, Paul. She's a fine-looking woman who knows what she wants."

Emma smiled at him. "I wish you would teach me to arrange flowers like that. You must be Paul."

"Yes, ma'am."

The man Emma knew she'd wanted stood behind her. Paul caught his breath, sure he was looking at the handsomest man in the world, a dark-haired Leslie Howard straight off the pages of his *Motion Picture Magazine*. Henry was tall, wearing a dark blue suit, white silk shirt, and red-and-white-striped tie. His light-brown wavy hair was combed back over a high forehead, and he looked at Paul with the most intense blue eyes Paul had ever seen.

This real-life movie star stuck out his hand and said, "Paul, I've heard so much about you."

Embarrassed, Paul hesitated for a second before placing his hand in Henry's. He felt too shy to say a word, thought he might faint on the spot.

With his heart pounding in his ears, he heard Lorene say, with some assurance, "Happy to have you here, Flight Lieutenant Gordon. Anything you need, just tell us."

If only he'd thought of something to say. After all, he and Lorene had been practicing Miss Sally's carefully written instructions on how to properly address Emma's new husband.

"Cat got your tongue?" Lorene cackled when she saw how flustered Paul was. "Couldn't even say hello to the man? You been saying it over and over again for three days. Call him Henry." She kept on and on teasing, understanding that if there was such a thing as love at first sight, Paul was in it. "You take over in the dining room tonight, just so you can keep your eye on him."

That evening, when he served at the table, Paul marveled at the way Henry held his knife and fork, never putting one down to pick up the other, and wondered at the differences between Henry and the Jacksons.

At first, Henry cut his fried chicken with a knife and fork until Emma urged him impatiently, "Oh Henry, please do pick it up."

On the other hand, when a plate of fresh green asparagus was placed before him, he picked one up in his fingers, after dipping it into the melted butter. Emma frowned while the Jacksons pretended not to notice.

When Paul went into the kitchen to get the cornbread and biscuits, he told Lorene about the asparagus, and she shook her head.

"Come back, tell me what else he does or don't do."

Later, Paul was carrying a platter of country ham to the table when Henry took his first sip of iced tea.

Miss Sally caught his fleeting grimace. "Have some more sugar, Henry," she urged.

"No, thank you. It's excellent," Henry said, and smiled politely.

Emma wondered, asking, "I remember how hot it was in India, darling. Didn't you put ice in your hot tea?"

Henry smiled gently, explained politely, "Heaven forbid, darling. For the British abroad, the higher the temperature, the hotter the tea and the more often we drink it. And we drink it all day long." Henry laughed at the thought and leaned forward as if confessing a secret. "No. After a good cup of hot tea, we break out into a sweat that cools us down."

Sweat? The very word wrinkled a tiny frown on Sally Jackson's forehead. "Sweat is what we call perspiration."

Then a rare observation from Walter Jackson, "Here, only mules and horses sweat."

Henry smiled. "Yes sir. *Vive la différence.*"

The Jacksons weren't sure about *Vive la difference*, but they laughed all the same.

Paul was in a swoon. After dinner, he stood beside Lorene, her arms deep in soapy water, drying each dish she handed him as if he were polishing a medal. He said, dreamily, "Always did call it sweat, but from now on, I'll pick up asparagus with my fingers."

"Now ain't that something? Mr. Paul Carew will *from now on pick up his asparagus with his fingers.* Since when you been picking up asparagus with a *fork*?"

He didn't answer, kept on drying the dishes, no use talking back to her.

Next morning, after the kitchen work was done, Paul begged Lorene to allow him to clean Emma and Henry's room. Emma's clothes were strewn across the bed; Henry's pajamas were neatly folded on top of his pillow. He picked up the book on Henry's bedside table, *Seven Pillars of Wisdom*, by T.E. Lawrence, and thought tenderly of Lily for making sure Miss Bessie had taught him to read and write. He opened the book to the first page dedication, feeling safe, knowing they were all out visiting Hidden River Cave. He read aloud slowly and carefully:

I loved you, so I drew these tides of
Men into my hands
And wrote my will across the
Sky and stars

He read it again, this time trying to figure out the meaning of those wonderful words. He promised himself that one day he would buy that book and read it. And every night for the next year, he said out loud before he went to sleep, "I loved you, and wrote my will across the sky and stars."

In the days that followed, he picked Henry Gordon's shirts out of the laundry basket and washed them by hand. He could not stop looking at this Englishman—who opened his beaten, silver cigarette case, pulled out a strange flat cigarette, and tapped it before flaming it with a silver Dunhill lighter. Paul listened carefully to the way

Henry spoke and rolled his words and sentences around and around, until he could say, "marvelous" and "absolutely" and "splendid" just like the Englishman did.

One day, after lunch, he was practicing in the kitchen. "How splendid," he said to Lorene as she cut up apples and blackberries for the cobbler.

"Ain't no use you talking to me like that, 'cause no one around here understand a word of it."

He ignored her, went right on practicing, and wondered why she couldn't see the beauty of those long foreign words. He liked to slip out after lunch, while Lorene ironed, and sit on a patch of flat green grass under the old hickory tree behind the greenhouse.

Today he took a deep breath before he sat down, put his arms out, and twirled around, fanning the heat inside of him. "I'm in love, I'm in love, you hear me, world?" he called out as he began to sing. *"For you I sigh, for you dear only, I'm all for you, body and soul."*

———

Later that afternoon, just as Paul was putting on his apron and beginning to sift cake flour, Henry strolled into the kitchen.

"Mind if I pay you a little visit?" He pulled out a chair and sat at the kitchen table.

Flustered, Paul took off his apron. "No, sir."

Henry opened his silver case and took out a cigarette. "I want to see for myself where all these marvelous creations are born."

Paul and Lorene looked at each other, guessing Henry hadn't heard how much Mr. Walter hated smoking.

Henry tapped his cigarette on the table, scratched his lighter, lit up, and blew out a double trail of smoke. He asked Lorene, "Where did you learn to cook?"

"Well, sir, I was born knowing it."

Henry smiled, took a few more puffs, looked over at Paul. "I see you're a true artist. Were you born knowing how to be a cook, gardener, and a florist, too?"

Paul felt his face flame. How could this man have guessed? "Yes, sir, far back as I can remember I liked to fool with flowers, help Mama cook and sew. Oh, and sometimes I made up stories about butterflies and told them at school."

Worried about his outburst, he studied Henry's face, looking for signs of disapproval, but all he saw was genuine interest.

"Wonderful, what splendid talents. You must write down one of your stories. I'd love to read it."

Paul was at Henry's feet. An artist. No one had ever called him that before. And talent. Did he really have *talent*?

"Any chance for a cup of tea?"

Lorene reached for the Lipton while Paul fetched Miss Sally's silver teapot.

"Hot tea, sir?"

Henry looked at his watch.

"Spot on five o'clock. Yes, please. By the way, have you ever tried an Indian curry?"

Lorene shook her head, while Paul jumped up and proudly fetched his tin of McCormick's curry powder.

"No, sir, but I put this into my deviled eggs and chicken salad. I never tried it with anything else."

He unscrewed the top, waited while Henry dabbed a little on his finger then to his tongue.

He frowned and said, "Bit bland. The devil's in the heat and that's how I like it—hot as a firecracker."

Paul ventured, "Might work up a sweat, sir."

Henry laughed. "Happy someone knows what to call it. Sweat is what you have to do in a hot climate. In the officers' mess in Quetta, we had a first-rate cook. Every day a member of my squadron chose a different curry, and Lord, did we sweat! Soon as I get back to England, Paul, I'll send you a few boxes of different powders and a recipe book."

Paul listened to every word, wondering what "mess" meant or where Quetta was. By now, he knew the importance of sweat.

Lorene, slicing country ham, muttered, "Might fire up Mr. Jackson's ulcer. I ain't sure about cooking with hot curry powder."

Henry sat, drinking tea with a twist of lemon, telling Lorene and Paul about his life in India, and "tackling," as he called it, one of Paul's cinnamon rolls.

By the time Miss Sally and Emma came home in a bad mood, patting their heads of too-tight curls from the hairdresser, Henry had finished his second cinnamon roll and his third cup of tea.

Emma was irritated to see him sitting at the kitchen table. "Come along, darling. Paul and Lorene have work to do."

He got up reluctantly and carried his plate and cup over to the sink. "Thank you both for the stimulating conversation."

After he'd left, Lorene shook her head and laughed. "What was that he called it? 'Stimulating conversation'?"

Whatever he'd meant, Paul would toss and turn in his head every word the Flight Lieutenant had said.

Before dinner, carrying a newly arranged vase of flowers, he tiptoed past Emma and Henry's bedroom door, and stopped when he heard raised voices.

"The way you're talking, Emma, it seems anything I do in this house is out of place."

Then Emma's voice, pitched a little lower, "But don't you see? That's exactly what you are. It's not your fault, you just need to learn the rules."

Paul wondered if the rules included coming into the kitchen, sitting down to have a cup of tea with him and Lorene.

———

Two days later, Paul was shoveling earth around a new magnolia. He stood straight when he saw Emma in a red-and-white polka-dot dress hugging her body, and Henry in his Royal-Air-Force-blue blazer, moving towards him arm-in-arm.

Emma had something on her mind. "Paul, we wanted to let you know we'll be leaving in a few days."

He knew they would be leaving, though he'd pretended to himself it would never happen.

She went on, "We're grateful for the way you look after Mother and Daddy. You and Lorene light up their lives."

Paul tried to hide his feelings. He could see Emma looking at him, curiously, wondering at the suddenly stricken expression on his face.

Henry stepped in, tried to give some comfort, "We've been here for three weeks. Don't worry, Paul. I'm not sure when we'll be back, but we will be. And then we'll have more chats in the kitchen. And next time I'll bring you some English tea. Trouble may be brewing, with Hitler's Nazi Germany on the rise. We will have to wait and see."

"Yes, sir." Paul could hardly keep back his tears as he watched them strolling back to the house. They talked about the deep impression he and Lorene had clearly made while Paul was left wondering what his life would be like without Henry in it.

———

After they'd gone, everyone in the Jackson house tried to cool the summer down with iced tea and electric fans, and when Lorene found Sylvester, the Jacksons' young yellow-and-white-striped cat, dead under a rose bush, Miss Sally reckoned he'd died of a heat stroke.

Lorene arrived early on these hot mornings, waited for enough light to go inside the chicken coop. She'd pick out a hen, wring its neck, pluck it to boil before six A.M. so Paul could make his chicken salad with chopped celery, scallions, and toasted almonds, and stuff it into ripe red tomatoes from the garden. Too hot to fry chicken. Lorene swore it was the first time she hadn't cooked a hot lunch since she'd been working there. The house was dark, the shades were drawn during the day, and, except for the people who had to work, everyone drank cold lemonade or iced tea and fanned themselves.

Nights, Paul lay on top of the covers, sweat trickling from his forehead and down the sides of his face. It got so hot he had to take off the head stocking that he put on to keep his waves down. Would he ever be free, find the chance to see what he could do outside of this life, without two old folks to look after and Lorene sitting on his head? He would never be like other men. Blessing had warned him. Not that he didn't like his work, but the curtain had come down for Paul since Henry left.

He sat in the kitchen, red-eyed, picking at Lorene's smothered steak, left over from last night's dinner. "Not hungry." He sighed. "Not even for your best in the world."

She unpeeled her glasses from behind each ear and snapped their metal case shut. "You listen to me, boy. You've got no friends. You don't go out chasing tail. Only time you leave this house is when you go downtown to the grocery with Miss Sally. You're stuck on the wall, Paul. No one to peel you off. You spend all day talking about Henry Gordon, but I can't see much in him. He ain't one of us. Can't understand a word he says, so full of precious good manners you can't see where he starts and where he ends. You can do better than going 'round trying to be just like him." Lorene crossed her arms and shook her head.

With every word, Paul felt hot blood rising.

"You're just picking up other people's crayons, Paul. You need to learn to color on your own, and you're free to do that. Walter told Elijah he wants to see your mama up here for a visit once a week. You see how those two old folks care for you? And your family loves you, too. Being cared for is what you need. If you're not happy, you're not right in the head."

Paul folded then fanned out a white damask napkin, carried it to the table, mad at Lorene for the way she talked, mad at her for making everything her business, even madder at the way she'd taken against Henry. He'd had enough. "You ever see any other White man come into our kitchen, want to spend time with us way he did?"

She sniffed and unscrewed a jar of mayonnaise for his chicken salad. "So what?"

Lorene was right about one thing, Paul thought. He hadn't been to see Lily for a while; he'd been getting news secondhand. Part of it was he couldn't stand to cross the tracks, walk by Moses's house, see Coralee sitting on the front porch, bone thin, a restless mind tearing at her sanity. He gave her some of his pay every week, but she needed more from him than that. He felt the sting of guilt. He was alive, Moses was dead. He'd wonder for the rest of his life if he should have paid more attention to those damned Hershey bars and warned his friend. Hadn't he known deep down there might be trouble? He'd denied his own feelings. Told himself he was not the same kind of dangerous person as Kenneth. He would never behave like that. How could he imagine the depths the florist would sink to? The guiltier Paul felt, the madder he got at Lorene. All she ever seemed to do these days was give him sass.

He picked up another white napkin, this time slapped it on the table. "How would you like to get up every morning, feel like one person, act like another?"

Lorene puffed up when she heard his tone. "Hold your horses, boy. We all feel that way." She banged a skillet down on top of the stove. "Better get used to it, coming to work, not being your real self. Might be for the best, far as you're concerned. As for happiness, that bubble bursts soon as you touch it."

It would take a day or two of angry silences in the kitchen before Paul slipped back into the groove with his cousin.

21

It was April when Miss Sally and Paul went out picking the first sweet peas. When he'd first arrived, she'd kept her eye on him. Now she trusted him to choose plants with suitable colors and to carry out the work as she'd taught him. She allowed herself to rest a little longer on the front porch on her chaise lounge. Most of the time in the garden she chatted freely, forgetting she was not talking to one of her friends. Miss Sally would never allow herself to complain, but at times, she would snap at Paul when her knees were on fire and every joint in her body throbbing with arthritis.

"Dig that hole deeper... Don't stand there like that looking at me... Give that plant more water."

He knew her temper came from suffering. He'd heard her talking the same way to Mr. Walter and even he never talked back.

She carried a wicker basket while he picked bundles of the scented flowers. When he had gathered the last sweet pea, she told him the exciting news.

"Emma's having a baby and Mr. Walter's bringing her home on the biggest boat he can find. Then we'll take Leroy, drive to New York to pick her up, and stay three days at the Waldorf Astoria. What do you think of that?"

Miss Sally was flushed and for a few minutes, Paul saw the young face behind the old lady's. "Sounds like a dream, Miss Sally."

A few weeks later, though, he watched her face fall when Walter changed his mind and decided to have a cousin meet Emma in New York and put her on the night train to Louisville. Her lips drew into a tight line and her arthritis brought out more winces than ever. He reckoned Lorene was right when she said, "Walter keeps his hand on his wallet where Sally's concerned. He ain't letting her loose to go on a buying spree in New York."

———

On Tuesday, August 27, Miss Sally flurried into the kitchen. The year 1935 had been full of promise and now it was all coming to a head.

"She'll be here any minute. Mr. Walter called from Elizabethtown a few hours ago. Better take that chicken off the boil. I hope you all made a couple of big jars of mayonnaise. No telling what the girl will want to eat. She was fussy even when she wasn't pregnant."

Paul stood on the front porch, waiting for the sound of tires on the gravel. When the dark-blue Buick pulled along the other cars in the drive, he ran down the steps and opened the car door. Emma took his hand and stepped out wearing a pale-yellow shapeless dress, which hung loosely over her large bulge. There were deep dark circles under her eyes, her springy blonde hair lay flat and had not been washed for several days.

"Oh, Paul, I'm so glad to see you."

He was surprised when Emma gave her mother a longer hug than usual.

In the days following, Emma was moody and tired. "Having this baby doesn't suit me." Paul overheard her tell Miss Sally.

He put sweet peas in her room every day, made a cheese soufflé from a recipe in the *Courier-Journal's* "French cooking week" column using Hart County cheddar. One evening, he carried hot sassafras tea into her bedroom, went in, smelled lavender oil, and found Miss Sally smoothing strokes from her daughter's toes to her knees and back again. She'd carried this practice down from Aunt Tildee, her own mammy.

Miss Sally loved Aunt Tildee more than anyone on earth, and she never forgot how when she was expecting Emma, Aunt Tildee had massaged her legs for her with a secret recipe of oils and plant extracts.

That was the only time Paul saw them sweet together and it didn't last long. Every morning after Miss Sally gave Lorene the menus for the day, Emma marched into the kitchen and changed them. Wearily, but with authority, she'd say, "Lorene, I don't want this heavy country food."

Miss Sally let it go. She wasn't fixing to fight with her pregnant daughter.

During meals, Emma hardly addressed a word to her mother, kept her eyes on Walter, while Paul served the cold chicken salad she loved. No one missed fried chicken and country ham except Mr. Walter.

After lunch one day, Paul went out to the smokehouse for Lorene. The air was hot and wet. He felt queasy. The back screen door slammed, and he heard Emma's voice calling him. She was standing next to the smokehouse, a shapeless and sleeveless white tent hanging over her huge belly and carrying her usual basket of Concord grapes. She could eat one or more baskets every day.

She'd pick one off the bunch, suck the insides out of that sweet, tight purple skin, and then spit out the rest. She asked Paul to ride out to Bear Wallow with her, said she wanted to see the farmhouse where she'd been born. He'd already made Chicken à la King with his new passion for butter puff-pastry sheets and all he had to do was fill them. The ham could wait.

Emma got into the car, wedged herself behind the wheel. After half an hour, they turned off the main highway and bumped down the old road leading to the farm. It was a pretty Kentucky house, white clapboard and tall front windows with a wraparound front porch. They got out of the car and found an old White woman sitting still in a rocking chair. Emma reckoned she must be Ima Burks, Sally's distant cousin. She knew her daddy had given Ima the house rent-free. Emma waddled behind her huge belly up to the porch. "Miss Ima, it's Emma Jackson, Walter's daughter."

Ima sat still, never moved, and didn't say a word.

Emma guessed she'd had a stroke. Someone hollered from inside the house, "Y'all need something, Miss Ima?"

Paul recognized Ruby Bisto as she came out of the screen door. She was one of Elijah's distant cousins, wearing down-at-the-heel slippers, walking like Humpty Dumpty, her top half was so heavy.

"What you all need? Land's sake, it looks like Paul Carew, Elijah's boy. That you, Paul?" Ruby wiped her hands up and down her apron. Not waiting on an answer, she continued, "They're all away. Family. Left me here with Miss Ima. They've gone to Sulphur Springs for the day, back tonight. Heard voices, knew it couldn't be Miss Ima, she ain't said a word, not for months. But you never can tell." Ruby cast a glance at Emma's swollen belly. "You all are welcome to stay till they come home."

Emma said they couldn't, she was wilting. But before they left, she pointed to the long window facing the front bedroom. "I was born in that bedroom, Paul, and I'm not looking forward to going through the same terrible ordeal as Mama did twenty-three years ago. She never stopped telling me bringing a baby into the world was hell."

Emma leaned on the car door, looking back at the house. "I got the whipping of my life in that front hall. Mama drew blood. In those days we lived out here in Bear Wallow, on the home farm." She pulled out a cigarette, forgot to light it. "When I wasn't running after my mammy's heels, I ran over to the Carews' to play with little Ed, one of your cousins."

Paul laughed. "Got plenty of 'em around."

She was staring at the house as if she'd forgotten he was there. "I'd run over to his cabin, on the edge of a field, about a mile from our house, almost every day. One day, when Aunt Hattie wasn't looking and Mama had gone to the hills to do good works, I decided to play 'Pretend Baptism' over by the pond with Ed. I put on the new white dress Mama had bought for my cousin's wedding, embroidered collar, lace around the hem. She did tell me, 'Don't you dare wear that dress.' Ed pulled on his shirt, ready to go, soon as I got to his shack. We called ourselves little ponies. He picked up a trot behind me and we raced through the fields. I remember yelling, 'Hurry up, we got a way to go for Jesus business.'" Emma giggled. "By the time I finished baptizing him, he was born again, and I was covered in mud like a catfish. I can see it right now. My dress was all brown and sticky. We ran home, scared Mama would see me before I could clean up. Sure enough, there she was looking mad, standing at the back door, waiting for me. She pulled a whittled birch out of a vase stuffed with walking sticks, raised her arm and laid into me, and kept on going until my backsides were raw. Right then, and I can see him now, Daddy came through the door and saw me naked, red welts all over my body. I started screaming, 'Daddy, she's killing me.' The sound of his voice, every word came out in ice-coated fury. 'Get out of my sight,' he said to Mama."

Emma looked down at her unlit cigarette. "Have one of these?" She struck a match, lit his, and then lit her own.

Paul held it between his thumb and forefinger. "I've never had one before."

She inhaled a long puff. "I've been smoking since I was fifteen. I guess you know how my daddy hates it. My baby boy's coming out with a Lucky Strike and a Concord grape in his mouth."

Paul took a puff, coughed a little, said, "Miss Emma, how do you know the baby's a boy? Might be a girl."

She smiled, ground her half-smoked cigarette out with her foot. "Simple, Paul. I don't want a girl. It's a boy."

On the road home, Emma struggled with the gearshift then kept her foot down, steady at forty miles an hour. "You know, Paul... Well, maybe you don't. I graduated from college. I have a master's degree in history. Now look at the state I'm in. What good was it all?"

He knew he couldn't answer for her. One thing that day he did do was share with Emma a lifelong taste for cigarettes and, like her, suffered the hidden scars from brutal beatings.

———

A week before Emma's time, Lorene arrived with the Kingdom's midwife, Sister Jessie Porter, who worked her miracles on both sides of the tracks. Part of those "miracles" was her use of herbs and barks, gathered from all over the countryside. Lorene swore she and Arletta owed her their lives.

Sister Jessie was over seventy; no one knew how far over. She was short, plump, her hair plaited into two long, gray-streaked pigtails behind her ears. Without wasting any time, she unwrapped her newspapers of dried herbs and threw them into the pots of boiling water.

While Sister Jessie waited, Paul sat her down, poured a strong cup of black coffee, and cut her a piece of his blueberry cake.

Sister Jessie sipped her coffee, looking at Paul over the rim of her cup. "I been keeping my eyes on you since you was little," she said. "You never been a child like the others."

Lorene scooted her skillets to the back of the stove. The kitchen filled with steam and the powerful smell of Sister Jessie's herbs. "You can say that again. He's not like the others. Only one of him."

Sister Jessie, with her eyes full of tenderness, looked at Paul. "I saw Blessing McCrae yesterday asking after you. I caught that poor child, but I couldn't save her mama. Poor Pearl, skin and bones, died in my arms. Blessing's a good girl turned bad. She got powers, she saw death coming to Moses."

Sister Jessie got up, took the long-handled wooden spoon Lorene handed her for stirring her potions, looked back at him through the clouds of steam. "Get ready for this baby, Paul. She'll be sitting on your lap for the rest of your life."

He picked the blueberries out of his warm cake and popped them, absentmindedly, in his mouth. "What do you mean she? And what have I got to do with her? And anyway, she better be a boy."

Sister laughed. "Wait and see."

———

Walter had insisted Dr. Grisham, at Louisville's Baptist Hospital, would be Emma's obstetrician. The Horse Cave ambulance, a converted hearse from the funeral home, was waiting to carry Emma to the hospital when her time came.

One morning, soon after Sister Jessie's visit, Paul was opening the oven door to slide in his tray of baked apples, Emma's favorite dessert. She came into the kitchen, sat at the table with a pencil and notepad balanced on her huge baby bump.

"Morning Paul, I'm ready to write your big apple miracle down in my recipe book... I feel so good this morning, for a change."

Paul spoke slowly as she wrote. "Steam the cored-and-peeled apples for a few minutes. Make a syrup of dark-brown sugar, apple juice, cinnamon, cloves, and pour over the slightly softened apples. Cook slowly, baste often, until the sauce is thick, and the apples are full of flavor."

"Oh Paul, I'm so hungry, can't wait to eat these apples with cold Straker's cream. I feel like going for a walk. I'm full of energy."

Half an hour later, a scream, followed by loud shouts, tore through the humid air of the early September morning.

Lorene looked up from her pea shelling. "I better tell Leroy to fetch Sister Jessie."

Paul dropped his eggbeater. "She was fine half an hour ago. You saw her. She sat right over there, talking about baked apples."

"That was half an hour ago," Lorene shot back, as she hurried out of the kitchen. "Don't stand there with your bare face hanging out. Boil some water. Get clean cloths. Anything can happen."

There was another loud yell from the front room.

Miss Sally was sitting beside the bed, her hand on her daughter's forehead. Mr. Walter was standing at the door wiping his face with a large white handkerchief.

Paul put the tray down. "Sister Jessie's on her way."

Emma was shaking, waiting for the next pain. "Do something, Daddy!" she screamed at Mr. Walter.

"Honey, I've called Dr. Grisham in Louisville. He'll be waiting for you. The ambulance will be here in twenty minutes."

Emma sat up, sweat pouring down her face. "I don't want this damn thing." She pointed to her stomach. "Take it out."

"You don't mean that, Emma," Miss Sally said.

"Hell, I fucking-well—damn-well do mean it."

Mr. Walter was sure he hadn't heard that language and went out onto the front porch to cool off and wait for the ambulance.

Sister Jessie arrived, carrying a bag. "Now you quit fretting, Emma. Sister Jessie's here. I've got what you need." She patted her bag. "Let me look at you."

Sister Jessie examined Emma and shook her head. "This ain't going to be easy. The baby's turned. She's coming out shoulder first, and she ain't ready yet."

Emma panted, "No, no," and threw her arms around Sister Jessie. "Don't leave me, don't leave me."

Mr. Walter knocked gently. "The ambulance is here."

Emma clung to Sister Jessie. "Come with me, please come with me. I won't go without you."

Miss Sally pleaded, "Go with her, Jessie. Roy Bird's driving the ambulance. He'll bring you back and drop you off at home."

Sister Jessie fetched her bag, took out a small glass bottle, and put it under Emma's nose "Sniff this, honey, take it in deep. I ain't leaving you."

————

When the ambulance arrived in Louisville, white-coated nurses and doctors rushed Emma into the operating room, leaving behind Sister Jessie, shaking her head, screwing the tops back on her empty bottles.

The baby turned, twisted, tried to swim back up the canal, and was finally pulled out with high forceps. A few days later, Emma was still suffering.

When the news reached Lorene, she shook her head. "When the time was right, Sister Jessie would have reached in with her magic fingers, turned that little thing around, and slipped her out."

They put the baby into Emma's arms. Jane lay with her open, red howling mouth, wanting something Emma did not want to deliver. Her breasts, full of milk, were pumped, while the nurses gave the baby bottles.

The second day, while they were visiting Emma in the hospital, before they drove home, Sally Jackson worried about the way her daughter felt about motherhood. "We got to find someone to really help us to look after this baby. It's got to be someone who can take over. We've got plenty of extra help. We need more than that."

Emma, sitting at the edge of her hospital bed, lit a cigarette, not paying attention to Walter's frown. "Send Paul with Leroy to pick us up. I'll be here for a little while."

A week later, Leroy and Paul climbed into Walter's new Buick sedan and set out early in the morning for the Norton Memorial Infirmary.

————

Leroy's father, Uncle Edgar, drank a lot and worked every now and then. His only son was tall and stocky, could look at a piece of machinery and fix it, and was the first person who could drive Mr. Walter without making him jumpy.

Leroy asked, "How you like working for Miss Sally?" He kept his eyes on the road, waiting for Paul's answer.

"If you have to know, I get on with her."

It began to rain, Leroy turned on the wipers. "Well, I don't like her. She's a bossy old thing."

"That's what she's there for, Leroy, to be the boss."

They stopped at a roadside café and Leroy asked for deep-fried catfish with French fries, followed by deep-fried pie for dessert.

Paul watched him eat like a farmhand, talking between bites with his mouth full. Paul, on the other hand, unwrapped two chicken salad sandwiches on thinly sliced bread, cut evenly into eight equal small triangles. He picked up one of the pieces, nibbled the corner, making sure to chew with his mouth closed. He remembered Henry's beautiful manners as he looked over at Leroy. All the way to the hospital, he watched his cousin's jaw move up and down, chewing gum. Paul reminded himself that Leroy had a kind heart and not everybody ate delicately.

They arrived, found Emma sitting on her hospital bed smoking a cigarette, dressed up in a chrysanthemum-gold wool dress and a fern-green cloche hat pulled down over her short blonde hair. Her suitcase was already packed and waiting. Baby Jane lay on the bed next to her, wrapped tightly in a blanket, with her eyes closed, mouth open, breathing in Emma's clouds of cigarette smoke.

Paul carried the baby, Leroy took the bags, and they settled mother and daughter in the back seat of the car. Ten minutes outside Louisville city limits, Jane tuned up and started to holler. Paul had helped with his little brothers and sisters, but he'd never heard anything like that.

They pulled into a roadside restaurant, and when Paul turned, Emma had pushed the baby onto the far end of the back seat while she sat at the other, red-faced, looking at it in horror. "Paul, this baby's having a tantrum. I don't know what to do. I'm whipped. Here, you take her." With that, Emma handed him the tightly wrapped bundle as if it were a ham.

When he pulled down the top cover, he saw a tiny pink tongue sliding in and out of pursed wet lips, eyes shut tight as the baby screamed, fists opening, closing, and legs trying to kick away the swaddle. Paul held her in his arms while Emma went inside the restaurant.

"Now you quit that, Baby," he whispered. "Stop your crying, little girl. Paul's here." He softly rubbed her forehead and her cheeks.

Leroy looked down. "Got us a miracle."

With a little snuffle, she'd stopped crying. Out she went; gone to Heaven, sound asleep. By the time Emma got back into the car, her daughter was a newborn little angel.

They'd passed the Horse Cave city limits when, from the back-seat, Paul heard his fate sealed.

"Now, Paul, when we get home, I'm going to give you extra money to sterilize these bottles, mix the formula, and give her the bottle. Mama's too stiff to help and Lorene told me you looked after all your baby brothers and sisters for Lily when they were born. We'll move you upstairs to the guest room above the dining room. There's a big bathroom. You'll have everything you need. I'll be so grateful. We'll hire someone extra to do the dirty work."

Emma hadn't asked him. It was more of a command than a question. He was shaking, his anger rising. What did he have to do with this little White baby girl? He had his own routine. He wanted to throw the baby back into Emma's arms. How was he any different from his great-grandmother Abilene, and her mother, Odella, both up and spent their lives raising a pack of White folks' children? He also wondered what "everything you need" meant.

After Leroy edged the car into the drive, they climbed the steps of the front porch where the old folks were waiting for Baby Jane. As she lay in Paul's arms, they pulled her blanket down to see their new "darling little granddaughter." Emma might as well have been invisible.

To make matters worse, Miss Sally went on to rile her daughter by saying, "Land's sake, Emma. Why aren't you nursing your own baby? That's a natural thing to do."

Later, with the baby asleep in her cot in the middle of the kitchen table, Lorene snapped a towel at Paul's head. "I got everything ready for you upstairs. Emma gave me strict orders. I'm to bring in Lizzie Campbell, she used to do for Mrs. Pettigrew across the street before she died. She'll be washing all those diapers, sterilizing the bottles. You'll be getting royal treatment; great big four-poster bed, anything your li'l' ol' heart desires. Mammy nurse, that's you, boy. Emma's never giving that little thing a bottle with you around. Watch it!"

Paul carried Jane, sound asleep in her basket, upstairs to their new apartment and looked around: two bedrooms, connected by a large bathroom, two giant cherrywood four-poster beds, both with heavy curtains of different tartan taffetas. It was private and comfortable. Every four hours he took a bottle from the warmer, shook a little sweet milk onto his wrist, then put the nipple into the waiting pink mouth.

Through the open window an owl hooted. The baby's eyes opened; her fingers held the bottle over his own. She looked up, kept him there with her unblinking blue eyes, like a fine silk thread was holding them, until the bottle was empty. He picked her up, rubbed his cheek on the top of her soft head as he gently laid her over his shoulder, tapped her back, and waited for the burp.

Mammy nurse, wasn't that what Lorene had called him? "Well, Babe," he whispered, "this is Paul Carew. I didn't ask for you, but from now on, I guess we'll both be feeling the mama in me."

22

Dozens of baby bottles with dark-brown rubber nipples were lined up on the kitchen counter, waiting for Lizzie. She'd had polio, limped, but she was strong.

Lorene had plenty to say on the subject of bottles. "Why can't the woman pull out her tits, feed the baby? Cow's milk formula ain't for humans. Makes their shit stink."

No one except Lorene had thoughts about why Jane stopped crying the minute she got into Paul's arms. The smell of his skin? The look of his face, sound of his voice?

"I reckon, Paul, that baby decided you're her mama. She won't go to Emma, and worse, Emma don't care. What'll happen to the poor little thing when they go back to England?"

Before it was Paul, now it was Paul and Jane. The baby was pasted and glued to him. The only time he got away from her was when her lids dropped. He'd give her a bottle, she'd reach out, hold on for dear life. Bone-tired, he'd get up every four hours—not her fault. Babies cry. Sometimes, her grandmother picked her up, took her for a rock on the front porch. When he tried to give her to Emma, all hell broke loose. Jane's little mouth opened; her tonsils vibrated with howls of fury. Her own mama handed her back to Paul. All it took was a few seconds, a sniff, hiccups—she recognized him, quieted down.

One good thing, having to settle Babe started him singing to her. He surprised himself. His velvet voice was as good as anything on the radio and Babe loved it. He crooned the latest songs and she'd turn relaxed and floppy in his arms.

————

One morning, Paul put Jane down in her crib, went into the kitchen, and found Emma twisting a Philip Morris into its black holder.

"Come sit with me a minute on the back porch, Paul." She patted the chair beside her. "I've been looking at all the new flowers you and Mama have planted. The way you've arranged the vases... I see you put a new one every day in my room."

"Yes, ma'am."

She lit her cigarette. "I wonder how you'd feel, Paul, about leaving Mother and Daddy, and joining Henry and me?"

Paul found his voice, with difficulty. "I hadn't thought about it."

Emma flicked ash into Miss Sally's gardenia bush. "You'll be in charge of Jane. We hope you find time to do a little cooking. Of course, there will be extra help, for cleaning and laundry. I may have to leave you here while I join the Flight Lieutenant and make arrangements there for you and Jane."

He tried to keep his voice calm and measured, "You'd leave me with the baby?"

"Of course," Emma said, lightly. "Just for a few weeks. When I return, she'll be ready to travel with us to England." She saw his expression. "Oh, I forgot to mention—I'll be paying you much more than you're getting now. Looking after a baby is a great responsibility."

The back door was open. He could walk out, go back to his family in the Kingdom. He wasn't a slave—he wasn't Odella. He thought of the crowded shack, without his own bedroom, and Elijah coming home every evening. "I'd like to think about it, ma'am."

Emma frowned. She'd been sure he would jump at the opportunity. "Of course, Paul, think about it. But not for too long."

Paul heard Jane's cry and hurried to change her. He fastened the safety pins of her diaper, laid her in her cot on the kitchen table. She giggled, reached up, put her hands on his face. A few minutes ago, he wanted to run away. Now he was thinking about New York, England, places he'd heard of in his movie magazines. It was easier to think of those places in his dreams or when they were safely tucked in magazines, he realized. Through the open kitchen door, he caught a warm familiar scent of honeysuckle.

Now, he saw himself reaching up beyond who he'd thought he was. Glimpses of Henry slotted into the puzzle. He could hear the whistle of the L&N train, carrying his dreams down the tracks. This time, he'd go with them. What else was on his horizon?

Early next morning, Emma found him alone in the kitchen. "Well, Paul, have you made up your mind?"

He cleared his throat. "Well, ma'am, I spent a while thinking about it. I'll be happy to look after Jane while you visit the Flight Lieutenant, though, I'm a little nervous about being in charge of a tiny baby. I'm also wondering how Miss Sally will feel about me leaving. Same time, I always wanted a job that takes me out into this here world. So, my answer is, yes."

Emma stuffed her package of cigarettes and lighter into her pocket. "Don't worry, my mother wants the best for us." She rubbed her hands together. "What a relief. That's settled."

A while later, he went in to check on Jane like he always did, to tell her the news. During the day they kept the baby in the kitchen or in the front guest bedroom when she was sleeping. He came out with Babe in his arms, stopped to listen at the doorway of the porch.

Sally Jackson set her chair to rocking while she spoke to her daughter. "I hear you offered Paul a job and Walter tells me he wants to go with you."

Emma exhaled a long line of smoke. "Well, Mama," she said, "Paul told me he didn't even need to think about coming to work for us. He's dying to get away. Imagine how he'd end up if he stayed here?"

Paul, standing in the hall, listening, shook his head. He'd never said any such things.

Miss Sally picked up her church fan and swatted away the cigarette smoke as she held Emma's eyes with hers in silent fury. "I guess you never thought about my feelings."

Outside, the tires of Walter's Buick slid easily over the drive. A door slammed.

Emma leaned towards her mother, spoke to her with a steely voice. "Just think for a minute about what you would have done without Aunt Hattie, Mama. You would've been lost. I was her shadow, you always said—but you know what? She was mean as stink to me. To keep me quiet, she put a hand over my mouth, told me she was stopping black spiders from coming out, said they'd eat me alive if I ever told you. She switched me hard and then took me in the kitchen and stuffed my face with jam cake. Paul would never be like that."

Emma ground her cigarette into the saucer while Sally turned her head towards the hum of sprinklers, showers of water catching the sun before falling onto the thick carpet of green grass.

Walter Jackson took off his Panama as he came up onto the porch, rolled the edges around in his fingers before putting it down on the table. He saw both his women looking at each other with red angry faces. To cool things down, he said, "Bound to be a while before Paul can leave with the baby. Hope so anyway."

Miss Sally, dabbing her tears with the thin light-blue chiffon handkerchief, said, "Neither one of you understands a thing. I've been teaching the boy all I know about the garden. Nothing coming out of the kitchen will ever taste the same without Paul there." Her mother looked at Emma with hatred in her eyes.

Paul tiptoed back to the kitchen, found Lorene beating cake batter. He spoke softly, "Those two women's at each other's throats."

Lorene handed him the bowl of chocolate batter. "That's nothing new. Fold that chocolate mix into my marble cake."

Paul tipped the bowl, and with a spatula, carefully turned dark chocolate ribbons through the white. "What will happen to that little thing?"

"You forgot what Sister Jessie Porter told you? She'll be sitting on your lap forever."

23

Emma's cases were in the car. Paul stood on the steps, holding Babe.

"Blow Mummy a kiss. I want you to wave goodbye to Mummy," he coaxed. Jane put her arms up, hid her face under Paul's chin.

Miss Sally said, "Look at that, Emma. There's a happy baby. You can leave feeling like a good mother, with a light heart. You're not taking her to foreign germs."

Miss Sally stood on the drive with Walter and waved to her daughter with one of Lily's hand-stitched, pink-chiffon handkerchiefs as if shooing off a bumblebee.

It didn't mean the two women never had a tender moment between them. Paul had seen Emma looking at her mother's swollen knees, her gnarled hands, and when Miss Sally winced with pain, he saw Emma put her arms around her mother, and for a few minutes, allowed love to overcome her memories of that vicious beating.

But after Emma left, Miss Sally's spirits lifted. She stood up straighter, flicked her flyswatter with authority, and directed everyone in the house to get back into their routines.

One day she came into the kitchen, as usual, to visit her granddaughter. "I ordered a new radio. Now I reckon we have one to spare. You could use it, couldn't you, Paul? I'll ask Leroy to take it upstairs and plug it in." She understood, from his shining eyes, she'd given him something he really wanted.

Paul wanted to reach out and hug her.

From that day on, he played the radio every evening, in the middle of the night, and in the early morning. He tuned into WHAS in Louisville.

Babe's musical education began with Duke Ellington. *"It don't mean a thing, if it ain't got that swing, doo-ah, doo-ah, doo-ah, doo-ah, doo-ah, doo-ah, doo-ah, doo-ah."*

The minute Paul sang "doo-ah," Babe got it, gave it right back to him. He danced, stepping up to the beat, swinging out into Babe's room. She'd stand, holding the bars of the crib, jumping up and down. Or she'd lie, listening to him croon "Stormy Weather," her eyes open, dreamily taking him all in. After the old folks had gone to bed, sometimes he'd put on a little pink lipstick, pencil in his eyebrows, spit into his Maybelline mascara box and brush up his eyelashes. Whichever way he came, Babe adored him.

Lizzie Campbell arrived every afternoon, went down into the basement to wash the diapers. There was plenty of work for two extra people. Miss Sally hired Petal Farlow, who came up every morning and minded whatever Paul and Lorene asked her to do. Petal's face was full, her breasts were round, her bottom wobbled, and, with her know-how, she made bringing up Babe a lot easier for Paul and Lorene. Petal cleaned the house, sat beside the crib and minded Babe when she was asleep.

The extra help left Paul time to train Leroy, showing him how to mulch, prune, and get ready for winter. When Leroy wasn't driving Mr. Walter, he was busy in the garden, where Miss Sally kept a sharp eye out, always ready to jump on him.

"Leroy, you haven't dug a hole deep enough. Ask Paul how to put in a new plant. Loosen up that dirt. You're choking it. Dig in compost. Plants scream at you and die. I don't want you killing my flowers."

Paul found Leroy in the kitchen, tattling to Lorene. "She says I'm killing her plants."

"Don't let it bother you."

Paul also tried to smooth Leroy's feelings. "Miss Sally's prickly. Old people don't like change."

Leroy looked down at his cold cup of coffee. "Hope she won't be this bad-tempered after you leave."

Paul couldn't answer that.

That afternoon, Paul and Miss Sally pruned the rose bushes. When they finished, she took off her gardening gloves, rubbed her hands, and held them up. "We can put this garden to sleep for winter, but I know when spring comes, you and the baby will be gone. I'm fifty-three years old. I had Emma when I was twenty-five. That nearly killed me. I could live to be ninety, but I can't count on it and with this arthritis, I wouldn't want to live that long. I don't suffer fools 'cause I'm suffering myself and ain't got time for them."

Paul understood and knew she didn't add what was really bothering her.

Leroy's irritating me and Emma never thought of how I'd manage without you.

Emma and Henry called from England every week and Paul told them what was happening. "Jane's beginning to play peekaboo and patty-cake. She saw herself in the mirror, can't seem to get enough of it. She's starting to crawl all over the place. She won't let me out of sight without screaming her head off. She's standing up, holding on to the bars of her crib. Me and Lorene smashing up vegetables, feeding her with a spoon. Her hair's growing in blonde. She's sleeping all night long."

Each time, Emma said the same thing, "I will come get you as soon as we know what's happening to us. In case you haven't heard, Hitler's building up his army in Germany. Henry is sure we will have another war."

If Miss Sally reached the telephone before Paul, she said the same thing every time, "Don't you dream of feeling worried about not coming home. Why, taking that baby to a foreign country where it rains every day would be crazy. She might get a foreign germ and die."

Miss Sally smoothed a torrent of words over any guilty feelings and prayed the same prayer every night: "Please Lord, don't let them come home too soon."

For the next fifteen months, the Good Lord must have been listening to her, and Paul saw Babe changing every day. She was crawling faster than an alligator and hiding all over the house, under beds, behind doors, anywhere she thought he might try to look for her, including the top of the basement stairs.

"You'll give me a heart attack!" He'd put her safely where he could see her.

One day in the kitchen, he took his time, waiting for Lorene's fresh-churned strawberry ice cream to soften. Babe was in her playpen. She'd learned to holler, "Paw-Paw."

Lorene, Petal, Lizzie, and Paul talked to her all day long. She handed them her favorite toys and screamed when they put them behind their backs to tease her. If they took her out of the playpen, she crawled all over the kitchen, laughing and babbling. She was getting to be too much for the old folks. They enjoyed watching her most while she slept.

Paul and Lorene were showing Babe how to eat properly, how not to shove fistfuls of mashed potato into her mouth. She'd been coughing for a few days, but they'd decided it was nothing to worry about. After all, they reckoned, she was singing at the top of her voice and playing peekaboo with Mr. Walter.

Petal lifted Babe into her highchair and put on her bib.

Lorene said, "Time for lunch, honey. You my good little girl?

What you doing? Tell Lorene, who's that?" She pointed at Paul, cutting up a piece of fried chicken.

"Paw, Paw, Paw," Babe shrieked.

Petal scooped a teaspoon of Lorene's ice cream from a bowl she'd prepared for the old folks' lunch and put a little in Jane's drooling mouth.

Paul grabbed the spoon. "What are you doing? Ice cream when it's cold outside? You'll give her pneumonia."

Petal huffed. "Babies love ice cream. You're too fussy."

In the early morning, Paul heard coughing and crying. He jumped out of bed, hurried into Babe's room, and picked her up. She felt like a hot-water bottle. Her face was scarlet, her eyes shining with fever. He put her gently back into her cot, covered her up, dressed quickly, and went downstairs to knock on the Jacksons' bedroom door.

"Jane's got a high fever, better call Dr. Jimmy."

Walter swung his legs out of bed and picked up the telephone.

Paul rushed back to Babe, his heart drumming, took her in his arms and whispered, "Don't get sick." She didn't answer, while he thought, if only he'd paid more attention to her cough. He wrapped her in a woolly blanket, sat down, held her close, and stroked her forehead.

Twenty minutes later, Dr. Jimmy was downstairs with a stethoscope around his neck. He took Babe's temperature and shook his head. "Hundred and four. Her lungs are congested. We'll have to wait and see. Looks like pneumonia to me."

Miss Sally groaned, Walter was grim-faced, and Paul tried to keep down panic.

Dr. Jimmy folded his stethoscope and, without a smile, clamped shut his black leather bag. "That's all we can do right now. Keep her warm, plenty of liquids, put on the kettle, get some steam. Watch that her breathing doesn't change. I'll be back in a few hours."

———

It was four-thirty in the morning. Miss Sally and Mr. Walter got dressed. Paul wrapped Jane in a warm blanket, laid her on a cot in the middle of the kitchen table while he made the coffee.

Mr. Walter, holding his car keys, rushed into the kitchen. "We're driving to fetch Sister Jessie. Miss Sally says she'll know what to do."

At five-thirty sharp, Lorene arrived, took one look at Babe's red face, heard her coughing and fussing, saw her waving clenched fists. Without pausing to take off her coat, she took an ice tray out of the freezer, placed the cubes inside a piece of flannel, and put it gently onto the baby's forehead. That only seemed to make her cry harder and cough more.

"We need Jessie Porter now."

No sooner had Lorene spoken, then they heard the bang of the front door, and there was Sister Jessie, hair wild, down around her shoulders, carrying a burlap bag stuffed with herbs and twigs. Without wasting any time, she took Babe in her arms, laid her down over a soft, thick blanket on top of the kitchen table, put one ear onto her chest, and placed a hand on her forehead.

She looked up. "Get two pots going. Boil up white willow bark to bring down the fever, another for the rest of my herbs." When she'd cooled down the bitter willow-bark tea, Sister Jesse added raw honey and dropped teaspoons of it into the little mouth Paul had coaxed open.

As Lorene would tell it in years to come: "Sister rubbed her hands together hard enough to set them on fire, puts them down on Babe's head. Child's coughing, but she ain't crying. Miss Sally and Mr. Walter stands there quiet, not sure what's going on, when all a sudden, Jessie says, 'Time's not right for what I needs to do. I'll be back. Meantime, wrap her up and give her my medicines.'"

When Petal and Leroy arrived, Petal began wringing her hands, Leroy was shaking his head, and Lorene let them have it, "Out of my kitchen. Petal, go to the laundry room and wash out these diapers. Leroy, get busy cleaning the yard. Don't you come back in here with those bare faces hanging out, looking like something serious wrong with our baby."

Paul had never been so worried. After three hours, Babe's fever was down, but her cough was deeper. Before anyone had a chance to send for her, Jessie slipped in by the back door.

"Time's right. Take her out of that cot, lay her on the table. Lorene, boil up more of them roots. Fold up towels, find me pillows."

She leaned over the baby and laid smooth, long, deep strokes from the baby's tummy, all the way up to her throat and back again, turned her over and did the same thing to her back, humming until Babe lay hypnotized. She turned the child over again onto her back and Jessie began deep breathing, finding her own energy. She placed the flat of her hand firmly across Jane's chest, arms stiffening as she began quick shaking movements that lasted a few long minutes.

After Babe had a violent spasm of coughing, Jessie stopped and listened to her chest. She turned her on her back again and cupped her hand to make a hollow tube as she lightly tapped against the baby's ribs. She kept on going, each time tapping a little harder. Fifteen minutes in each position. There was quiet, except for the sound of tapping.

Half an hour later, she sat the baby up, put a pillow on her tummy and stretched her over it. Jessie's patting took on a new rhythm, a drumbeat that led to the spasm of coughs she was looking for. She turned Babe back quickly onto her tummy, lifted her in the air while she was coughing hard. Suddenly, with a choking sound, a large yellow and green ball of phlegm shot out of the baby's mouth. Jesse put her ear to Jane's chest, listening carefully, and then examined the ball of phlegm. Satisfied, she smiled, picked Jane up, stroked her head, and handed her to Paul.

"It's over. She's fine."

And she looked fine, smiling, turning her head and gurgling. No more coughing.

With tears in her eyes, Miss Sally put her arms around Sister Jessie. "You saved her life."

Walter wasn't sure he'd seen what he had seen. "And to think I almost stopped the treatment. Looks like a miracle to me."

"No." Sister Jessie smiled. "It ain't no miracle. I learned all this from my mama. She learned it from her mama, all the way back to my great-grandmother, Jessie Lavender, a slave on the McQueen Plantation in Louisiana."

Walter jangled the car keys in his pants pocket. "Beats me why you can't teach Dr. Jimmy."

"'Cause he ain't asked me."

After lunch, Dr. Jimmy's car pulled up in the driveway. "How is she? Let's have a look."

Paul was holding a wiggling, giggling baby playing peekaboo with her grandfather.

Dr. Jimmy looked carefully but didn't dare take her out of Paul's arms. "Not sure how we explain this."

With a grin on his face, Walter took out his wallet. "Maybe you want to knock on Sister Jessie Porter's door."

"Don't tell me, Walter Jackson, you believe in that mumbo-jumbo?"

Walter smiled and said with the kind of authority no one in Horse Cave would ever dare to mess with, "I didn't before, but I sure do now."

The next day, alarmed by the dark circles under Paul's eyes, Miss Sally urged him to take a few hours for himself and Lorene refused to let him help with the dishes.

"You're a tired-out mama. You've had a shock, take time for yourself. She can stay with me in the kitchen. I'll pick her up if she fusses. We get on just fine."

Paul untied his apron, and with a sigh of relief, went out the back door to his own neglected house. It smelled musty, and when he pulled the curtains, the windows were dirty. He lay down on top of his bed and wished he could stay there forever.

After what Miss Sally now called "the moment we near lost our little grandbaby," she set sail on a new adventure, one that became her weakness and Paul's delight. Every month, before dawn, Leroy drove the Jacksons to Louisville. Miss Sally shopped for baby clothes while Walter sat in the front seat talking to Leroy and dreaming of lunch at the Brown Hotel. They ordered the same thing every month, a Hot Brown sandwich, which was lightly toasted bread covered with rare roast beef and topped with gravy and Parmesan cheese.

Miss Sally shopped at Byck's department store where she bought as many baby dresses, coats, shoes, socks, and hats as she could find.

When it came to Jane, Walter had no limit. "Charge as many things as you need."

After lunch in the Grill Room, and a brief stop at the Mysterious Rack Hat Shop—Walter tried on Panama and Stetson hats, ending up with one more of each to add to his collection before they headed back to Horse Cave.

A little later, Paul lifted the lids of box after box, and pulled out dress after dress: red velvet with white lace, yellow organdy with puff sleeves, a fluffy full-skirted pink taffeta, a dark blue coat with a velvet collar, and after that, he went on to the shoeboxes full of matching pairs of baby shoes.

Paul dressed his Babe up in front of a long mirror.

She never fussed, seeing how much fun he was having.

"If I can't dress up, least I can turn you into my own pretty little baby."

Jane looked at herself in the mirror, up at him, clapped her hands and giggled.

————

Two weeks before Jane's second birthday, Betsy Lou Bybee at the Horse Cave switchboard, connected Paul to Emma Gordon, outside Portsmouth, England.

"Paul, I'll be home at the end of next week, pick you all up just as I promised, and we'll join the Flight Lieutenant in England. After that, it's on to Ireland for us. I'll explain when I see you."

He could hardly hear himself speak, much less Emma.

Jane was singing at the top of her voice and banging pot lids together. Since early morning, he'd been shutting himself in closets, crawling under beds, playing hide-and-seek while she scooted around on her new riding toy like a demon, looking for him.

"I can hardly hear you, ma'am."

Emma shouted into the phone, "Please, Paul, start getting ready. I'll only be there for a week."

Getting ready sounded overwhelming.

Emma must have sensed this. "Don't worry about playpens and strollers. We can buy all of that over here."

He took a deep breath before he answered, "I'll do my best."

"That's all I ask."

As he hung up the phone, he muttered, "On top of everything else."

24

Emma got out of the car in her tailored yellow-and-gray-tweed suit, hair combed back into a chignon. Right away, Paul saw she looked more like England than Kentucky. He stood holding Babe's hand as her mother came up the stairs of the front porch.

"Look at your beautiful red velvet dress, Jane. What a pretty girl you are. Tell Mummy where you got that."

Babe pointed to Miss Sally.

Emma knelt and tried to take her daughter in her arms.

Paul whispered in Jane's ear, "What do we say to Mummy? Give her a kiss."

A shy, "Hello," escaped Babe's lips. She then stuck her neck forward and planted a smacking kiss on her mother's cheek, then turned around, holding on to Paul's leg, hiding her face.

Miss Sally looked on as Emma rushed to put her arms around her father. Their daughter had arrived already in a hurry to leave. Henry had been posted on a special mission to Ireland. They'd found a house near the base, with plenty of room for Paul and Jane.

"Paul," Emma told him later in the kitchen, "there will be lots to do there. I've bought the basic furniture but it all needs fixing up. We'll have fun doing that together. You'll be brilliant at decorating, I know."

Paul wondered. He'd never done any decorating before.

————

After a few days at home, Emma decided to take Miss Sally and Mr. Walter out for a night at the Brown Hotel. She and Miss Sally had a shopping spree in mind. With Emma driving, they all left after breakfast.

"While we're away, take all the time you need, Paul, to say goodbye to Lily and the rest of the family," Mr. Walter told him.

Paul waited until after lunch, telling Jane a butterfly story, and sang her to sleep with Lead Belly's "Good Night, Irene."

On his way out, the back screen door slammed behind him. He was halfway down the drive and whistling when her screams brought him running back to the kitchen.

"Paw-Paw! Paw-Paw!" Babe was sitting on Lorene's lap, yelling. The sight of him brought her back to sniffles and smiles.

"I fixed this visit up a week ago. The family will all be waiting for me," he told his cousin.

"You ain't going anyplace where this little thing can't see you."

Leroy heard the commotion and came in from the garden. "Only one thing to do with a car sitting in the drive. I'll run you both over to Lily's. Nobody's going to find out."

Tabby and Tallulah had been waiting since after breakfast, all dressed up in their yellow ruffled cotton skirts, while Ernest and James had covered their new shorts and shirts with dirt, digging for worms in the backyard.

When the shiny Buick slipped in front of their house, Tallulah shouted, "He's here, he's here," and ran to open the door of the car. As usual, Tabby held back, waited for her sister to test the water.

Lily came out onto the porch, wiping her hands on a tea towel.

She took a deep breath when she saw Paul lift Babe out of her seat. "What in the world have we got here?"

"Take care of her for a minute." Paul leaned down and hugged his brothers and sisters. "Come on, give Babe a hug, too."

Tallulah lifted her up, smacked a few kisses all over her face, followed by Tabby.

The boys hung back, wondering what she was doing there.

Without waiting for Paul, Tallulah told them, "She's Paul's little girl. We got to be nice to her."

Inside their shack, dishes were still in the sink, and Paul noticed Lily's sewing strewn around her machine in untidy piles. He was reminded how he'd once put away the dishes, organized his mother's sewing, and tidied the house. Now he was used to being in the Jacksons' kitchen, the size of this entire place.

Babe didn't notice the difference, too excited to meet Tabby and Tallulah.

A few minutes later, Coralee came over from next door—thin, silent, and haggard—to visit with Paul and have a piece of coconut cake. They all had to plead with Leroy to leave the car and join the party.

The table was laid, and Lily stood at one end behind her chair. "You all come and sit down—Jane next to me and Paul on the other side. We've got fresh lemonade, chocolate chip cookies, and coconut cake."

"We made it—we made it," shrieked Paul's brothers and sisters. The twins poured the lemonade, Lily cut the cake, and the questions began.

"How far away is Ireland?"

"Why are you going?"

"How you going to get there?"

"When'll you be back?"

"Are you sure you're coming back?"

Coralee stared absentmindedly at Jane as she ate her cake. Jane stared back at Coralee who suddenly smiled for the first time since Moses's death.

"Li'l ol' thing, fits right in. Wish Moses was here to see her."

After a while, the boys were fidgety, so it was Tallulah's idea to play hide-and-seek.

"Tabby, you and James take her and hide. Me and Ernest will come and find you." Tabby and James took Babe by each hand and led her into Lily and Elijah's room where there was a large hanging closet. Tabby opened the doors and helped a giggling Babe get inside and hide behind all the hanging clothes, warning her to shush while she and James hid under the bed.

"Ready? Coming."

Within a minute, Tallulah and Ernest saw Tabby's shoes sticking out from under the bed.

"Where are you, Jane?" they called.

They heard tapping.

"Here, here."

"Where are you, Jane? We can't find you."

They all began to tease and call out, "We can't find you."

This time her tap was followed by screams. "Paw-Paw! Paw-Paw!"

They opened the cupboard door, lifted her out. Paul was there in a second and spent the next five minutes calming her down.

Tabby smoothed Babe's hair. "We didn't mean to scare you, Baby."

Ten minutes later, Babe wanted to play hide-and-seek again.

Paul told his sisters. "She's overexcited." He turned to Jane. "Enough, Babe, let's stick with peekaboo."

———

It was late afternoon when Blessing called from Coralee's front porch, "Where is everybody?" She was pretty as ever and on her way to getting prettier. Red high heels held up a curvy girl, wearing a tight pink skirt and red elasticated top. Blessing had the true measure of herself and everyone else. No one could fool her.

"Let me look at you, you sweet little thing." She headed straight for Jane and gave her a hug. "Sister Jessie told me all about you."

Blessing kept a dazzled Babe on her lap at the kitchen table while she cut up small forkfuls of cake. "One for me... One for you... Another one for you."

Paul fretted, "She's already eaten two pieces."

"Ain't going to hurt her none."

Paul looked out the window. The sun was halfway down behind the trees in the backyard.

"Time to go."

"No, no, no!" Babe screamed.

Blessing put her down.

Tabby coaxed Babe, taking one hand, Tallulah the other, and they led Babe to the car with promises of, "We'll come up to your house and play with you."

On the front porch, Blessing caught up with Paul. "It ain't right, Elijah getting up in the pulpit, shaking his fist, preaching over the evils of adultery. Everybody's talking about him carrying on with Sissy Cole and how tired and sad your mama looks."

"What can I do about it?"

"Nothing. Lily's trapped like all women, bringing up the children."

Paul had tears in his eyes as he hugged Coralee and Lily goodbye. He felt he was running away, abandoning his family.

Leroy drove slowly on the road out of the Kingdom. On Paul's lap, Babe dropped into a deep sleep. They passed Elijah on his wagon coming back from the fields. A furious Paul watched his father turn his head and look back at their car.

What could Paul do to fix things for his mother?

Lorene was waiting for them. "I reckon she'll have to miss her boiled eggs and toast. She looks all tuckered out." She saw Babe lay like a ragdoll in Paul's arms.

"She ain't never played so hard. Had herself a big time. She doesn't need brothers and sisters."

After putting Babe to bed, Paul tucked into Lorene's chicken-fried steak with onions, and told her what Blessing said about Elijah.

Lorene pointed her knife at him. "You ain't got no power to fix that. We'll be keeping our eyes on Lily. Nobody in the Kingdom loves Elijah the way they love your mama."

————

They were leaving. Paul found a new suitcase from Miss Sally inside the door of his little house and another one from Emma. After breakfast, Mr. Walter invited him into his study, opened a drawer, handed him an envelope, and said, "Paul, you're in charge of my grand-daughter and her mother. You're taking part of us with you." He added, clearing his throat, "We'll miss you."

Back in the kitchen, Paul peeped into the envelope, counted four ten-dollar bills. Some extra on top of his regular pay. But no matter how many crisp bills Walter Jackson put into his hands, Paul would never forget what happened the morning he got up the nerve and crossed the line, looking into Walter Jackson's stern face, asking him to save Moses. He would take that lesson with him. A Colored boy like him could be kicked out of a White man's world whenever he put a foot wrong. They tell you their secrets, talk to you about their problems, but don't get any ideas of doing the same thing back.

Lorene counted cases in the front hall. There was Emma's large dark blue steamer trunk with narrow layered bands of wood and round brass locks, along with her four other suitcases. Petal and Lorene folded and packed all the baby's new clothes. Paul's cases sat underneath the others, all waiting to be taken down to the train depot.

"Looks like the Queen of England taking her leave," Sally Jackson's voice was sharp.

Walter stood quietly, taking cloudy glasses on and off, wiping the lenses with his large white handkerchief.

Miss Sally rushed around, hoping her hustle and bustle would hide her sadness at losing Paul *and* the baby. "I see you're all packed and ready, Paul."

Lorene handed him a large brown paper bag of chicken and egg-salad sandwiches. "Better take these with you. Ain't no dining car on the train for the likes of us."

He'd miss that voice of hers, the sharp cut of her sarcastic advice.

"What you doing halfway out of the door forgetting all about me?"

He'd been sure she was coming to the train station. She'd promised she would never miss waving him goodbye. His feelings for her rose behind a rising lump in his throat. "I can't say goodbye to you, Lorene." His voice broke, "I just can't do it."

"Just like I can't go down to the train station, saying goodbye to you."

Awkwardly, she put her arms around him, and through his tears, he saw hers. He took Jane by the hand; he'd dressed her up in a dark-blue wool coat with a velvet collar over a light-red wool dress, with white tights and black patent leather shoes.

She put her arms around Lorene, "Bye-bye, La La."

"You better miss me, child, else I'm coming to get you."

Waiting in the front hall, Emma shook her head as Paul hooked a small leather purse over Babe's arm. "Lord, Mama, never seen so many outfits. She's better dressed than I am."

Emma smoked furiously as Leroy took all of their cases and put them into a truck from the tobacco plant.

Down at the train station a great black engine stood steaming in front of smooth silver Pullman cars with redcaps on the platform, waiting to help passengers climb on board.

Everyone in the Kingdom had turned out to say goodbye to Paul —everyone except Elijah. There was Lily, holding her head high, so as not to tip into tears, his brothers and sisters, first cousins, second cousins, and even Miss Bessie who took off her glasses after she'd hugged him tight.

"Remember, Paul, keep your butterflies flying."

Paul caught sight of Coralee next to Blessing's bright red skirt, saw them waving and pushing through the crowds.

"Hurry up, Paul," he heard Emma calling. "We'll miss the train."

He took the extra time to put his arms around Coralee and Blessing.

"Don't you forget Moses," Coralee whispered. "Don't you ever forget what happened to Moses. Carry him with you."

Paul took her hands. "My brother, how could I forget him?"

On the train, he pulled down the window in one of the Pullman drawing rooms Emma had reserved for her party and waved from it as the cries of "All aboard" threaded through the pounding chug of the great black engine. The last views he had were of Lily running down the platform, holding onto the last sight of him, and Sally Jackson sadly waving her pink chiffon handkerchief. He would never be sure, but as the train gathered steam, rolled over the crossing where he and Moses had laid Clarence on the tracks, he thought he saw Elijah, sitting in his wagon, waving his old straw hat.

"The porter will take your order while I go to the dining room," Emma told Paul. "Order anything you want from the menu—just ring for service. There are two beds, next to each other. You all have plenty of room. I'll be in the next compartment."

She closed the door, leaving Babe and him as they had always been—together.

Paul had never put a foot outside Horse Cave, except for the one time he'd been to Louisville. Now here he was on a train to New York City, closed into a first-class drawing room, Babe beside him, with porters knocking on his door, asking him what he needed.

Paul snapped his fingers, she kicked her heels on the seat, and they began their duet. *"You are my lucky star,"* he crooned.

She shot her finger up to the sky, the way he'd taught her. *"I'm lucky where you are."*

They pointed to each other.

She knew the tune, sang along, patted her chest and put her arms out, the way he'd shown her. "That's it, Babe. Give the world a great big hug."

When it came time to open his package from Lorene, at the bottom were enough sandwiches with razor-thin cuts of country ham wrapped tightly in wax paper to last for two or three days. Lying on top were egg-mayonnaise and chicken salad sandwiches. She'd sliced the bread thin, used Paul's recipe, and put in lots of chives and chopped celery. He handed Babe a small triangle, and they sat together, quietly munching. He'd taught her pretty fine manners, showed her how to nibble. He pulled her onto his lap so they could both look out of the window.

"Wave bye-bye to Kentucky, Babe." They sped past fields, watching Colored workers taking their hats off to salute the train, maybe wishing they could be sitting right where Paul was. He felt glamorous in his new blue suit and his first passport. He looked down, *Wait a minute, I have on blue pants...* Nothing to worry about. He was on a train, but it was pulling away from Great-grandma Abilene's world.

25

"Blue pants, eh? You better come with us."

Paul woke up in sweat, lifted his shade, and waited for dawn to ease his terrors. He pressed the call button, relieved to hear the gentle knock on the door.

"Could we order hot oatmeal, milk, orange juice, and coffee? And can you tell me where we are now?"

"We're in New York State, couple of hours away from the city." The porter avoided eye contact.

After a short cab ride from Penn Station, they stepped into the lobby of "the tallest hotel building in the world," the Waldorf Astoria. Babe held on tightly to Paul's hand. He did not notice the doorman's frown; he did not hear Emma explain to the manager that he was the child's nursemaid. He had two American passports, one in his pocket, the other holding his hand.

"Are we dreaming, Babe?" Paul whispered, as she sucked her thumb, wide-eyed. There was marble everywhere and they stood on a floor with gold tiles. Paul felt bewildered by how far he'd come, from shacks and unpaved red dirt roads to here.

"What would your daddy say?" he asked Babe. "'Marvelous, extraordinary, splendid.' That's what he would say."

He tried not to stare at the gorgeous women all around with their low voices, expensive perfume, and high-styled clothes. He wondered how many movie stars and singers were right here. Might even see Fred Astaire; there were lots of men who looked like him, with slicked-back hair and nifty suits. The atmosphere was so rich, he felt dizzy.

"Going up!"

In the elevator, a young Black man wearing white gloves turned a golden wheel to indicate the floor they wanted. He raised his eyebrows, and his smile grew wider when he saw Babe standing next to Paul. He wasn't the only one staring. The other passengers had never seen a Colored man in the front elevator, except for the people who operated it. They couldn't take their eyes off lean, tall, handsome Paul Carew, dressed in his new blue suit.

Emma offered to look after Jane, insisting Paul go out for a walk around Manhattan. He'd dreamed of seeing Radio City Music Hall, only a few blocks away.

After lunch, he sang "Embraceable You" soft enough to put Babe to sleep. She lay arms up, lights out. That was the only way he could sneak out of the bedroom.

Outside, the doorman gave him directions and Paul set off along Park Avenue. He knew where he was going. Rockefeller Plaza—Radio City Music Hall. Under his breath, in his head, he tapped out, "Wake up, Paul Carew, you're in New York City."

All down the Avenue, giant buildings overshadowed a road packed bumper to bumper with automobiles, loudly honking their horns. He saw a dark blue Chrysler, just like Mr. Walter's, pull up at the red light and stop. He could hardly believe it. A Colored man in a pinstripe suit with a wide red-silk tie sat in the driver's seat. Must be the chauffeur. Paul looked again. There was a Colored girl sitting beside the driver, with a red-feather boa slung around her neck, big gold earrings, and a bright red mouth. He stood for a minute after the light turned green, watching the taillights disappear. Those people owned that car. They looked rich. Anything was possible in New York.

While threading his way along the packed sidewalks, he'd noticed a few dark faces. Some of them looked like they were going somewhere important, dressed up and cityfied; and there were plenty of women, carrying paper bags, wearing shabby clothes, on their way to clean.

Suddenly, there it was, all lit up and right in front of him, the sight straight out of one of his magazines. Radio City. A few years before he'd read that Katherine Dunham, with her Colored dancers, had been the star attraction. Now it was Barbara Stanwyck in *Stella Dallas*, and the Rockettes, too. Paul closed his eyes, allowed his mind to wander, playing out his deepest desires. He was alone onstage, dancing and singing "Sweet Georgia Brown." And this time there was no Elijah, no beating, only the sound of people clapping and clapping and clapping.

Paul opened his eyes to honking horns and saw traffic all around him. Better not hope too hard. Time to turn around, he told himself. Babe might be fussing, and he was the only one who knew what to do about that.

He strolled back, found a new doorman on duty: long gray coat, gloves, top hat, whistle in his mouth.

He put himself in front of Paul. "Hold on. Where do you think you're going?"

"I'm staying here with—"

"Wait a minute. Negroes are not allowed in this entrance," the doorman said, putting his arm between Paul and the revolving door. "What makes you think you can walk through the front door?"

"Well, sir, I came in through the front door and went back out this way too."

The assistant manager arrived. Heart pounding, Paul asked him to call Mrs. Gordon's room. The manager picked up the telephone, looking sideways at him.

"Yes, ma'am... Right away, ma'am. We'll send him right up. I'm sorry, but we do have a policy here..."

A few minutes later, a Negro bellhop escorted Paul to a back elevator. "What made you think you were better than Jesse Owens?" he asked Paul, looking at him and grinning.

"I have no idea what you're talking about."

"Believe it or not, I took Jesse Owens up in this same back elevator last week. He was standing where you are now. Even a hero rides back here with me if he happens to be Black. "'Mr. Owens,' I said, 'you ought to be coming through the front door of this hotel, riding in the front elevator.'"

Paul had heard on the radio and read in the papers before he left Horse Cave about the American Negro athlete who had run away with four gold medals at the 1936 Olympic Games in Berlin.

"He showed them what a Colored man can do." The bellboy stopped the elevator and put it on hold while he told Paul, "Jesse talked to me—he took the time to talk to me. He said, 'You know, they got it wrong? The German people cheered me, and Hitler even waved at me.' And that ain't all Jesse Owens said to me. Jesse didn't go up in any back elevators in Germany. He said the biggest insults to our people are delivered right here in this country. He said, 'Even the President of the United States hasn't shaken my hand or sent me a telegram.'"

Paul stepped out of the elevator, already hearing howls from down the hall. He opened the door with his key. Emma stood holding her daughter in front of her, jiggling and shaking her at arm's length. Babe's face was screwed up and her legs kicking furiously at her red-faced mama.

"Take her, Paul," Emma said, tersely.

Safe in his arms again, it took only a second for the child's fury to settle. She was back to being Paul's good, sweet Babe.

———

The next day, on board the *Queen Mary*, Paul and Babe looked out the portholes of their first-class drawing room.

"Babe, there's my schoolteacher, Miss Bessie's, famous Lady Liberty. Look at her, holding up a light meant to welcome people from all over the world to the United States of America.

"Miss Bessie always said she wasn't sure what kind of welcome light's shining for us Colored folks." He remembered the sting of the hotel doorman's words. "Never mind, we're on our way to see the handsomest man in the world, your daddy. Are we excited about that?"

With the gentle rolling of the ship, they had both taken a while to settle. Paul had kept her close to him. He'd got into the habit of telling her his deepest feelings.

"Your mama, Paul, is a rare bird, a lot more mama than papa." Paul looked down, seeing that after all their dancing, she'd fallen asleep on the floor.

"I'm not sure how good a parent I can be to you. Most of all of me loves you, another part wants to be somebody, and the rest of me wants to be with your daddy." He sighed. "We'll have to see which part wins."

After the steward knocked on the door with dinner, Paul sat and carefully spread goose liver pâté on the hot toast before cutting it into tiny pieces.

"One for me, one for you—one for me, one for you."

"More, Paw, more!"

Anything Paul put in his mouth, Babe wanted to put in hers. He lifted the silver dome hiding his Steak Diane, cut off tiny pieces of meat and mixed them with the sauce and mashed up vegetables, to feed to Babe. He reckoned this was the first time in his life he was excited by someone else's cooking, and swore he'd learn to make goose liver pâté and Steak Diane.

After a stormy day at sea, looking through portholes at waves going up and down, he felt sick. He gathered up Babe and went out for fresh air and sat on deck in a chair, Babe on his lap, a steamer rug pulled over their knees. He closed his eyes, sang a line from a new Gershwin tune: *"The way you hold your knife, the way we danced till three, the way you changed my life..."*

Next thing he knew, he heard *"No, no, they can't take that away from me,"* and recognized a silky voice like pouring molasses. He opened his eyes to his echo and there was a woman with curly, silky, short dark hair. And what a figure!

She sat beside Paul, cupping her hands around a mug of bouillon, and asked, "Are you a singer? Or a dancer maybe?"

Prettiest Colored girl Paul had ever seen; she peek-a-booed with Babe and wondered where he came from. The answer, "Horse Cave, Kentucky," made her giggle.

"How in the world did you get from Horse Cave, Kentucky onto the *Queen Mary*?"

Paul pointed to Babe. "Got my little passport right here."

"She's a lucky girl. By the way, you've got a beautiful voice."

He smiled. "Thank you, ma'am. So do you."

On his way out, a steward asked, "Did you have a nice time talking to Miss Lena Horne?"

Paul knew she had to be Lena Horne. He had remembered her from the pictures in his magazines. Hadn't she told him he had a beautiful voice?

He looked at Babe and said, "I'll be singing that song for the rest of my life."

After that, he went on deck every day hoping to see her again. Waited... Waited, but she never came back. The sweetest part of their meeting was that she'd treated him like an equal, taken him for someone. He never liked to think of himself as the help.

————

They stood on the crowded deck as the *Queen Mary* slid into Southampton dock, Babe in her yellow dress, struggling to remove her yellow lace-trimmed bonnet. Emma looked nervous, smartly dressed in a new red-silk suit, ankle-length skirt, and a red hat Paul called "the helicopter," with a stem on top and darker red wings flying in all directions. He was in his blue suit worn with a yellow tie to match Babe's outfit.

It took a while before Henry found them in the crowds. He wore a blue blazer, red Ascot Cravat, tall and handsome as ever, his dark brown hair combed flat. He'd tamed those waves.

"Darling, it seemed you were gone forever!" He hugged Emma so hard he seemed to forget about anyone else. At last, his hand was resting on Paul's shoulder. "Paul, we're so happy you're here. And this must be my beautiful little daughter."

Henry put out his arms to lift Babe up and give her a kiss, but she struggled, latched on to Paul's leg, and began to fuss. Henry laughed and said, easily, "Give her time to get to know me. She's better off with you for now."

There was a change of plans, an overnight stop in Brighton for a visit to Henry's mother. On the train, he invited Paul to bring Babe into the dining car. The steward greeted the whole party politely and ushered them to a table. Was Paul dreaming?

"No segregation here," Henry said, proudly.

Babe sat across from him and after two bowls of Brown Windsor soup, fed to her by Paul in tiny mouthfuls, they both watched the waiter lift fillets of Dover sole off the bone and lay them tenderly on Paul's plate for them to share.

Emma, sitting with Henry at the next table, leaned across, and explained, "Paul, there are not many Negroes in England so no race problems here. You can go anywhere you feel like. Well, almost anywhere."

A cotton ball of fog covered Brighton. They stepped off the train into thin gray needles of rain, took a taxi, and stopped in front of Granny Gordon's home, a large, white Georgian house in a crescent facing the sea. Henry's father, a naval officer, had been killed in the First World War, leaving Esther Gordon to raise her son alone.

Paul had heard Emma call her "an absolute Tartar," with a will even stronger than her daughter-in-law's.

The car door opened and Mrs. Gordon, a plump woman with coils of white hair and Henry's blue eyes, sailed right by Emma and Henry and made a beeline for Babe.

"Come to Granny," was followed by terrible screams as Babe's grandmother tried to pull her away from Paul.

The furious child punched the old lady in the stomach, howled herself into a tantrum, and lay on the ground screaming, her back arching like a fish out of water.

When Emma tried to explain, it all came out in a jumble, "The baby's tired—trains, boat. She stays with Paul. He's the only one in the whole wide world who knows what to do with her. We never keep them apart. They're a pair. Just one rule: leave them alone."

Granny Gordon looked down, astonished at the angelic blonde curls and angry face of her only grandchild. Paul took Babe back into his arms, brushed her off, calmed her down, and was finally led into the kitchen by a disappointed Granny Gordon, where Flora, a skinny little maid with uncombed hair and a runny nose, took orders from the fat cook. Mrs. Carlton's bulk was contained by a starched gray dress, and she wore a white cap pulled low over her eyes. Both of them stopped what they were doing and stared at the tall young Colored man with the child in his arms.

"This is Paul Carew and Jane, my granddaughter," Granny Gordon said, tartly.

Flora and Mrs. Carlton remained speechless.

With a smile, Paul asked, "Never seen one of us before?"

Embarrassed, they wished him a good afternoon.

"Perhaps Mr. Carew and Jane would enjoy a cup of tea and a piece of cake." Straight-backed and icily polite, Granny Gordon left the servants' domain.

Paul looked forward to this visit to Henry's mother in her house. It wasn't supposed to turn out like this, he thought, when he heard Granny Gordon's voice raised.

"Put them together? What could you be thinking? She can't sleep all night next to a native man with his hair all stuck up and waving?"

Babe, still hiccupping from her tantrum, sat beside Paul while he cut up a freshly baked piece of gingerbread and waited for a cup of tea to cool so he could share it with her.

He reached into his pocket, pulled out a package of cigarettes, and was told firmly by Mrs. Carlton, "I'm sorry, Mr. Carew, no smoking in the house."

He thought of going into the garden, where he was sure he would find Emma and Henry puffing, but when he looked at Babe sitting beside him, drinking her tea, he decided against it.

After they'd shared a second piece of gingerbread, they were taken up to their room by Flora. He looked around at the polished antique mahogany furniture, a large double bed, a crib in the corner, and heavy blue-and-white curtains pulled across the long windows. Granny Gordon, perhaps sorry for the way she'd behaved, had given him one of the best bedrooms. Paul put Babe on the floor to crawl around, opened a window, sat down heavily on his bed, and began to bounce up and down on the hard horsehair mattress. The more he bounced, the more he laughed.

Babe picked up his mood, got excited, giggled, and reached out her arms.

"All I can say, little dickens," he told her as he picked her up and put her on the bed, "is I hope you don't have too much of that mean old Granny in you."

After he gave Babe supper and put her to sleep, Flora was sent upstairs to mind her while Paul ate dinner in the kitchen. The table had been laid properly. There was even a glass with a bottle of red wine next to it. He'd never tasted red wine. He poured himself a glass, took a sip, then another and wondered if Henry had thought to offer him this.

The food wasn't bad: roast lamb, mint sauce, au gratin potatoes. The best part was dessert, English trifle. Paul wrote down the recipe and instantly saw how he could make it better. While he was eating, he tried not to listen to Henry's mother's raised voice coming from the dining room. He'd already heard enough to know what she thought of Colored people. All through dinner, the two women cooking in the kitchen carried on as if Paul weren't there, but the English, as Emma had warned him, had a way of blanking out people who were not like them.

Up the stairs, on his way to bed, Paul heard Granny Gordon say, "Why aren't you caring for your own baby, Emma?"

Paul remembered Sally Jackson's outrage on the front porch, right after they'd brought Jane back from the hospital. *"Why aren't you nursing your own baby, Emma?"*

Maybe those two grandmothers had something in common. It seemed to Paul it wasn't a long way down the road from the Jacksons' front porch to this cold house in Brighton.

While he was getting ready for bed, there was a knock on the door, and when he opened it, there was Emma. "Paul, don't unpack. We'll be leaving after breakfast."

"I'll be ready."

Wind rattled the windows as he tossed and turned on the hard, old horsehair mattress. Babe slept like an angel in her crib.

Next morning, Granny Gordon tried to kiss Babe goodbye. Paul felt sorry for the sad-faced old lady, as he waved Babe's arm goodbye.

After a short ride in a taxi, Paul found himself on another train. In his new compartment, he sat across from Babe. He'd dressed her up in a red-smocked blouse, matching red-corduroy skirt, and white tights. "British outfits" bought especially for their trip by Miss Sally.

He wiggled his fingers, she giggled. "You are a real little dickens, yelling at your grandmother. You sure didn't look as sweet for her as you do now."

Paul smoked half a cigarette. He wasn't feeling good, and wished he had someone to try and help him make sense of what was happening. What had Colored people ever done to Granny Gordon?

"What do you think about it, Babe? All your grandmother did

was take one look at my brown skin. Wonder what it feels like to only see Colored people, not to have White people looking at you the way they do or telling you what to do."

Sitting beside him, with her eyes wide open, unblinking, it seemed the more he talked to her like a grown-up, the more Jane seemed to be looking at every word he said, as if she understood exactly what he meant.

"I thought I'd be happy if only I could get away from Elijah. After that, it was trying to forget what happened to Moses, and then it was if only I could leave Horse Cave and the Jacksons, get out into the big wide world. Well, now I'm over here, I'm still not happy. I'm not sure people here are that much better than the White folks I left behind."

Out of his window, the green fields of England speeding by, he saw Great-grandma Abilene's face, heard her saying: "I'm old now, Paul. I've passed all my days, all my years, working in White pockets. Who knows who I might have been somewhere else?"

Babe snuggled in closer, as if to give him comfort.

"Want to hear the real truth?" he murmured. "I'll always be on that train, waiting for a rope around my neck. Don't know if I'll ever be able to take it off."

PART TWO

26

Paul picked up the humming sound before he saw the airplanes. Jane was asleep on a blanket beside him. Even though she was growing up, she still napped in the afternoon. He stood poised with his secateurs raised above the white rose bush he'd been meaning to prune since moving into the Manor House on the edge of Ballygreen, Ireland, eighteen months ago. Settling in had proved no problem. Indeed, for the first time in his life, Paul felt more a part of life in this village than he'd ever felt in Horse Cave.

He looked up, the quiet of the moment shattered as a dozen or so planes flew over his head, the lead aircraft dipping its wings before pulling the whole group up into a steep climb that rattled the windows of the house. The planes spread, a multi-colored fan opening high against a blue sky. He knew they were coming—the endless questions.

"Why do they go up there? How do they get there? Can you fly, Paw-Paw?"

"Look up, Babe. That's freedom. It's your daddy. I don't know how they got up there. I haven't learned to fly."

Paul's heart beat harder. Henry and his Spitfires, coming in straight from England; that meant the squadron leader would be home for dinner. Paul undid the brake on the stroller, left the roses unpruned, picked up his pace and hurried down the drive and into the village. He had a long shopping list, with everything on it for the dinner he'd be cooking that evening.

He looked down at Babe as if she had been reading his thoughts and said out loud, "And now your daddy's been chosen to command the first squadron of Spitfires. Hear that, Babe? Spitfires."

The way he hissed the "s" tickled her. "Spitfire, Spitfire. My spit's on fire," she said it over and over again as they made their way into the village.

Eighteen months in County Down had left him wondering if a fine rain was good Irish weather. If he hadn't been so busy, helping Emma to move into the new house and looking after Jane, he'd have thought more about it.

"We can't live in a tin of sardines." That's what Emma had said when Henry had showed her the squadron leader's quarters on the base. A young Irish real estate agent in a tweed hat and poplin rain-coat took Emma in his Hillman Minx to a house just outside the village. He opened iron gates and motored along a short drive up to a chalky-white Georgian manor house, in the middle of a garden where roses tangled with lavender. Emma made up her mind, then and there, to move in—and not just because the house was on Lord Castlederry's estate.

Together, she and Paul hung curtains, visited antiques shops, moved furniture, and squared-up pictures. Everyone in the village had something to say about the American girl from Kentucky who had fixed up the house beautifully; her husband, the handsome Air Force officer; and the Colored man in charge of their baby.

"Food for thought, Paul." Emma had lost no time in plunking a stack of cookbooks on the kitchen table.

After tucking in Jane, Paul was required to study Mrs. Beeton's classic English recipes. The volume now opened automatically at Henry's favorite—jugged hare.

"You'll soon get the hang of it, Paul," Emma promised.

"Want to bet?" he muttered, under his breath.

Emma could talk. She didn't have to unwrap the butcher's paper, look at bloody pieces of hare, like a large naked, skinned rabbit, much less cook it.

From the minute Paul woke up in the morning until he laid his head on the pillow, never before ten o'clock, there was always Babe to feed, entertain, and watch over. And in between baby-minding, he helped Emma decorate and cooked for the family and more, as sometimes the chaps from the squadron came for dinner.

"Elastic Boy," he called himself.

Emma thought it would lift the pilots' spirits if she could just lay on a bit of entertainment after a real squadron dinner party, only there was none to be found anywhere. Until she looked at Paul.

"Heavens above, why in the world didn't I think of it? I'm snapping my fingers when I hear you singing to Jane all over this house. If there's only one thing in this whole wide world I know, Paul, it's that you can sing."

What made him say it, he never knew, "Well, ma'am, whenever I get a little time on my hands, I'm practicing my own dance routines to go with my singing."

"Why, Paul, I had no idea." Smoothing the back of her chignon, Emma went on, "Would you ever think about putting on a little show for Henry's boys?"

He pretended not to hear as he went out the door to pick up Jane.

———

With Jane now talking a mile a minute, Paul pushed her, as he did every morning, in the stroller, down the drive, and into the village with its narrow lanes. He was decked out in his Irish tweed hat, set on his head just lightly enough to keep the waves in place, and covered up in his coat of knobbly gray Irish tweed, which kept him toasty dry and warm, a gift from Emma and Henry.

Paul knew Henry would be back, after the wing-wagging flyover, for the jugged hare, now bubbling on the wood-fired stove back in the kitchen. Paul was managing, after all, he felt, life here was pretty good.

First stop, as usual, was Willie Donnelly, the fishmonger. When they reached the shop, Paul lifted Jane out of the stroller, saying, as he had every time they'd gone together to Willie's, "Now remember, Babe; it's Alma, not Ayma."

"Paw-Paw, I do 'member!"

Paul laughed. She was smart as a button in her red-tartan skirt, green pullover, white socks, and shiny black shoes.

Jane stood on tiptoes to open the door, and a hint of smoked fish drifted onto the street. Inside, Willie, as broad as he was tall, had the wide mouth of a passionate man. He could fillet a fish as fast as he could lay out a man on the sawdust.

Alma, his red-haired lady friend, wore bright orange lipstick. She wrapped the fish, worked the till, greeted customers, and flirted with the lads. From the very first moment Paul entered the shop, he'd called her "my lovely" while gently suggesting she keep Henry's kippers away from the Dover sole because "their smell goes right through paper, onto other fish."

He was liked by Willie who'd told Alma from the beginning, "Paul's different from most Americans, a real gentleman."

Pushing back a ringlet of red hair, Alma came from behind the counter. "How are ya, darlins?" She planted a smacker of a kiss on Paul's cheek before delivering the same to Jane, leaving each of them with a cheek bearing the imprint of a pair of orange lips.

Willie, in a blue-and-white-striped apron and a floppy cap of Donegal tweed, stood admiringly by. "Quite a show! Quite a show! And what'll it be today for the squadron leader? He'll be coming home for dinner."

The thought of Henry's return was enough to raise Paul's sights from lemon sole to the line of lobsters cooked to a burnished red, arranged on ice.

"Willie, just tell me those beauties are from Leggan Bay, and I'll tell you the squadron leader and Miss Emma would kill for a taste of one."

"Strike me dead, sir, if they weren't bathing yesterday in the Leggan water, cooked this morning by Alma's own fair hands. How many could the squadron leader manage?"

"Two would be fine, Willie. Thank you."

"Make it three, Sir Paul?" Willie added, "The third a gift from Ireland."

Paul turned to Babe. "So, young lady, what do you think of that?"

Until then, Jane had not said a word. Now, she pointed at the line of lobsters. "One for Jane, one for Paw, one for Jane..." She paused. "An' one for Ayma."

Alma clapped.

"Then that's a deal, Willie."

"Yes, sir! On the account?"

"Same as always, sir."

They all laughed as Alma wrapped the lobsters, handed Paul a carbon copy of the bill, and with a now-off-with-you-darlins peck, she left a second pair of orange lips on Paul's empty cheek.

Jane, holding a new large red lobster claw, twirled madly about as Paul took her hand and pulled her out of the shop, yelling, "Bye-bye, Ayma. Bye-bye, Willie."

Then on to the butcher, where three middle-aged women in the line stopped their gossiping. They no longer looked at Paul as if he came from another planet. Now it was, "Morning, Paul. This is a fine day for flying!"

He bought ground hamburger steak for another of Henry's favorites, English mince. Paul made it with tiny pearl onions, fingers of toast, and, of course, add Worcestershire sauce and a little extra butter, a must for Henry.

Then on to the greengrocer for broad beans, cucumbers, and

potatoes. There again, whispers behind his back had given way to, "How's the wee lassie, Paul?"

A shopper observed to her companion, "You'd swear from the way the child talks back to him, she's a grown up."

————

That afternoon, Jane wanted him to play hide-and-seek, but Paul had had enough distraction for the day. He picked her up, put her down outside in the playpen she was growing out of, tucked her in under lots of warm blankets, and she soon fell asleep.

Back at work, he sliced pieces of brown bread, razor-thin, cut off the crusts, then put a knife into the great yellow lump of good Irish butter he'd taken out of the cooler—they didn't need refrigerators. He spread an inch of butter on each piece. He took the cold bowl of drained, salted cucumbers, pronged each one with his long nail, and layered them onto the bread. Then he ground and sprinkled pepper, gave a crush of rock salt, and finally, carefully, put the pieces together.

Henry would be home for tea at five for the first time in weeks. Paul looked at his watch, reached for the silver teapot, noticed a few spots clouding the surface. Unfolding a yellow polishing cloth, he rubbed up and around one way, then the other, shot a few sprays of spit, and polished harder, until his face bounced back at him. He shook out a Chesterfield, stuck it between his lips, and pulled the Gable squint he'd seen in a copy of *Motion Picture*. Just like in his movie, a hand appeared, flicked up a flame on a silver cigarette lighter, and lit Paul's cigarette.

"Good show, Paul," Henry said.

Astonished, he looked around to find the squadron leader in his blue RAF battledress. Paul was still struggling to his feet when Henry started opening cupboards and looking for canisters of tea.

"Mrs. Gordon tells me you want a lesson in brewing a good cup. I'll show you how, it's simple. Ready?"

"Yes, sir."

"First, bring a large kettle of cold water to the boil. God forbid the hot tap."

As Henry ran the water into the kettle, Paul admired Henry's strong hands, the perfect pink half-moons on his fingernails.

"Second, boiling water goes in, to warm the teapot. Third, pour the hot water back into the kettle and boil again. Fourth, wait a minute, let's not scald the tea leaves. I allow the bubbles of boiling water to settle, and then pour over my own mixture of Earl Grey and Ceylon—one teaspoon per person, one for the pot. Remember, Paul, bring the kettle up and pour gently, not to bruise but to infuse the leaves." Henry performed each action as if tending a sensitive piece of flying equipment.

The steam raised the smell of dry tea leaves. When Henry moved his face away, Paul noticed a fine bead of sweat on his upper lip. He smelled aftershave.

"Now, it's made. How about serving it in the sitting room with—dare I hope—one of your cucumber sandwiches? And do I detect the scent of jugged hare?"

When the squadron leader finally left, Paul's face was flaming.

In the sitting room, Emma had lit the fire.

Henry laid on a couple of logs and flopped into a deep armchair. "Lord, it's good to be home. I'm whacked... Got a bit of a headache."

When Paul arrived with tea and sandwiches and set the tray on a low table in front of the fire, he found Emma and Henry with their heads together.

"Thank you, Paul," Emma said. "Look, you may as well stay and hear this. We've had dinners with most members of the squadron, but this time we're going to have a real party. I was just about to tell the squadron leader how, when we finally do invite all the pilots, you're going to make the evening with your dancing and singing. Henry had no idea you could dance, did you, darling?"

"Well, of course. I know Paul can sing." Henry stood. "Wait a minute, Paul. Let's discuss the details now. Sit down." He pointed to the wingback armchair.

Paul stood, looking at Emma, wondering what to do, but then saw her smile.

"Come along, sit down," Henry urged. "Have a cup of tea."

Paul sat uneasily on the edge of the chair.

Emma twirled a cigarette into her holder.

Henry said, easily, "We'll leave the entertainment entirely to you, Paul. Now let's discuss the menu."

Paul sat back comfortably and grew less uneasy as the three planned the dinner together—a fine large Irish salmon, curried lamb for those who'd prefer it, half a Stilton, a whole cheddar cheese, and for dessert, a pineapple upside-down cake. They set the date: three months from today.

Henry remembered his new electric HMV portable gramophone had laid idle in the basement since the move to Ballygreen. There was a stack of records to accompany any dancing and singing. Then he said to Paul, "Wait a minute. I might have the perfect partner for you. Perry Beaumont's wife, Kitty, was a dancer. That is, if you need a partner?"

Paul had never danced with anyone before. He'd never danced in front of an audience. He'd worry about that later.

Much to Paul's relief, Henry said he would arrange for Bill McNabb, the mess sergeant, to come over, set everything up, and serve drinks. Their kitchen maid, Kathleen, together with Mara the housemaid, would bring in the food. It was all set.

As Henry rubbed his red-rimmed eyes, Paul wondered if he'd slept for days. "Getting his boys ready for war" was what Henry had said was his first priority.

After Paul had eaten three of his own cucumber sandwiches and drank two cups of tea, poured by Emma, he stood. "I'd better go see to Jane."

———

Paul had a lot to prepare for the big party, and now Emma wanted him to organize a tea party with Olivia Castlederry. Both events weighed heavily on his mind. It had been so long since Emma had written to her mother to ask for the ingredients needed for his famous jam cake that Paul had entirely forgotten he was counting on it to provide the tea table's centerpiece.

As he was lifting Babe out of her stroller, Emma came into the kitchen, carrying a large package.

She turned it over. "Our lives are saved, Paul. Must be blackberry preserves for the jam cake. Now we can have a trial run for our Castlederry tea."

The brown paper was shredded, the string loose. Customs had already lifted the top off the box inside, just as Paul was doing now, pulling out Ball jars of blackberry preserves, unwrapping the many layers of white tea cloths around each one. When he reached further down, there were two McCormick tins of allspice, and at the very bottom, two ivory-colored envelopes marked "Paul." He recognized Sally Jackson's wobbly slant on one and Cousin Lorene's tiny scrawl on the other. It was getting late. He'd take his time with Lorene's letter. He put that away in his pocket and opened Sally Jackson's.

April 8, 1938

Dear Paul,

These blackberry preserves are for your jam cake, and I put in the allspice because I am not sure they have it over there. Your cousin, Leroy is helping me in the garden, but nothing seems the same since you left. I hope you are happy over there.

Yours, as ever,

Sally Jackson

P.S. Hope you found soft brown sugar for the caramel icing.

Paul looked out of the window at the heavy gray sky and dreamt about the warm, sunny days in early September when he and Miss Sally went up the lane behind the smokehouse to pick blackberries.

He picked and Miss Sally held the basket. Every now and then, she put a few of the warm berries into her mouth.

"Ain't nothing better. Go on, have some," she had said, and giggled.

In the kitchen Lorene's copper pot would be ready with blocks of unrefined sugar. Soon the room was filled with the flowery scent of the boiling fruit.

He picked up a jar. He'd be making the best jam cake anyone had ever tasted. Paul knew that Sally Jackson cared about him. She had hoped that he was "happy over there." But what did that word mean anyway? Happy? Can't look into the mirror to find that out. For Paul to be happy, he needed to first be sad, recognize the difference. For him, happiness was just an idea floating around, popping like a bubble whenever you touched it.

He couldn't wait to make his jam cake. He took cinnamon down from the shelf and with it, his secret—black pepper. He fluffed up the butter and sugar, already thinking about the long dark-brown vanilla beans he'd found that morning at the grocery store in the village. Once he began to cook, he forgot everything else.

———

On the day of "her ladyship's" visit to the Gordon household, the front doorknocker was buffed to a high shine; even the gravel driveway was raked. Lady Castlederry stepped out of a silver Bentley, one arm supported by a chauffeur dressed in spotless livery. Her tweed skirt was flecked with the colors of a cock pheasant's tail, and when Emma greeted her, and led her into the sitting room, Paul picked up her musical voice, hitting a succession of highs and lows.

Lady Castlederry lavished praise on Emma. "My dear, you've done wonders with the house—so comfortable. You Americans are such whizzes—endless hot water, every room heated, even the bedrooms so cozy. Whereas we love going to bed with icicles inside our windows!" She laughed, chattering on without drawing breath.

"By the way, I've heard so much about your manservant, Paul. In the village they adore him. They're simply intrigued, especially with how he's teaching your baby to talk. Wanda O'Callaghan, the baker's wife, says the child is like a sponge, listens to his every word, and never takes her eyes off him."

Olivia Castlederry and Emma sat facing each other in front of a roaring fire.

Emma poured two cups of tea. "Milk?"

Lady Castlederry raised her hand as if stopping traffic, smiled, and replied, "No milk, thank you, but I'd love one of these." She helped herself to a cucumber sandwich and leaned forward as if confiding a secret. "I've just come back from the most marvelous trip to Berlin. Have you ever been?" Not waiting for an answer, she rattled on, "Yes, our old friend, Joachim von Ribbentrop, just retired as German Ambassador in London. He arranged for us to have dinner with Chancellor Hitler."

Emma looked intently at her guest. Her face showed nothing of what she must have felt. Only the night before, Paul had heard Henry describing to his wife the scandal caused by von Ribbentrop's recent Nazi salute on arriving at Croydon Aerodrome.

"And how was Berlin?" Emma stabbed the jam cake, slicing off a piece for Olivia.

Olivia accepted it with a murmured, "How very American this looks." Then continued brightly, "My dear, it sounds trite, but Herr Hitler was completely hypnotic. I was caught, a rabbit in his headlights. However..." she leaned forward and added in a low voice, "...he has the most atrocious table manners I've ever seen.

"On the other hand, Hitler has done wonders for Germany in spite of what you might have read. National pride is quite restored. Factories are hiring many more workers. I'm sure that when Herr von Ribbentrop comes here for a shooting weekend, he will tell you all about it himself. Oh, this scrumptious cake! How lucky you are to have Paul."

Emma steadied her nerves and remembered her manners as she

poured her guest another cup of tea from the silver pot Paul had polished to a silken sheen. Nothing Olivia Castlederry could say would diminish the shock that had been widely felt when it was widely reported the Duke of Windsor had exchanged the Hitler salute with the Führer at his retreat in Bavaria.

Lady Castlederry, reading Emma's set expression, and seeing her own enthusiasm for the Nazi leader unreciprocated, tried to find a subject to flatter her hostess. "Your wonderful Paul," she plowed on, "would it be terribly indiscreet of me to ask if you would ever allow me to borrow him? To teach my kitchen staff a thing or two."

Emma sat straight, bolt-upright in her chair. Unsmiling, she gave a clipped response, "Well now, Olivia, I'd have to ask Paul about that." Her face had gone quite red.

Paul, standing behind the door, heard every word. As far as Lady Castlederry was concerned, he was no more than a bit of furniture she could move around. He wished he had Lorene with him. She'd have something to say about that to Her Ladyship.

Before making her way down the steps to the waiting Bentley, Lady Castlederry gave Emma a kiss on her cheek. "What a lovely time I've had. Marvelous." She glanced back at the house. "Oh, by the way, please thank your wonderful young man for those heavenly cucumber sandwiches and—what was it—oh, yes, jam cake! Too quaint. You and Henry must come for dinner again soon."

Paul heard every word, smiled, and stuck his tongue in his cheek, and turned to Jane.

"Paw-Paw, why did she have that funny feather in her hat?"

"Because people like Lady Castlederry like to stick feathers all over themselves from the birds they've killed."

"Why do they kill birds?"

"Because they have nothing better to do."

Emma, as she waved goodbye to her guest, realized having Paul around gave her that upsweep out of ordinary into a kingdom where she was envied. And thanks to him, Jane had learned to talk earlier than most children. Emma had noticed how, since leaving Kentucky,

Paul's accent had veered in another direction, stretched from Horse Cave like taffy pulled from one side of the Atlantic to the other. Surprised, she'd said he was sounding more and more like Henry. Now she took a moment, detouring to the kitchen to find him cracking lobster claws.

"Paul, that was a great success, but I'm not sure about Lady Castlederry's politics."

Dinner with Hitler, indeed. She'd been having such an interesting time with Olivia recently, but Henry had warned her to be careful what she said to her Irish friend about the RAF's recent expansion, and now Emma thought she could see why.

27

Paul watched from an open window. At the appointed hour on Friday, August 12, 1938, a Wellington bomber broke through the dark cloud cover hanging low over the Royal Air Force airfield, circling once before making a landing on the grass strip, scaring off the resident flock of seagulls.

The birds' angry shrieks sliced through the roar of 3000 horse-power engines, which soon turned into a throaty growl as the bomber rolled toward the cement apron where Henry headed up his squadron of pilots, lined up in front of their Spitfires. The Wellington's engines shut down, the deepening silence only adding to its menacing air, the red light blinking on its tail fin, the only sign of life.

Paul turned to look at the Spitfires sitting there like toys. He counted the twelve planes in a line, their pilots alongside in gray-green overalls; behind them were forty ground crew and a red fire engine.

Paul watched Air Commodore Oliver Griffith step from a ladder onto the apron. Gold-trimmed cap, two rows of Great War medals, and a magnificent pale-gray mustache. An exchange of salutes and the inspection started. The common thread: Ready for action. It was time for Paul to move on to the planning room where Sergeant McNabb would be waiting for him.

Sergeant McNabb greeted Paul, standing at the entrance of the planning room's long corridor in his three-stripe battledress, blue eyes dancing in his red face. "Come on in, young fellow. You're part of the team now."

Paul laughed. He liked McNabb.

They'd worked well together at the manor on dinner parties for the pilots. Paul liked the way McNabb talked with a Scottish accent, rolling his 'r' when he spoke. Now Paul slipped on his black butler's jacket, and with McNabb's help, set about arranging large copper urns on each table, filling them with boiling water, dumping into each a full bag of tea leaves. Next came seventy mugs, jugs of milk, bowls of sugar, and what McNabb called "tea-break wads," circular, oven-gold buns sticky with white caster sugar.

Paul smiled, and imitating a Scot's accent, said, "I bet the boys love these, you ken?"

"Paul, what you're looking at is our secret weapon. The Huns don't stand a chance when our boys are armed with tea and buns."

When the men came in for their tea and buns, the Air Commodore's ebullience, and Henry's high spirits, all heightened the growing conviction. Something big was up. By the time the break was over, pilots and ground crews, along with the Wellington's crew, had moved over to the planning room where they sat in silence looking at a blackboard, a film projector, and a screen.

Paul and McNabb watched and listened from the door. The squadron leader, followed by the Air Commodore, strode in purposefully.

Unmoved, straight-faced, the Air Commodore, Oliver Griffith, stood, looking around the room of cheering men. He raised his hands for quiet. "Gentlemen, please be seated." He turned to the squadron leader. "Thank you, Henry."

"Gentlemen, we've work to do. First, some background, none of it pretty." He looked around. "You know what happened: Hitler re-armed the Rhineland, then marched into Austria and swallowed it whole." Oliver Griffith's mustache bristled. "You ask, why?" He scanned the room, the tense jaws, eyes bright with growing anger. "You chaps deserve the truth. Henry, let's hear it." He turned to the squadron leader standing at the blackboard, who began to write.

The words and numbers formed fluently as if pouring from the white chalk, the underlinings fast and heavy, the chalk breaking and falling to the floor with the final THEM.

Henry stood back from the blackboard. "There you have it, gentlemen. That is why not a shot was fired."

Paul saw Henry's lips drawn tight against his teeth; a dog about to bite.

Us: Fighters. Spitfires, Hurricanes 95

Them: Fighters: Focke-Wulf, Messerschmitt 1,500

Us: New bombers 300

Them: New bombers 1,000

Us: Army throughout the Empire 200,000

Them: Army in Germany 850,000

The army figures appeared, and the broken stick of chalk was reduced to dust under the squadron leader's heel. There was anger and concern among the men who shifted uneasily in their seats, muttering swear words.

The commodore stepped forward. "Go in now, gentlemen, and we'll lose the bloody war. The numbers don't lie. But hang on, chaps." He took a step closer to the men and spoke quietly, "The Prime Minister's deal with Adolf, call it what you will, bought us something priceless: time, gentlemen. Time to prepare ourselves to fight—and win!" The mustache took on a jaunty air.

"The Treasury's opened up. From now on, it's airplanes, airplanes, airplanes; guns, guns, guns—and men, men, men. War effort full steam ahead."

If Oliver Griffiths thought the men might jump up and down at this bit of good news, he was disappointed. They needed something more. Again, he took a swipe at the mustache, notching it up a fraction as he turned to Henry. "The chaps want something to level the playing field." He stepped back as the squadron leader moved in close to the men.

"Okay, lads. You asked for it. Here we go. First, as of today, the squadron is designated Bomber Attack Squadron one-o-one, the first in the R-A-F. Our key mission: knock Jerry's bombers out of the sky before he knocks us out."

A bolt of electricity couldn't have galvanized the men any quicker than this announcement. Shoulders were squared, backs straightened, every eye quickened.

Paul stood with Sergeant McNabb and listened intently, shocked by what he was hearing.

"Finally, the squadron will be assigned to Group Eleven, the frontline air defense of London."

Perry Beaumont raised a hand.

"Yes, Perry."

"When do we leave, sir?"

The air commodore looked at him coolly. "Perry, soon enough. Though I'd be careful what I wished for if I were you."

"Sir!"

———

The pilots of RAF Squadron 101 filed out of the airfield bus the following Wednesday evening: Matt, Ian, Curley (with the bald head), Perry (the oldest at twenty-five, with the whopping handlebar mustache), Marco (the youngest at nineteen). For all their different characters, they dressed the same in dark blue single-breasted blazers with RAF or Cranwell crests, gray flannel trousers, white or blue shirts with RAF ties, brown-suede or black shoes. Their hair was brushed and shining with pomade. The odd man out was Perry, in a double-breasted blazer. All the men were clean-shaven except for Perry, whose handlebar mustache curled perkily on either side of his long narrow nose.

Henry looked at his watch. "Slap on time, chaps." He paused, and then added, "Naturally."

They all laughed.

"You all know my bride, of course, and I see some of your sweethearts and wives are here."

Emma waved from the steps. She ushered everyone into the Manor. The tone had been set. The men were ready to have a fine old time.

Paul stood with Mess Sergeant McNabb, who saw to it no one went thirsty. Beer and Irish whiskey flowed, perfectly partnered with Paul's melty cheese sticks and stuffed eggs.

Emma felt she owed the squadron a real party. She'd told Paul, who now understood what could be at stake, that she wanted the men, if only for a few hours, to forget "deflection shooting," whatever it was, along with all the other stuff Henry was drilling into their heads.

Emma looked around the room, appreciating the lusciousness of Paul's arrangement of deep-red Dublin Bay roses in a silver bowl on the center table; the glowing logs in the grate chasing away the chill. Above the wide stone fireplace was a large painting of a baby elephant hanging onto the tail of its lumbering mother, a gift to Henry from the Maharaja of Khairpur for teaching his son to fly. The room was abuzz with chatter and laughter. It felt good to be sharing her life with the boys on the base—a home away from home. Wasn't it something Americans had been doing since the colonists landed in Virginia? The thought that she was now in a foreign land was interrupted by her husband's voice rising above the babble and cigarette smoke.

Back in the doorway, Paul announced, "Ma'am, ladies and gentlemen, dinner is served."

That brought forth a noisy round of applause.

Henry clapped his hands. "Let's go, chaps."

Emma led the way down the corridor into the dining room. The room was large, cozy, lit by another log-fire burning brightly in an open fireplace. There was a glow of candlelight from a pair of silver candelabras reflecting off the starched-white tablecloth of Irish linen. On the wall, picture lights shone above artists' colorful Mughal-style paintings of imaginary wild animals. Emma had picked them up at an Antiques Fair in Bombay. She admired the Waterford crystal vases containing Paul's arrangements of roses and parsley, placed at regular intervals down the middle of the long mahogany table set for eighteen.

Paul stood at a side table, prepared to serve a large, steamed salmon decorated with transparent lemon and cucumber slices, and dishes of buttered new potatoes, young green peas and carrots, together with bowls of his thick mayonnaise.

By a serving table to the other side of the room stood Mara, who came every day to clean the house, now wearing a black long-sleeved dress with a white-lace collar and frilly white apron, ready to serve Paul's curry, cooked with spices from the Quetta region, where Henry had served much of his India time. There were side dishes of mango, tamarind, green and red chutneys, sliced bananas, crushed pine nuts and peanuts, chopped onions and tomatoes, along with rice, white and brown, decorated with lightly fried chopped onion. All the dishes gave the table the festive air of an Oriental bazaar.

Standing by was Ben McNabb with bottles of Pouilly-Fuissé and red Burgundy, or Guinness for the curry lovers.

Paul took all this in at a glance. Not a bad show, as Henry would say, for a boy from Horse Cave, Kentucky. He felt curiously uplifted by the evening's developments. He had a mission. He would do his utmost to bring relaxation and enjoyment into the lives of these young pilots. Nothing was too good for them.

Turning to look at her guests, Emma sang out, "On the left, Paul and salmon. On the right, Mara with Henry's curry, by Paul." She paused before adding, "Sit wherever you please, and bon appétit."

Men peeled off to the left and right.

Emma buttonholed Perry to sit next to her, his wife, Kitty, on Henry's right. Francis Peregrine Beaumont, alias Perry, youngest son of a Scottish earl, pulled out Emma's chair for her before taking his own seat.

Perry had followed his dream of flying, breaking the family tradition of Eton, Sandhurst, Coldstream Guards. Achieving a first in physics at Cambridge had been enough to earn him his severely traditionalist father's approval of Cranwell and the RAF: "So long as you stay safely up in the air, dear boy."

"Perry, how's it all going?" asked Emma, smiling warmly at him.

Perry gave the left handlebar of his mustache an upward flourish. "My shooting has improved to no end since flying with the squadron leader. Those high birds are goners."

"Oh, Perry, I can't believe you've much time for shooting pheasants."

"Can't avoid it, I need the practice."

Perry tucked into his curry while Emma marveled how easily the pale pink flakes of a perfectly cooked fresh salmon slipped onto her fork. "Well, Henry's never brought a pheasant home. Bad shot?"

"Up there, in his kite, he's the master. Believe me, Emma."

Emma frowned as she forked up the rest of her salmon. "What's going to happen?"

Perry put down his glass and rubbed his forehead. "We are going to war, Emma. That's what's going to happen."

She quickly put down her knife and fork. "If war is declared, Perry, you won't be on your own. I'm sure my country will help Britain." She lowered her eyes to the table.

Henry was busy with Perry's wife, Kitty—fair curly hair, blue eyes, an easy, wide smile. Dance was in her blood. She had been in the middle of a brilliant career in Sadler's Wells Royal Ballet company, in London, when Perry had caught her eye at the Café de Paris. Six months later, she became the wife of the dashing young RAF officer.

Emma turned to Marco, the dark-haired officer on her left, and with a solicitous smile said, "Marco, I need your help. Perry's about to explain how shooting up there—" she pointed to the ceiling "—improves shooting down here."

Marco laughed. "Perry is the ace in our pack. He'll put you in the picture."

She turned to Perry, who began with an upward flick of the left handlebar. "Take a pheasant."

Emma groaned, "No! No! No more pheasants, Perry. In Kentucky, we shoot doves."

He paused, pensively holding a finger along his nose. "So, let's go for a... Now let me see... A dove."

"Why not an ostrich, Perry?"

"Can ostriches fly? I think not, Emma. Let's just settle for..." he paused "...a Messerschmitt?"

"God, no. Let's stick with your pheasant, Perry."

"Emma, truth is, the end result for both is the same—in the bag."

Spoken quietly, without a trace of bravado, the words hung in the air between them and Perry turned to look, a little wistfully Emma thought, directly into her eyes, and raised his glass.

"Here's to now."

"To now, Perry."

Paul stood behind the buffet table where most of the guests were serving themselves second helpings. He watched Cayzer, a short red-haired Flight Lieutenant put three heaping tablespoons of lamb curry onto his already full plate. He'd overheard Henry tell Emma that Tony Cayzer was the only "nasty piece of work in the squadron." He hadn't meant to, but now caught Cayzer's eye.

The Flight Lieutenant looked at him and asked in a conde-scending voice, "Eat curry where you come from, young man?"

"No, sir," Paul answered.

"Where do you come from?"

"Kentucky."

"I might have guessed. The old plantation and all that?"

"No, sir, no more old plantations. Not now." Paul smiled,

stretched up to his full six-foot-four inches so he could look down on Tony Cayzer.

It was nearly time to bring in dessert. Paul's heart thumped against his perfect white shirt. He looked over, and saw Emma deep in conversation with Perry. He prayed as hard as he could that everyone would forget about the dance number. He'd been practicing but didn't feel ready for any display in front of all these people.

————

Sergeant McNabb saw to it that no glass remained empty, and Paul's two upside-down cakes served with thick yellow Jersey cream had already become a delicious memory when Perry stood, quieting the hubbub with a clink of his glass.

"Ladies and gentlemen, let's raise our glasses, first to Squadron one-o-one's leader and his lovely bride for their generous understanding that while Army lads tread the sod on their stomachs, bless them, us chaps rule the sky on ours. To Henry and Emma!"

They rose to their feet and cries of "Henry and Emma" filled the air until Perry raised a hand and restored quiet.

"And now, to Paul—for the magic he has worked in creating this sumptuous feast."

They all raised their glasses. "To Paul! To Paul!"

Paul was too distracted by thoughts of the dance to do any more than smile and nod his head. He wondered about his partner. He'd spotted Kitty, the pretty blonde lady among the guests. Lively, easy-going, the only possible dancer in the room.

Kitty felt him looking at her and came over. "I'm Kitty Beaumont, your partner in an impromptu number. Paul, I can't wait for our duet. Dare I ask what we will be dancing to?"

"'Anything Goes.'"

"Wow." She laughed and pointed a finger, saying, "Well, hello, Fred."

Paul hesitated. "Hello, Mrs. Beaumont."

She took his hand. "Call me Ginger."

"As soon as I've changed, Mrs. Beaumont, and put Jane to bed."

When Babe was settled, Paul was back downstairs in narrow black trousers, black socks, black polished shoes, creaseless white shirt, smoothed-down shiny dark hair. All six-foot-four inches of Paul Carew, from Horse Cave, Kentucky, stood in the shadows, behind the door and waited for his cue.

Henry spotted him first. "There you are, Paul. We're all agog." Henry clapped his hands, and the room came to attention. "Time for Paul and Kitty to entertain us."

Sergeant McNabb passed a tray of cognac, whiskey, and port. Already the air was heavy with the rich smell of Montecristo cigars.

Perry, the only man in the room taller than Paul, spotted his arrival and danced Kitty over to him, her pleated white silk skirt curling around her long legs.

"Before we begin, Paul, what'll it be?" Kitty raised her glass to him.

"A glass of wine would be fine, Mrs. Beaumont."

"Kitty, please," she insisted.

Then, turning to Perry, "Darling, have a glass for Mr. Carew standing by."

Henry took a record out of its sleeve. "As requested, 'Anything Goes'."

Kitty curtsied.

Paul smiled, ready for Henry to drop the needle.

Kitty's hand in Paul's, they took it easy, waiting for the first verse to kick up their heels. He got the beat from the top of his head, took the swell into his shoes, and with a smile, pretended it was nothing. Then all hell broke loose. Paul knew where he was going, Kitty followed.

In a crazy swirl, they deviled it up then paused and took a few seconds. Paul cooled it down, snapped his fingers to a half beat. His black shoes tapped, and Kitty's answered back.

The world has gone mad today

And good's bad today
And black's white today
And day's night today...

Paul's arms, right to the tips of his fingers, followed his feet, sweeping up higher and higher.

Kitty danced for a while inside his circle before cutting loose, then off they went together, turning around each other, faster and faster, until the last line of the song.

Kitty, out of breath, gave Paul a hug and called out to everyone in the room, as she held up his hand, "A star is born. Three cheers for Paul."

The men of RAF Squadron 101 rose to their feet, applauding wildly.

Kitty and Paul looked at each other, astonished by their own perfect timing, then burst out laughing.

Everyone topped up their drinks and lights were lowered. Flames from fresh logs cast a fluttering patchwork of fire up the chimney.

Emma shook her head, tears in her eyes. The evening had been every bit the success she had hoped for.

Paul, glowing in his moment, was the first to hear the screams.

"Paw-Paw, Paw-Paw!" Babe was standing at the open door, a tiny figure in a red nighty, waving a lobster claw. She began to wail, this time, she meant business. "Paw-Paw. Now."

He knew that tone. "Good night, everyone."

———

Kathleen swished flakes of Rinso washing powder in a sink full of water, stacked the pots, and waited for Paul to finish serving before she soaped each plate with a carry-on of constant chatter, her red curly hair framing a face scattered with freckles. For all the time he'd spent in Ireland, Paul still had a hard time understanding a word she said. It didn't matter. She carried on talking, never stopping for an answer.

Her brother, Michael, managed the Cut & Snip Beauty Salon in the village. On most days, Michael waited to catch a glimpse of Paul walking by with Babe. On his day off, Paul often went in for a trim, not a cut.

Paul enjoyed putting his head forward while Michael washed his hair with a scented shampoo, carefully never to get it in his eyes.

Michael took his time, massaging Paul's scalp, then rinsed out the first shampoo and began all over again. The second time, the massage was harder. Then the hairdresser's long fingers began a tender rub that slid down to the nape of Paul's neck.

Paul wasn't sure about this.

"That's fine... Enough, Michael. Thank you."

Michael, who was only five-foot-eight, stood on a stool. From the chair, Paul watched him in the mirror.

"How about a few pin curls, Paul?" Michael giggled.

"Not today, thank you."

Most of the time, Paul kept to himself behind a copy of *Photoplay Magazine*. Today, he considered the Irishman. Michael's skin was so white, he wondered if it had been bleached. Unlike his sister Kathleen, not even one freckle marked the features framed by his curly red hair.

Michael was fussing around Paul in the salon like a chicken in a ruffle, offering him a cup of tea. "And what have you seen of Ireland, Paul? Sure, you must get a day off. I bet you've never been to a night-club in Belfast?"

Paul sighed. For the last twenty-two months Michael had been nagging and pulling at him. He liked Michael but that's where it ended. Michael was no Henry. Still, he thought, it might be a new experience to see the inside of a Belfast nightclub.

————

Michael picked Paul up the following Saturday night in a battered Austin 7.

Paul left his cranky Babe asleep and in the care of Mara. "Don't fuss yourself, Paul. Sure, I've raised eight children. If she wakes up, I'll pick her up and play with her."

Michael parked in the middle of Belfast. They walked for ten minutes to a pub he knew well up a side street. Inside, across a smoky room, stood a gleaming new American jukebox.

"Joseph Hoban brought it all the way over here on a boat from America," Michael proudly explained, as he ordered.

Later, a plate of bangers and mash was slung onto the table together with pints of Guinness. Under the watery blue fix of Michael's worshipping eyes, Paul got up, went to the bar, and traded Irish coins for American nickels to put in the jukebox.

A few tables had been cleared in the middle of the smoky pub and no one was dancing. Paul sat, feeling queasy from the warm smell of beer, the loud chat, and the hot red faces all turned in his direction. He decided to wait to put in his money, while Louis Armstrong was finishing "All of Me" when, at the next table, a tall young girl with long red hair tied back with a bright green ribbon got up, came over, and held out her arms to him.

"I'm Eileen. Dance with me?"

Paul did not hear Michael whisper, "Watch out."

Paul got up slowly, aware of eyes fixed on them as he and Eileen moved onto the small dance floor in the middle of the room.

Paul waited for the music, the first words of "Sweet Georgia Brown."

She just got here yesterday,
Things are hot here now they say

"Ain't that the truth?" Paul smiled to himself, remembering standing in front of his mama's mirror in her pink dress, swaying to this same song.

Paul pulled Eileen in, then with his hands gently on her shoulders, danced her away to the beat of the music. She followed his steps, forward, backward, to the side, until he brought her in closer, his hands around her waist. They glided together, smooth as ice skaters. Everyone in the room held their breath.

Without any warning, a man weaved out of the crowd and edged between them—short, stocky, and reeking of whiskey. Through the music, Paul heard a slurred voice say, "That's my girl."

Eileen reluctantly unwound herself from Paul's arms and moved away. Her man swayed unsteadily, throwing one punch, and then another into the smoky air.

Paul stood, arms hanging loosely by his sides, dodging every drunken blow in time to the music. He swayed like a bird on a branch in the wind. The blows missed him time after time. Paul stepped lightly backwards, smiling, snapping his fingers to the beat.

Laughter all around. Someone shouted, "Come on, Paddy. Be a good sport, he's taken the piss out of you."

The music stopped. The drunk tripped and fell forward into Paul's arms.

Eileen stood by balefully, hands on her hips. "I asked this Yank to dance."

Paddy was beginning to see the fool he'd made of himself. Bleary-eyed and exhausted, he looked at Paul and a slow grin spread over the Irishman's face. "Friends?"

Paul put out his hand. "Friends."

The barman called out, "Drinks on the house."

Michael was standing at the door, ready to go. "Come on, Paul, we're late."

Paul waved goodbye. "So long, folks. Look forward to that next dance."

Outside in the car, before they got started, Michael shook his head and warned, "That was Padraig Hannigan you were hugging. He's a dangerous man, Paul, Republican Army. That could have gone either way. You need to watch your back."

Watch your back? Paul had not heard that one before. This was Ireland, not Horse Cave. He had fairly well-developed hackles. He'd been growing those hackles ever since the last time he danced before the mirror.

————

It was raining and it was late. Only a few lights were on in Belfast. Michael sped up, skidding around the corners. As soon as they left the outskirts, he pulled into a lay-by and turned to look at Paul with soft blue eyes.

"Won't you come home with me and spend the night?" he asked timidly, reaching over to touch Paul's cheek. "You're the most gorgeous man I've ever seen."

Paul looked out of the rain-splashed windshield. "Michael," he said gently, "drop me off at the manor. I'm sorry. I don't want the same thing as you do."

Michael looked smaller than ever behind the steering wheel. He spoke softly, sadly, "You danced like a star tonight. I knew I didn't stand a chance with someone like you."

Paul shook his hand before getting out of the car. "It was a great adventure. Something I won't forget. Thank you, Michael."

He liked and sympathized with the Irishman. If there was one thing Paul understood, it was the pain of loving a man who would never feel the same way.

28

After their grand dinner party, leaves blew off the trees, and winds brought rain, and winter social life in Ireland stayed within the family. Paul never took another day off. Not because he didn't have any due, he didn't want a day off. His night on the town with Michael in the pub had left him a little wary. He knew his way between the Manor House and village. Any detours could only bring trouble.

One night, he got into bed, breathing in the deep quiet of his room, and realized the letter from Lorene was still unopened in his top drawer. He pulled out her letter, written on grocery-pad paper, and sat atop his bedspread to read it.

Dear Paul,

I'm sitting on the back porch, waiting for Larkin's to deliver the groceries, killing time, waiting for it to kill me. Almost two years run away with us, and I've written you ten letters. Boats sink carrying your answers?

I'm looking at Miss Sally, standing with two canes now, next to Leroy. She's fussing at him. Her mood went down when you left and it ain't come up. Lily has shingles, she's worn inside and out, thinner than a pencil!

Mr. Walter got terrible indigestion all the time, but he still finds the pickles I hide from him.

Pick up a pen, Paul Carew. I know you learned to read and write. Won't matter to me if you don't spell so good.

Love, Lorene

His cousin Lorene had seen right smack dab into his heart. Paul could read, he could write, he just wasn't so sure about putting down on paper what he really felt. But what a friend to him she had been; up in the air, high on his fancies, she'd bring him down, leading him in the right direction. How he missed the flash of her gold tooth and her hot sass.

Paul missed his mother too, the way she looked up from her sewing machine and smiled whenever she felt him looking at her. And Tallulah and Tabby, with their feisty ways, waiting for him to pay attention. They grew up at his heels, and now they must be young ladies. His scoundrel brothers too, always running to get away from trouble.

And Blessing... His heart yearned for her wise words, her sweet protection, her terrible angry determination to get justice for Moses. Most of all, he missed Moses. Every time he thought of him, the lump in his throat brought him to tears. If only he could get back to the pond, see the sun shining through Moses's frizzy hair as he threaded Paul's worm onto the hook. If only, if only.

Well, he could write a letter to Lorene. He pulled out a pencil and paper and began:

Dear Lorene,

I've been getting your news secondhand from Emma. I know Miss Sally's telling you mine. I'm in a new world here. Pilots, airplanes, and there's a war coming. We had a big party for all Henry's pilots in his squadron and I made your pineapple-upside-down-cake recipe. Couldn't find tins of pineapple, so I caramelized apples. It turned out, but not as good as yours.

Jane is growing like a weed. That's what I call her. Emma says when she was Jane's age, her head was empty—not like Jane's. She wants her daughter to learn to read and write. Tomorrow morning, we have a teacher coming from the school in Ballygreen. Emma says she's marvelous. We'll see if Jane thinks so.

Meanwhile, I'm learning plenty too. I can go anywhere I want, sit downstairs at the picture shows, walk into a restaurant, eat with White folks, go to their bathrooms. No "Whites only" in Ireland.

I'm the only Colored person around here. I reckon I miss seeing people like us. I wish I had a piece of your hot-water cornbread with a big pat of cold Straker's butter. Never thought I would say it, but I sure do miss you telling me what's what. Say hello to Leroy.

Love Paul, and from Babe

————

Emma, Paul, and Jane were at the door when the new teacher arrived.

"My name is Abby. I'm from the South, Donegal, and I've never met an American before. I'm honored—" She laughed. "—no, exalted, to meet you." She put out her hand, thought better of it, and gave Paul a kiss on the cheek. "Welcome to Ireland." Then, "I'm best friends with Lena Horne, Count Basie, Bessie Smith." She tapped the side of her head. "Know what else is in there?"

Paul, amazed, shook his head.

"I've read everything by Zora Neal Hurston. And, of course, Langston Hughes."

Paul knew the music, he'd never read the writers.

Abby Kelleher's curly, dark red hair was tamed by a very short haircut. Paul took in her long tweed coat, admired her ankle-length red-wool skirt, tight black sweater, and dangly jade-green earrings.

"Come on, Jane, let's get going," she said.

Jane snuggled in close to Paul while Abby held up cards she'd painted with flowers and birds with large letters of the alphabet in the middle. Paul and Jane read the letters together out loud until Jane could repeat the alphabet by heart.

Next, Abby told Jane stories. "Leprechauns were tall fairies who would appear as old men." She related the story of the King of Erin and the Queen of Lonesome, and another, and another. She told one tale after the other, taking on all the voices, sometimes scaring Jane.

"Have you had enough, my darling?" she asked, eventually.

"No! More, more, more, please." Babe snuggled closer to Paul.

After an hour and a half, Abby said goodbye and promised to come at the same time the following day.

"Babe, let's go and say thank you to Mummy for sending us Abby. It's time you learned to say Mummy and Daddy nicely."

"Mummy and Daddy nicely," she repeated with a devilish grin.

––––––

Whenever Paul wasn't cooking, he was talking to Jane. "I want you to listen hard, and listen good, Babe."

She'd listened hard. She'd listened good. And she talked back.

For weeks, they'd been singing "Flat Feet Floogee" by Slim and Slam.

Paul said, "It's time for you to stop saying you and he to your Mummy and Daddy and calling me Dada. I'm not your daddy."

"Dada," she said, looking at him and laughing. "Dada, Dada, Dada," she shouted.

They practiced.

He told her, "You look at them, then say, 'Good evening, Mummy and Daddy.'"

Jane stood straight, gave a little curtsy, exactly as Paul had taught her. "Good evening, Mummy and Daddy."

Paul dressed Babe up and took her into the drawing room for six o'clock "parents' time." He turned her around to face Emma and Henry, who were just about to take a sip of their first martini.

Babe curtsied, raised her hand, then with lots of spit, she turned, looked behind at Paul like a baseball pitcher and gave her "Good evening, Mummy and Daddy" right where it belonged, to Paul. Luckily, Emma and Henry, not noticing a thing, were halfway down their first martinis.

"Yes, sir, you're my baby," they hummed together, as he tucked Babe up in bed.

———

As time went by, with news of Hitler's build-up in Europe coming every day, in the newspapers and on the radio, Paul understood the danger ahead. Every day it got worse.

Henry spent at least two nights a week on the base with his squadron. "We get up too early in the morning for me to come home every night, darling," Paul overheard him tell Emma.

And when he did come home, his face was white with exhaustion, with frequent headaches driving him upstairs to his room.

One morning in the dining room, between bites of toast and marmalade, Henry announced to Paul, "Thanks to that softy, Chamberlain, we've been appeasing the Nazis. An appeaser, as Winston Churchill said, is someone who hopes that 'if he feeds the crocodile enough, the crocodile will eat him last.' War is the only solution. And war is what they will get." With that, Henry got up quickly from the table and was out the door.

Paul tried to put the idea of crocodiles and war out of his mind. He concentrated, instead, on cooking Henry his favorite recipes. But the fear wouldn't go away. War meant flying, war meant killing, and worst of all, war meant dying.

———

Paul could not remember one day of full-on sun under the Irish sky. Low clouds, and what he called falling wet, meant he could not tame their garden the way he had with Miss Sally in Horse Cave. Even the lady's mantle hung heavy and low; the flowers and bushes went inside themselves, all tangled up with wet weeds. So, when Paul got a chance, he took Jane, put on his garden gloves, sat her down beside him, and set to work. Jane filled her bucket with dirt, mouth open, as close as she could get to Paul's every word.

"Babe, when my Great-grandmama Abilene got too stiff to work in her garden, she used to keep a bucket of dirt on her front porch. Every few hours she'd pick up a handful, rub her hands in it, said something in that black dirt was going right inside, making her feel better. You do just like Great-grandma did, stick your hands in this little pile here; make something with that dirt."

"What did Great-grandma make?" Babe took her hands and covered her face with wet earth, started making dirt balls and throwing them.

"She made cakes."

"Here, Paw-Paw, me too?"

That's all it took to set both of them laughing.

They did not hear Emma open the back door or notice her until she was right beside them.

"Good Lord, what a sight you are, Jane Gordon. Let's take a hose and wash that dirt right off your face."

With those words, Jane screamed, "No, no. We're playing Great-grandma Abilene. You go away! We don't want you."

"Maybe I better leave this to you, Paul." Emma left, pulling furiously on her cigarette.

Paul took his time, stayed outside weeding and pruning, while his girl settled down and covered herself in more mud.

———

Emma took to coming into Paul's kitchen more and more often. A little visit with Paul could calm her worries over Henry's headaches and the coming war. Something else was coming too. Emma and Henry were expecting a second child and Paul listened to her worries about that. Emma was happiest when Jane was asleep and Paul was free to concentrate on her.

One morning after Henry had left, she burst into the kitchen. "I can't believe another year has rolled us right around to the King's birthday flypast on Thursday. Paul, look at this kilt Olivia Castled-erry sent over yesterday."

So, she was still friendly with the enemy.

Emma held up the green-and-red-plaid kilt. "Your little girl can put this on with the ruffled blouse from Mama—bit frilly, but never mind," she told Paul.

"I think she wants to put on that twirly pink skirt your mama sent."

Emma mashed a cigarette into her holder. "That is quite enough of what Jane wants. You're spoiling her rotten. Lady Castlederry's coming to collect us, and we'll be together in the grandstand for the flypast. Jane's a little girl. You go and tell her what she'll put on. It's the kilt or else."

In the end, Jane had the last word. The kilt was too big. It was the "or else" twirly.

————

You couldn't miss it: a beautiful Spitfire airplane flying out of a white cloud with green fields below. The poster had been printed in color, "Courtesy of The Castlederry Estate Office." Paul could see Henry grinding his teeth at that.

The RAF policeman had saluted Lady Castlederry's Rolls-Royce as they'd swept through the gates of the airfield after a simple lunch at The Manor—cold salmon, Paul's warm potato salad with thick dill mayonnaise and chives, a fresh spinach and endive salad, finishing with raspberries and whipped cream. Paul loved hearing her lady-ship's envious swooning to Emma about his cooking.

Ronald, the chauffeur, followed directions to the visitor's car park where Paul unloaded the pushchair, and they made their way to the grandstand.

The sleek, graceful Spitfires were drawn up in a line, wingtip to wingtip, the pilots and crew besieged by visitors. They negotiated a path through clusters of picnickers spread out on tartan rugs enjoying the blessed sunshine. Paul spearheaded their procession. Anyone looking up at him would have seen a tall, fine-looking young Colored man in a blue blazer with a white shirt and red tie, trying to maneuver a pushchair with strapped inside a pretty little four-year-old with blonde curls, arms waving as if she were leading an orchestra. Behind them, treading carefully since she was noticeably on in her second pregnancy, came Emma.

Finally, a colorful pheasant tail bobbed along poking up from a floppy green-felt hat worn by a tall and elegant Olivia in a simple autumn-colored tweed suit. Her ladyship was intrigued by the number of people calling cheerily to the young fellow pushing the little girl ahead of him.

When they arrived at the edge of the landing strip, Olivia Castlederry sought Paul out. "Why, Paul, you have so many friends out there."

"Well, ma'am, these are the folk who make life here a pleasure."

"You know something, Paul?" Olivia hesitated, looking him straight in the eye. "You Americans are much better at making friends than us old stick-in-the-muds. You could give me a lesson one day." She laughed, adding, "Though, I don't think Mrs. Gordon would approve. What do you think?"

What Paul thought was what he said. He looked steadily into Lady Castlederry's eyes, surprisingly speckled with tiny dark flecks scattered on a golden green background. He spoke slowly, gently. "You know, ma'am, I've got more friends here and now than I've ever had before. You wonder why?"

She nodded, lowering her eyes.

"Because these folks don't care a damn about the color of my skin, ma'am."

When she looked at him then it was, he would recall later, as if she were seeing him for the first time. Her eyes were bright with interest.

Reaching out, she touched him on the sleeve. "That, Paul, is all you ever need to teach me."

Time for the show. The dogfight was about to begin. Henry simply looked at his watch, then signaled up at the control tower with a raised arm, setting off the loudspeaker.

A crackly voice echoed across the airfield, "Ladies and gentlemen, welcome to RAF Ballygreen. Would you kindly make your way off the airstrip? Time for the show."

The crowd had met the pilots, seen the Spitfires up close. They wound their way back to seats in the grandstand or the grass verge around the airstrip to watch the action.

———

From his seat in the grandstand, Paul looked across to the airstrip, where the pilots stood at alert beside their Spitfires. He recognized each of them from the dinner. And there was Henry, dashing in white overalls.

Just then, a voice on the loudspeaker blasted out, "Scramble! Scramble!" sending Babe into a fit of wild waving, yelling, "Bye! Bye! Bye! Bye!" as all the pilots climbed into their cockpits.

The engines roared, propellers flashed, spinning in the sun. The sky filled with green flares, signaling each airplane to move from the lineup.

Babe climbed onto Paul's lap, put her arm around his neck, and watched how all the airplanes, in little groups of three, sped along the ground, rose into the air together until they became as small as birds in the sky. The fight began, planes chasing and diving on each other; you could hear shooting, before they zoomed back into view. Not for a minute had the loudspeaker man been quiet. He knew all the turns and twists the airplanes made, calling out their names as they chased each other: barrel roll, wingover, scissors.

Everyone was thrilled at the spectacular display.

"You can see it right there, Olivia. Hitler would be an idiot to tangle with the R-A-F," Emma said, proudly.

Olivia smiled at her as if Emma were an ignorant child. "Emma dear, believe me, Hitler has no argument with us. He's said it a hundred times. The last thing he wanted was a war with Great Britain."

Paul saw it happen then; everyone saw it happen. A Spitfire kept on, and on, and on diving.

The crowd stopped cheering when the announcer called out, "Pull her up, damn it! Pull her up."

Paul watched as the plane fell like a stone from the clear blue sky, smoke and flames billowing as it crashed in a field across from the landing strip nearby. He pulled Jane in close and stood to his feet, holding her in his arms, pressing her head to his chest.

Emma was unconsciously cradling her stomach, eyes wide with terror.

The eleven Spitfires circled and prepared to land.

Emma grabbed Paul's hand. "Tell me when Henry's landed."

There was an awful silence. Two by two, the pilots brought their planes down with the deafening roar of the 1000-horsepower Merlin engines scorching the grass landing strip before coming to a stop in front of the grandstand.

Perry and Curley, Marco and Matt, Ian and Harvey... Ten of them. One more to go.

Emma shut her eyes and squeezed Paul's hand. "Dear God, please make it, Henry. Make it, Henry. Make it, Henry!"

Olivia put an arm around her. "The leader lands last, my dear."

Paul muttered under his breath, "Make it. Make it."

The last airplane came in slowly, gracefully, flaps down, wheels brushing the grass. When it came to a stop in front of the grandstand, the canopy opened. Henry stepped out, ripped off his helmet, and waved to Emma and Paul before joining the others in a huddle.

Babe began to cry. "What's wrong? Paw, what's wrong?"

Paul couldn't answer. He was shaking so hard.

Henry did not come home that night. Paul found out it was Tony Cayzer who had hammered in vain on his glass cage as he burnt alive. In the kitchen he sat with his cigarette and a double whisky.

Emma had gone to bed. He'd spent an hour calming Babe, answering her questions: "Why did the plane fall down? Why did it burn up?"

That poor young boy. Paul had forgiven and forgotten all his nasty comments.

29

On Sunday, September 3, 1939, Henry telephoned Emma to say he would be home in minutes. He asked her to gather everyone in the drawing room to hear the Prime Minister, Mr. Chamberlain, make a radio broadcast at 11:15 A.M.

They were all there with the radio on when the squadron leader arrived just in time to hear the BBC announcer: *"In two minutes, the Prime Minister will broadcast to the nation from the Cabinet Room of Ten Downing Street. Please stand by."*

Blankly, they looked at each other: Henry, holding Emma's hand, Mara, Kathleen, and Babe on Paul's lap.

Mr. Chamberlain's voice broke the silence, *"This morning, the British Ambassador in Berlin handed the German government a final note stating that unless we heard from them by eleven o'clock, that they were prepared at once to withdraw their troops from Poland, a state of war would exist between us. I have to tell you now that no such undertaking has been received, and that consequently, this country is at war with Germany..."*

Henry stood and looked intently at each of them in turn when the broadcast was over. "There it is. We're at war with Germany, as expected. Our marching orders came in this morning. The squadron is expected at RAF Duxford on Monday. In a moment, we'll talk about getting you home."

Paul could not recall ever seeing Henry so determined. Nothing would be allowed to stand in the way of beating the Germans.

Before they left the room, Henry thanked Kathleen and Mara for all they had done to make the family's stay in Ireland comfortable and happy. "We're together in this," was his parting shot to the girls as they headed back to the kitchen.

It took him only a few minutes to lay out the plan ahead. In a week's time, the Mauretania would be leaving Liverpool for New York. That morning, he'd managed to get a suite for Emma, and one for Paul and Jane. They'd arrive in the U.S., and a few days after that, they'd be back in Horse Cave.

Arrangements had been made with the Londonderry Estate Office about The Manor. Emma could expect a call to confirm what she wanted sent home or sold. Nothing had been overlooked. She was surprised by what a relief it was to have all this taken off her shoulders. Jane would be well cared for, Paul would always be there for his Babe.

———

Paul looked out the car window at fields of tobacco and corn growing in rich red Kentucky dirt. The car bumped as they crossed the railroad tracks from the Kingdom into town. He was home.

Emma, in the front seat next to Leroy, was holding onto her almost seven-months-pregnant belly. Jane, in the backseat, was holding Paul's hand.

Paul knew the two old folks would be waiting for them. He wondered if their familiar ways would have changed. Most important of all, in a few minutes, he'd be hugging Lorene.

Walter Jackson sat waiting on the front porch, his spotted blue-and-white bow tie a little tight around the collar of his cream shirt, his dark blue Shantung-silk suit smart under his thick white combed-back hair, his Stetson on his knee. Ready since 6 A.M.

Sally Jackson had pumped her swollen arthritic knees up and down at least ten times that morning, getting in and out of her chair, dressed in her freshly ironed, powder-blue organdy with a lace collar. The old maids from across the street had copied the dress for her from a picture of Eleanor Roosevelt in *Life Magazine*, not that Sally approved of the socialist ways of the President and his wife.

"They're here!"

And with a wide fat roll of the white sidewall tires, there they were. The door slammed. Emma got out first, lumbered up the porch steps.

"Oh, Daddy, I'm here." She ran into his arms.

Sally pushed down on her two canes to raise herself up.

"Is that my little girl hiding behind Paul's leg? Give your grandma a kiss."

Babe pushed her dolly forward.

"You, sugar, not Raggedy Ann."

Jane mashed her face into the back of Paul's leg and held on.

"Paul, I have your little house all fixed up," Miss Sally told him.

Emma's arms did not go all the way around her mother, and her kiss was a light touch on Sally Jackson's cheek. "She may be growing up, but Jane can't sleep without Paul—not yet, Mama. She can't be where Paul can't hear her. Put them upstairs, together."

Lorene was waiting for him, standing in the background. She kept her feelings hidden, but Paul spotted her bright eyes and her trembling lips. The time away had made a difference: lines had sunk into wrinkles. She was fatter and he could hear her breathing.

"'Bout time you got here. Been waiting too long." Almost shyly, she held out her arms.

He spent a good long while holding her solid body close to his heart. "I missed you, Lorene."

She purred, "That's what you say to all the girls. What's that little thing plastered onto your leg?"

"Say hello to Jane. Babe, you give Lorene a great big hug."

A flicker of memory... A sense of safety? Jane handed Raggedy Ann to Paul and put her arms up for a cuddle from this woman she scarcely remembered.

At last, Paul was in the kitchen with the familiar smell of fried chicken and new-cut mint. He watched his cousin put her hands on her hips.

"Let's have a look at you. Handsomer than ever, all dressed up like a fancy Englishman in them gray pants and dark blue jacket. Ain't that a pretty red-and-white tie you got 'round your neck. You look mighty fine to me—too fine for my kitchen."

She winced as she bent down to get a good look at Babe. "Girl, let go of Paul's leg for a minute and come on over here. Why, I could be looking at your daddy. She's like Henry, but blonde like her mama. Come on, Jane, let La La see Raggedy Ann."

Jane shook her head sadly, "Poor Raggedy Ann. She's a dirty dolly."

"Well, I'll just throw her into the machine—she'll come out brand new." Lorene turned back to Paul. "Before I forget, Walter asked Leroy to bring Lily up here later on. Everyone's anxious to see you."

Mid-afternoon, Jane was fast asleep upstairs, under a slow fan, when Lily came into the kitchen with Cousin Leroy.

"Mighty long time, son, too long."

Paul held Lily close. "Never far. I got you in my heart, Mama."

He'd forgotten how tall Lily was, how her smile came with a flash of gold, her high cheekbones and the arches of brow over her black-rimmed eyes. She held him again for a long while.

"Paul, we can't pack all your time away into this visit. You'll be coming over tomorrow afternoon while Jane's asleep. I'm not mad at you for not writing, son. You're just like me. I don't feel like talking 'bout what I did yesterday."

Sitting beside his mother was like being in front of a mirror—

smooth and clear. He tried to look away from the fast, heavy rise and fall of the brooch in the middle of her flowered cotton dress.

"Don't worry about me. Are you all right, Mama? Shingles gone?"

"I'm fine." She lifted one of his hands. "Look at these nails. How in the world do you keep them this long?"

He spread a hand on top of hers. "I try to look after them."

Lily trailed one of her fingers down the white frost on the outside of her glass of iced tea. "Lorene tells me you're raising Jane all by yourself. I'd like to have a look at her."

"Well, people say she walks like me, talks like me, sings like me— and that means she's a whole lot like you, Mama."

Lily took a forkful of Lorene's triple-layer coconut cake. "Watch out they don't get jealous, son."

"What do you mean?"

"Paul, it's our job to do their dirty-baby work. We wipe the soft cheeks, cuddle them, and before you know it, we love those babies, and they love us. Day comes, and it does come, they're going to take them back."

Through the window, he saw Leroy dragging the hose, turning on the sprinklers in the garden. "Mama, she's a Little Miss Copycat. She's my girl, anyone can see that. They don't want her back."

Lily smiled, shook her head. "Son, don't say I didn't warn you."

"I'm going to wake her up. You'll get to meet her."

He wondered why Lily didn't understand his place in the family. There was no letting him go. He woke Jane from her nap, brought her downstairs, rubbing her eyes.

"Babe, say hello to Mama. Last time you saw her, you were a tiny little thing."

"Come over here and let me see you, Jane. Look here, child, I'm cutting you a piece of this cake."

No one asked Babe to put her arms around Lily's neck, but she did. She climbed onto her lap, gave her a long hug, and a kiss on the cheek.

Sally Jackson came out onto the back porch. "Well, look here at my little precious girl on your lap, Lily. No time to give her grand-mama a cuddle? Jane, you come with me right this minute and see the new dolly I have for you. We'll call her Miss Pretty."

Lily smiled, set the child down, told her to go see her grandmother.

That night, Paul tucked in a clean Raggedy Ann alongside a blonde curly-haired, blue-eyed, porcelain-faced dolly bound up in a pink organdy dress. But Jane, holding on tight to her cleaned-up Raggedy Ann, would not allow the new Miss Pretty under her cover.

Emma unpacked her suitcases and set about organizing the house her way for the next two months until the baby was born. She hired Birdie Barlow, another Carew cousin, to come up and do for her and the new baby.

Meanwhile, Paul would have to listen to the damn crickets. He missed the squadron, the shopkeepers, and most of all Henry. Every time he heard the phone ring, he ran to pick it up.

Finally, it was Henry and he ended with, "Paul, take care of your-self. I really miss you. Have you given any more thought to joining us over here?"

Paul thought of nothing else. How could he forget the Air Commodore's words? "Henry, why not ask Paul if he would like to join you over here, as your Batman. Put on the RAF uniform?"

Paul lived on seeing himself joining Henry and the squadron, and "I really miss you." He said it out loud, took it to bed every night, and held on tight, while listening to "Paw-Paw, please, put a stocking on my head. Can't sleep without one. Can I have some of your cream? My face hurts. Put polish on my nails," and so on and so on. But Paul never felt scratchy. He put Elizabeth Arden's eight-hour cream on Jane's face, pink polish on her fingernails, and bought her a stocking to put over her curls when she went to bed. She lay, in Heaven, listening to him read Raggedy Ann.

Before she went to sleep, he tried again. "Let's talk about your new brother or sister."

"Nighty night, Paw-Paw."

Next day, at breakfast, he made up his mind. Babe kept sweeping her plate with toast.

"Let's talk about the new baby," he said, firmly. "Your mama's fixing to bring over your cousin, Virginia, to play with you."

Jane shook her head, and between bites with her mouth full, said solemnly, "I don't want to play with her." She dug her nails into Raggedy Ann and threw her across the kitchen. "No! No brother or sister."

"Jane, you pick up Raggedy Ann right this minute." The lower his voice, the louder she heard it. "Babe, I'm not telling you again. Pick up dolly now."

Jane slowly got down from her chair, picked up Raggedy Ann, and shook her doll as hard as she could. "You're a very bad girl, Raggedy Ann."

30

Paul and Jane had time on their hands. Sally Jackson had an idea. "I'll ask my sister, Ruth, to arrange for you all to take the boat trip through Hidden River Cave."

Every week, when Jane was a baby, Paul had wheeled her buggy downtown to visit Miss Ruth in the Cave office. When tourists came into the office, Ruth liked to tell them proudly, "We have the largest cave entrance in the world. Dr. Thomas, my late beloved husband, bought this cave in eighteen-ninety-five. By nineteen hundred, Horse Cave was all lit up, thanks to my darling Harry putting a hydraulic dam into the underground river. And that's not all."

Paul knew it by heart. She flicked a duster over all the polished rock samples for sale in the cave office. "We have air-conditioned tennis courts down by the entrance."

Paul wasn't looking forward to walking down 250 stone steps to get on a boat and row into a black hole, half a mile down from the sidewalk. If he'd known what was waiting for him, he would have dreaded it even more.

Lorene tried to stop him. "Colored people don't take cave trips, Paul. And, that little thing will be scared to death." Lorene had been simmering ever since Emma came in and told her not to fry the quail but *sauté* it instead. Worse, Emma wanted Paul to show Lorene how to make a mushroom sauce with white wine—no more Kentucky cream gravy. Or as Emma put it, "No greasy southern food."

Lorene's last furious words were, "We're in Kentucky, we cook this kind of food, and just so you know, all the garbage in Hart County drains into that cave, and it's starting to stink up the whole town. Jane will get polio, wait and see."

In the afternoon, Paul picked Babe up after her nap, curls in a tangle, kissed her forehead, washed her face, dressed her in her brand-new pink piqué dress, socks, shoes, and a sweater. He wore a black cotton shirt, and a red-and-white polka-dot Ascot Cravat, a Christmas present from Henry.

They set off to walk downtown. Babe held his hand and pulled on his arm, while skipping over all the cracks in the sidewalk. They strolled down Main Street, past the neon sign outside the Baptist Church.

"What's it say, Paw-Paw?"

"It says, Jesus Saves."

"Who does Jesus save?"

"You and me, Babe."

"Why?"

"Because why. If you're a bad girl, you can ask him to save you."

———

The Hidden River Cave office was smack in the middle of town. Aunt Ruth, a well-padded version of Miss Sally, was waiting for them, and handed Jane a Coca-Cola.

"Paw-Paw wants one too."

"Of course." Aunt Ruth wiped a powdered forehead with a pink chiffon square and handed Paul a bottle.

Jane held onto hers and drank it so fast her eyes watered. She paid no attention to Paul's frown when she made a rude noise at the bottom with the straw. They sat for a while.

"I want you all to say hello to the two boys giving you the tour. You'll be spending the afternoon with them."

Aunt Ruth opened the screen door, called outside, "Terry, Joe, come in here and meet my family. These boys have been with me a while. Best guides we got."

There they were, Terry Weaver, who'd kicked over the geraniums when he was gardening for Miss Sally, and his brother Joe, both dressed in black pants with "Hidden River Cave" written on the back of their white T-shirts. Paul took a moment. They were the same two spindly boys he'd known, with bad skin, greasy hair, and narrow eyes. He remembered Lorene's warning, "Don't ever mess with the Klan. They'll find you if they want you, and when they do want you, it ain't for no good."

Paul made up his mind to pretend he'd never met Terry Weaver.

"Hello, boys," he said, politely, with his new mid-Atlantic voice. He watched their faces as they took in the "boys."

"Jane, put out your hand, say hello."

Babe put out her hand the way Paul had taught her. "Hello, boys," she echoed.

Aunt Ruth must have smelled some trouble. "Terry, Joe, you all give my family a royal tour. I want them to enjoy every minute of Hidden River Cave. They've just come home from Europe."

"Yes, ma'am."

The boys looked at Paul, none too friendly, while Aunt Ruth ordered the two of them outside to sit awhile. She wanted to tell Jane a story before the visit. Aunt Ruth was a little like Lorene, carrying a bag of tall tales around her neck, weighing her down until she got them told.

"Jane, did you walk down here on the sidewalk?"

Babe nodded her head, sucking the Popsicle Aunt Ruth had just given her, orange juice dripping down her chin.

"Honey, I bet you didn't know, under that sidewalk you got great big sinkholes. In bed, you're sleeping over miles of tunnels in the ground. I bet you never heard of Floyd Collins?"

Jane shook her head, sat on the edge of her chair, waiting. "No."

"No? I'm going to tell you a true story." Aunt Ruth scooted her chair closer to Babe's. "Floyd Collins, a poor farm boy, lived in Horse Cave, on the edge of town. One morning, it was winter, a cold fine rain was falling. Floyd went out walking and stumbled on a big sinkhole. He got down on all fours, wiggled in a little way, and saw a tunnel. He'd been looking for a connection to our caves. Find them and his family would be rich.

"He hurried back to the house, fetched a lamp, and began to explore the tunnel. He slowly pulled himself along an underground passage, through mud and slime. He went further and further. Suddenly, his flashlight went out. A shower of gravel rained down on top of him, kicked up a big old rock, came tumbling down, and broke his foot. Floyd was in the dark, with water drip, drip, dripping on his face. His leg, pinned under the rock, was throbbing. He lay there, hour after hour, day after day—and night after night."

Ms. Ruth fluffed the top of her white ruffled blouse, paused to observe the effect of her story.

Jane was quiet, Paul wide-eyed.

"Rescuers were working round-the-clock. The passages all around him were closed with the heavy fallen rocks. Only way to get him out, if they reached him, would be to cut off his leg. They were almost there, when, at the last minute, the rescue shaft fell through. By that time, the radio had taken the story around the world and twenty thousand tourists poured into Horse Cave and gathered to hear Floyd's last weak words." Aunt Ruth took a sip of Coca-Cola.

"That was that. He was just a poor farmer looking for a new cave. Time they finished with the story, the rock weighed two tons and Floyd was a hero."

"Did he die?" Jane was taking Aunt Ruth's story in.

"Honey, what do you think? He died as if someone had put a pillow over his face."

"Where did he go?"

"Don't know, sugar. Wherever the finger was pointing for him." She called in the guides, waved them off. "You all have a good time going through the cave."

They followed the two boys. At the top, Paul felt safe; the sweet sidewalk, trees, leaves, burning bright in the hot sun.

"Paw-Paw, I'm scared. I don't want to die."

Paul stopped to smooth her hair and give her a hug. "I'm here. Nothing is going to happen to you."

They started down the 250 stone steps. Halfway, Babe got stubborn, taking one slow slippery step at a time. "I don't want to do it."

"No, come on now, put your arms out." Paul picked her up, with her arms tight around his neck, her hot cheek next to his. He carried her into a dripping, cool bowl of limestone. He slipped, caught himself, grabbed the iron railing with his free hand, and when he looked up, saw the circle of light getting smaller and smaller. Water beaded onto ferns, dripping from cold rock. The bottom was a big black hole, cut out of the stone. A rowboat lay waiting in a dark pool.

"Here we are, folks—entrance to Hidden River Cave. All aboard."

The boys had been told to give them a full guided tour. Terry sat in the front of the boat, Joe rowed, and both of them had their flashlights ready. Paul and Babe sat in the middle, waiting as a swish of oars slid them into the cave.

All Paul could think of was, *Hell's down, Heaven's up, and right here's in between.*

They entered an enormous cavern, cold, damp, dark, quiet as a church. Terry turned on his flashlight. "See them things hanging from the ceiling like icicles?" Terry's voice echoed as his flashlight picked out horns—yellow, pink, and purple—twisting down from the ceiling. "Them's stalactites, growing from the top; from the bottom, stalagmites. We ain't got none coming up from below, 'cause we're on water."

Joe rowed on.

Paul wished he'd slow down. Sure enough, after a while he

stopped, and Terry shone a beam into a clear pool of water, lighting up tiny pink and white fish. You could almost see through them as they chased each other in circles.

"Here we have Hidden River Cave's eyeless fish. See them bumps? That's where their eyes should be. They don't see, don't need to 'cause they live in the dark. Lot of people live in the dark, they still got eyes."

That seemed to tickle them.

Joe said, "Darkies—they got eyes, do they live in the dark?"

They laughed.

Paul felt cold and shivered. Babe climbed onto his lap, and he felt her arms tight around his waist.

In the dim light, red pimples stood out on Terry Weaver's face. "Joe, you think about it—these fish are color blind, get it, color blind."

Joe whooped. "You're right, Terry, they must be; not everybody is. We're not."

Suddenly, both flashlights went out, they were cast into pitch black. The little boat began to rock. Sounds of laughter came from the boys.

Paul felt himself losing balance. Afterwards, he swore on his memory, he'd felt a push from Terry Weaver.

Where would that leave Babe?

Paul heard his own voice strike fury out of the wet dark rock, "Turn the lights on! Right this minute."

Babe took her thumb out of her mouth and shouted, "Paw says turn on those lights."

Inside the dark cave, came echoes, one after the other: "Turn on the lights turn on the lights turn on the lights."

The two boys could smell Paul's anger. It didn't take a second for them to get their lights on. "We always do this," one of them said. "People liked to get scared—it's part of our tour."

But after that, they stayed quiet, knowing they'd gone too far, and rowed the boat back, gently.

Eyes blinking in the light, Paul and Babe got out, almost running up the steps into summer heat. Aunt Ruth was waiting for them in her house, right next to the cave office, in her sitting room full of antiques. She gave Jane a Snickers bar, asked her how she enjoyed the cave.

"Thank you very much, Aunt Ruth," Babe answered, politely.

Aunt Ruth handed them each a silver cup of freshly made lemonade. "You're welcome, Jane. Funny, those eyeless fish. Nature switches off what she doesn't need—dark all day, all night. Maybe they're extra sensitive in other ways. Feeling, not seeing. By the way, how were your guides?"

Paul put in quickly, "We got your Royal Tour."

Babe looked at Paul. She knew when to keep her mouth shut.

They said goodbye, Babe kissed Aunt Ruth, and they set off. On their way back, Mr. Dorsey was closing his drugstore and Sue-Lou Dunagan was staring out the front window of the Bee Lovely Beauty Salon.

As they passed the neon sign: Jesus Saves, Baptist Church. Babe piped up, "Why couldn't Jesus save poor Floyd Collins?"

"Because he couldn't see him way down deep in that dark, dark cave."

Paul couldn't stop thinking about those little pink and white blind fish and how things turn out for some, having to live forever in a deep black hole.

———

Miss Birdie Barlow, a fully qualified registered nurse with a degree from Bowling Green, sashayed into the kitchen, put her suitcase down, pulled out her hat pin, and took off her hat. Her hair stuck out in neat plaits all over her head, and she was dressed from head to toe in medical white.

Paul remembered what Elijah said about the Barlows. "Just

because those children got educated, doesn't mean they have to go round with their noses in the air."

"Put this in my room, next to the baby's." Birdie Barlow pointed to her bag and ordered Leroy, who was gnawing on a leg of fried chicken at the kitchen table.

Lorene, rolling out biscuit dough, cocked her head and put her hand on her hips. "Looka here, Miss High-and-Mighty Barlow. Leroy's your cousin. Last time I looked he ain't the porter. Pick up your own suitcase. I'll show you to your room."

Birdie settled in. She, Paul, Leroy, and Lorene gathered around the kitchen table, Lorene at the head, waiting every day for Baby John to arrive. When he finally arrived, he came on time, slipped out easily, and looked adoringly into his mother's eyes.

Later, after she recovered, Emma carried John Lindsey Gordon around the house as if he were a golden trophy. "Look at his little hands. See how happy he is in my arms. Hardly ever fusses or cries."

Miss Sally cooed, "Look at Grandmama's beautiful precious baby boy."

In the kitchen, Lorene whipped cream. "Ain't never seen a tiny baby as pretty as he is."

"I have," Paul said, waggling his spoon at Jane.

Jane stuck her thumbs in her ears and wiggled her fingers at Lorene.

Lorene muttered under her breath, "He's happy 'cause Emma offered a little of what God gave her to feed him."

Emma cradled him in her arms and nursed her newborn.

Sally Jackson was sure she'd never seen her daughter so content.

Birdie swept through the house, laying down the rules. Everyone had to wash their hands in hot water before they touched the baby. Every diaper had to be boiled and ironed with a hot iron. Every window was closed tight, to keep away germs.

When Jane asked if she could play with the baby, Birdie answered, "Babies don't play. They're not dolls."

Jane kept away, stood watching from a distance while the grown-ups fed and cuddled this new little person.

When Birdie crossed the line from carpet to linoleum, she knew better than to mess. She looked forward to meals around the kitchen table. Lorene and Paul filled platters with the most delicious food Birdie had ever tasted.

"How can Jane love the baby if she can't touch him or play with him?" Lorene held her spoon in the air.

Birdie held out her plate for a second helping of chicken and dumplings. "Baby's too little for her kind of love."

Paul took his time pouring tea over cracking ice and looked straight into Birdie's eyes. "What happened to babies in your house, Birdie?"

Birdie looked down at her plate and waited a few moments. "Abe came first, then me, and five years later everyone got excited when little Jewel was born."

Lorene served Birdie an extra spoon of gravy, took off her apron, and took a seat. "Ain't never heard tell of a Jewel Barlow."

"Let me tell you all." Birdie sighed and put down her knife and fork. "Jewel was six months old when she took a high fever. Everyone was beside themselves with worry. She'd been sick for a few days, and it was my turn to mind her when Mama went to the store." Birdie picked up her glass and took a long drink of the sweet, iced tea. "When she came back from the store, I was playing out on the porch. I'd only left the baby for a few minutes. She threw down her shopping, ran in to get her, and carried poor baby Jewel in her arms, ran out, screaming, 'I told you to mind her. You killed her, Birdie.' I never got over it. That's why I studied nursing and made up my mind to save every baby I could in this here world." There were tears in Birdie's eyes.

———

The only time Babe was quiet was when she was reading books. All during the day, Paul heard her calling, "Look at me, Paw-Paw," when she was skipping rope or riding her tricycle.

When she wasn't playing, and Paul was busy in the kitchen, she'd gotten into the habit of standing outside Baby John's closed door, holding on to Raggedy Ann while the grown-ups chattered on the front porch.

Birdie noticed. "Something's wrong. She's got a funny look on her face. Better keep an eye on her."

One afternoon, everyone was asleep. Paul was out in the garden raking leaves. He looked over at Babe's empty sandbox. Uneasy, he hadn't seen her go back into the house. He ran through the kitchen, into the hall where he found the baby's door open. He rushed inside. Jane was holding the pillow down over the baby's face.

Paul pushed her aside and picked up John struggling for breath. The baby began yelling at the top of his lungs.

Jane stood stone-still, holding her dolly.

They all flew in from the front porch—Miss Sally, Birdie, Emma, and Mr. Walter.

"What in the world?" Emma grabbed the baby.

Paul thought quickly. "It's not her fault," he said. "Jane was only playing. He must've gotten scared when she showed him Raggedy Ann."

With the baby's terrible screams, no one believed him.

Jane stayed quiet and watched them all carry on, holding, kissing, cuddling, and soothing, until the baby was cooing.

Paul took Babe upstairs, sat her down and told her good and hard, "Sit and think about what you've done. That poor tiny baby might have died."

She shook her head, whipped her curls as hard as she could. She looked at Paul, her bottom lip wobbling. "Dead, like Floyd Collins?"

Then Paul remembered Miss Ruth's words: "Snuffed out, as if someone had put a pillow on Floyd's face."

"Aunt Ruth didn't mean for you to go around putting pillows over people's faces. Say after me, Babe: 'I'm sorry I tried to hurt my baby brother. I'm ashamed of myself.'"

She replied, "I'm sorry I tried to kill my little brother, but maybe Jesus will save me anyway."

31

Eight months they'd been there, and Paul was getting tired of Horse Cave, Emma, Birdie, and the sick baby. They all lived in their private circle.

Every day, Dr. Jimmy Burks knocked on the door. He came in for coffee and slice of whatever cake was being served, took out his stethoscope, and checked the baby's heart. He prodded tiny swollen ankles, then left with a worried look on his face.

Emma showed the good sense not to bring Paul into it. He'd never told her about Jane, John, and the pillow incident. He didn't need to; she'd felt the danger coming from her daughter.

Birdie came prancing into the kitchen with her "good news." William Dorsey, assistant treasurer at Mr. Walter Jackson's tobacco plant, was going to drive her "royal lowness" (which is what Paul called Birdie) with Emma and Baby John to Boston for a few days of tests at Boston General Hospital, "staying in fancy hotels on the way," Birdie boasted.

Lorene stood, hands on her hips. "People in those hotels will put you in with the help. When you get back here, that stuck-up nose on your little face will get mashed in so fast you'll never see it in the mirror again. Back to the Kingdom where you belong, no one's ever going to hear about you, Miss Priss, or your trip to Boston."

Birdie turned on her heels, flashed back, "Well, that's just how much you all know about it."

———

One evening, Mr. Walter asked Paul to see him in his office. "Remember Billy Thurlow, my manager at the plant?"

Paul did, because he was Lily's cousin.

"His boy, Willie, joined the Army last year. Now he's back telling big tales about how badly he was treated, pushed down and put down, cleaning latrines day after day. So bad he was trying to get discharged, even dishonorably. What would happen if we go to war and you get drafted? We'll have to find a way, Paul, to keep you safe."

Back in the kitchen, any idea of being in the American Army made Paul feel sick and worried. He'd seen pictures—how you got your head shaved, the baggy uniforms the men wore. They made you look like you were in jail. An American Army made up of the likes of Terry and Joe Weaver.

The day before Emma left, she invited Paul to drive out and pick up some buttermilk from Straker's dairy. "Paul," she said, staring straight ahead at the road, "war is coming. The Flight Lieutenant agrees with my father. You'll be drafted into the army. So, he wanted me to tell you that and something else."

Paul looked out the window, closed his eyes, waiting.

Emma went on, "'Tell Paul I have a place for him in the RAF. We need him.' Those were his words, but he will call you himself later this afternoon." Emma turned off the main road and drove along the tree-lined avenue into the dairy.

"What about Jane?" Paul asked.

"Don't worry about Jane. She'll be six years old soon. Mother, Daddy, Lorene, and all the other help will be there to look after her."

Paul murmured under his breath, "They're not me."

Henry called that evening. "Paul, what do you think? There is a place for you here, with me and the squadron. Mind you, it's not without danger."

Paul knew there was only one answer. He was afraid. At the same time, he'd left some of his best memories with Henry and his squadron in Ireland. *Dammit, Paul*, he thought, *here goes*. "Yes, sir, I'd be proud to wear the uniform."

"Good show. You will have another month in Horse Cave and then I'll arrange for you to take a military plane from Washington. You'll be met in London and go through the medical induction. After that, it will be RAF Padmore for basic training. No worries there. I almost forgot to tell you, once you're an aircraftman, the Air Commodore has arranged for you to be my batman. That means you will be looking after me, and in your spare time working in the officers' mess."

After Paul hung up, Babe came running.

"Who are you talking to, Paw-Paw?"

"Talking to your daddy."

"Come on, let's sing our songs, dance, and play movie stars."

"You're a little dickens, Babe."

He had time. A whole month. He'd try not to think about war. He knew he should have been more frightened than he was. They needed him. Hadn't Henry said so?

———

Emma came back from Boston General Hospital and Johns Hopkins. No one was smiling. The cruel diagnosis of Baby John's illness came with the first flakes of a rare Horse Cave snow, now shimmying down outside the kitchen window. Icy weather, terrible news.

Paul, Birdie, and Lorene sat sadly around the kitchen table drinking their coffee. Miss Sally had delivered the bad news last night before supper. Emma was too distressed.

"John's a mighty sick baby." She reached up with her purple

chiffon handkerchief and dabbed her eyes. "Lorene, you remember my cousin, Ada Burkes, came to visit last year, one who married the famous heart doctor from New York, now lives near Tampa, Florida? They're finding Emma a house next door to them, so they can keep an eye on her and the baby. She'll take Birdie with her."

The nurse nodded to Lorene a silent "I told you so."

"What about Jane?" Paul wondered aloud.

"Jane's staying right here, where she belongs." Miss Sally was sure of that.

Babe moved closer to Paul. "With Paw-Paw."

No one would contradict her.

Outside the kitchen, a cold wind blew through the poplar trees and ruffled the feathers of the rooster with his chickens, sending them scurrying back into the henhouse.

Emma put her foot down. "Don't let me catch anyone in this house with gloomy faces. My baby will get better."

After that, no one talked about dying but Mr. Walter put down his knife and fork before he had finished his pancakes, and Mrs. Sally said no to Lorene's ice cream and coconut cake. Emma lived on black coffee and cigarettes. Miss Sally, said in a happy voice, that she was sure all those oranges from Florida would soon make him better.

In the kitchen, Lorene banged her rolling pin on the counter. "Shut your mouth, Birdie Barlow. Not one more word about the baby. Just get on and look after him."

Jane had bad dreams. "Paw-Paw, I don't want Baby John to die. The bogeyman will come and get me."

"No such thing as a bogeyman. Babe, come on, let's quit this."

That evening, Jane watched Lorene whip potatoes. No one could whip like Lorene. She didn't stop until she had a creamy white fluff of butter and hot milk.

Paul was stripping silky threads from newly picked ears of corn.

"Have a taste, honey." Lorene passed the almost empty bowl to Babe who stuck in her finger and licked the rest clean.

Paul could not imagine saying goodbye to his Babe.

She jumped up and ran to put her arms around his legs. "We'll have fun here, Paw-Paw."

He smoothed her hair. "You bet we'll have fun." After all, he had a whole month before leaving. There was plenty of time.

Soon after breakfast, Miss Sally insisted on taking Emma and Babe to the hairdresser in Glasgow. Elsie Pence, wife of the mayor of Glasgow, had a hairdressing salon that was the center of gossip in the county.

"Paw-Paw, I don't want to go," Babe pleaded.

"Go on, Babe, just don't let Elsie put your hair in pin curls. Remember how it looked the last time."

Permanents took all day. Lunch would be tuna fish sandwiches under the dryer. Miss Sally and Emma ruled; they were swept into the salon as if they were Royals. Babe was fawned over and sat with a Coca-Cola and comic books to wait her turn.

Paul looked forward to a day on his own. He'd left Birdie with Baby John and Lorene in the kitchen. On his way out to water plants on the front porch, he saw Emma's bedroom door was open, her bed unmade. He went inside, surprised to see her makeup strewn across her dressing table, pots without their lids. She must have been in a hurry.

He went over, pulled out her stool and sat down. He picked up her ostrich feather powder puff, still full of powder, dabbed a little on his nose. He giggled out loud, not quite the right color. He smiled at himself, then filled in his lips with a pink Elizabeth Arden lipstick, spat into the black mascara, and tried brushing it up his long eyelashes.

"What are you doing?"

The voice froze him to his stool.

In the mirror stood Birdie Barlow. He'd been sure she was in the kitchen feeding the baby.

"You think Mrs. Gordon would like to see you using her make-up?" she said it in a low, sneaky voice.

Paul pulled out a Kleenex and tried to wipe his face, stood, turned, and looked fiercely at Birdie. "Don't think for a minute Mrs. Gordon would appreciate you telling a lie about me. Go on, try. You might find yourself out of a job. Who do you think means more to this family, you or me?"

With that, Paul took the watering can he'd left on the floor and handed it to her. "Why don't you take this out to the front porch?" He could tell from the way Birdie lowered her chin, she had understood him perfectly.

For a moment, he told himself that was the end of it. *Was it?* He stood outside Emma's door and wished he could kick Birdie's fat ass all the way back to the Kingdom. Would she really keep her mouth shut? After all, she was Emma's pet. And did he really believe Emma and Henry would not mind him putting on makeup, dressing like a girl? In the kitchen, Birdie gave him a sly, sidelong glance as she gave Baby John his bottle.

How could someone like him feel safe or be sure of anything?

———

That evening, Paul was checking on his wobbly cheese soufflé. He'd give it ten more minutes to turn golden-brown, cracked on top. The phone rang and he ran to answer. Emma was there before him. He heard her give Henry the doctor's verdict about Baby John.

"Nephritis, the doctor gives him a year, maybe two. 'Spend time with him in a warm climate,' the doctor advised. He said, 'That's all we can do for you.'"

Paul imagined Henry shaking his head. He didn't need bad news, couldn't handle it at the moment. Paul had seen how he reacted to his daughter in Ireland. He was getting ready for war. Nothing else mattered. Henry could fly his plane through stars, find his way up, up, almost touch the moon... But when it came to a woman's worried heart, he'd lost the map.

Paul tiptoed away from the sound of Emma's flat voice.

"It's all right for you to say, 'Don't cry, darling, everything will be all right.' Damned well won't be!"

Paul tried to sidestep all this, to concentrate on his last weeks with Babe. He had work to do looking after his little girl.

"There's not a whole lot for Jane to do in Horse Cave, Kentucky." Lorene was pulling turnip greens, stuffing them into a great big black pot with a ham hock. "Why don't we call Jane's cousin, Virginia? She could come over and play."

Jane shook her head. "No, I want to play with Paw-Paw."

Lorene was full of ideas. "Old Man Brandstetter has gone and put himself a pet shop in the back of his hardware store."

Babe instantly raised her voice. "I want a pet!"

Birdie, sterilizing baby bottles, sniffed. "You ain't bringing no pets into this house with a sick baby."

Lorene turned, put her hands on her hips, and flew at Birdie. "Better shut your mouth. You ain't got nothing to say one way or another."

———

Paul and Jane set off to go downtown and visit the pet shop that afternoon.

"If I miss all the cracks in the sidewalk, what'll you give me?"

Paul knew this bargain by heart. On the way downtown, he held her hand as she skipped every crack before they reached the Jesus Saves sign at the Baptist Church. Her prize was a package of bubblegum.

Mr. Brandstetter was a short, plump, bald man in his forties with a gray beard.

Babe whispered to Paul, "Mr. Upside-down Face."

"We ain't got many pets yet. Supply and demand. I got pictures. You can choose. Right now, we only got smaller ones." He proudly showed them a corner in the back of his shop. A canary was sitting silently on its perch. Hamsters were scurrying back and forth in a cage.

They stopped in front of a small glass box. "Look at this, Paw-Paw." A chartreuse chameleon was sitting on a green leaf, eyes like shining raindrops.

Paul lifted the lid. There he was, green as a frog on a lily pad. "Mr. Brandstetter, do you mind if we pick him up?"

"Go ahead. Put him on your shirt, he'll turn the color of anything you're wearing."

Paul put the chameleon onto his red shirt. It took tiny, deep, swelling dragon puffs, and slowly turned cranberry-colored.

"We'll take him. What do we give him to eat?"

"You all can have fun feeding him tiny little balls of hamburger meat. A few worms... Crickets if you can catch them. Tell Lorene they love raw turnip greens, kale, and lettuce."

Jane insisted on carrying the little glass case all the way back. When they got home, they fixed the creature a leash, a fine thread around his neck, and he crawled from Paul's hands onto Jane's yellow sweater, gave up his green, inhaled, and turned yellow. After a while, they could hardly find him.

They called him Camey. Lorene loved him, liked to cut up vegetables to feed him. Miss Sally put him on her purple dress and watched him huff, puff, and turn purple. Mr. Walter tried putting the little lizard on a striped tie. Camey got confused and remained green. Birdie was the only one who screamed every time she saw him.

"Paw-Paw, why does he turn red on red, or yellow on yellow?"

"That's how they hide, Babe, keeps anything from killing or eating him."

She looked up into his eyes. "Why can't we do that, Paw-Paw?"

"Wish we could, Babe, but we got to make do with the color we were given. If you're a chameleon, color don't matter."

She rested her head against his chest. "Look at me, Paw-Paw, sitting on your lap. Am I turning brown? I wish I could."

That did it. They both giggled.

———

Together they fed Camey freckled lumps of meatballs and watched his tiny tongue stab for more. Every day they found new colors for him to turn, kept him busy, loved him more. He never disappointed them.

At night, upstairs in his room next to Babe's, Paul tucked Camey into his striped pajama pocket and slept on his back.

Next morning, tree branches scratched at his dark windows. He heard Lorene's voice calling, "Paul, where are you?"

Oh, God, he'd overslept. He threw on his clothes and rushed to Babe's room. "I'm late, come on, Babe. Get up, up, up."

He didn't have time to help her get dressed. He hurried down to the kitchen and got busy helping Lorene cut grapefruit.

Jane, at his heels, sat down at the kitchen table, hair in tangles and dress on backward, beating out "Jumpin' at the Woodside."

"Give me a ride, Paw-Paw!"

He put her finger on his Adam's apple, swallowing, "Going down, first floor!" To her squeals and giggles, he turned back to making scrambled eggs and told her to be quiet until breakfast was over.

"Paw, where's Camey?"

Paul had forgotten all about their little chameleon. He ran to his bedroom, leaping up the stairs two at a time. His striped pajamas? Gone.

In the basement laundry room, in front of the wringer, legs apart, cigarette hanging from the side of her mouth, Birdie pulled at flattened layers of mangled clothes.

"Stop!"

She looked up, heavy pouches under her eyes. "I went upstairs to pick up you all's laundry. Only had a few baby clothes for that big machine. Miss Sally told me to always fill up the clothes washer. Ain't my fault."

She held Paul's pajama top; a stain flowered over one pocket.

"You've killed our pet, our beautiful boy."

Babe sat on the basement stairs waiting, mouth open. "What's happened? Where is he? Is he dead?" Then, "Don't cry, Paw-Paw. Don't cry."

They hugged each other and cried together.

After telling Lorene the news, Paul cut out his pajama pocket, found a box, and got a ribbon. Out in the garden, they dug a hole in the soft earth.

"Let's sing to him, Paw—he's on his way to Jesus."

"Might take more than that to get him to Jesus." Paul took Babe back indoors, put a marshmallow in her hot chocolate.

An accident? They couldn't help blaming Birdie.

"Paul," Birdie huffed, when no one spoke to her in the kitchen. "It was only a little lizard. I didn't mean it."

It was too late. Behind her back, Babe and Paul stuck together. "Paw, she killed him. We'll hate her forever!"

Poor little Camey, always turning colors, trying to be something he wasn't, trying to fit in and disappear. When Paul had calmed down a little, he thought about Birdie doing her best to look after John. He felt sorry he'd been so rough on her. When she came into the kitchen for lunch, he put his arm around her shoulders. "Don't worry, Birdie. Wasn't your fault."

She had tears in her eyes. "I don't like lizards, they scare me, but I wouldn't kill a living soul. I'm sorry."

"We were too hard on you." He looked over at Babe. "Jane's sorry too."

Babe nodded when she saw tears running down Birdie's face. "Don't cry, Birdie. We're not mad at you." She ran over and gave Birdie a hug.

That evening, as Paul rubbed butter, pepper, garlic, raw onion into the T-bone steaks, he asked Babe, "Ever see Camey turn white when he was sitting on you?"

"No, Paw-Paw, never did."

He guessed he'd been a little careless leaving Camey in his

pocket; he looked down at Babe, thinking he'd make sure to take better care of her. But how could he do that, now that he was leaving?

32

That morning, they all tiptoed around Emma's mood. Her suitcases were almost ready for the trip to Florida. She had enough on her mind without this news.

In the kitchen, Paul found that for a joke, Babe had dressed herself back to front, in her dark blue dress with white daisies. She held onto him.

"If you go, Paw-Paw, I'm coming too."

"Not this time, Babe."

Outside the window there were new green leaves on the large sycamore. Paul untangled Babe from his leg.

"I'll be back to put you to bed."

"Promise?"

"Promise."

He crossed the railroad tracks into the Kingdom. A fine spring rain spattered red mud along the unpaved road to their shack. Paul buttoned up his raincoat. He was living in two worlds, one rich, one poor. He would remember this sight, he decided, and think about it when he was overseas.

Saying goodbye to his family this time was like going to his own funeral. He felt Lily's bones through her thin gray cotton dress as he hugged her. Tabby and Tallulah kept on and on.

"Why are you leaving us again?"

"Yes, why are you?" James and Ernest echoed.

Coralee came over, and when he hugged her, said sadly, "Another dead boy."

He tried to cheer them up. "I'll be back. I'm not running into danger. You can be sure of that."

They were not sure of that.

After a long visit, on his way back across the tracks, Blessing caught up with him.

"Paul, stay safe. Nothing's going to happen to you. I feel it in my bones." She hugged him and ran off, trying not to get too wet and late for business. The rain was getting heavier. He stood looking over at the bushes where he, Moses, and Blessing hid all those years earlier.

————

After lunch the next day, he read Jane her favorite *Peter Rabbit* book then told her, "Babe, I have something to tell you. Let's walk over to the Methodist church."

"No," she said, angrily. "Let's go downtown and get me a Popsicle."

He didn't argue.

She got dressed up in her fancy Sunday School dress.

He tried to stop her. "That's for Sunday."

"NO."

They set off. When they reached the Jesus Saves Baptist Church sign, he decided it was time. "Babe, do you remember in one of your *Babar* books when the elephants went to war? Well, Germans are bad people, and they want to kill us. I have to go away for a while, join your daddy in England, to make sure they don't come over here, get anywhere near you."

Jane shook her head, looking up at him, her face crumpling. She began to cry and plead with him, "No, no, no, you can't do that! Go away? Pretty, pretty please. No, no, no, Paw-Paw. Babar's not real. He's an elephant. You're my everything. You can't leave me. I'll give you anything. I'll be a good little girl. Please, please, don't go. I won't let you go. I'll die without you."

Afterwards, he had to carry her home, put her into bed, sit with her while the heavy sobs turned to jerking hiccups. On the pillow, her tangled curls were soaking wet.

"I'll be back before you miss me, Babe." He tried singing all the songs he knew, all night long—looking into her blue eyes that stayed wide open way past dawn.

Finally, there were no more tears.

They gathered outside on the front porch, Jane, Miss Sally, Mr. Walter, and Lorene, to see Paul off.

"You got a mighty big trip ahead of you, son." Walter was close to tears.

Jane stood, unmoving, like a rock.

Paul lifted her up, rubbed his cheek on hers. "It won't be long, Babe. Don't forget, you're my girl," he said tenderly, and handed her back to Miss Sally.

Miss Sally took Jane's hand and tucked straggly strands of hair behind her ears. "Now Paul has gone to look after Daddy and beat the Germans. Mummy's gone to look after baby brother, and you're going to live here in Horse Cave with your Grandmama and Grandpapa."

Paul rolled down his window and waved until they were out of sight. This was for Jane's own good. One day she would understand, he had no choice.

His war would end years later. Hers had just begun.

33

On the front porch, Grandmama tried to roll Jane up, gathering her close to her cotton dress, smothering her in the sweet smell of lily of the valley. She called her "sugah" and told her she'd be her very own baby.

But Babe remembered that song Paul sang: "I'm Nobody's Baby." Pulled close to old, perfumed, powdered skin, she found her Grandmama's necklace, twirled each pearl between her fingers, tried to cry, and wished she could.

Miss Sally asked Lorene to bring Jane a cup of shaved ice and a cold *Coca-tingle-nosed-Cola.* "My little precious can have anything she wants. Let's see you smile." That included cinnamon Red Hots, bubble gum, and popsicles.

Lorene was waiting for her in the kitchen. Jane started to cry. She put her arms around Lorene, her face against the starched apron.

Lorene undid her hands. "I'll go upstairs, pack all your things, and bring them down here. You get to sleep in the front bedroom with your own bathroom, girl, and don't you let me catch you making a mess in here."

A giant four-poster bed stood in the middle of her new room, with a faded quilt on top of a white bedspread. Heavy yellow-brocade curtains were pulled across long French windows leading out to the garden. Jane watched Lorene hang up her dresses in the dark polished-wood wardrobe and fold the rest of her clothes into a large chest of drawers.

"You have a grown-up bedroom. Better act like a grown-up girl, hear me?"

That was the beginning of life in Horse Cave without Paul. Lorene, though Paul's first cousin, wasn't like him, singing while he worked—she never sang. Paul always said she had no rustle in her bustle and didn't know how to shake it. She was grumpy. Maybe the idea of working there without Paul put her in a bad mood, more for her to do.

In the kitchen, slamming cupboards and banging skillets, Lorene said, "We're always the ones to pay, Colored blood will run." She'd heard from Mr. Walter it wouldn't be long before America went to war. "Negroes in the American Army are treated like dirt," she said. "Even lower than hillbillies."

"And what about Paul, Lorene?"

"Paul ain't in the American Army. He's gone to England."

Lorene wore her apron all the time. She was never not busy. She baked, made cobblers, chicken potpies, and one day that gave Jane an idea. She was over by the hollyhocks, mixing dirt and water, making mud pies, looking for ways to feel good in the hot sun, patting her mixture into play baking-set dishes. She pulled flowers from her Grandmama's plants and was sticking different colored petals on top of the mixture when she hit on an idea. She waited for Lorene to go to her bathroom out back in Paul's little house. Once Jane asked her why she couldn't go to the bathroom in the house, she put two fingers up, pinched her nose and said, "'Cause I can't stand the smell."

Jane ran into the kitchen and slid her pies on the top shelf of the oven. She hadn't noticed, and she'd filled her mud pies too full.

Lorene had put her corn pudding, fried chicken, and cherry cobbler on the rack underneath.

Smoke poured out of the oven, just before Lorene rushed into the kitchen. "What are you doing in here? What's this awful smell?" She yanked open the oven door. "What the hell is this?"

She pulled out Jane's pots, now dripping dirt all over her fried chicken, corn pudding, and cherry cobbler. "I'll whoop your little ass, you spoiled brat. The shit I have to put up with. Don't you stand there with your bare face hanging out."

Lorene took the dirty, smoking lunch out to the chickens.

Jane followed. "I'm sorry, Lorene. I didn't mean it."

Lorene threw spoonfuls of spoiled corn pudding at the chickens. "Everything was fine. Now I'm losing my mind because you're driving me crazy."

Jane, red-faced, stuck out her tongue at Lorene. "You're driving me crazy too. I hate you."

Miss Sally opened the back kitchen door. "What's going on out there?"

Before Lorene could say a word, Jane confessed. "Lorene's mad 'cause I put my mud pies on top of our lunch."

Miss Sally shook her head and went back to the front porch to wait for whatever was coming.

Back in the kitchen, Lorene opened tins of tuna fish, sighing, "If only Paul were here."

Jane ran to lie on her bed and read her *Raggedy Ann* books.

After a while, Lorene came in, and said in a softer voice, "Old folks waiting for you. Come eat your lunch. Tuna fish sandwiches, ain't the end of the world."

———

Jane's feelings were bruised. She stayed away from Lorene and spent more time with Grandma, Grandpa, as she now called them, listening to the radio. President Roosevelt and commentators,

Edward R. Murrow and H.V. Kaltenborn, talked about war, more war, men dying.

Jane sucked on candy canes and spent hours in her room reading *Raggedy Ann, The Tale of Peter Rabbit,* and other stories by Beatrix Potter. She found a way to get right out of herself and inside those pages. She went to live with Peter, Jeremy Fisher, Mrs. Tiggy-Winkle, talked to them all the time, drank chamomile tea like Peter did, and felt she belonged inside their world—especially since she didn't like her own. She'd hoped Lorene would get used to her. She wanted to be in the kitchen all the time because Lorene was a Carew and that was the closest Jane could get to Paul.

On her way out to the porch, she heard an announcer on the radio, "Now the Andrews Sisters singing the all-time hit of this war, 'Beat Me Daddy, Eight to the Bar.'" Jane knew those words by heart. She stopped right where she was and went crazy, danced her head off, boogie-woogie. She was back with him—and knew that nothing, nobody could ever keep her away from Paul.

Grandpa switched off the radio, saying, "Too much racket."

Jane listened at the door.

"Walter, what's got into Lorene? She's mean to Jane."

Hard to believe that her grandpa answered, "Sally, I think I know what's going on. I heard it all at the plant from Abe Barlow. Her mama's been sick. They thought Severine had cancer; turned out it was an ulcer. Lorene has to pay someone to mind Arletta."

"Don't you think we give her enough for that, Walter?"

"Well." He paused. "Tell me again, how much do we pay her?"

We give her thirty-four dollars for a six-day week."

"Seems plenty compared to everyone else."

"She's been with us almost twenty years, Walter."

"Truth is, Sally, Lorene's got big ideas for Arletta. She wants to give her a real education. That's not a bad idea. I think we should raise her salary. Let's say five dollars more a week."

"I reckon that's fair, Walter."

"Well then, that's that. I'll tell her."

Standing there listening, Jane thought how she'd seen Lorene working hard all the time. She'd noticed Lorene's worn-down shoes. She always came to work in the same old brown skirt and white blouse. When she undressed and slipped into her white uniform, Jane sometimes wondered if she had any other clothes.

She raced back into the kitchen. Lorene was slicing big bright red beefsteak tomatoes from the garden.

Jane ran over and put her arms around Lorene's waist. "I want to help you, tell me what to do."

Lorene nibbled a piece of juicy tomato from the end of her knife.

"Looka here, girl. What kind of help will you be giving me with your mud pies?" She laughed and flashed her gold tooth.

Jane loved to see that.

Lorene took a bushel basket of fresh green peas and put it down on the kitchen table.

"Go on. Get your fanny up on this stool this minute and get busy shelling."

———

In those days, Jane had time to sit with her Grandmama.

From sideways on, Miss Sally looked old. She turned, faded blue eyes behind dirty glasses. "Is my precious missing Paul?" She was good at catching Jane's feelings. "Hard to see you, sugah, cataracts. Must be God's will. I believe He slowly covers up what we see in this world and gets us ready for the next."

When Miss Sally rolled down her elastic stockings, Jane saw her grandmother's knees, two bulbs of swollen pain; her legs seemed to sink all the way down into her ankles. Maybe, Jane wondered, God wanted to stop her moving all together. Every morning, out in her garden holding a hose, Jane watched her grandmother walk like a penguin on slippery ice.

Jane remembered seeing an old photograph in a silver frame showing how her grandmother had been long ago; white lace blouse, tight collar, under a chin, determined, as any young, strong Kentucky girl. In the photo, the young woman's long white fingers and pink nails lay on a silver silk dress. The minute the camera snapped, and there she was, forever young. Now she ran her fingers over swollen knuckles and a too-tight large diamond ring. Jane shivered; swore she'd rather die young than get old.

Miss Sally reached into her jar of candy canes and handed Jane one. Jane whittled; her tongue was sweet and stinging at the same time as she sat listening to stories of her grandmother's life. She'd led a group of good church ladies, gone into the mountains and delivered babies in hillbilly shacks. She got going on stories the way Lorene did.

"Sugah, women in those hills, they're old at fifteen, up at dawn, fixing breakfast for mean, sullen, sour-breathed men, drunk on corn liquor. They all got too many little ones falling out of their nests with their mouths open, front porches with boards loose, sagging old pieces of junk piled up, chickens scratching, running inside and out. I went in with soap and towels and found one woman in her bed pouring more sweat onto dirty sheets, knees into her belly, an old rag between her teeth, stuffing down the screams and moans. When their time came, they were grateful for me holding their hands. I cleaned up, fed the children. I pulled out their babies from many of these poor souls. Sad to say, I delivered a few dead ones." Miss Sally got up, teetered. "Come upstairs. I want to show you something."

On one side of the room sat two large camphor chests from China. Her grandmother opened the lids. "Some of these are presents from those hill women." She laid one quilt after another on the four-poster bed.

Jane felt she was looking through her kaleidoscope as her grandmother went on.

"You'd see some of these prettiest ones lying over the dirtiest sheets. The families would never allow me to leave their houses without one of their best."

Tired out with telling, quietly, Miss Sally and Jane looked at a "Crazy Quilt," a jumble of colors every which way.

"No flowers in my garden could ever compare with these patterns. I'm sad to say, Abigail, I will always remember her name, died. I send money every month to her children. Before she left this here and now, she knew what was coming. On my way out, her daughter handed me this, her last quilt."

Miss Sally lifted out others. Different colored bricks lying not quite straight on top of each other, finely hand-stitched sideways. On some quilts there were circles, looping inside and out, wedding ring quilts.

Jane's favorite, "Lone Star," was patched in every color of her crayons on a dark blue background. Jane felt dizzy looking. She wanted every one of them. "Grandmama, can I have these quilts when you die? Pretty please."

Miss Sally smoothed, pushed the last quilt down, and closed the chests. "Your mama's already been up here, taken what she wanted, paying me no mind. She changes everything in my house, tells your grandpapa what he can do or not do." Her lips wobbled, tears fell, she took off wet cloudy glasses, and rubbed her eyes. "Never mind now, you're my little girl. Mighty young to be thinking about me dying and leaving you my quilts. Don't you think so, sugah?"

Jane put her arms around her grandmother. "I didn't mean it. You'll never die."

———

Jane was sitting at the table with Lorene, drinking chocolate milk, when Leroy came into the kitchen clutching a handful of the mail he'd collected from the post office box in Horse Cave.

"Here's something for you, Jane." He pulled out a postcard, turned it over, and looked at the picture. "What have we got? A picture of a girl in a uniform."

"Leroy, give it to me quick."

Jane jumped up from the table and reached for the postcard. Out of breath, she whispered, "It's from Paul. Oh, look, it's a picture of Princess Elizabeth in her uniform. Here's what he says: 'Dear Babe, I put on my own uniform this morning. I'm now L.A.C. Carew, in the Royal Air Force. Here is a picture of Princess Elizabeth in her uniform. She'll be Queen of England. You're my princess. I miss you and love you. I'll be back. Paw-Paw.'"

That night, Jane was too excited to sleep. She put her postcard under her pillow and tried to imagine her Paul in a uniform. After a while, she heard music playing. She pulled back covers, slipped down from her high four-poster bed, and followed the twanging of a guitar. Across the hall, she saw a pool of light under her grandparents' door. *They must be awake.* She lay and listened.

"Walter, turn down that *Grand Ole Opry* caterwauling right this minute."

"Hush up, Sally, go to sleep."

Clear as a bell, Jane heard, "Now ladies and gentlemen, let's give a big welcome to the Carter family and everyone's favorite, 'Poor Orphan Child.'"

We see so many children now
Poor little boys and girls
Who want that mother's loving hand to smooth their golden curls

Tears poured down Jane's face. She had to stop her sobs before they turned into hiccups.

Roy Acuff singing, "Great Speckled Bird" was next. *"What a beautiful thought I am thinking, concerning a great speckled bird..."*

Jane listened and tried to sing along quietly until the radio was turned off, and she ran back to bed.

―――――

Prudence Christian, a schoolteacher from Boston, was married to Matthew Christian, the principal of the Horse Cave high school. He was a learned man with a dry sense of humor.

Grandmama said, "They don't mix with folks from Horse Cave."

Emma had laid down the law; her daughter was to be taught by the best teacher in the county, so Miss Sally reluctantly approached the principal's wife who agreed to tutor Jane outside regular school hours.

Miss Prudence wore horn-rimmed glasses over bright blue eyes. Her light brown hair was parted in the middle, and she wore bandanas around her head like an Indian chief. She was spider-thin, with legs, as Lorene said, like "two tobacco sticks." She came carrying a satchel full of books. She sniffed when she saw a stack of *The Little Colonel* novels on the hall table.

"*The Little Colonel* books are a must read for any child in Kentucky, sugah, you'll love them," her grandma told Jane.

Miss Prudence thought otherwise. "You cannot tell who really won the Civil War when you read those books." She undid her satchel and pulled out two other options.

"We'll introduce you to *The Wind in the Willows, Winnie the Pooh*, and after that, we'll make our way into *The Secret Garden*. Your grandmother tells me you're ahead of your age with reading."

Jane nodded happily. Stories and dramas swirled in her head all day long.

Miss Prudence wondered, "Shall we try writing a letter to your daddy over in England?"

Jane pulled out her postcard. "No, no, not to Daddy. I want to write to Paul."

"Let's do Daddy first."

Jane stood up. "Paul is my daddy."

Miss Prudence played along.

They sat in Jane's grandfather's office. The room was full of dark brown leather and polished wood, with a large glass case of rifles in one corner of the room. It was a clear spring day. Miss Prudence opened the windows and the French doors leading out into the garden before sitting behind Walter Jackson's great mahogany desk with Jane on a chair beside her.

Miss Prudence took off her glasses and looked at her pupil. "I'm going to take you out of yourself. I'll teach you to read to me with passion. You'll be dying to turn the pages. Today, I'll introduce you to Mole, Rat, Mr. Toad, and Mr. Badger in *The Wind in the Willows*. I'll read a page to you, then you'll read it back to me."

Jane nodded happily.

"Shall we begin by writing a letter to your daddy?"

Jane shook her head and pulled out her postcard frayed at the edges. "No, no, Miss Pru. I have to write to Paw-Paw first."

Prudence smiled. "Your grandmama told me all about Paul. Very well, let's write to him. I'll help you. What do you want to say, Jane?"

"Dear Paw-Paw, I can sing 'Little Orphan Child' and 'Great Speckled Bird.' I've been an orphan since you went away. Maybe 'Great Speckled Bird' will carry me over to England to see you. I love you. Come back soon."

Miss Prudence put her arms around Jane's shoulders. "You must have been brought up by someone who talked to you as if you were a grown-up. I see you love the rhythm of words."

"Paw-Paw told me secrets. We sang songs, danced, and he told me stories about a butterfly called Muriel."

Miss Prudence smiled and gave Jane a hug. "Now I know why you want to write to him."

They read, heads together, two pages of *The Wind in the Willows*, Jane imitating Miss Pru's clear way of speaking, quickly moving her finger over the words as she read them back. When they were finished, they folded the letter to Paul into the envelope, printed the address, and went into the kitchen to give it to Leroy to mail.

Miss Prudence shook hands properly with Lorene and Leroy and called Lorene "Miss Carew."

Grandma was in the kitchen. She laughed afterwards and said, "That's the way they do things in Boston."

————

Everyone was nice to Lorene, tiptoed around her feelings and bad moods. Jane saw her grandma give Lorene scarves, stockings, and dresses. Jane innocently asked Lorene if everything Colored people got was second hand.

"Go on, get out of this kitchen."

Jane started to cry. "All you think of is being mean to me."

"If you opened your eyes, you wouldn't need to wonder why I get mad."

Jane guessed what she meant. Once, when she asked why Negroes went to their own churches, Lorene told her, "White people think we got second-hand churches, go to second-hand Heaven, 'cause we're second-hand people."

"Lorene, Jesus says all God's children go to Heaven, even if they can't go to church together."

Lorene laughed at her. "That's what you think."

Every night, Lorene put leftovers in a bowl, wrapped them up in a white tea towel, made a handle from the cloth, and carried it out with her when she left.

Grandma was finishing her coffee on the front porch one evening as she watched Lorene go off down the sidewalk, and said, "There she goes with her totes."

Jane asked her what that meant.

"Totes means carrying. We give her what we don't eat during the day." There it was again—second-hand.

Jane waited all week for Methodist Church Sunday school. She got all dressed up in Grandma's latest present, a dark blue linen dress with a white piqué collar, and shiny red shoes with a bag to match. Grandma loved to buy her new outfits.

When the children filed out of church into the Sunday School room, Jane sat behind Mary Bell Bybee, whose daddy owned the ten-cent store.

Hands clasped, eyes shut, her golden pageboy shaking when she sang, "Jesus Wants Me for a Sunbeam," Mary Bell got so fired up, tears ran from under her glasses.

Jane clasped her hands and prayed as hard as she could. "Jesus, bring back Paul. Don't let him die."

The hymn was over. Miss Francis Talley, her grandfather's secretary down at the plant, opened her arms out of the wide sleeves of her creamy beige blouse and in a trembling voice, said, "Children, He loves us all, each and every one of us, in the whole world."

Jane raised her hand. "Does he love Colored people the way he loves us? If he loves them, why can't they come to our Sunday school?"

Miss Francis, fluttered, "Of course, he loves them too. They have their own Sunday school and church."

"Is their Jesus Colored?"

"Jesus is White, Jane, wherever he is."

"No, Miss Francis. He's white here and brown over there."

On Monday morning, first thing, Jane asked Miss Pru, "What color was Jesus?"

The teacher took her time and answered carefully, "He's a chameleon."

"Oh, Miss Pru, I know all about chameleons. We had one for a pet. Wherever he was, he turned that color."

Her teacher laughed. "Well, there you are, then."

PART THREE

34

RAF Padmore Training Center. Monday, June 3, 1940

Still in his blue-gray battledress, Paul lay on a thin horse-hair mattress. His boots hung over the end of the iron bed. The barracks room had two windows with blackout blinds pulled down, wooden walls painted with white shiny paint, and a coal-fired stove.

He swung his legs off the narrow bed and walked over to his cupboard. He could feel his three roommates' eyes following his every move. There was Andy the joker—shiny, greasy blond hair, quick-witted; Tommy—stocky, short, a tough fighter; Willie—spiky, short black hair, sharp and suspicious, with hard blue eyes. They were all wearing regulation shirts and shorts.

Paul hung up his battledress, stowed his vest and pants, pulled out his red-and-white-striped pajamas, a Christmas present from Emma and Henry, and put them on.

The room exploded with laughter.

"What the blazes?" came from Andy.

"That'll scare Jerry away," came from Tommy.

"Blind the buggers," from Willy.

Paul walked quickly back to his bed.

Andy sat up. "So, what can we call you?"

Tommy had an idea. "How about Fireball Paul?"

"No, no." Willie scratched his head. "Let's keep it short and punchy. I've got it: Blaze."

Paul got into his bed and lay with his arms behind his head, not sure of his roommates' tone. Were they teasing or were they mocking? Time would tell. He remembered Henry's advice to him: "Close to your chest, Paul. With the chaps, keep your own counsel."

"Blaze will do fine, boys," Paul said, laughing. He knew there was no room for his glimpses of Muriel during this war. He had a job to do.

After lights out, Andy asked Blaze if he knew where he was going after the basic training ended.

"Thornfield," Paul answered.

"Jesus, you'll be right in the line of fire at that air base. 'Blaze' might fit the bill."

Paul laughed uneasily, for the sake of keeping it friendly. After that, he closed his eyes and thought about seeing Henry again.

———

The Mess smelled of floor polish, frying bacon, and Old Spice shaving lotion. Paul and his hut mates plonked their plates on the table. Fried eggs, floppy bacon, squishy tomatoes, black-edged white toast, ugly mugs of gray tea.

Paul watched the young men filing into the room—pink cheeks, hair slick with pomade, their battledress pressed and new, just like his. Did the uniform make him one of them? He'd soon find out.

He tried to bury a whiff of fright at the thought of Thornfield under fire. Then he made for the door with his mates, already on their way to the parade ground. He reached for his forage cap. Damn.

He'd left it in his room. He raced back to the hut, just as a Spitfire engine kicked into life. After Ballygreen, he'd recognize it anywhere.

A few minutes later: "Where've you been, Blaze?" Andy stood with the rest of B Company, milling around on the edge of the square.

Puffing, out of breath, Paul was about to answer when a sharp voice cut in. Jerking his head around, he looked straight into the iron-gray eyes of a sergeant standing stiffly beside him.

"Would you kindly look at your watch, AC Carew, and tell us what time it is?"

"Sir. Sorry, sir. I'm late, sir. I'll make it eight-thirty-five, sir."

The sergeant stared at Paul from in close, his short cut mustache bristling. He shouted, "You lost nine minutes of RAF time, AC Carew."

The sergeant stepped back, his voice steely, "AC Carew, ten paces forward march, left right, five six seven eight nine, halt."

Towering over the men who quickly made way for him, Paul marched forward.

The sergeant looked up fiercely into his eyes. "AC Carew? Is that marching?"

"No, sir. Not if you say so, sir."

The sergeant turned to his men. "This is marching."

Never had Paul seen such precision, power, and drive, concentrated in a single figure, with the hard crunch of boots shaking the earth beneath him.

"That, men, is drill. And you, AC Carew, step over here." The sergeant faced the squad. "Let's get some order here. Form up five ranks. Ten men in each." He put Paul on the right, in the front line. "Right marker, AC Carew. No one can miss you—like a bleeding lighthouse." He looked grim as he started his pep talk.

"Listen to me, men. My name is Sergeant Worrall. You'll have heard about Dunkirk. They're calling it a miracle, getting our chaps off the beaches." He paused. "That's no victory. Still, a damn good effort. Reports say the RAF excelled." His eyes ranged the lines of B Company. "But, lads, Jerry's quiet right now. Soon, he'll throw the works at us. The key to victory then will be the three-Ds: discipline, detail, determination. That's drill."

Sergeant Worrall stepped back a pace. "Squaaad, atten—shun. Tomorrow you will be in competition with all the other companies— boxing, cross country shooting. B Company will be the winner." He stepped back a few paces. "Make sure of it. Squad, dismissed."

Squad dismissed. The most beautiful words in the English language. Paul understood that for the next four weeks, Sergeant Worrall would monitor his recruits' every move until he was satisfied they were working together like clockwork.

Paul showered and joined his mates for supper in the mess. Halfway through grey mince and mashed potatoes, the station commander's voice came over the loudspeaker.

"Group Captain Richards here. Gentlemen, here is a replay of Prime Minister Churchill's speech given in the House of Commons this afternoon."

They all put down their knives and forks. There was total silence as the men listened.

With a tight throat and his heart beating, Paul marked the moment, as they all did, when the Prime Minister addressed the RAF after the Dunkirk evacuation.

"This was a great trial of strength between the British and German Air Forces... We got the Army away; and the Germans have paid fourfold for any losses which they have inflicted. Very large formations of German airplanes have dispersed in different directions. Twelve airplanes have been hunted by two. One airplane was driven into the water and cast away by the mere charge of a British airplane, which had no more ammunition. All of our types—the Hurricane, the Spitfire, and the new Defiant—and all our pilots have been vindicated as superior to what they have at present to face...

"I will pay my tribute to these young airmen. They... deserve our grati-

tude, as do all the brave men who, in so many ways and on so many occasions, are ready, and continue, ready to give life and all for their native land."

When the speech was over, Paul was not the only one clapping. He thought of Henry and his squadron and felt proud to know them.

35

The slow days passed into months. Jane followed Lorene into the kitchen, still trying her best to keep her happy, telling her stories, singing her songs. She followed Leroy out into the garden, always looking to him for a flash of Paul.

"Pretty please!" Arms-around-the-neck cuddles were not enough to melt her grandmother's heart and allow Jane to go visit Lily.

"No, sugah, you can't go there. Now you just trot into the kitchen and help Lorene to get ready for tonight."

As soon as it got dark, it was time for Jane's lightning-bug party. Grandma had invited her Sunday school class, and Lorene was baking coconut cake, making pimento cheese sandwiches, and iced raspberry Kool-Aid.

"Lorene, how many lightning bugs do I have to put in a jar to get first prize?" Jane climbed up on a stool, watched Lorene wrap up J.C. Penney coloring books and crayons in red tissue paper.

"Jane, put your finger on this knot. You listen and listen good. This is your party, so you don't get a prize. You *give* the prize! Got it?"

Jane pulled out her finger before Lorene could nail it down.

When she went back into the kitchen to get ready for lunch, she watched Lorene hit the biscuit dough so hard with a rolling pin it jumped right off the counter.

It was after dark before the lightning-bug party got going. They'd invited Virginia Anne, Jane's cousin. Virginia Anne was seven years old and acted stuck up. Jane didn't feel like chasing dots of fire all over the place, especially after Lorene told her she couldn't win the prize. Everyone else spent hours chasing bugs and slapping them down into their jars, before eating watermelon, coconut cake, sugar cookies, and drinking Kool-Aid. Jane ran the slowest, never put one in her jar.

That night, Grandma sat on her bed before she went to sleep, and asked Jane what she thought of the other children.

"I can be friends with my cousin Virginia Anne when she quits being so stuck up."

Grandma, who loved gossip, was sure it was because Virginia Anne's mother was beautiful but crazy and full of drugs. "Take Doris Carter. Her mama needs to take her to the hairdresser for a haircut. And poor Joanne Brandstetter—fat as a little pig. I saw her eating three pieces of coconut cake. Let's have another party next week, sugah."

———

The sun reached toward noon the next day when Jane, sitting on the front porch, saw her grandpapa roll slowly up the drive in his sleek, new black Chrysler with whitewall tires. There followed an almighty clatter, and when she peeked over Grandmama's porch ferns, she saw Elijah following behind, slapping the rumps of four black mules, straining to pull a long wooden wagon up the hill to the house. Even when Elijah lifted his dirty old straw hat, his face was so puckered up, she could hardly find his eyes. Lorene said he could be the meanest man alive, even if he was a Baptist preacher.

Jane waited until their business was over on the porch and her grandpapa went in to get the news on the radio. Elijah pulled up the side of his mouth, clicked a few times to turn the mules and the wagon around, when his eye must have caught her red sundress behind the porch pillar.

"Howdy, Jane."

"Howdy, Elijah, how you doing?"

He lifted his hat. "Can't complain."

She skipped down to join him as he *whoah-ed* to halt the mules.

"Lorene says she wants me to come home with you, so I can tell you all about Paul." She pulled her worn out postcard from her dress pocket. "Look, he's written to me."

Before Elijah's scowl said no, Jane jumped up on the springboard and got right in beside him. "Come on, Elijah, giddy up!"

They clattered down Horse Cave Main Street. She spotted Mr. Dorsey outside his drugstore locking up for lunch. "Hi there, Mr. Dorsey." He shaded his eyes, trying to see who was behind the words.

Elijah had a cheek full of chewing tobacco and sweat streamed down from under his straw hat.

"Watch this, Jane." He moved his front teeth forward over his bottom lip, caught something, then puckered up and blew a wad of spit and tobacco all the way to the curb in front of Bybee Five and Dime.

"Wow, Elijah! Do it again."

Jane held on tight to the sides of her seat, jutted out her chin, and stared straight ahead. When the wagon wheels took the railroad tracks, her bottom lifted, then smacked down so hard she felt tears sting.

They were in the Kingdom, where Lorene, Leroy, Lizzie, Paul, and all the other Carews lived. Standing beside small newly-built houses, old shacks sagged, their porches on either side of the narrow unpaved streets. It was noon. Everyone was inside eating lunch.

Elijah lifted her, then placed her down in front of the torn screen door. She remembered her last visit; Tallulah and Tabby, playing hide-and-seek, eating cake and ice cream, sitting next to Blessing.

Here she was, right back in her memories. Tabby and Tallulah ran out; they'd spotted her red sundress. Lily followed.

"What in the world, child?"

Jane ran to be hugged and stopped when they all kept their distance. Lily's deep-set brown eyes looked wary.

Tabby was the first to say, "Come on in, Jane."

Tallulah took her hand and led her into the house.

A large plate of chicken, cornbread, and a big bowl of turnip greens lay on top of the stove.

Lily said, "Elijah, what are you thinking about, bringing her here?"

Jane found her tongue and put herself in front of Lily. "I've come to tell you all about Paul, how he's in the Air Force over in England, killing Germans so they won't come over here and kill us. Look at my postcard." She whipped out the picture of Princess Elizabeth. The words on the card were blurred from tears.

"We got one too," James and Ernest cried out at the same time.

"I'll read you mine, if you show me yours," Jane said.

Lily read out loud, "'Dear family, I'm wearing a uniform. Haven't seen any war yet. It's raining every day, freezing cold in England. I'm doing exercises and training. You'll see lots of muscles when I get home. Love Paul.'"

Jane quoted her card by heart, and then asked, "Can I have lunch with you? Let's all of us sit down and talk about him. You can tell me stories about when he was little."

For a second, Lily's front gold tooth flashed behind a smile, but then it disappeared right back into her pursed mouth.

"Come on, Mama," Tabby pleaded. "Let her have lunch with us."

"We're having the same lunch as always. Nothing special."

Jane looked at the food on top of the stove, nodded. "You're having the same thing we have every day. Please, can I?"

Lily wondered, "Does your granddaddy know you're here?"

Jane nodded her head and tried to swallow.

"Mama, can't she sit with us and eat some fried chicken?" Tallulah begged.

Elijah went to the sink and washed red dirt off his hands. "You're lucky, Jane. Only reason I'm here today is I got the afternoon off to look for extra field workers."

Lily moved to answer a knock at the door. Before she could open it, Jane's grandpapa stepped inside, Panama in hand.

"Afternoon, Lily, I think Jane might be here." He filled the room with his six-foot-four frame, add an extra inch for his thick silver hair.

"Sir, she just took a notion to come here, only wanted to tell us about Paul, didn't mean harm." Elijah let the hush fall where it lay for a few moments.

"Seems to me, Elijah, you might've imagined the child would be missed. Her grandmama's in a terrible state. Just thank the Lord that Mr. Dorsey telephoned from the drug store to ask if that was really Jane on your wagon."

Jane looked around the room, couldn't find one face to smile with. Her cheeks were on fire. "No, Grandpapa, I'm staying right here, having lunch with Lily. Elijah can bring me back on his wagon."

Lily quietly gathered her children and put them in the bedroom, shutting the door. She took their uninvited guest by the hand, and said, "Now, Jane, you listen here. We weren't expecting company. I want you to mind your grandpa. Go on home with him."

Grandpapa said, "Jane, you go climb in the car. Lunch is getting cold here, and I reckon at home, too."

He closed his granddaughter into the car and on the way home, his jaw never moved under the Panama. When he pulled up the drive and turned the key, he sat a while and then looked over at her. "We don't do that. We have our lunch here, and they have their lunch there. Do you understand?"

Jane said, "I can't see why—tell me why I can't eat lunch with them. What's wrong with that? Why did Lily look at me in that funny way?"

Her Grandpapa took off his hat, pulled out his handkerchief, and wiped her tears. "That's just the way it is. We don't mix things up."

Grandma was lying back on the front porch rocker, whipping the Methodist Church palm fan. "Sugah baby, we gave you up for being kidnapped!" She pulled Jane down into her Coty-powdered neck. "Old Elijah ought to be shot for taking my little precious without a word."

Jane could have killed her grandmother, talking like it was Elijah's fault. "I climbed up on Elijah's wagon. He didn't even see me until we got clear across the railroad tracks."

"Lunch is on the table," Lorene called. "You come in here this minute." She pulled Jane into the bathroom to scrub her hands.

"Hey, Lorene, that water's burning."

She held both Jane's hands firmly under the tap. "Burning? What you really need is a good whipping."

At the table, Jane nibbled the crunch off her chicken leg, tasted tears.

Grandma twisted a sprig of mint in her iced tea. "Lorene, please pour a little bit more sugar in next time, it's too puckerish."

Jane asked, "Can I get a new coloring book after my nap?"

Lorene passed biscuits. "Are you looking for a reward after that kind of acting up?"

"That's enough, Lorene." Grandpa, feeling sorry for her, put his hand on his heart, pulled out his wallet, and gave her a dollar.

On the way to the five-and-dime store, Lorene did not hold Jane's hand except for crossing the road, still mad at her for hopping onto Elijah's wagon. At the cash register, she put down some paper dollies, coloring books, and a packet of crayons. They came to one dollar ten cents.

Jean Ann Bybee at the till shook her head. "Got an extra dime, Jane?"

Lorene fished a red leather change purse out of her pocket. "Here, I got it."

On the way home, Jane said, "Thank you, Lorene. I'll get Grandpapa to give it back to you."

"Don't you dare. Think I ain't got a dime to give you?"

Jane sat on the kitchen stool, took out her paper dolls.

Lorene poured a cup of coffee, got up on the stool across from her. "You need to get one thing into your little head, Jane, right now. You think you're Paul Carew, part of him, and you're not, 'cause he's a Negro. Time for you to be what the color of your skin makes you, 'cause that says who you are. Otherwise, you'd be part of his, part of ours—and you're not. You'll be running around the rest of your life looking for somewhere to sit down and be comfortable. Are you listening?" Jane cut out her paper dolly. "You hear me, girl?"

I'm gonna buy a paper doll that I can call my own. A doll that other fellows cannot steal... She looked at Lorene, crooned her best.

When she stopped singing, Lorene gave her one of her rare smiles. "Guess I can't stop you being who comes naturally. Lord knows you do sound just like him."

"Lorene, does that mean if you're born one color, you can't be part of another?" Jane pinched the skin above her elbow to check.

"I don't see you cutting out any colored paper dollies."

She couldn't understand what Lorene meant. Feeling angry, hot, sick, and ashamed, Jane went to her room, tried to read but couldn't stop crying.

36

Late afternoon on a Sunday, Paul lay on his bed, longing for a puff. He'd heard smoking was bad for him, and Sergeant Worrall told him to rest up before the final boxing competition the next day. He knew his roommates thought he was nuts. First, he'd quit smoking, then he'd taken up running at night and putting in extra workouts in the gym. Sarge's pep talk on the square had stuck. Life was competition. He had to do twice as well as everyone else.

"We'll be there for you, Blaze," were the last words he heard before he turned out his light.

The room was silent. The chaps were in his corner.

———

Unable to find an opponent of Paul's height, LAC Blossom, the boxing trainer, put him up against Ben Callaghan, red hair, big, broad, and Irish.

"Watch out, Blaze, Ben's a bruiser," Andy warned him.

The match was set for four o'clock that afternoon. Paul hardly ate lunch. He could feel Muriel and other butterflies in his stomach.

All of the 100 recruits stood around the small boxing ring in the station's large gymnasium, waiting for the fighters to come out. They were taking bets and getting ready to cheer their boys on.

Paul, a white towel around his neck, in red shorts and black boxing gloves, was helped through the ropes by his three room-mates. Callaghan, already prancing around in the ring, wore black shorts with black boxing gloves. The bell sounded.

Ben lumbered out, swinging his arms, swishing the air like a windmill gone wild. Right from the start, Ben saw that the tall, thin, spidery fighter in front of him wouldn't stand still. Paul was there one minute, the next he had Callaghan wrapped up in his arms like a fly unable to move. Ben charged, time and time again, with his head down and his fists forward.

Paul was dancing to his own tune: "Anything Goes."

In Paul's corner, Sergeant Worrall leaned across the ropes. "Paul Carew, round three. Go get him." He patted Paul on the back. "You can do it."

The bell rang.

Circling, Ben snorted, wiping his nose with his right glove. For two rounds, Ben's bloody nose had been Paul's target, repeatedly peppered by Paul's left-handed jabs. Only once had Ben ducked low, then, coming in with a short hard punch to Paul's solar plexus, had doubled him up.

The referee restrained the fighter from piling in until Paul stood up straight; that was Ben's best shot.

The referee called, "BOX!"

Now Ben came in with a wild left swing that went nowhere, leaving his head uncovered as he dropped his right hand to deliver an uppercut.

Sarge yelled, "Legs! Carew, legs!"

Paul saw the opening, moved in fast, for the first time using his right hand. Unseen by Ben, the haymaker exploded on the side of

Ben's head. He stood rigid, staring dull-eyed at Paul before collapsing onto the canvas.

B Company was on its feet cheering, hollering, "Blaze! Blaze!"

Sergeant Worrall clapped, nodding his head at Paul, whose only thought was, *What the hell have I done?* as the referee raised his right arm. The winner!

————

Paul was too excited to sleep. Every hour stuck to the one before. At last, Parade Day had arrived; the day he'd been training for—five weeks of the hardest work he'd ever known. He reached up, felt the new muscles in his arm, and smiled to himself. He'd shown them. He and Muriel had made it.

Up late, he and his hut mates were spitting on their shoes, polishing their belt buckles, rubbing up a shine you could shave by.

The sun shone over the company square and on the heads of the smart young recruits, forming their squads for the final parade. They all quickly and quietly formed ranks.

Group Captain Hawthorne, the officer taking the parade, was a gray-haired veteran of the Royal Flying Corps, with two rows of faded ribbons.

After he'd inspected the three companies, he gave a short, rousing speech to the men, "Gentlemen, congratulations. It's chaps like you, working together, who keep our aircraft flying and our pilots in the air. You lads will help make sure the Luftwaffe goes down in flames. Today you're all winners. But this time, B Company is first across the line. Well, done, Sergeant Worrall! Well done, men!"

One by one, Worrall marched B Company forward, starting with Right Marker AC Carew.

Paul marched with precision, as if his life depended on it, to receive the Best Company Award. Chin in, he sharply saluted the Group Captain, who, with a smile, shook Paul's hand and presented him with the company certificate—and another one: "Best Aircraft Man, AC Carew."

"Thank you, sir."

"You earned it, Carew."

Paul looked across at Sergeant Worrall, who stood impassively, staring straight ahead. He wondered, as he accepted the award, what Elijah would think of him now and winged a prayer to the Good Lord for sending him Sergeant Worrall.

At the "Belt and Garters" going-away party that night, the company showed what they thought of Sarge. Paul lifted him to the ceiling, where to cheers he scrawled, "Worrall, Best Company Sgt., July 1940," a pub tradition reserved for RAF winners.

The last to leave was Sergeant Worrall, shepherding out the last few boozy men, pointing them in the direction of the airfield. He was the only one dead-cold sober.

Up to this point, everyone had treated Paul well. The elderly RAF officer swearing him into the Air Force, said, "Paul Carew, reach up. You'll pull the Hun right out of the sky." The rugged Scotsman, who'd issued his uniforms, said, "You'll be wearing shorts, Laddie." The camp tailor who lengthened them, said, "Now they're fit for a giraffe, son," and the camp barber, as he chopped into Paul's waves, said, "This hurts me more than it hurts you."

Paul wondered if they were all colorblind. Suddenly, he snapped out of his meandering. The Camel had burned down to his fingers. There was ash on the blanket, and he couldn't afford a blister.

He packed his bag for Thornfield and wondered about the days ahead. He imagined Great-grandma Abilene and Odella, sitting up in Heaven shaking their heads with a few, "Oh, my Lords," and, "What's next?"

37

Cousin Virginia Anne was a year and a half older than Jane, but at times she seemed much younger. Vicky, as she liked to be called, came more often these days to play with Jane, who read her books out loud to her new friend.

On Saturday afternoons, Leroy walked the girls down to the picture show. Inside, they waited on the edge of their seats for the serial, *Tiger Woman*. They'd left her the Saturday before, mouth gagged, all tied up, head turning her spotted ears this way and that, ready for next week's rescue. After the serial, they waited for the *Pathé News* rooster to crow.

A deep, serious voice followed, "England under attack."

Jane nudged Vicky. "That's where Paul is."

"I know that, silly."

The voice went on, "Hundreds of German aircraft are on their way to bomb England, while the RAF pilots run out to jump in their Spitfires and defend their homelands."

"Spitfires, see that, Vicky? Paul and Daddy's planes."

They showed London's broken buildings, flames coming up out

of windows, air-raid sirens screaming. Then a fat man with a cigar and a funny hat, making a V with his fingers.

The voice, "Normal life goes on in war-torn Britain."

There were pictures of children with arms full of books, picking their way through rubble. As the curtain went down, the voice said, "And, at the end of the day, there will always be time for a cup of tea."

Both girls stuffed popcorn into their mouths between hiccups and tears.

———

Lorene didn't think Baby John would last the year; she said that the same way as she might, "My cornbread's done." At the same time, she tried to tell Jane her mummy was all by herself, looking after a sick baby, and the child needed to understand how hard that was. Those words were getting nowhere near Jane. All she could remember hearing over and over was "Be seen, not heard."

Her mummy had such a long shadow, she tried to make Jane's disappear. Paul had always said, "Here comes the Queen of Sheba."

And then, there was a small change. Emma telephoned Jane from Florida every week, asking how she was getting on with Miss Pru. Jane forgot she was talking to her mother, sat on the chair by the telephone and told her all about Mary, the little girl in *The Secret Garden.*

"And how do you like your teacher?"

"I love my teacher, Mummy."

"I'm glad to hear that. Good night, Jane dear, be a good girl. I'll call you next week."

———

It was the worst summer they had ever had, and Grandmama couldn't get a minute's peace because of the humidity.

"It's hotter than a firecracker and my knees are killing me."

Pots of ferns hid the front porch from the street, but the heat rolled through anyway and the air tickled up a sweat. Grandmama spent all her time watering her plants.

Leroy slowly raked leaves and stopped to lift his baseball cap and wipe his face. "Sure is hot, Miss Jackson."

Grandmama picked up her glass of iced water between vigorous sweeps of her Methodist Church palm fan.

"Leroy, hot or not, you get on and deadhead those geraniums. Jane, call Lorene, and after Leroy's finished here, he can drive you both to Larkin's for groceries."

Lorene and Jane got out at the same time as Cousin Eva, Vicky's notorious mama, parked her baby-blue Studebaker convertible. Eva opened the door, placed one green ballerina shoe on the pavement, followed by orange hip-hugging shorts and a tight white halter-top. Long, blonde Veronica Lake hair shrouded half her face. She peered at them with one eye and brushed back a dangling rhinestone earring.

"Hi there, Jane, where've you been? Come on over later and play with Virginia Anne."

Lorene took out a long list and went on ahead while Jane followed Eva into the grocery.

Eva did not need to be reminded to put packets of Kool-Aid and boxes of Twinkies and Hostess Cupcakes into her cart. Jane watched her gold charm bracelet slip and clink every time she raised her hand; she smelled so good she seemed to have bunches of lilies of the valley growing under her arms.

When Lorene and Jane lined up their cart behind Eva's at the checkout, they watched her pull out a nickel and put it into the bubblegum machine. Jane guessed she saw her wishing, because she pulled out one ball after another as she fed in nickels and more nickels, staring at the black licorice as it slipped down the chute.

Cousin Eva gathered them all up, took Jane's two hands, opened her palms and filled them with sugar-gumballs. She popped two in

Jane's mouth. She saw Mr. Larkin staring so hard at Eva, he needed to count the items twice.

Lorene shoveled herself heavily into the front seat of the car next to Leroy, while Jane edged against the brown bags in the back.

"Did you see that woman's outfit?" Lorene's neck was too stiff to turn her head around, so she talked to the front window. "How in this world did she squeeze into those pants? She's three months on the way with another one. Imagine carrying on like that. I remember when Dr. Jimmy picked her up in Chicago eight years ago. She was popping out then and I knew she was made for the city, not for Horse Cave.

"Lizzie, the Pettigrews' maid, told me Eva Burks was invited for lunch last week and when Lizzie served the perfection salad, Eva was so full of drugs she knocked that plate full of Jell-O and whipped cream onto the floor, eyes popping right out of her head. Then she pulled out a cigarette, lit it, hanging out of that red mouth, right there at the table. Nothing good ever came with that one."

Jane tore off a corner of the brown paper bag and wound it around her tired old wad of bubblegum, fished in her pocket, found a new one—this time a licorice ball—and popped it in her mouth. "I don't care what you say, Lorene. Cousin Eva's pretty, and I like her, so there—and *now*, I love my cousin Virginia Anne."

After lunch of biscuits, covered with cream chicken gravy, and turnip greens, Jane climbed into her four-poster bed for nap time, opened *The Secret Garden*, then settled down not to have a nap. After a while, she heard Lorene open the basement door to go down and iron. Jane hurried to take a bubble bath, put on her yellow sundress and started off down the path through the front yard, past a snoring Grandmama in her porch rocker. She was allowed to walk the four blocks by herself to see her cousin. The sun was hot, still at the top end of the sky, as she skipped over cracks in the sidewalk. Dry drifts of old brown weeds heaved hard upwards to break the concrete into puzzle pieces. Cold tickles of sweat ran down the front of her sundress and the backs of her legs.

Virginia Anne was in her front yard spread out like a cross, blonde plaits on the grass behind her head.

Jane said, "I saw your mama in the grocery store this morning." Virginia Anne lifted her hand to shade her eyes as Jane pulled her up. "I think she got Kool-Aid. Let's make some."

The screen door slammed behind a low moan from the living-room sofa. Long legs sprawled to one side. Jane tiptoed across the room to find Eva's head rolled over, mouth hanging open, eyes half shut.

"You better call your daddy. She looks awful sick."

Virginia Anne was in the kitchen. "I can't call him every time she looks like that." The pink Kool-Aid frothed up under the cold tap. "Jane, stand up there on tiptoe; get the Twinkies from the second shelf. Look at this. We've got orange popsicles too!"

On the way out, Jane noticed one of Cousin Eva's ballerinas had slipped off her heel and was dangling from her big toe.

The girls settled down on the long grass in the front yard, picking dandelions, crowning their heads over and over with the long chains they made until they looked like two golden sunbeams. Vicky flowered a few red spots around each side of her nose, but she still looked pouty and pretty.

"I'm getting a baby sister. She's baking in the oven right now, and I bet you wish you were getting one too, Jane."

Jane finished her Twinkie and broke the cellophane with her teeth to start on her second. "I already got a baby brother, and he wasn't what I asked for."

They lay back, flat on the ground, shading their eyes against the hot sun. Jane pulled out a blade of grass and stuck it between her front teeth. "I keep on praying for a sister. Maybe one day Jesus will answer my knock on His door."

She was on her way home when Dr. Jimmy's car scorched the curb. As he got out with his black bag, she heard, "Jane, how you doing?" The sun was falling into dusk, so she had to hurry home, but she set her mind to skipping over every single crack in the sidewalk.

38

RAF Thornfield, Monday July 8, 1940
Paul watched the WAAF corporal skillfully weaving her way through the mass of soldiers and airmen waiting for transport outside Thornfield Station. Breaking free from the crowd, tall and sharp in her blue-gray uniform and cap, she smiled, holding out her hand.

"He was right. The Squadron Leader said to look for the lighthouse." The woman's grip was strong. When she spoke, her tone was warm yet business-like, "Carol Fleming. Welcome, Paul Carew. Please follow me."

Paul walked behind her out to the car, a camouflaged Hummer, parked in a slot reserved for RAF Thornfield. Corporal Fleming drove more like a man—in silence, jaw set, eyes focused on the narrow road busy with military vehicles.

It was only after the armed guard at the airfield's guardhouse had checked their identity cards and raised the red-and-white boom to let them through, that the Corporal said anything. "Strict security, everyone's scared to death. No one trusts a stranger these days."

Paul took in the anti-aircraft gun placements and searchlights, trenches and sand-bagged windows. There'd been nothing like this at Padmore. Though there were no planes flying, the air was filled with the rich, throaty sound of Rolls-Royce engines being tested. He remembered Ballygreen, the smell of high-octane fighter-fuel mixed with the faint smell of cigarette tobacco. The ground rose gently to the Officers' Mess, a large old, red-brick country-house, the largest of many buildings facing a long line of trees and a green lawn with flower beds, separating the buildings from fields, with a few cows grazing. If it weren't for the noise of the engines and the smell of the air, Paul felt he might be a million miles from anything like a war.

Leaving the car at the Officers' Mess, Corporal Fleming led Paul, with his suitcase, along to the Other Ranks quarters and up to the second floor.

In the distance, through the trees, he made out camouflaged hangars and bunkers with men working like ants around a large, winged insect—a Spitfire.

Opening No. 7, Corporal Fleming showed Paul into his room. "Welcome to the front, Aircraftman Carew. The Squadron Leader hopes to see you in the Mess at six-thirty. I'll be there if you need any help."

Paul stepped promptly through the door to the Officers' Mess. He'd showered, shaved, put on the service uniform, magically converted to his size.

Corporal Fleming, at the reception desk, stood and saluted playfully. Smiling broadly, she walked to where Paul was standing, reached up, straightened his tie, eyes never leaving his face, reached for his forage cap, folded it, tucked it into his belt. "There. The Squadron Leader's with the lads in the bar. Give it to them, Paul Carew! You look great."

Paul felt as if he was floating as she led him to the bar, a huge, paneled room filled with young fliers in battledress, mostly holding mugs of beer.

Seeing Paul, Henry broke off talking with Perry Beaumont. The room quietened as the Squadron Leader strode over to Paul, the only man in the room in service dress and the tallest. He cut a fine figure.

"Aha! At last, reinforcements from across the Atlantic." The Squadron Leader shook Paul's hand warmly, raising it in the air. "Best Aircraftman, LAC Paul Carew, a Sergeant Worrall graduate. Welcome back to one hundred and one." He turned to face the chaps. "If this man can't get you lot out of bed at four A.M., nothing will but a Jerry bomb. Let's give him a hand."

The first to step forward was Perry Beaumont, mustache riding high. "We've missed you, Paul." He paused, smiled. "Or is it, Blaze? Whatever, Kitty's looking forward to seeing you again. That evening... Still feels like a dream."

"No time for dancing now, sir."

"When this job's done, Paul, there'll be reason to dance. Believe me."

The Squadron Leader had to pull Paul away, the lads crowding round, throwing out questions about Padmore and Sergeant Worrall who'd drilled his Ds into several of them before they'd gone on to pilot training.

With its comfortable armchairs, a center table loaded with magazines, and a vase of white roses, the Mess library retained only one reminder of battle—a wall covered with old photographs of Great War pilots and their flimsy planes. There was a smell of floor polish and flowers. Henry and Paul sat facing each other, old friends as well as squadron leader and aircraftman.

"Paul, you made it with honors. Well done. Tomorrow, the tailor will put up your stripe. Here's how we read it: Jerry's knocked us for a six, out of France. A home run in your lingo. Right now, we're both making up the damage we did to each other, and Jerry's putting his fleet together just across the Channel. Our Intel knows it. We're in the center of a storm about to break." He paused, pulled out a cigarette case, offered one to Paul.

Paul dug into a pocket for a lighter, doing his best to control the shaking of his hand as he lit Henry's cigarette.

"Now here's where you come in, Paul. In the short time it took Jerry to overrun France in the air, we beat them three to one. We have to keep it up, make it four to one. You will have so many duties it will make your head spin. Begin by getting me and Perry up on time and then see to it the men of one hundred and one are fed and watered. Be in the dispersal hut when we leave on sorties and try and be there when we return."

Henry studied his cigarette thoughtfully. "I don't need to tell you, Paul, that the men know you. They're fond of you, and seeing you around is good for morale. Speaking of morale, find a way to tart up the hut, will you? Bloody disgrace... Nowhere to sit... Blankets on the cots old and scratchy. Take a look, see what you can do. I remember you and Emma working magic in Ireland. McNabb will drive, take Fleming. See what you can rustle up. When you look for furniture, tell them it's for the boys in blue."

Paul stood, saluted him. "Yes, sir. Right away, sir."

Henry laughed. "I can see you've been to Worrall Camp."

———

Paul took a look around the wooden dispersal huts. Pilots snatched sleep here between sorties on camp beds that sagged. There were two wooden tables with uneven legs, their tops ring-marked and scratched; springs were markedly absent from the armchairs. Paul poured tea into chipped cups and saucers.

"Sir," he said to Sergeant McNabb, "we need new comfortable chairs, decent tables, pretty new China, some posters, and a picture or two on the wall."

Sergeant McNabb pulled himself up, affronted, and shouted back, "Where in the bleeding blazes do you think you are? Buckingham fucking Palace?"

Paul stood his ground. "Orders from Squadron Leader Gordon."

"Why didn't you say so?" Sergeant McNabb, for all his blustering, buckled down immediately. "All right, let's get to it."

Flight Lieutenant Rowley Ballie grudgingly gave RAF funds for the "beautification" of Squadron 101's dispersal hut. "Or Squadron Leader Gordon's chateau," as Ballie acidly called it.

"It's the least we can do for these men," Paul insisted.

He brought in comfortable new camp beds with colorful woolen throws. A large polished mahogany table was introduced, always bearing a bowl of fresh flowers arranged by Paul. Comfortable old chairs were slip-covered in blue-and-white chintz. Paul and Corporal Fleming, with McNabb driving, had scoured the country-side, begging antique furniture dealers to lend the pilots the best they had in stock.

In another touch of genius, Paul found a gramophone from the Salvation Army.

"Belonged to this poor woman's eighteen-year-old son, just got himself killed in France. He'd be happy to know you boys have it now, I'm sure." The Sally Army lady pointed to several large stacks of 78s. "We picked it up this morning, along with these."

On the way back to base, Paul sifted through the recordings. "If I Didn't Care" by The Inkspots; "Body and Soul" by Coleman Hawkins; "Just a Kid Named Joe," The Mills Brothers. Not bad.

Boris, the fat and temperamental Mess cook, found movie posters and calendars featuring publicity stills of Betty Grable, Lana Turner, and Rita Hayworth. And especially for Perry, on a separate wall, a sympathetic antiques dealer lent them colored prints of pheasants and grouse.

Perry was ecstatic. "Crikey, Paul, you are a wonder."

"I think," Henry said, as he took off his silk scarf and stepped out of his flying suit, "as do we all, you've made this a place worth coming home to, Paul. Thank you."

———

Henry wondered if Paul dared brave the blitz, come up to London and have a drink with him at Claridge's. Funny thing—and how Paul loved it—that Henry wouldn't stop and think about how it looked, walking into a fancy hotel with him. Paul guessed, Henry thought as long as he was with him, it wouldn't matter, and it never did. They took a car, Henry drove.

They arrived, parked near the hotel, got out and walked. They heard footsteps coming and going, as they blew cigarette smoke into a thick London fog. Paul was beginning to wonder how they would find their way when a siren wailed. They ran, following other footsteps down into a subway shelter.

Paul found a seat across from Henry's, next to a platinum blonde with dark roots; a toothy fox-head wound around her neck snapped the other half of its tail.

They heard bombs landing, thuds, explosions. There was a hit in the distance then one almost on top of them. Platinum pulled out a cigarette, stuck it in her mouth. An old man began singing, *"Keep the home fires burning, while your hearts are yearning. Though your lads are far away they dream of home..."*

Around him, people's eyes shone with tears. Paul tried to be quiet but something inside had to get out. Must've been the Andrew Sisters, his all-time favorite girls, because he got up in front of everyone, and jittered his bug with "Beat Me Daddy, Eight to the Bar."

It surprised him that lots of people knew the words. He hit them with his boogie-woogie, jumped up and jived. The last verse got so crazy, it knocked them out, right there in no-man's land. They forgot everything else. By the time the all-clear sounded, they'd raised the roof with their spirits and shouted, "Bugger off, Nazis!"

Paul hurried outside after Henry and an air-raid warden. They dug into smoking rubble; in still-burning buildings. They moved beams, raked through debris, lifted bodies out, got them onto stretchers, and into ambulances.

Through the heavy dust, Paul heard Henry, "Paul, over here!"

Paul almost broke his neck climbing over pieces of smoking rubble. She was lying on her side, a little girl in a blue and white polka-dot dress, buttoned up the back.

"Sir, she's no more than four." Her hair was short, dark brown curls. She was holding a raggedy teddy bear next to her now-still heart.

Henry knelt, took off his leather gloves, and closed her blue eyes.

Like a bullet into Paul's heart, he saw Babe, her sad little face, all they were to each other. In that second, he understood, looking at the dead child, all he was, all he would ever be till the day he died, was Babe's Paul. He stroked the little girl's dusty white forehead.

Paul and Henry looked at each other, tears streaming through their fingers. First thing when Paul got back to his room, he picked up Babe's picture on his bedside table, kissed her cheeks. He hoped she knew how much he missed her. No stopping the mama in him.

39

Early spring, 1941, red measles broke out. Jane figured Virginia Anne must be sick when she missed seeing her. Jane picked up the telephone and called. Dr. Jimmy answered, mumbled like he was pushing cotton balls down the receiver and hung up. Jane heard Lorene calling her to supper and decided to try again later.

Grandpapa held out his plate and waited for Lorene to scoop out an extra dollop of ice cream onto his blackberry cobbler. Jane watched melting white vanilla run down and trickle into the hot, dark blue juice.

"Grandmama's got something serious to tell you, sugah." Grandpapa's spoon stopped on the way to his mouth, as he turned to Miss Sally and added, "Be careful how you tell it. Let's not have any unnecessary details."

Grandmama helped herself to another piece of cobbler. "Eva Burks is dead."

The words came out of her mouth like they'd been backed up for a while. Jane hardly caught the second to say, "What?"

"Well, Lorene heard the whole story from Becca—she works for Dr. Jimmy—who was in the kitchen when she heard Eva fall down the stairs. She said it was an almighty clatter. Becca ran out to find her out there with her legs held right up to the baby bump, groaning and shivering. By the time Dr. Jimmy arrived, the pains had started, her water had broken, she was bleeding all over the floor and screaming her head off. When they finally got her onto the operating table in Glasgow, they had to cut the baby out—"

Grandpapa raised a finger. "Watch out, don't go too far."

Grandmama picked up her cup for a quick sip of coffee. "Walter, I'll stop this story when it reaches the truth. Anyway, they wrestled Becky Lewis out—that's what they've named her—but Eva died."

Grandmama settled the cup back in its saucer. "They tried everything to bring her back. Jimmy was thumping her poor little chest for hours. Gone, just gone." She looked up from the table. "Lorene, didn't you tell me your Cousin Becca goes over every day to help?"

"Yes, ma'am."

"But it's Virginia Anne who takes care of the baby at night." Grandmama continued, "They say Jimmy's fallen to pieces. He pours more whiskey out of his bottle than Becky Lewis drinks milk out of hers. That's right, isn't it, Lorene? Now, put the rest of the fried chicken and cobbler in a Tupperware and I'll send Jane over with Leroy."

Jane thought about Eva Burks' blonde wedge of hair and that sweet blue eye blinking at her.

Jane found Virginia Anne on the porch, rocking Becky Lewis.

When Virginia Anne saw her visitor, she put the tiny baby down in her cot and the two girls hugged.

Jane felt Vicky's ribs and when she got a good look at her, it seemed she had gone straight from eight years old to thirteen, with a new haircut and short shorts. Becky Lewis lay on her back, arms jerking up and down, and spit drooling out of her little mouth.

"Virginia Anne, I'm so sorry about your mama."

She smiled back at Jane's serious face. "Well, I'm not sad or sorry, not even for one little minute. She did it on purpose. It's the best thing that ever happened to her. Jesus just called her home and she needed to go. We went up to Chicago for the funeral to stay with Aunt Trudy—and you know what? She told me she saw Him, plain as freckles, with Mama sitting there right beside Him. I talk to her every day, and she has more to say from there than she ever did from here."

Becca—tall, skinny, and bossy—was one of Jane's favorite Carews. She'd been looking after Dr. Jimmy for years. Becca brought them orange popsicles and they set to breaking them into two pieces, sucking them into sharp points, and dipping them into Welch's grape juice.

"Boy, oh boy, Vicky. Ask Jesus to call up my Paul, so I can talk to him."

Then Dr. Jimmy pulled up in his dirty old Chevy, got out with his hair sweaty and his shirt unbuttoned all the way down his chest. He walked right by the two girls, slamming the screen door behind, filling the early evening air with bourbon breath.

Jane looked at the black doctor's bag he'd thrown on the porch chair and thought of Eva.

Virginia Anne waved her goodbye and Jane climbed into the back seat of her grandpa's car. She could hear Becky Lewis tuning up as Leroy banged the car door closed.

"Don't worry, Vicky, I'll be back tomorrow," Jane called.

Eva went out like a smoked cigarette—dead in no time. Everybody got used to it, except Jane. She could still see Eva putting in all those nickels, saw colored balls snapping out of the machine, feel her teeth cracking into black crunch, melting into soft licorice bubblegum.

Every day, she thought about Eva sitting next to Jesus, Him patting His hands on top of her golden head. More she thought about it, more she wished she could go there too. One way to get to Jesus was to end it all here on Earth, and once you were there with Him, you could live in Heaven all the time. Jane wasn't feeling happy on Earth without Paul, not for one minute. Maybe Eva's death was telling her something.

———

"We're getting you ready for school, girl."

It sounded like a punishment. Lorene's list of dos and don'ts came with Grandma's new school outfits, shiny red satchel, and a blue lunch pail. Miss Pru had decided that Jane was ready for regular school although they would still be meeting up for extra tutoring from time to time since Jane enjoyed their lessons together.

Lorene wrote "Jane Gordon" all over everything and told her to mind her manners. "Remember who you are. Make us all proud of you, especially Paul."

The day before, Leroy came into the kitchen waving a letter. "It's from him!"

Jane jumped up and down. "He must have been talking to Jesus." She sat at the kitchen table and read quickly:

Dear Jane,

Lorene says you're going to school soon. When I get back, tell me all the stories from the books you'll be reading. We're in the middle of a war here. I'm looking after pilots who go up in airplanes every day and night. Horse Cave seems a long way away. Remember the song we used to sing together? "Don't sit under the apple tree with anyone else but me." Wherever you are right now, sing it.

I love my Babe.

Your Paul

A pale September sun shone through white wisps of early morning fog, hanging over the trees.

"Put this sweater on. Give me that lunch pail." Lorene grabbed Jane's hand. "Come on, hurry up."

They set off on a good grass path that led past Paul's little house, the chicken run, and smokehouse, and came out on the other side of town. The closer they got, the tighter Jane held onto Lorene's hand.

By the time they reached the sidewalk and crossed the street, Jane's heart was thumping, and her hand in Lorene's was sweating.

The large redbrick building was set back from a green lawn

where a large white pole flew the America flag. Children of all ages were streaming into the building. Miss Prudence stood at the door and greeted each one.

"Come on in, Jane. I'll take you to your classroom and introduce you to Miss Hortense."

"Let go of my hand, girl," Lorene said, gently.

Jane took her lunch pail and looked up at Lorene.

"Don't worry. I'll be back to get you at three o'clock. Don't act up."

Cousin Vicky was standing in the corridor. "Hi, Jane, meet you at recess. You can see the hillbilly children who just started here too."

Mary Lou Bybee and Wendell Cherry from Sunday school sat on either side of Jane. She recognized some other children from her lightning-bug party. Sneaky Jean Palmore, as Grandma called her, sat behind her.

———

When the bell rang for recess, Jane raced outside to get a good look at the hillbillies who had started coming to school because President Roosevelt wanted every child in America to get an education. The mountain children hung out together. Snotty faces, shirts hanging, hair cut every which way. In the middle of the crowd, taller than most, was a girl called Luretta. Her hair, long and black, stuck together in small curls. She had a soft red mouth, clean white cheeks, blue eyes. She wore a full, whirly-twirly skirt made of faded leftover quilts.

Jane could see Luretta was the boss. She went over, asked their names, wondered if they wanted to play. At first, they laughed at her; she was only six and a half.

After a while, Luretta came over and they started to talk. She had a voice like a country-music guitar; strings pulled tight. Luretta was nine, the younger Jane was grown up for her age. They became friends. Luretta had never been to school before and had no idea how to read or write. Jane looked out for her and because Jane's class teacher, Miss Hortense, loved Roosevelt so much, she softened and allowed them to spend time together, especially when she saw how quickly Luretta caught on. Anyway, Luretta was pretty and clean.

When they ate lunch, Jane watched her new friend unwrap sandwiches of white bread, crusts on, filled with lard. That evening, she asked Lorene to make her two extra chicken salad sandwiches and put in two slices of caramel cake.

"What in the world? You'll be bringing home half your lunch."

No point telling her. She'd get fired up and tattletale then stop Jane from talking to her new friend.

Luretta took the sandwiches and told Jane about life in the hills. Her mama made quilts and sold them in Berea. All her mama made, she told Jane, "goes down the throat of my no-good daddy. He's twenty-five years older, raped Mama when she was twelve. She had me two days before her thirteenth birthday. I got two sisters and two brothers."

Jane wanted to invite Luretta home, ask Grandpapa to help, but she knew Lorene wouldn't stand for it.

One day, she trusted Luretta enough to tell her all about Paul, and how he'd come to work from the Kingdom when he was a young boy. "Now he's over there killing Germans and winning the war to keep us safe in the playground." She told her new friend how beautiful he was, how his waves folded, pushed up into place on top of his head—a Kentucky cardinal, bright like a bird.

"Paul and me played dress-up. He told me stories better than any books. He looked after me every minute. We sang songs and danced. Every day with him was a picture show, with movie stars, what they were doing and wearing. He'd move the dial on the radio, find The Ink Spots for us. That was all we needed. He'd light up his cigarette, take a sip of coffee, and before you knew it, we'd be singing 'If I Didn't Care'. I'm his baby. They gave me to him. Anyone bad comes near me, he'd kill them with a butcher knife. You know what? He's gone, and I'm not happy anymore." She'd forgotten Luretta was there, and by now, was listening to her own voice.

Luretta was laughing; the girl had no manners.

"Why are you laughing?"

"You're talking about a nigger boy? Calls himself a boy, dresses up with you and acts like a girl? Is he your mama or your daddy? That's funny!"

Soon as those words came out, Jane punched Luretta in the stomach; the first time hard, second time harder, then again, until her friends pulled her away. Miss Hortense came running with two other teachers and marched them both to the principal's office over in the High School.

Boy Joe Lafferty, sitting in his chair, looked at Jane gently. As for Luretta, when he looked at her, he could have been smelling a bowl full of rotten eggs. "What's this all about?"

"Nothing," was all Jane said.

"Don't know," from Luretta.

Jane was told not to fight and sent home.

That afternoon, on the path home, she smelled warm grass. She tried to run away from that word "nigger." She'd heard Lorene call herself that many times, along with everyone else Colored she'd ever known. But she'd never heard the word come out of a mouth in her family. Something about it made her feel sour-sick in her throat. If Luretta said it again, she'd kill her.

She slipped through the back door, snuck as far as the dining room, and dropped her satchel.

Lorene called out, "Come back here, girl, let me look at you. Boy Lafferty was on the phone, said you'd been attacked by one of them hillbillies."

Up on her stool, Jane stared into a bowl of vanilla ice cream and caramel sauce and told Lorene she wasn't hungry. "No one hit me, Lorene. I hit Luretta. And next time I'll kill her."

Lorene left off rolling dough, sat on a stool, her face almost on Jane's. "Nothing comes from nothing. Messing with White trash, you start acting like them. We take what happens, color it the way we feel, not the way it is. You can make blue eyes pink with your crayons, but it's just coloring in."

Fingers in her ears, Jane ran into the garden.

Lorene came after her, saw how much she'd been hurt, how mad she was.

Jane couldn't stop crying.

Lorene put her arm around her. "Paul loves you more than anything. He'll soon be home. You're his precious baby." She waited a minute. "You're mine, too."

————

The white flowering magnolia trees inside the playground gave shade to Jane and Virginia Anne as they ate their lunches. It was spring, the warm air carried the flowers' scent of lemon and roses. The girls turned their faces to the sun.

Luretta stood apart from her friends, turning her hips, and swirling her patchwork skirt. She watched Jane and Virginia Anne.

Jane saw her face had become freckled, red with pimples. Months had gone by since their fight. Jane had stopped hating her so hard. She took a bite out of her chocolate cake and gave the rest to Virginia Anne. The bell rang. They dusted their skirts and filed back into class.

Luretta, though nine years old, was still in grade one. She'd never learned to read, and Miss Hortense had put her in the back row, well away from Jane. She never called on Luretta to read out loud.

The windows were closed, and it was warm and stuffy in the classroom. They all pulled out their first-grade readers.

Jane looked around; Luretta smiled at her. After the class, she stopped in front of Luretta's desk. "Want to be friends?"

"Yes. I'm sorry for what I said." Luretta gathered her books and got up from her desk. "See you tomorrow."

They became close again and talked to each other in the playground. Virginia Anne was a little jealous, and for a while, went off with other girls to eat lunch.

Luretta scratched her spots until they bled.

"Come on home with me after school," Jane said. "I'll put on calamine lotion, make those go away."

Grandmama had given her permission to cross the street on her own, which meant she could walk home without Lorene.

After school she held Luretta's hand, crossed the road, and they walked down the lane across the field and past the smokehouse. Jane stopped and whispered to her friend, "Listen, Luretta. We got to go behind those bushes in front of the house, up onto the front porch, and sneak in the front door."

"Why, Jane?"

"'Cause Lorene doesn't let me bring anyone home, that's why."

Grandmama was out in the garden with Leroy and Lorene was in the basement ironing. The girls slunk around the porch pillars and ran into Grandma's bathroom.

"Hurry up, Luretta, push that stool over here."

Jane climbed up, opened the medicine chest, and pulled out the calamine lotion. She reached for the cotton balls on the top shelf, fell off the teetering stool, and the bottle of lotion fell and broke all over the floor.

Lorene came running right into the racket. She went after Luretta, flicking her tea towel like a whip. She only had to see the way Luretta was dressed—the dirty worn-out shoes, the old, faded patchwork quilt skirt. Lorene chased her out of the bedroom through the dining room, out into the kitchen, and finally out the back screen door, waving her tea towel. She didn't stop there. She chased the poor girl halfway down the lane to school.

Jane, red in the face, ran after Lorene but heard her yelling, "We don't want no poor White trash in this house!"

When she caught up with Lorene, tears of fury were running down Jane's face. Lorene put her hands on her hips and turned to face her.

"You can't have that White trash here. 'Sides, I reckon she's got the itch with those red spots all over her. She'll give it to you."

Jane stood her ground. "You can't talk to her like that, calling her White trash. What if somebody called you names? She's only a little girl, just like me. What if somebody hurt your feelings?"

Lorene answered in a dead cold voice, "We got to swallow it."

They walked back to the house together. Neither one of them said another word.

————

The following morning, Jane woke after she'd stewed all night trying to figure out what she couldn't know—how it felt to be Luretta and Lorene.

In the kitchen, she watched Lorene turn over pancakes. Jane liked to eat with her in the kitchen instead of with her grandparents.

"Getting too hot for pancakes, girl."

"Ain't too hot for me."

"You better cut that 'ain't' out."

"I'll cut it when you cut it."

"Don't you sass me."

They were back to normal. Lorene cut up sweet pickles to put in her tuna fish salad. She laid eight pieces of bread out on the counter.

"Why are you making so many sandwiches today?"

"You can give the ones you don't eat to that hillbilly girl. She needs fattening up."

————

It was the last day of school before the summer holidays. Luretta acted like nothing had happened when Jane asked her to eat lunch under the magnolia tree. The bell rang at noon. When they sat down under the shade, Jane saw what Lorene must have seen. Luretta's skirt had patches over the patches. The white was turning gray. Jane had never seen her wear anything else. She opened her lunch pail at the same time as Luretta opened her paper bag of lard sandwiches.

"Wait a minute, Luretta, I got something for you."

"For me?"

She handed her two of Lorene's sandwiches and a big piece of angel food cake.

Luretta took her time opening the wax paper before eating what was inside. "Tell her, 'poor little White trash' says, thank you."

40

The 0630 wake-up calls done, Paul walked up to the Officers' Mess. Peering through the chestnut trees lining the road, he hoped to spot the Jersey calf born the day before. All he could see was the early morning mist of August still hanging low over the field, a soft, smoky veil blurring the view. He remembered the young tobacco leaves in the spring at home. Only in Kentucky, the sun burnt it off early.

He quickened his pace. For two days, headline talk on the *BBC* had been on little else. *"Fighter bases across the southern counties bombed. The Luftwaffe, determined to smash the RAF. The Battle of Britain has begun."* So far, Thornfield and Biggin Hill had escaped attack.

Paul had just stepped into the Mess dining room when a serviceman blared out over the loudspeaker, "One hundred and one squadron. Fifteen minutes ready. Transport at the door."

Sixty seconds later they were all in the transport, followed by Paul clutching a tin of hot sausage rolls he'd snatched from the kitchen.

Inside a bus that was fogged with tobacco smoke, most of the men were looking out the windows. There was no chatter.

Henry lit a Balkan Sobranie and handed it to Paul. "How does that song of yours go? 'There'll be a hot time in the old town tonight.'"

"That's it, sir."

In the hut, there was silence as the minutes ticked by—five, ten, fifteen, twenty. The telephone rang. Lindsey Campbell, the brawny Scot, picked up the phone. "One hundred and one squadron... *Scramble!* Protect base. Stukas. Angels ten."

The boys ran, wearing bulky Mae Wests and flying suits, their heavy boots pounding the grass. Paul watched them as the fitters helped them into their planes, engines already warmed by the ground crew that Henry called "the spine of the Squadron." In seconds, the Spitfires trundled onto the airfield, turned into the wind, were off, speeding down the runway up into the dawn of a summer day. Three and a half minutes. They were gone.

Paul was alone with half-eaten sausage rolls, stubbed-out cigarettes, and the full cups of the tea he'd just poured. Feeling jittery, he picked up a sausage roll, took a bite, put it down, and admired his full-blown white rose, stuck in a brandy bottle, cut from the beds in front of the Mess.

He was in deep, deep water. He'd just seen Henry take off; his love for the man was almost unbearable. There were times he felt he'd explode. If it hadn't been for Padmore, he'd be drowning. Discipline, discipline. That's what held him together.

Moments later, the loudspeaker blared across the airfield. "Hats on. All non-essential personnel take shelter. Attack imminent."

Paul, tin hat slipping over his face, did not waste a second. His long legs whirled him into the nearest trench alongside a hangar.

"Morning, Corporal, I didn't hear you knock."

Paul recognized Chiefy, Flight Sergeant Alf Boynton, the key bloke of the ground crew. He was also the joker of that pack.

With one finger, Alf, slowly raised Paul's lopsided helmet. "If we'd known it was you, Blaze, we'd have dug a lot deeper."

A siren's high-pitched wail was followed by the roar of an aircraft engine and loud explosions. The ground shook.

Terrified, Paul watched the dirt sliding on the side of the trench.

"Fucking Stukas!" Alf pulled his tin hat lower. "Keep down, mate."

One by one, the German planes came screaming down across the airfield. Paul heard the sharp *crack crack* of anti-aircraft guns. Everyone in the trench stood up and watched as a Spitfire, guns flashing with a brittle crackle, closed in fast on a German bomber. Too late, the Jerry pilot put his Stuka's nose into a near-vertical climb, smoke pouring from the engine, the plane hanging like a black kite for what seemed forever, before flipping onto its back and plunging down beyond the end of the airfield. A loud crash, an explosion, then smoke and flame.

"That's it, poor bastard. Serves him right, though," Alf said.

In seven minutes, the attack was all over, leaving the field full of black craters and Paul's nerves shattered.

"First time with Stukas for me too, laddie." Alf paused, then said in a shaky voice, "You know what, Blaze? If it hadn't been for that early warning, and our lads going up like bloody grayhounds, they'd have been sitting targets."

Paul saw the tremor in Alf's hands at the thought.

The all-clear sounded, the trench emptied.

Paul watched Alf run into the hangar, returning with an armful of small bright red flags. Paul reached out, without thinking. "Here, let me give you a hand."

Alf handed him half the bundle. "Did Padmore teach you what to do with these?"

"Yes, sir!"

"Remember, Blaze, the Stukas are dropping some delayed-action stuff nowadays, so watch where you put your feet."

Paul wished he'd kept his big mouth shut. Now there was no going back. He could see a couple of bulldozers, working fast, filling in the craters, the drivers signaling to the mounds they'd spotted.

Alf and Paul zigzagged across the airfield, sticking in flags alongside UXBs.

Don't think about what could happen to you, Carew. Do it! That's your job, he told himself.

Paul and Alf moved fast. On a cool early-summer's day, they sweated with nervousness. The red flags fluttered merrily on the mounds.

———

Relieved to get back to the dispersal hut, Paul fixed himself and Alf a cup of tea, tidied the place up, changed the water in the brandy bottle.

Outside with his cuppa, Alf looked across the airfield. "Take a look, Blaze. The bomb-disposal boys are on the job. They'll be clearing a path for our fellas to put down. Better get a move on." He looked at his watch. "Back soon."

Paul's hands were still shaking. Planting flags, he'd been scared and excited. Since joining the RAF, he'd been putting himself forward, daring to be more than he had ever imagined he could be. Back in Horse Cave, he'd felt his limits, stayed inside the lines. Here, there was danger, but no limits. He could go where he pleased.

Paul, with heart thumping, counted the pilots in. All present except for Henry.

"Latest Intel said Marlin leader caught a packet," Perry informed him tersely. "Undercarriage shot up. He's coming in. Fire truck, ambulance standing by."

The whole squadron, including Paul, lined up outside the dispatch hut. The bulldozers had been ordered off the field, a few of the craters already filled in. They'd made a narrow landing strip, marked with yellow flags, a few red ones fluttering close by.

Perry turned to Paul, still sweating, beside him. "The boss is good. You'll see." Perry saw Paul was suffering. "Hell, Blaze, that man can land a crippled Spitfire blindfolded."

From the east, Paul picked up sight of Henry's plane. Low, slow, very slow, it made its approach. The canopy was open. He could see Henry looking down and from side to side.

"He's talking to control," Perry muttered.

Suddenly, Henry gunned the engine. The Spit surged forward, gaining height, circling, back above the trees.

"He's checked out the landing." Perry was rigid with tension, unable to look away.

Every pilot standing there with them saw themselves in the cockpit of the crippled plane. The morning sun shone from a cloudless blue sky. A couple of sparrows had just landed in front of them, stabbing hopefully at the grass.

"What's he doing now, sir?" Paul's voice was almost a whisper. He'd closed his eyes.

"Balancing, Blaze, balancing." Perry said it under his breath. He'd recognized Paul's feelings for Henry. Perry put an arm around his shoulders. "I know how you must feel, but here he comes. Open your bloody eyes, Blaze. You can't miss this."

Paul opened his eyes. The Spit had landed. It was bumping over the field on one wheel, lopsided. One wingtip pointed to the sky, the other scythed the grass, clipping a yellow flag, then a red one. Paul's heart was slamming in his throat.

Henry cut the engine. The absence of sound was a shock. The plane was still careering over the bumpy outfield.

"Stick back, stick left, stick right. Brake, brake, brake," cried Perry.

The propeller had stopped. As the wings leveled, the Spit looked as if it hovered just above the ground before sliding onto the field with a slight swishing sound.

The pilots and ground crew cheered. Henry climbed out of the cockpit, pulled off his helmet, unwound his white silk scarf. "Gentlemen," he said, "thank you. One Spit delivered, a little shop-soiled. Let's see what we can do to get her ready for the tea-time merry-go-round, shall we?"

41

Winter and spring faded into summer. Rumors began to fall like leaves. Something big was happening. Fifteen German pilots were brought in for interrogation and held in guarded barracks across from Operations HQ.

On his way back from work, Paul passed their barbed-wire enclosure and saw them talking, smoking, walking around, waiting their turn for questioning.

From behind the wire, a blond, thick-haired young German called out in perfect English, "Hello, where are you from?"

Paul stopped and went over to the fence.

"Hello," the prisoner said to him, again in English. "My name's Max von Essen." He put his hand up against the wire.

"Lance Corporal Paul Carew." Paul placed his hand briefly against the prisoner's.

They talked a while. The prisoner was a captain in the Luftwaffe, from Dresden, flew a Messerschmitt, but did not want to talk about how he had been captured.

The next day, Paul decided to take him a ham sandwich wrapped in waxed paper and a piece of fruitcake.

The German looked up at him under long sandy eyelashes. "I've been waiting for you, Lance Corporal Carew."

Paul felt himself shiver at the words. Did not like to admit he thought it, even to himself, but the German flyboy was handsome in his Luftwaffe uniform.

Max said, "We've never had a Black man in our Air Force."

"Is that so?" Paul smiled. "Maybe that's why you're losing, Max."

"Are you sure we are?"

"You bet, I'm sure. We have four hundred Colored men from the Caribbean in RAF bomber command. Best navigators and gunners in the business. Wellington pilots as well."

"Really, Paul? Yes, I think I heard that somewhere."

Paul felt the heat rising and said, "These guys know how to find Messerschmitt, shoot you down, knock you out."

"Wait a minute, Paul. You picked the wrong guy to preach to. I'm not in the Nazi Party. I'm happy to eat with you, fly with you, and happiest of all to share your music."

It seemed Max was a big fan of the blues, knew most of Paul's favorites. The two of them, barbed wire between, got themselves going, singing Fats Waller's, "Your Feet's Too Big," and ended up with Billie Holiday's "I Can't Give You Anything but Love."

Paul allowed himself to overlook the fact that he was enjoying his meetings with the enemy.

One day, arriving at the POW barracks with a fresh pork pie and some chocolate for Max, he found him gone.

"Your new friend is being interrogated." A thin, haughty German SS officer, immaculate in his high-buttoned uniform, was standing at the wire waiting to explain.

Paul thanked him, lowered his eyes, and hurried away, the gifts for Max still clutched in his hand.

After a few days, Max was back, wearing a clean shirt and with a shorter haircut. He said he'd run out of cigarettes, so Paul gave him a few of his. Max smiled as Paul lit one for him through the wire and stuck two more of Paul's Lucky Strikes behind his ear. Just then, the same haughty officer from the other day walked over to where they were standing.

"Let's go, Max. We have a meeting." The rest of his sharp-toned command was given in German.

Max looked at Paul, regretfully, over his shoulder as the officer hurried him away.

Paul decided to tell Henry over his early-morning cup of tea the next day about his contact with the German.

Henry listened carefully, an expression of amusement on his face at first that gradually changed as all the implications of Paul's confession sank in. Instead of being alarmed or angry, though, Henry looked excited. Color mounted in his face and flushed the fine skin at the bottom of his neck.

Paul had to force himself to look away.

Henry plonked his teacup down on the tray and rubbed his hands together. "I'll set up an urgent meeting with our intelligence corps. You may be able to help us, Paul. And just so you know, I'd heard about your little chats with von Essen. Thank you for coming to me about this. You've done the right thing. Now let's use it."

The following day, Henry and Paul met the intelligence officers in a private room. There was an MP stationed at the door. The Group Captain, a wing commander, Henry, and Paul sat around the table in the middle of the room. A heavy WAAF officer came in with tea and biscuits and slopped milk all over the plate.

Paul was unimpressed.

The Group Captain began, "Paul, we're getting nowhere fast. German night fighters are right on top of our boys, finding us quicker, coming in faster than before. Far more crews are being shot down in recent months." He leaned forward. "We're interested in knowing what has changed in their night-time capability. We believe they've installed a better forward-view radar system, independent of ground control. If they have, you can bet your pilot friend will know about it."

Henry took over. "If you can get a conversation going about night flying, Max might just let something slip. Our scientists need all the info they can get."

"Tea, sir?" The WAAF poured Paul a cup of the strong Assam blend he detested.

"Use your wits," the Group Captain instructed him. "Pick a quarrel with him... Goad him about Luftwaffe losses—he won't know any different. But don't, for God's sake, say a word about our civilian death toll, thanks to him and his chums. Report to Wing Commander Gordon if you learn anything at all.

"Oh, and one more thing, Carew. This von Essen chap may seem a perfectly decent type, but you must stay on your guard with him at all times. I can't go into specifics, but we're hearing some very disturbing information about measures taken against the Jews in Germany and Occupied Eastern Europe. Never underestimate the enemy, even when he is apparently at your mercy."

Paul made a few more visits to Max, remaining vigilant at all times and changing the subject whenever the German asked him about life outside the RAF base. One evening, he left the Mess after an early dinner. It was a windy, rainy night. In the distance, Paul could hear the night fighters revving up, waiting for darkness to fall before they took off.

Max hadn't shaved that day. His blond stubble made him look rougher than usual, more of a brawler than a gentleman pilot. Paul pulled himself up sharply. He must remember what the Group Captain had said and treat this man with proper caution.

The German waited without speaking while Paul lit a cigarette for him, took it, and commented, "I count the planes taking off. I wonder which of our cities they're laying waste to tonight."

"Let's not kid ourselves your countrymen are all innocent victims, Max. You talk about bombing raids. What about the cities you've targeted here?" Paul was careful not to mention the death toll in coastal areas and the Midlands, let alone London, which had suffered greatly.

Instead of retaliating to this, the German deflected it. "Let's talk about something else."

"Sure, Max. Look how dark it is tonight. No moon—good for our boys. Bet you miss being up there, hunting like an owl at night."

"You're right, Paul," he said, instantly. "And these days we German owls have sharper eyes than you do—eyes in the back of our heads."

Max laughed heartily at his own observation, and for the first time, Paul could see past the cute boyish good looks to the ruthless fighting man beneath. He made his excuses, told Max he'd see him the next day.

Henry was in the Mess having a double whisky at the bar, when Paul told him about his conversation with Max and what he'd learned.

Henry finished his drink at a gulp then slapped his leg and smiled. "Bravo, Paul. That's just what we're looking for. Do you see what this means?"

"Not exactly, sir. But he was definitely thinking about some important advance, I knew that much."

"Eyes in the back of our heads, that's what we need—otherwise known as rear-view radar. Max has to have meant Jerry *already has it.* Our boffins are working hard on it, but it seems they've missed the bus. They'll have to run and catch up and this is just the kick up the backside they need to motivate them. Lives will be saved because of your good work today."

Henry was off to the dispersal hut, but before he left, he patted Paul on the back. "Owls... Brilliant of you. Well done. I shan't forget this, and neither will Bomber Command."

42

J une 6, 1944

"Almighty God: Our sons, pride of our Nation, this day have set upon a mighty endeavor... To set free a suffering humanity. They will be sore tried, by night and by day, without rest—until the victory is won.

"With Thy blessing, we shall prevail over the unholy forces of our enemy. Help us to conquer the apostles of greed and racial arrogancies. Lead us to the saving of our country, and with our sister Nations...

"Thy will be done, Almighty God.

"Amen."

President Franklin D. Roosevelt

In his room later that evening, before stealing a few hours' sleep, Paul looked out the window at line after line of tents. Through the trees, on the far side of the airfield, in the purplish half-light, he could make out the shapes of over sixty Hurricanes and Spitfires. What had Henry said yesterday? "Tomorrow could be the big day."

Early wake-up call at 0100 hours. Paul knocked loudly on Henry's door and went in.

"Hell's teeth." Henry pulled himself up in bed. *"Parlez-vous Français,* Paul? Looks like we're crossing the Channel all right." With that, he made straight for the shower and called out as he turned on the cold water. "Tea can wait till I'm in the dispersal hut with all the chaps."

Next call on his list was Flight Lieutenant Beaumont. "Sir, it's one-fifteen A.M."

"Bugger off, Paul."

Laughing, Perry pulled the covers back over his head, before coming out from under. Handlebars pointing down, eyes shining with boyish enthusiasm. "We're off then."

After breakfast at 0230, transport picked up Squadron 101. It was still pitch-black outside, clouds hiding the early light in the eastern sky. Henry held a cigarette between his lips, handed it to Paul.

When no one was looking his way, Paul stubbed it out, rolled it carefully in a handkerchief and stowed it away in the breast pocket of his battledress tunic.

————

In the dispersal hut, Paul followed his routine, lighting up the tea urn, laying out sugar and milk for anyone looking for a last cuppa. He helped the pilots sort out their lockers, found Harvey's silk scarf, handed Will his gloves, Marco his goggles. A lot of the boys needed him to help them get into their bulky Mae Wests. It reminded him of Babe struggling to find a sleeve-opening in her cardigan, putting it on back to front. This was stuff he did every day. Only Tuesday, June 6, 1944, was like no other day.

On the wall of the hut's planning section was a map of Operation Overlord. The chaps were bound for Normandy to offer as much protection as they could to the troops being landed. Gold Beach was circled in red. Perpetual air cover, five sorties. Take-off 0330. Paul looked over at Henry. He was smoking, talking things over with Perry, who looked pretty cool, puffing on his pipe, sipping a glass of water.

Perry saw Paul watching him and flicked up his mustache. "'I'll be seeing you,'" he sang out, and laughed.

Henry checked his watch, looked up at the clock on the wall. "Okay, chaps. Check your time and remember, radio silence is imperative if you value your balls. And put in your second breakfast orders with Boss Blaze here." Henry paused, checked his own watch. "Okay, fellows, let's go!"

Parachutes slung on shoulders, helmets in hand, the pilots trooped out of the hut, walking to join their crews at the planes. At 0330, Marlin squadron was in the air. D-Day was officially underway.

———

All day long, Paul cycled back and forth around the airfield, pedaling furiously from dispersal hut to the Mess, making sure he was there after each sortie with sausage rolls, hot tea, apple cake, and tender care for the fliers.

"Paul, I'm knackered," he heard on every side.

He picked a slow soft jazz number from his large store of 78s to soothe the boys smoking quietly or resting on the cots. There were the inevitable losses.

Quiet, sweet Tubby Abernathy didn't make it back from the first sortie; Lindsey Campbell, the loud brawny Scotsman, ditched in the Channel and the spotters found no signs of life. Jaws tense, eyes red from tiredness, the pilots marked their missing without a word and got on with it.

It was seven-thirty, the end of that long summer's day. The 101 Squadron had completed four sorties. Charlie and Martin were successfully picked up from the drink and were on their way back; Freddie, the youngest and newest in the squadron, had pancaked at

Formont on the Norfolk coast and was now looking for a ride home.

Paul was in the dispersal hut. Overhead, planes were circling, some coming in two at a time, flying on empty, desperate to land. Alone, Paul waited for his boys, lit a cigarette. They were due back. He heard a fire truck screaming and ran outside. Across the landing strip, two Spitfires had collided. They were burning, lighting up the far side of the airfield.

When the telephone rang, his stomach convulsed. Running back into the hut, he lifted the receiver.

"Corporal Carew. Controller here, Marlin Leader Blue called in. Heavy damage. ETA five minutes. Airfield clear for solo pancake landing."

That's Perry. Slamming the phone down, Paul smashed the glass of the emergency cabinet, grabbed the heavy long-handled axe, lifted up the fire extinguisher, and was out the door, heading for the middle of the airfield. On the far side, through the dusk, in the light of burning planes, he could make out the busy fire trucks and ambulances.

Overhead, circling pinpricks of light showed a dozen planes in a holding pattern. The night sky was thick with the roar of Merlin engines. Paul knew they'd be running out of gas, pleading with control for permission to land. Paul picked up the shape of a Spitfire above the horizon spiky with pine trees, silhouetted against the fading light. No landing lights, one wheel hanging crookedly from the undercarriage.

The plane glided over the end of the airfield. The propeller had stopped. But for a high whistling sound, the approach was silent. On and on, the plane seemed to float across the ground, until, right where Paul stood, it slid onto the grass, gouging a deep furrow, throwing heavy clods of earth into the air.

The Spitfire lay hissing and smoking. Paul could see Perry feebly raise his hand, only to let it flop down as he slumped forward in the cockpit. The plane had tilted over, propped up by one wheel. Flames spurting out of the exhaust broke the spell rooting Paul to the spot. Grabbing the extinguisher, in four steps he was at the plane, directing the foam as he'd been taught, smothering the flame. There was a scary smell of high-octane fuel. Axe in one hand, Paul clambered onto the wing; he banged on the canopy. Slowly, Perry raised his head.

Seeing Paul, he signaled to the upper edge of the canopy window where two star-shaped bullet holes were just visible.

Paul could see the blood seeping from under Perry's helmet, down his forehead, across one eye, and dripping from his mustache. Paul raised the axe high above his head, and, marking the space between the two bullet holes, slammed it down with a force that shook the plane. Again and again, he wielded the axe, widening the hole, showering Perry with broken glass. Smoke, now pouring from the engine, started to fill the cockpit.

Perry slowly lifted his head, looked at Paul, then at the hole in the window, and raised his hand to touch his mustache.

Paul understood *this was it.* He dropped the axe, braced his legs against the cockpit, thrust his body through the hole. The Lord was listening. The Flight Lieutenant had released his safety harness. Wrapping his long arms round Perry's shoulders, Paul tried to heave him up and out of the cockpit. They were stuck. Smoke, orange, acrid and hot, roiled. Babe's voice rang in his head: *Dance, Paw-Paw. Dance, Paw-Paw.*

Tightening his grip around Perry's shoulders, thrusting his knees against the plane's body, he unwound his legs like a piston, yanking them both free from the cockpit. Together they fell back onto the wing. Sliding off, Paul hauled the pilot's inert body to the ground. With one final burst of energy, Paul dragged Perry away from the burning plane. It was only then he noticed one side of his own uniform tunic was soaking with blood. Through the smoke and glare of the burning Spitfire, he heard voices, the wail of an ambulance. Dimly, he made out Henry's familiar rangy figure running towards them. And then... Only darkness.

———

Paul woke up in the hospital. He was alone in the room. Outside his window he saw a flock of starling, swooping, hitting on a heavily laden cherry tree. His head was splitting. When he tried to move, he felt a sharp pain in his side.

A knock on the door. Henry pulled up a chair and sat down beside the bed.

Paul asked, weakly, "How's the Flight Lieutenant?"

"He'll have a sore head for a while. The bullet missed his brain—not that there's much there to miss. Just a flesh wound, like yours. You must both have charmed lives. Another bit of luck—Feather Lynette was duty surgeon. He sews the daintiest stitch in the business. Both of you will have your beauty unimpaired."

Paul smiled weakly, "Yes, sir. Lucky, sir."

"Oh, I almost forgot to tell you." Henry laughed. "The docs shaved off Perry's mustache along with his hair. He looks like a young boy. He'll be along to visit as soon as he can. Might be a few days."

Paul tried to pull himself up in bed.

"Not yet, old chap. Doc wants you to rest. You lost a lot of blood. In the next few hours, you'll be seeing every member of One-O-One. And that's not all, *Sergeant* Carew, I'm recommending you for a medal." Henry pulled out two cigarettes, lit them both, and put one in Paul's mouth. "I hope what you did for Perry will be the end of the heroics. I've spoken to Emma; she got in a flap when she heard you were wounded and called her mother. They'll be going over to tell Lily and the rest of the family all about this caper."

"Sir, I hope they won't tell Jane."

"Absolutely not." Henry took a deep puff of his cigarette and said, with some emotion, "I've let Sergeant Worrall know. And everyone in Brighton sends you their best. Mother wanted to come and bring Winnie with one of her sponge cakes."

Paul was surprised. In such a short time, Henry had told so many people.

Henry stood up and put his pack of Balkan Sobranies on Paul's bedside table. "Reckoned you always fancied these. I'm on call. Here, I'll let the nurse know to make sure you put out that cigarette."

Paul drew the smoke deep. Closed his eyes, just for a moment.

43

Paul got off a military transport plane in Washington, on a cool rainy fall afternoon in 1945, feeling dazed, as if coming down from a ladder with the last step missing. The night before, he'd said goodbye to the men in the Mess and the chaps in the squadron.

Percy had seen to it that Paul was given the rousing send-off he'd earned; rounds of whiskeys and sodas, followed by bangers and mash. There were cries of "Well done, that man!" "Yes, damn good show, Paul." Pats on his shoulder. Murmurs of, "Keep in touch."

Best of all, was Henry's toast to him in front of the whole squadron. "We got through this war with your help, Paul. Jerry didn't stand a chance."

He stood for hours in a taxi line with GIs and sailors on their way to Union Station. He finally shared a cab with two other Colored soldiers, one on his way to Louisiana, the other to Mississippi.

One asked, suspiciously, "Where are you headed?"

"I'm on the overnight sleeper to Louisville."

"Sleeper—where have you been? We'll be riding all night long in the cattle car, and so will you. Never mind a sleeper."

Paul had no idea what they were talking about.

Carrying his big heavy suitcase, the porters directed him to follow the crowd of other Colored men, wearing uniforms with duffel bags slung over their shoulders. He'd left his own uniform in his suitcase and wore a dark blue blazer with an RAF badge, white shirt, and gray flannel trousers.

He made his way down the platform, past the Pullman sleeping cars, and saw White folks being tended to by Negro porters carrying their bags, and conductors taking them to their wagons. Then he saw where they were pointing for him: "Colored Only."

On board the Jim Crow car, he looked around. There was no room to move, and the seats were tattered with springs sticking out. After waiting in line for the bathroom, he tried to wash his hands in a dirty sink. No water came out of the taps.

Watching him come out, a little girl clung to her mama, a young woman, looking fresh and pretty in a white blouse and a cotton flowered skirt.

The woman looked at the handsome, tall young man, and said, "Bet there's no water in there. That's the way it is." She opened a pack of sandwiches. "Ham and cheese, want one?"

Paul shook his head. "No, thank you, ma'am."

The train moved jerkily out of the station. There was no room to sit. He looked up for a luggage rack.

A sailor eyed his big, heavy bag with sympathy. "They don't put luggage racks in for Colored folks."

Paul had to crouch, hunched up in the aisle beside his suitcase. On the seat beside him, a tall, skinny GI with his leg in a heavy cast wanted to talk.

"Name's Phil. I see you don't know the ropes, you didn't bring food or water with you. What's that badge with the gold wings on your jacket?"

"Royal Air Force, and my name's Paul."

"You mean to say you were in the *English* R-A-F?"

"Yes, sir, I was."

Heads turned all around. The young mother sitting behind him leaned forward and wondered, "Did they let you fly a plane?"

"No, ma'am. But I was part of a fighting squadron. I got the boys ready to fly."

"The R-A-F, huh? That's something."

Another GI, waiting against the scraped door of the restroom, raised his voice above the rest, "In the American Army, I must have peeled thousands of potatoes. We were segregated till the end of the war when they needed bodies to take German bullets. Fit to die for them, but not to fight with them. At least, not till the end."

A few passengers clapped.

A sailor sitting on his duffel bag next to Paul, asked, "How did they treat you in the R-A-F?"

"Like one of their own, sir."

The stale air was full of cigarette smoke. The car swayed as the train rattled through the night. Everyone, except Paul, seemed to have brought sandwiches.

Hands reached out to share their food with him, along with offers of bottles of soda pop and water. He stood up, stretched, and lit a cigarette, grateful he was in such good shape. When he sat back down, he looked over at his neighbor and saw, from the strained look on Phil's face, that he was in pain. Every few minutes he tried to move his leg in its heavy cast, cramped under the narrow seat.

"Where were you, Phil?" Paul asked him, in a low voice. Some of the passengers had begun to doze.

"Patton's seven-sixty-first, outside Nancy, France." Phil patted the cast. "This leg won't be much good anymore." He closed his eyes. "We showed them though. The sons of bitches in our top brass didn't think we had it in us, but we came out on top. We did it then, Paul, and we'll do it again." Phil made the V sign with each hand. "Know what this means?"

"Sure, Churchill's V for Victory."

"No, look, a double V for Victory. The enemy over there, and this one—" he held up his other hand, "—for our enemy over here."

"Who do you mean?"

Phil pointed to the rotting seats, the dirty sink, and the long line waiting for the stinking toilet. "I mean, the White folks who keep a knee on our necks."

———

In the morning, Paul said goodbye to his new friends, changed trains in Louisville, and boarded another segregated car on its way to Nashville. This time, he sat on a broken-down seat and slept until he heard a loud call, "Next stop, Horse Cave."

He stepped down from the train in front of the Owens Hotel, carrying his heavy suitcase. A gusty warm wind was blowing through the locust trees and swirling up dust in front of the hotel. It was hot. Paul unbuttoned his blazer, took it off, rolled up his shirt sleeves, and looked up at the sun. He'd forgotten.

A little way down the platform, Leroy whirled both hands over his head then ran to hug his cousin. "Mr. Walter's expecting us to stop and see Lily."

Paul, his body stiff from the train, climbed into the soft, comfortable front seat of the Chrysler, smelled new-car leather. The road was paved and smooth until they bumped over the railroad tracks onto the rough red-earth track leading through the Kingdom. He noticed how small the houses now looked.

They stopped in front of his house, and when Leroy cut the engine, Paul heard an almighty clatter behind the car. He looked around. It was Elijah, his face scrunched up, same old tattered straw hat down low, sitting in his wagon, pulled by his old mule.

"Whoah! Whoah, there."

Paul got out of the car and watched his father shoot a wad of tobacco juice into the dirt.

"Howdy, Elijah," he said.

"Howdy, son."

He'd said it—*son*. Paul's lip trembled.

"Glad to see you back. Everybody's talking about you in the Kingdom. Hear you won a medal?"

"I did, sir."

Lily appeared on the front porch, shaded her eyes, and hurried out to meet him. "Is that really you, son? I prayed and prayed."

He folded her in his arms. Next it was Tallulah and Tabby's turn. They were young ladies now, all dressed up in light-green short cotton skirts and yellow embroidery blouses.

Paul wished they hadn't felt the need to straighten their hair, which lay in flat and stiff black wedges. He'd loved seeing their wiry halos around chubby cheeks.

They both said at once, "We told Mama every single day you'd be coming home in one piece."

James and Ernest, hair combed, wearing their best shirts and blue jeans, said hello, shyly.

They all sat on the front porch, drinking Lily's spring tonic, sassafras tea, and eating freshly baked coconut cake, while Elijah went to put his mules away.

Lily leaned over and whispered, "Your father says you're living proof of God's holy miracle."

"And what holy miracle would that be, Mama?"

"The war, son. He believes Jesus brought you home."

Paul took out a white handkerchief and tenderly wiped a crumb of coconut cake from Lily's chin.

"You mean he's happy I wasn't killed?"

"That, too. We all are. He's sure the war's turned you into a real man."

"And what do you think, Mama?"

"I reckon you toughened up who you were in the first place. Ain't changed nothing."

They sat back and laughed together.

Paul watched as every few minutes Lily smoothed fine gray hairs away from her face. Since he'd last seen her, she'd become thinner, the paint scrapes on the front porch deeper, and the swing creaked louder.

"Where's Coralee?"

Tears filled Lily's eyes. "She sat over there on her porch every day talking to an empty chair; she put a glass of lemonade for Moses on a table beside the empty chair. She barely stopped to draw breath. 'What happened today at Larkin's? You and Paul going fishing tomorrow?' On it went till I took her over supper.

"A month ago, early one evening, she was sitting there same as she always was. Next time I looked, she'd gotten out of her chair, was sitting up on the edge of the front steps, you recall those steep rickety steps of hers. I watched her slowly put her chin on her chest, lift her arms and topple, head-first all the way down. I reckon it was the way she planned it. When we got to her, she was lying there dead with a broken neck, gone home to Jesus."

"Coralee... Moses," Paul said, bitterly. "They didn't stand a chance in this world."

Lily sighed, pulled out a chair for Elijah, and said, "Well son, that's all we know. Let's not dwell on it right now. You're back with us." She looked over at Elijah, just back from tending to the mules. "Ain't we proud of our boy?"

"We're proud, Lily."

Paul wasn't sure what had come over his father.

Lily moved her chair closer to Paul's. "Coralee willed her house to Blessing. That girl watched over Coralee, made sure Moses's mama wanted for nothing. Blessing says tell you she's mighty anxious to see you."

Tabby and Tallulah sat quietly at Paul's feet, taking it all in.

Lily passed a plate of coconut cake to Elijah and smiled. "Your father got used to her being next door. Not so's he'd approve of her ways... Still. You'll see, she's changed."

Tallulah brushed the cake crumbs off her skirt. "We love Blessing more than anybody. She buys us presents, always something we've been dying for." She pointed to the two pink flying-butterfly barrettes, pulling back her straight wings of black hair on either side of her face. "Like these."

After a while, Leroy looked at his watch. "Someone's been counting the seconds for the last four years."

Lily echoed, "Son, you better hurry on up there, and say hello to your little girl."

He got in the car. "I'll be back, soon as I can." He waved until his family disappeared in a cloud of red dust.

Back over the tracks, on up Main Street, past Larkin's grocery, the picture show, Hidden River Cave, the five-and-dime store, Paul tried to lighten his mood, take himself back into his *Paula* world. He wished he could stop, get out of the car, go in and buy some new beauty supplies. He couldn't wait to dress up, be all by himself in his own little house. He'd hum a few songs, take out one of the dresses he'd left in his trunk, put on his face, look in his mirror, and sing to Muriel, *"Lovely to look at, delightful to know and heaven to kiss."*

As the car slowed to go through town, Paul saw they'd fixed the humps in the sidewalk in front of the cave office. The former "Bee Lovely" had a smart green awning and new sign declaring itself "Quick Snip." The "Jesus Saves" sign was still all lit up in front of the Baptist church. They turned into the Jacksons' drive lined with white summer-flowering magnolias.

Lorene ran down and opened the car door. "You're here. 'Bout time."

Miss Sally, wearing her purple voile, her hair a little whiter, her waist a bit thicker, clasped his hands. "Mighty proud of you, Paul."

Mr. Walter, standing beside his wife, cleared his throat. "Happy to have you home. Seems you distinguished yourself."

Miss Sally remembered, "Someone's missing. Where's our own little precious girl? Come on out here, sugah."

Paul caught a movement behind the pillar.

Lorene clapped her hands as if she were scaring up a chicken. "Jane, we're all calling you. He's back." She turned to Paul. "For a whole month, ever since she heard you were coming, you couldn't count the ants in her pants. She's hiding back there, her heart in her mouth, holding onto a two-week stomachache."

Jane, in buttoned patent-leather shoes, dressed-up yellow organdy, with a big bow tied behind, long blonde hair in curls, took aim and arrowed down those steps, two at a time. She put her arms around his waist, face pressed into his shirt buttons. Everyone else melted into the cool air of the fine morning.

In the kitchen, Jane scooted her chair as close to Paul's as she could. "I knew you'd come back."

Lorene laughed at this. "Like hell you did, Jane! You flapped around like a headless chicken." She handed them cups of hot water with Lipton tea bags floating on the top, noticed Paul's disdain. "That's how we do it here. Ain't used to your fancy ways."

He was thankful he'd put two tins of the best Darjeeling loose leaf into his suitcase. He poured the milk the way he always had into Jane's cup, telling her, "You're all grown up, Babe."

"Oh, no, I'm not. I'm still me."

He looked into her blue eyes. She might be nine years old, but those were the blue eyes of his newborn baby. He stood and reached out his arms to her. "Come here, Babe. I need another one of your hugs. And this time, let's make it a long one."

Their memories filled up a quiet that lay between them until Lorene banged a skillet onto the stove.

"All I can say, better make the best of the next few days. Miss Sally told me Emma's coming with your daddy and little brother next week, and thanks to some new medicine called sulfa, that poor sick little boy will live forever."

Leroy stood in the doorway twirling his battered straw hat. "Where you want me to put this big suitcase, Sergeant Carew, sir?"

"No need, Leroy. I'll carry it to my house by myself."

———

That evening, Lorene had grilled T-bone steaks brushed with garlic butter, served with French fries and a head of lettuce in French dressing. She told Paul she knew they didn't have food like that over in "poor old England."

"Skinnier than ever, Sergeant Carew," she observed. "Jane's just like you."

They all sat down at the table together, Lorene jumping up every now and then to fill Paul's glass with iced tea. When he tried to help, she shooed him away with her dish towel. "Don't you move, hear me? It's my turn tonight."

After supper, he went to say goodnight to Babe. She'd put on a pretty pink night gown. He brushed her hair; they sat on the edge of the four-poster, and he told her stories about her daddy and the rest of the squadron.

Before she went to sleep, he asked her if she had something on her mind. One jumble of words tumbled out after another. A whole pile of tangled-up mess he couldn't make sense of. Eva Burks killed herself to get to Jesus. Her best friend at school wore old quilts and had nothing but lard in her sandwiches. Then there was Miss Pru and all the books they'd read together, and how now they were reading *A Tale of Two Cities*. She couldn't wait to tell him the whole story and he would have to read it too.

"Oh, Paw, and one more thing before I go to sleep, and pretty please will you do it?"

"What's that?"

"Do you think you could put on your uniform and walk downtown with me tomorrow?"

"Why, Babe?"

"Because I'm so proud of you, that's why. Pretty please?"

He kissed her goodnight and walked outside into the cooling air of a fall night, down the familiar path to his house.

Inside, Babe had picked rainbow-colored flowers and put them in jars and glasses all over his bedroom and bathroom. She'd drawn and colored pictures of a little girl smiling and written underneath: "Welcome back, I love you."

There were new pictures on his walls: a painting of Daniel Boone wearing his coonskin hat, holding his musket, and standing beside a group of Indians; a larger painting of red and pale pink roses spilling out of a white alabaster vase; a colored print of Victorian ladies sitting on a blanket having a picnic, in full crinoline taffeta skirts, holding onto straw hats with colored ribbons.

Paul smiled and wondered what those dignified ladies were saying to each other; then he whispered, *"What kind of world is this?"*

Miss Sally had put a new radio on the table in the corner of his bedroom. Best of all, along one wall, there was a big, full-length mirror. He snapped open his case, took out his slate-blue RAF uniform, and hung it up in his cupboard. There it was, first on the line of his war service awards with red, white, and blue stripes—his military medal.

Opening the small blue-velvet box from his suitcase, he looked at his decoration, silver with the head of the King of England, remembered the afternoon Henry received his D.F.C. from the Air Marshal, and another medal was awarded to Perry, Paul heard his own name being called.

"Military medal to Sergeant Paul Carew, RAF Squadron One-O-One, who took it upon himself with great courage, Tuesday, June sixth, nineteen-forty-four, to rescue, without thought for his own safety, a pilot and fellow squadron member from his burning aircraft." Paul stood stiffly at attention. He could feel the air marshal's hand brush his chest while absolute silence filled the parade ground.

He wondered, as he brushed his teeth and waited for his steaming hot bath to run, what the people in the Jim Crow train car were doing right this minute. He had Phil's address in Mobile, Alabama. He'd write and send him a postcard with a picture of Hidden River Cave. Before going to sleep, he saw an image of Lorene standing at the kitchen door, looking tired, after she'd washed the dishes, untying her apron, getting ready to walk home.

He slept. Lord only knows he needed it. Breakfast turned into lunch, and afterwards, he went upstairs to put on his uniform while Jane went to her room and dressed in a bright red cotton skirt and a purple blouse.

"Ready, Paw?"

"Ready, Babe."

He said it first. "Hubba-hubba. Love those colors."

"Hubba-hubba to you too, Paw. You're beautiful in your uniform." She picked up a corner of her skirt. "Grandma says purple and red clash. I told her that's what I wanted."

"What did she say?"

Jane smiled beatifically. "She said I belong in the Kingdom. I told her she was right."

———

While the old folks were napping on the porch and Lorene was ironing in the basement, Paul and Jane skipped through the garden, down to the sidewalk, happy to feel a warm sun heating up the afternoon.

She held out her hand, he took it. "Oh, Paw, you look so hand-some. Promise with a pretty please you won't leave me again."

"You'll be the one leaving me when you grow up, Babe."

"Not ever, I promise, not ever."

After a ten-minute walk, they'd reached the drugstore. Jane tugged on his sleeve. "Let's go in and have a lemon fluff. I've been bragging about you. I even showed Mr. Pettigrew your postcards."

He looked inside and saw two young White girls sitting at the counter, twirling on the bar stools.

"I can't sit down in there, have one of your lemon fluffs. It's for Whites only."

Jane argued, fretted, and got mad. "Come on, we'll go in, and sit down. They can't say anything. You've got on your uniform."

"That's not turning me White." He put out his arm, pinched a bit of skin. "I still got this."

She pulled back the sleeve of her sweater, pinched her skin. "Still hurts. What's the difference?"

"You know better than that. How many Colored people have you seen on those barstools?"

"Not even one, Paw. Never mind their dumb lemon fluffs. Let's go to the picture show." She tugged at his sleeve, as people on the street stared at them.

Jane, in step and as close to him as she could get, held his hand tight, with her chin in the air.

"Babe, you thought these people would stop, shake me by the hand, and say, 'Welcome back'?"

"I guess I did."

There were billboards outside the movie house, ads for *Back to Bataan* with John Wayne and Anthony Quinn.

"Come on. It's starting in ten minutes."

Paul pulled out his wallet and stuck five dollars through the hole. "Two, please."

The girl inside was yanking a wad of chewing gum, taking it from one side of her face to the other. She looked at Babe.

"So, let's see, that's one ticket downstairs for Whites and one ticket upstairs for Coloreds."

Paul remembered there had been no trouble in England or in Ireland buying a movie ticket and sitting where he felt like sitting.

"You go on in, see the picture show, Babe. I'll take a walk."

"Go in without you, are you crazy? Let's both go up to the balcony."

"Get one thing straight, Babe. *We're* not going up to the balcony."

She went back to the window. "This is a dumb town with dumb people in it and I hate all of you!"

The girl kept on chewing. "I don't make the rules."

Babe tried to hold back tears.

Paul saw how bewildered and angry she felt. She'd missed the movie, the lemon fluff, and worse, she lived in a world she hadn't properly seen before. They couldn't go anywhere and sit down together except for her grandparents' house.

On their way home, they ran into Ida Larkin on her way out of Larkin's grocery store. She stopped to talk. "You're looking fine in your uniform, Paul. We heard all about you being over there. Ain't it sad Moses can't see you now? He'd be proud."

"Thanks, Mrs. Larkin."

Dragging her feet on their way home, Jane asked Paul, "Tell me the Clarence and Moses story, please."

"You've heard it a million times."

"Do you miss Moses?"

"All the time."

'Where is he now?"

"You know he died in an accident."

"Lorene told me. There's more to it than that. Tell me."

"Let it lie for now."

He sat with Lorene after supper while Jane got ready for bed. "I'm bone-tired, Lorene, and not from fighting a war. We got shut out of the drugstore, couldn't sit next to each other in the picture show. Over there, I was treated with respect. I was Paul Carew, a person, not a Negro."

The Seth Thomas clock in the dining room chimed nine.

Lorene replied, "I don't care what you say; people like us got no business fighting in a White man's war."

"I was happy to fight in the R-A-F."

"Ain't the same White men over there as we got over here?" She picked up a clean tea towel, wrapped it around a bowl of leftover supper. "Time for me to go home."

———

"Paul, we got a lot of pruning to do. I appreciate your taking your time off with me. Does my heart good to have you here again." Miss Sally lowered her voice. "Leroy's no damn good, least he's nowhere near as good as you in the garden. Only thing he can do is drive a car."

"That's pretty good, Miss Sally. I can't drive a car."

As soon as she came home at four o'clock, Jane sat down as usual at the kitchen table, looking forward to the surprise Lorene fixed for her every day. Lorene took an angel food cake out of the oven and a pack of fresh strawberry ice cream from the freezer.

Paul sat with them, confessed he was dying for a cigarette.

Jane said, "I'd like to try one, too."

Lorene cut in. "Over my dead body."

"You in a bad mood, Lorene?"

"You'll soon find out."

Jane ate her ice cream in tiny spoonfuls, the way Paul had taught her. "Miss Pru says we need a new Civil War. She said no one paid any attention to the first one."

Lorene cut a piece of the cake and passed a bowl of fresh sliced strawberries and sugar to go over the sweet strawberry ice cream.

"Ain't no use carrying on, Miss Smarty-pants. Your grandma's going to whip your ass good, hears you talking like that. Now you eat that ice cream and stop licking at it like a newborn pussy cat."

Paul had had enough. "I'm the one teaches her manners, Lorene, not you. That's the way I want her to eat ice cream."

Before Lorene could answer, Miss Pru appeared at the kitchen door wearing a long blue-and-white-striped skirt with a high-necked white blouse and a red bandana tied around her forehead. "Here comes Pocahontas," Lorene muttered.

Babe jumped up and led her over to the table. "Here he is, Miss Pru. You said you were dying to meet him."

Paul got up to shake Miss Pru's hand.

She said, "It's an honor to meet you, Sergeant Carew. Perhaps I can come back in the kitchen, after we finish our lesson, have a cup of tea together, and hear any stories you feel like telling us about the war. We're all so grateful to you."

Paul sat back down with Lorene at the kitchen table to finish his cake and ice cream.

"Pitiful." Lorene shook her head and took a sip of coffee.

"What's pitiful?"

"Ever ask yourself what a little White girl's got to do with us? She's awful close to you. She's nine years old. How's she going to get on in life if she thinks you're her papa and her mama? Most of them grow out of that."

Paul felt heat rising. "She's been my child right from the start."

"I ain't seen much of you around the last four years. She's been right here most of the time with me in this kitchen. We raise them, then what?"

"What do you expect?"

"Nothing. Which is just as well."

————

"Jackson residence." Lorene picked up the phone in the kitchen. "Miss Emma? Yes, ma'am, we're all fine. He's right here." She'd put her hand over the receiver. "Paul, it's Emma."

Paul hadn't spoken to her in almost four years.

"Good lord, Paul, it's you! It seems like a lifetime." She sounded happy and excited. First, she told him how John was a miracle baby. He'd been cured completely thanks to sulfa drugs. "I'm so happy you're back. How does it feel to be home?"

He took a moment and said, "A little bit strange. There's a lot to get used to."

"I've been getting most of your news, Sergeant Carew. I know you were wounded. Are you all right?" She waited for a moment. "Are you still there?"

"Yes, ma'am, I'm fine. I'm here."

"Oh, Paul, the good news is—the Group Captain was promoted

yesterday, and I hope we'll all be heading to Stockholm, Sweden. Would you like that?"

He didn't have to think. There was nothing else on the horizon. "Yes, ma'am. I'll take a look at a map for Sweden."

She added, "We've talked about what your job will be. It'll be more like a manager, Paul, in charge of the kitchen, the ordering, the staff, and Jane. Of course, we'll talk later about your salary. And one more thing: I'll be arriving in a few days, and I can't wait to see you."

He knew where Sweden was from the RAF ordnance maps of Europe, and it was a long way north.

When Lorene heard the news, she pulled a face. "Off again? Hope you know what you're getting into this time."

———

Paul left the house early the next morning to see Blessing and visit with his family. On his way through town, Miss Ruth was standing outside the cave office, unlocking the door.

"Land's sake, it's you, Paul Carew. I heard from Ida Larkin you came to town with Jane in your uniform." She came over and shook his hand. "My sister Sally says you made a hero of yourself over there. Seems you got a medal and a promotion. Planning on staying with us long?"

"No, ma'am, not long."

"Why don't you bring Jane and go through the cave again?"

"Thank you, Miss Ruth. I'll bring Jane to visit you next time I come to town. We may not have time to go through the cave but thank you for asking us."

A few minutes later, Paul climbed the steps of Moses's porch where Blessing sat pushing the same creaky old swing.

She stopped and got up to give him a long hug. "Let me look at you. Handsomer than ever." She took his arm. "Wow, feel that muscle. I hear you're a war hero, Sergeant Carew."

Her light-blue cotton dress reached just below her knees and buttoned up as far as a small white collar. Her shoes were simple dark blue sandals. Her makeup was a fine dusting of powder, no lipstick, no eyeshadow, no earrings. She was lovelier than ever.

"For Pete's sake, Blessing, what's happened? You been born again?"

She giggled, sat back down on the swing, as Paul took his old familiar frayed white-wicker chair.

"I'm a retired lady. Truth is, I'm working full time for Boy Lafferty. Don't know whether you remember his wife, Doreen, the one who was paralyzed. She died two years ago. Boy asked me to be his housekeeper. Linda Joe, Dead Eye Farlow's daughter, used to do for Boy. But she got married and moved to Munfordville. He offered me a full-time job with a salary so high I couldn't say no. 'Sides that, I don't have to work too hard at night."

"Does that mean you're doing everything for him?"

"I reckon it does."

Paul closed his eyes. At least Moses wasn't around to hear this news.

Blessing picked up his thoughts. "I knew how sweet Moses was on me. Reckon he loved me. Wait a minute, Paul. I forgot to offer you a root beer."

She came back out with two cold bottles, fizzing white at the top. She stuck in a couple of straws before handing one to him. "I might have married Moses one day. I kept it in the back of my mind." She set to swinging again and sipped her root beer. "What about you, Paul? Feel like talking about the war?"

"No, Blessing."

"Have you found a love yet?"

"Let's just say I'm not looking."

"Remember what I told you?"

"What was that?"

"You won't wonder anymore when you find it." She put her hands behind her waist and gathered her skirt. "Ain't that the whistle for noon? Let's go. Lily's invited me over to your house for lunch. Made chicken and dumplings."

He and Blessing tipped carefully down the ten rickety wooden steps of her front porch. At the bottom, she reached out and tenderly touched his cheek.

"Both of them gone, Paul, almost like they never was."

"Blessing, long as we're here, so are they."

———

"Paul, watch out. They'll all want a piece of you," Henry had warned him before his return. "Everyone has their own ideas of what we've been doing over here. Chaps like us who've been in action, don't want to be reminded when all people at home want are the gory details."

Every morning over breakfast, Mr. Walter kept him hanging around in the dining room answering question after question.

"Did you carry a gun?"

"No, sir, I didn't carry a weapon, but the pilots were given revolvers."

"What kind of revolvers?"

"Well, sir, I'm not sure. I do know the NCOs carried Sten guns and Enfield three-o-threes."

"Did you see any Germans over there?"

"Yes, sir, I saw a few Germans."

"Weren't they carrying Luger pistols?"

"No, sir, they were behind barbed wire."

———

At five o'clock precisely, Paul poured boiling water into a China pot, over Darjeeling tea leaves. He'd cut thin slices of brown bread and layered each piece with Straker's unsalted butter. Jane and Miss Pru joined him and Lorene for tea when their lesson was over. That evening's hot topic was how the end of the war would change their lives.

Babe's turn was first. "Paw will be here with me, every day. He won't be getting wounded, and I won't be getting scared anymore."

"Your turn, Paul." Miss Pru helped herself to another piece of brown bread and butter.

He thought for a few seconds. "So far, nothing has changed except for me."

Before they had a chance to put any more heat in their hot topic, Miss Sally filled the doorway. "What are you all talking about this evening?"

Lorene slowly untied the back of her apron and sighed. "We're talking about how happy we are that the war's all over. Reckon we'll all go right back to where we were before it started."

44

Paul sang softly to himself on his way to bed, *"And so with time on my hands and you in my arms..."* It was a warm night, even for June. You could hardly see the trees behind a thick white fog. An owl hooted. Paul wondered if it was the same one he'd heard every night before he left. He waved his hands through the mist.

"Abracadabra! I can't see you, spirits, but I know you're there. Coralee, Moses, Great-grandma Abilene... Come back and haunt me. I miss you all."

In his room, he closed the curtains, pulled his old trunk out from under the bed, opened it, and took out his dress-up dress, floor-length, yellow silk with long sleeves and a full skirt. Miss Sally wore it back in the old days, she'd sworn, "when I had my figure." Luckily for him, she'd always been plump, and in those days, she was a lot taller.

He shook out the full skirt and let the silk slide through his fingers. No one could have been happier than he was at that moment. He undressed carefully down to his shorts. Looking at the stitch marks of his jagged wound, he stepped into the pool of yellow silk and struggled with the zipper all the way up. He clipped on the broken pair of dangly diamante earrings he'd fished out of Emma's wastebasket all those years before and mended.

In front of his new full-length mirror, he put on makeup and dusted fine, light, toast-colored powder, over-foundation. He wet his mascara brush with lots of spit and wound the black onto his lashes. A spray of gardenia perfume, and he was all ready to go. He swished, turned, and twirled the full yellow skirt before he switched on the radio. He couldn't believe his luck: Billie Holiday singing "Body and Soul." He swayed a little from side to side, dancing with the girl in the mirror, Billie's voice like a prayer hitting home. Lost in himself, he was in a swoon.

The song ended. He opened his eyes. In the mirror standing beside him was Babe. He hadn't heard her open the door. He was sure he'd locked it. She was all dressed up in her new blue and white striped cotton dress with a white lace collar, her blond hair combed down over one eye.

She clapped her hands and sang out, thrilled with surprise and excitement, "You're beautiful!"

Speechless, shocked he'd been found out, he stared at her.

She twirled her full skirt, flashing her petticoat.

"It's you, Paw, both of you," Jane said. "Don't worry, I've always known it."

His heart was thumping so fast he could barely breathe.

"When I was just a little girl in Ireland, I sneaked out of bed one night, watched you put on lipstick and rouge and dance around, but you never dressed up like this. I love it! Let's dance together. Please?"

He wanted to reply but seemed to have lost his voice.

Jane giggled, went and turned up the radio, raising her finger. "Listen."

They heard the disc jockey say, "And now, ladies and gentlemen, I'm going to play a song from the original score of *Born to Dance*, the nineteen-thirty-six MGM movie. Ready? Here goes."

When the orchestra struck up, she came to him, holding out her arms.

"We know this one by heart, don't we, Paw-Paw?"

He slid one arm around her waist, and they began to dance and sing softly together.

I've got you under my skin.

I've got you, deep in the heart of me.

So deep in my heart that you're really a part of me.

I've got you under my skin.

THE AUTHORS' NOTES

Jane Scott Stuart's Note

"Tell my story—your story—our story."

I thought no more about keeping my promise to Paul until years later, early one wicked winter's morning in northeast Scotland when driving snow rattled my windows.

I was struggling in this cold country, missing Paw-Paw. Putting another log on the fire, I took out an empty notebook. I began writing the story he told me many times about the day his father beat him almost to death. Pages filled quickly. In my sitting room, I felt his presence, he was with me, Paw-Paw and I were together.

Hours later, when the storm had passed, the telephone rang. "Paul died today. Try and be brave." My mother sobbed.

When I finally decided to honor my promise, I was in my late seventies, living six months of the year in a lovely house in northern Scotland, surrounded by woods with endless paths for walks. The rest of the year, my husband and I live in a small village in Provence, France, with views out onto a garden with white roses and a large, reaching willow tree, a perfect atmosphere for reflecting.

I began my task with determination and purpose, counting on my passion from childhood for literature. I found inspiration in the deep reflections and recollections of my thirty years of psychoanalysis. Most of all, I recalled, in my daily practice of meditation, the sharp memories I have of Paul, not to mention the part of me he formed.

The computer became both my savior and foe. I was a novice who only wrote and read emails. I wrote by hand. Transcribing the text, fluffing up my eighty-year-old brain. I counted on Apple and Google, memorizing an entirely new language, losing pages of text, shooting my blood pressure up to stroke levels. "Don't forget to SAVE. Don't forget to SAVE," bounced off the walls of my sleepless nights.

I knew all along I was not Paul and not Black, and yes, it would have been better if he had written his own story. My family, others, all of them White people, shook their heads. "Can't do that."

After one of my many sleepless nights, I decided to go where the story belonged. I fell into the arms of Michelle Chester, a Black woman and owner of an editing firm in Dallas, with her sympathetic voice and uplifting message. "I have someone for you, Jane."

Elaine, with her sharp eyes and love for this story, began to polish and direct. I realized this novel was more for Black people than anyone else. Elaine has become my rock and my co-author and my friend. She brings our story to you with love and deep devotion.

We are writing the sequel, which keeps Paul right here beside me.

At eighty-six now, I have a fitness coach. I ride my bike every day, meditate for hours, do Yoga, Qi Gong, and walk daily, not to mention healthy eating. Perhaps I can stretch in a year or two more.

"Strut your stuff, Babe."

"I hear you, Paw-Paw."

He is still shaping me: I love to get dressed up more than anything in the world. My closet is full of every color of the rainbow, quirky jackets, tight jeans, and long flowing skirts. Like him, I spend hours putting my outfits together, and even more time looking for new ones. *Where do I get it from?* The apple never falls far from the tree.

If for some odd reason, you did not like our novel and put it down, all I ask is that you do so GENTLY.

Elaine Flowers' Note

It started with an email. Like so many other times, my colleague, Michelle Chester, had a project land in her inbox she thought was well-suited for me. Most of her emails to me began with: "Here's a project you may be interested in... Hey, you like period pieces, right... I know you like race matters, here's something for you to check out..."

On this day, I could see the preview text, reading, "Here's something you should love..." so I reheated my cup of Lemon Zinger for the third time, took a seat in front of the computer, and clicked it open. Michelle went on to say in her email, "I think this lady is in Europe. If you contact her, let me know how it works out." To make a short story shorter, Jane and I exchanged emails before she called from Scotland, sharing the story of her life with Paul, a Black man who had taken care of her, and how he was her world from the day she was born.

Of the many things she shared—how dear he was to her and the promise she made to tell his story—she voiced concerns with the novel she'd started being racially sensitive. Because she was White, she needed the eyes of a professional Black writer/editor to ensure there was nothing that could be deemed offensive. I was more than happy to take a look.

I received the first drafts of the first few chapters and—Michelle was right, the people, the places, the times—I was in love. I went to work, falling deeper with each collection of chapters coming my way —ultimately, and over the years, I was committed to the work, which delightfully morphed into co-author. The diamond, coming into view, each point shining brightly with every revision and rewrite.

Not in This World, an untold story beginning in the 1930s is, perhaps, a story that could only be fully appreciated in this day and time. Trusting the timing of a Greater Work at play, my friend and co-author, Jane, welcomed me aboard to help her keep the promise made in what was certainly another lifetime—and not in this world.

———

Contact the authors at NotInThisWorldBook@gmail.com

Printed in Great Britain
by Amazon